SILVER-TONGUED
Devil

SILVER-TONGUED
Devil

PORTLAND DEVILS, BOOK 1

ROSALIND JAMES

Synopsis

♡

No more wild rides. No more wild side.

Blake Orbison's pro football career with the Portland Devils may have come crashing to an end, but not calling the signals anymore just gives him more time to devote to his business enterprises, including the latest and greatest: the opening of the Wild Horse Resort in scenic north Idaho. And that other one, too. Blake's on the marriage track now, and he's got a game plan. But when he runs into a trespasser leaping from his shoreline boulders into his lake, what's a good ol' boy to do but strip down and join her?

Dakota Savage is nobody's temporary diversion, least of all the man responsible for her family's semi desperate circumstances. Some people may think she has a piercing too many, but she's had more than enough of being called trash in this town. She's come home to Wild Horse to run her stepfather's painting business, and any extra time she has goes into creating her stained glass. An overpaid, entitled, infuriating NFL quarterback is no part of her life plan, no matter how sweet he talks. No matter how slow he smiles. No matter what.

Author's Note

♡

This is a work of fiction. Names, characters, places, and incidents are products of the author's imagination or are used fictitiously and are not to be construed as real. Any resemblance to actual events or persons, living or dead, is entirely coincidental.

Table of Contents

♡

Life is what happens while you're busy making other plans.

(Attributed to many)

Hot and Bothered

♡

"Man, I'm hot." Dakota Savage tossed the paint roller back into the pan, then wrenched off her respirator and goggles with a sigh of relief.

"Well, I wasn't going to say anything. I'm classy like that." Her partner, Evan O'Donnell, was already methodically stacking materials on the bare concrete floor of what would eventually be the Tamarack Suite. After weeks of work, the Wild Horse Resort, one hundred sixty rooms and suites of town-transforming luxury destination, was barely more than a week away from being completely painted. Which was good, because the sooner they were done, the sooner M & O Painting would be getting their next check. And bad, because the sooner they were done, the sooner their nice big job would dry up. Literally.

"What? Oh. Yeah, right." Dakota scraped a couple random flecks of white paint from her glasses with a fingernail, squirted the lenses with water, then dried them on a somewhat-clean section of her white overalls before grabbing a rag and the bucket of water and starting to wipe down the windows. Everything stunk now that her respirator was off, but, hey— stink was her life. "Soon as we're done, I'm swimming. I mean

1

as *soon* as we're done, I'm in that water, baby. Treat time."

Now that she was clearing the glass of its protective film of hairspray and could see the lake again, she was tugged toward it by a nearly physical force. Today was only Wednesday, with two long days still to go before she could disappear into her workroom. She had this idea… but it would have to wait. Meanwhile, the temperature outside was hotter than north Idaho had any right to be in late May and even higher in here, especially beneath her layers of clothes. No A/C for the crew. No matter how "luxury" the resort was going to be or how rich its owner, the budget was everything. People, on the other hand? Not so much. She wouldn't have taken this job for any money if she hadn't needed—well, any money.

But out there… out there were celestial blue sky, rippling blue water, and the cedar-clad mountains rising beyond. Directly below Dakota's vantage point on the resort's fifth floor stretched the marina, its neat rows of newly constructed docks as yet boasting only a handful of boats instead of the crowd that would eventually—everybody said—fill every slip. And then, of course, there was that long crescent of sandy beach off to the left beneath a golf course that had once been a residential neighborhood. The golden sand of the private beach glittered under the afternoon sun, beckoning her with the promise of a refreshing swim in water that was still nearly winter-cold, but who cared?

Of course, she didn't plan on using the beach.

"Go on." Evan shrugged a big shoulder toward the door, since his hands were full. "I'll finish up here, check on the rest of the crew."

"Nah. I'm good." Evan was looking fairly tired himself, even though somebody else might not have seen it. His pale-blue eyes seemed shadowed in his craggy face, and he'd grown even quieter than usual during the past months. When she was stressed, she got testy. Evan just became more stolid than ever, until he seemed carved from an especially hard block of wood that you were surprised could actually move and speak. When she'd told him she was taking over her stepdad's part of M & O Painting five months ago, he'd said, "Fine," and that had been it. Of course, he'd been *really* stressed then. Just like her.

Now, he shrugged. "You covered for me the other day when I had to take Gracie to the doctor. Plus all those other times. You're due."

She kept working on the windows. "Necessity versus luxury. No comparison. And I know you want to get home to her."

"I'm sick of you anyway. Get out. But don't swim here," Evan added. "Show some sense. Ride on into town and go from there. You know what tightasses they've been about that, and I'm not bailing you out."

Dakota finished the windows, then started peeling tape off wooden trim. "You'd bail me out in a heartbeat and you know it, but you aren't going to have to. You don't go to jail for trespassing, Mr. Straight Arrow. It wouldn't be that big a deal. Here's what happens. Jerry Richards or one of his henchmen yells at me to get out, and I act like I can't hear him at first. Then I climb out of the water, dry myself off real slow, and act sorry. You know Jerry's a dirty dog, and most of those guys aren't any better."

Evan jammed the lid on the five-gallon paint bucket with a couple blows of his big fist, then hefted it with ease. "Right."

"Hey. It could work."

"You ever get yourself a bikini?"

"Well, no. I swear, the smaller the suit, the more it costs. So what? It's still a swimsuit, right?"

"I'll get my bail money ready. Not saying you don't have a—well, anyway." The tips of his ears were turning red. "But I've seen that black suit, Grandma."

"It's navy blue."

"Even worse."

♡♡♡

So far, Blake Orbison's new life plan wasn't meeting his expectations. Or maybe that was him. All he knew was—if he'd been his employee, he'd have fired himself. The Wild Horse Resort needed his attention now, weeks before the grand opening, but he kept… lapsing.

"Buck up, punk," he muttered.

"Excuse me?" Jennifer Cardello, his north Idaho assistant, asked, looking up from her phone and stumbling over a tree root.

"Sorry." He'd already grabbed her arm. Now, he hauled her upright. "Am I walking too fast for you?"

"Oh, no. I love speed-walking and typing, especially when it's about a hundred degrees out. I often ask myself, why has this been missing from my life until now? And then I answer myself. Because it sucks."

"Not loving the walking meeting concept, huh? I think better when I'm moving. Well, I used to, back when I was able to move." The bum knee still took him by surprise sometimes, when he started to run and then remembered it didn't work so well anymore.

"Oh, yeah," she said. "You're totally a loser now." At his surprised bark, she added, "Switching to voice dictation. Hang on."

"Right," he said. "Strike that from the record, though. The part where I feel sorry for myself."

She was still fiddling with her phone, but now, she sighed. "Blake. I work for you. I'm not allowed to judge even if I were, you know, judging. Which I might be, but I'm not saying, see?"

"That's right. Somebody told me you were professional. Who was that? Oh, yeah. The mayor."

"So fire me. It'd be a blessing. I'm just saying." At his grin, she said, "We're both grumpy. You're allowed to be. I'm not. So grump ahead, and I will pretend to be cheerful."

"I'm done," he decided. "Complaining *and* moving. Besides, it's probably time for you to go do… whatever."

"Leave work? Nah. I live for you." When he grinned again,

because she'd just about jollied him out of his bad mood, she said more seriously, "I'll type this up and update your calendar. And then—yeah, I'm out of here, if you're OK."

"Go. And thanks."

She hesitated, though, for once, and he shot a look at her and realized that asking her to walk beside the lake in heels and a slightly too-tight skirt probably hadn't been his best idea. She was looking sweaty and decidedly redhead-flushed. He sighed and said, "You've got me all guilty. Get out of here before I have to give you a bonus or something equally horrible to make up for it."

"Nope," she said, back to brisk again. "I said the thing about you being a loser. I was being ironic, for the record. Plus grumpy."

"Got that. Head on back. See you in the morning."

He watched her pick her way over the uneven ground and felt another unwelcome stab of conscience and irritation. What the hell was going on with him? He didn't do weather. Rain, sleet, or sun, you got the job done. He didn't do moods, and he didn't do doubt. Except that he was doing all of them right now. He'd gone through some life changes, sure, in the too-quick transition from NFL quarterback to full-time businessman, but uncertainty was part of the deal, and so was injury. And so was taking what came your way, dealing with it, and moving on.

That was just about enough of that. He didn't do introspection, either. Hell, most people would have doubted that he knew what the word meant.

To his relief, he rounded the corner of the bluff path and saw Jerry Richards, head of security on the project, standing around with a couple other guys, all of them looking excited.

He headed on over there. If you couldn't do discipline, do distraction. Not a motto he'd be hanging on the wall, but it worked for now.

"Hey," he said, approaching the three men with SECURITY emblazoned in white on their black T-shirts.

"What's going on?"

The other two looked at Jerry, who said, "Got a trespasser out there." He hitched his belt up under his gut. "I'm on it. Headed down there right now to deal with it."

Blake took a look and saw the swimmer moving parallel to shore. Going fast, probably because it was freezing out there. This was the big security risk? North Idaho could be a little short on excitement at times. "Swimmer in the water, yeah," he conceded. "But I don't own the lake."

"Gym bag on the shore," Jerry said. "Stuck it behind a rock there, see? Little bastards think they're cute. I'll run him off right now."

"Nah," Blake said. "I'll do it. It'll do me good to kick some ass. Not literally, of course," he figured he'd better add.

"Hey, do what you gotta do," Jerry said. "You're the boss. Nobody's going to say a damn thing." He looked at his guys, who nodded hastily back, and Blake remembered the rumors he'd been hearing about his security chief's methods and made a mental note. And gave a mental sigh. This project…

Well, he'd wanted a challenge.

Badasses Gotta Badass

♡

Dakota was about thirty degrees cooler already. Literally. She couldn't feel her feet anymore. She headed to shore, scrambled up the highest of the weathered gray rocks that lined the shoreline in the little cove, and bounced a couple times on her toes.

She was just about to jump when she heard the "Hey!" from behind her. It startled her so much that she stubbed her toe, shrieked, fell, and hadn't righted herself by the time she hit the water fifteen feet below with an enormous slapping sound.

It was a belly-flop. No other way to describe it. She remembered why you didn't do that, too. Because it *hurt*.

She came back up to the surface spluttering, treaded water, and hauled air back into her lungs while trying to ignore the sting from her abused face and belly and, she would swear, her internal organs. She might not have had the breath to say "Asshole" out loud, but she thought it.

She squinted toward shore and saw somebody. She couldn't tell without her glasses, but she thought it was a guy, and he—she—might be wearing a black shirt.

Jerry Richards, probably, excited about getting a chance to be official. What did he have, binoculars?

7

Well, she'd figured it could happen. Whoever it was, they weren't going anywhere, and the water was cold, so she swam back in and hauled herself back up the smaller rocks onto the shore. Not too close to him—it *was* a guy, she thought—but he headed right on over, unfortunately.

She wasn't sure she could pull off "cute," now that she was faced with it. She'd never been blonde, she'd never been anything close to perky, and she'd never been good at flirting. This had probably been dumb. Good thing they were almost done with the job.

Except that there was Evan. Oh, shoot. Evan. Who needed every day of the job. Heck, *she* needed every day of the job. Irresponsible, that's what this idea had been. However irresistible it had seemed or how rebellious she'd felt.

It wasn't Jerry. That much, she could tell as he got closer. It was somebody a whole lot slimmer. Tall, check. Short dark hair, check. Black shirt, check. But no gut, and she thought there was some darkness around the jaw that wasn't quite a beard. Another security guy. She could be cute enough for him. Maybe. What would he care, really, what she did?

"Hi," she said as he approached. "Next time maybe don't yell right when I'm jumping." Taking the initiative. Projecting confidence. She was better at that than "cute."

"Hell of a graceful landing," he agreed, and glasses or no, she could see the flash of white teeth through the dark stubble just fine. Also that he had a pair of shoulders to die for, and some very nice arms in that T-shirt. Not to mention long legs in dusty jeans and work boots, and about six foot three of lean muscle. Nobody she knew, because she'd have noticed him. She might not be able to *see* him, exactly, but she could see enough.

"If you're security," she said, "I was just going."

"I'm not security. And I hope that's a lie that you were just going, because that looked real fun."

He had a Southern drawl she'd surely never heard in Wild Horse. Slow as molasses, and just that thick and sweet. *Ah hope thass a lah that you were juss goin'.* "Let me guess," she said, feeling a sneaky little surge of excitement. "You're out here to do wrong. Sign says 'No Trespassing,' and you've been given the big lecture, but you're not worried, because you're a badass like that."

Some more grin. "Could be. Is that water deep enough to be safe? We're both too pretty to get ourselves paralyzed."

"Oh, yeah," she assured him. "Best spot on the lake for it. No place else has rocks like this or a pool this deep. Which means, of course, that the Man comes and fences it off and tells you that you can't use it anymore, even if you're working out here. Gotta love capitalism, and this is about the worst."

He gazed into the distance and scratched thoughtfully at his cheek. "Bad place to work, you think? Huh."

"I wouldn't do it for a heartbeat if I didn't need the money. You could say that I'm not in love with Mr. Blake Orbison or his company. But you know, we all need the money."

"That we do. Arrogant guy?"

"Let's say that I don't like the way he treats people. On an… institutional scale." *Whoa, girl,* she told herself. *Lose the bitter and get back to reckless. More attractive, and a whole lot more fun.* Trust her to meet a truly prime specimen of manflesh for once and immediately put him off. "So I'm sure I shouldn't jump off his rocks. But hey, what's life without a little danger?" There, that was better.

"Now, see, darlin'," he said, his voice getting even deeper, the accent going a shade richer, "that's what I tell myself all the time. It's a real shame that so few people think like us."

"Hmm." She might not be good at flirting, but he clearly had enough flirt for two. "You on the project yourself?"

"Sure am. Mind if I join you?"

"They're not *my* rocks."

"Well, that's true." Hot Guy's irresistible, crooked little grin was still going on like gangbusters, and she remembered with a stab of something too much like chagrin that her swimsuit *was* navy blue and a one-piece style that had been on clearance for $7.99, but that her grandma would have flipped past with a "Boring, baby. I might be old, but I'm not dead." Her hair was in a messy, dripping braid, she wasn't wearing any makeup, her nose was probably running, and she was nobody's dream girl.

Nothing she could do about it now, though. She was about to turn and head up the rock again, but she may have gotten a little distracted. Because Dream Boy was pulling up that black T-shirt, and glasses or no… she could see that he didn't have a six-pack. He had an *eight*-pack. And then he kept going, and her mouth might have gone a little dry. It had been a while. And it had been longer… no, it had been *never* that she'd seen a chest that good. Not up close and offscreen.

When he dropped the shirt and his hands went to his belt buckle, she realized she was standing there staring. And what was he *doing?*

"Ah…" she said. "Around here, people generally wear clothes to swim. I mean, I'll just get kicked out, but you could get arrested."

"But then," he said, "like you say, we live dangerously. Badasses gotta badass." He sat on a rock and started untying the laces of his work boots, which was when she realized that standing there gawking at him as he stripped was probably not her smoothest move. So she turned around and headed for the rock again.

This time, she jumped off cleanly. And if she looked back when she heard the splash behind her… well, she couldn't really see him anyway, not unless he got *really* close. Which wasn't happening.

Which was fine.

♡♡♡

Blake didn't know who she was, but he was going to have to find out. She had a weird squint, her body was more athletic than stacked, and that was one of the ugliest swimsuits he'd ever seen on a woman below the age of forty, but she had enough attitude for two, honey-colored skin that was already touched by the sun, a set of cheekbones that his thumbs needed to brush over while he held her head for his kiss, and legs that wouldn't quit. If he'd been in charge of her, he'd have had her wear something cut all the way up to her waist, just so he could look at those legs. Her ears had been pierced in a couple places, and then in a couple more, because she had two piercings at the top of the left ear with a ring through each and a tiny silver chain joining them.

If anything had looked more like a pair of handcuffs, he didn't know what it would be. That chain was hot as hell.

And then there was that other thing.

When she'd turned around and walked away, then started climbing up that rock, he'd discovered that she had exactly the kind of ass that a Southern boy loved best. The kind that took two hands to hold. Firm, round, and downright juicy.

Hell, yeah.

When she got up there, she got a thumb under each side of the navy-blue material and snapped the suit down over the gorgeous curve of butt cheek, and he thought he'd have a heart attack. And then she jumped off, and he'd just say that following her up there didn't take any decision-making at all, and swimming behind her to shore to do it all over again was a foregone conclusion.

After the second time they'd jumped, she turned to him in the water, treading water with one hand while she slicked her dark hair back from her face with the other, and said, "Too cold to stay long. Anyway, I have to get going."

"Aw, now, darlin'," he complained, "those are words that cut a man to the bone."

He was rewarded by a smile that lit up her whole face. That was some mouth, too. That mouth said *generous* and *good time*, not to mention *Lay me down and love me right*.

"Anybody ever tell you that you're forward?" she asked. "Stripping to your underwear in front of a woman you've just met and all? Black might have been a little less obvious than fire-engine red, too, not that I looked."

"Can't get anywhere if you don't try," he said. "Words to live by. And I thought we'd established that I'm a badass. Two badasses ought to get to know each other better, don't you think? Maybe have a drink, do a little dancing, see if they get anywhere they want to go. I'll bet you know the spot for it, too."

She didn't answer. She was looking past him, and he turned in the water and saw Jerry Richards checking them out, his hands on his hips.

"Shoot," his new friend said, nearly under her breath, through teeth that had started to chatter. "Is that security?"

"Yeah. Head of security."

"Jerry? Shoot. Look, I'll go in first, swim around to the left, up to the beach. You go on over to the right behind the rocks. There's a place you can slip out of the water there. Give me five minutes. I'll either talk my way out of it, or he'll haul me off. He'll leave, and you'll have a chance to get out."

"Uh…" He didn't even know how to answer that. "I don't generally let women take the fall for me."

"He knows me, and he doesn't like me. As soon as I get closer, he'll recognize me no matter what. But he'll just call me a name or two, look me up and down, and threaten me some, because he's a sleaze. With you—who knows. I have a feeling you don't respect authority, and Jerry isn't too good on 'reasonable use of force,' especially when he feels disrespected. And he feels disrespected a lot."

Just what he'd thought. He was going to have to do something about his security department. "I tell you what. We'll call it Opposite Day. Go on behind your rocks. I've got this."

He didn't wait to hear her answer, just swam for shore. Stupidest argument he'd ever heard anyway. She must have met some real princes if she'd known any guy who'd go for that.

Unfortunately, she followed him. She might have the kind

of mouth he loved both ways, she might have a body that made his palms itch and the kind of spirit that called his name, but she was lousy at following directions.

Taking her to bed would be a power struggle all the way. Of the most delicious kind, because you never wanted to play the easy game. The best wins were the ones you fought for, and the best opponents were the ones you had to work on. Long and hard.

No more bad girls, he reminded himself. *No more wild rides. You're looking for sweet. We're going for classy here, remember? It's time to find wife material.*

But there was one part of him that tended to talk the loudest in these situations, and unfortunately, he'd never yet succeeded in making that be his brain.

Wild Child

♡

Dakota followed him in to shore, mentally slapping herself around some.

She'd *known* this was a bad idea. She took responsibility; that was her deal now. Besides, she couldn't stand to get somebody fired just because she'd longed to leap off those rocks like she was sixteen and… and life was different.

Or more like she was twenty-nine, had longed to do something reckless, and had found somebody who seemed to long for exactly the same thing. Which didn't mean she should be leading him, all unsuspecting, down what she *knew* was the wrong path. He wasn't going to like her much when he was unemployed.

He was pulling himself up and onto the rocky shore, she could see that much. She climbed up behind him, and he put out a hand onto her arm and steadied her, which was nice of him.

His briefs were sure-enough red, and… well, there was this pouch. Outlined with black, in case you'd missed it. This close up, she could see that just fine. If there were any shrinkage going on there, she'd just say that the un-shrunk version must be…

She jerked her eyes back up to his face, and there was that half-smile again, like he knew exactly what she'd been thinking. He was still holding her arm, too. She wrenched it away and paid attention to Jerry, because of course he'd come to bust them. And whether Mr. Hotness liked it or not, she was taking this one.

"My fault," she said, talking right over whatever Jerry was saying. "I jumped off the rocks and did a bellyflop, and he… uh… thought I was in trouble and jumped in to rescue me."

She wished she could see Jerry better, because he wasn't talking, just staring at her, she thought. "Hang on," she said abruptly, and stumbled her way across the rocky ground to the spot where she'd stashed her bag. It was under a big bush, which she saw as a fuzzy circle of green. She always picked a landmark like that to avoid wandering in circles and having to quarter the ground for her belongings.

"This some kind of ritual? Pacing the area off?" It was her dream guy. He'd followed her, still wearing only his briefs. For some reason, Jerry had let him go. Not like Jerry at all.

Ah. Red bag spotted. She patted around the top of it, found her glasses, and shoved them onto her face with a sigh of relief. Then she stood up, took a look at her companion, and just about fainted.

"Oh, sh— shoot," she stammered. "Tell me I did not just do that."

"Do what? And I've got to say—I'm kinda digging the librarian look here."

She barely heard him. She saw Jerry clearly enough now, coming up to join them and saying, "I'll just take off, then, Mr. Orbison, go check in with my evening shift."

"Yeah," he—friggin' Blake *Orbison*—said. "You go on and do that."

"You take care, Dakota," Jerry said with what she guessed was supposed to be a paternal smile but instead was just sleazy. "You want to watch out jumping around those rocks. I know you wouldn't want Mr. Orbison to be sued, and your—well, I guess we'll call it your family—doesn't need any more accidents, do they?"

She didn't slap him, but she sure wanted to. She didn't look at him at all, just went for her towel, then realized that she was giving both men a great view of her butt, which wasn't the part of herself she liked to lead with. So to speak. She stood up again, wrapped the towel around her waist, tried to ignore them while still talking to them, and said, "You're right. We don't need any more accidents on Mr. Orbison's property." And picked up her bag and left.

She was still barefoot, and the rocky ground was bruising the soles of her winter-tender feet. She didn't care. She was out of here.

♡♡♡

"What the hell?" Blake muttered, then went for his jeans and hauled them with difficulty up his still-wet legs.

Jerry cleared his throat. "I told them all to do the job and get out. They know they're not supposed to be hanging around afterwards or going into anyplace they're not working."

"What do I care if somebody takes a swim?" Blake buckled his belt, then shoved a foot into a work boot without bothering with socks. "Is she one of the cleaners or what?"

"*Dakota?* You'd never catch Dakota Savage doing anything that feminine. She's one of the contractors that took over the painting after you canned Steve Sawyer's crew. Course, she's normally all covered up."

Blake looked at him more sharply, then went back to tying his bootlaces. "Let me guess. You think firing Sawyer was a mistake."

Jerry gave a shrug of a meaty shoulder. "Steve's a good man. Dakota's… well, that whole family's pretty much trash. But hey, sometimes trashy's exactly what you're looking for, know what I mean?"

If Blake hadn't, the smirk on Jerry's face would have told

him. And even though it was what he'd been thinking a few minutes earlier, it annoyed the hell out of him. Anyway, he had his boots on. He grabbed his shirt and socks and took off.

He caught up with her not in the parking lot, as he'd expected, but around the side of the building. He wouldn't have noticed her except for the flash of orange in his peripheral vision.

She was tying her shoelace when he came up to her. She was wearing shorts now, which wasn't a bad look at all. She had some leg on her, that was for sure.

"Dakota," he said, and she whirled to face him and didn't lose her balance. She was still crouching, which meant he was looking down the front of her suit. It was covered, not very thoroughly at all, by an orange tank top. Her hair wasn't looking too good. Her body was looking just fine. And "Dakota Savage"? That was a *name*. Looked like she could live up to it, too.

She stood up straight, shoved up the severe rectangular black-framed glasses that had "sexy librarian" written all over them, and said, "I have to go."

She wasn't smiling anymore. Her face was all the way closed down. Nearly severe in its lines, cheekbones and nose and jaw all firm, strong, and sharply drawn. Somebody might have called those looks "exotic." He couldn't imagine anyone would ever have called her cute, but he couldn't see how they'd call her trashy, either. Other than that chain in her ear. That chain was giving him definite ideas, even as her body language and ugly swimsuit said exactly the opposite. "Challenge" was the word all the way around.

"You know," he said, "you've got me all confused. I thought we were getting along real good, and here I've gone and driven you away somehow."

She wasn't looking him in the eye. "I shouldn't have been swimming out there. Forget it, OK?"

"Ah…" He scratched his nose. "Let me guess. You need the job."

Her gaze finally swung around to him. Fierce, that's what he'd call that. "Here's a tip. Down here at the bottom, we all need the job."

"You don't like rich guys."

"Gosh, you're quick." She yanked a helmet out of her front basket, jammed it onto her head, and shoved the fastening closed. "Your name's on my paycheck. I'm not going to say anything else. Except that I don't think much of a guy who lets somebody go on like that, listens to them digging their grave, disguises his voice, and laughs at them."

"You weren't going to say anything else, huh. Except that." He considered telling her that he got more Southern as things heated up, but it didn't seem like a good idea.

"I'm a good painter. So is my partner, and he *really* needs the job. He has a baby. One more week, and we're gone. Just forget it."

He sighed. "Whether you swim with me, whether you tell me what you think of me—hell, whether you go for that drink with me, or anything else—that doesn't have anything to do with the job. I'm not that kind of guy."

"Now, see, I'd have said you're exactly that kind of guy, letting me go on like that, putting me at that disadvantage. But I'll tell you another thing. I don't care what Jerry said. Or I do. I do care. But I don't accept it. Whatever he said, I'm not that kind of girl. And even if I were, you'd be the last man on earth."

I'm not that kind of girl? Had anybody actually said that in the last forty years? He would have laughed, but then again—no. She was really upset, somehow. She straddled the bike and said again, "I have to go. I appreciate you not letting him bust me. And I'll appreciate it more if you'll forget all about this."

She didn't wait around to hear his answer. She just rode away.

♡♡♡

18

By the time she'd ridden the three miles home, Dakota had herself under control again. Sure, it had been stupid. Sure, every bit of it had been impulsive. Sure, she had nobody to blame but herself. Well, and Blake, but she'd known for a long time that you couldn't control what anybody else did, and he was a rich, arrogant guy who didn't care about other people. You could only control yourself, and she *did* control herself.

Usually.

Once she'd put her glasses on, she'd recognized him right away. The resolutely square jaw might be covered with stubble now, the dark hair might be longer than in any publicity photo, and there might have been a few lines carved into his brow and fanning out from the corners of his eyes that she hadn't noticed in his pictures. He might have deepened that accent in a way she'd never heard in an interview, back when she'd been researching him… maybe a little obsessively, but who could blame her? But the strong nose was exactly the same, and so were the hazel eyes. Nearly gold, with a rim of dark green around the iris. Not many men had those eyes, or looked at you that way out of them, with a gaze so intense it was nearly hypnotic. Not many men looked like that, period.

Tough, that was the word. Not quite handsome, and all male. Some people might have called it "confident." She'd have called it "entitled." Like he thought he was king of the world.

It had been harder to hold that thought when he was standing over her with those shoulders, those arms, that chest, and those rock-hard abs displayed above a pair of low-slung, dusty Wranglers. Looking like a Coke commercial, like the construction worker who'd be setting down his jackhammer, pulling his T-shirt over his head, and turning the head of every woman from eight to eighty. Before tipping his head back and downing his drink with the kind of abandon that got your imagination working overtime.

She'd sure never seen a picture of him like *that*. Football uniform, yes. Business suit, yes. She had plenty of defenses against suits, and more against privileged, arrogant athletes. Not so much against long, lean, sculpted muscles that looked like they'd been built the hard way. With work. And none at all against the ugly white lines of scar tissue that showed where a man had hurt and healed.

All right, then. So she'd had an unfortunate encounter with an NFL quarterback-turned-ruthless-businessman who was too compelling for her peace of mind. So what? Time to shake it off. Which she did, though it took all three miles of her ride home to get to that point.

As soon as she opened the back gate, Bella was there, her ears pricked high and her tail going fast.

"Hey, girl." Dakota gave the dog a thump on the shoulder. "Did you and Dad have a good day?"

In answer, Bella went and grabbed her rubber Kong, dropped it at Dakota's feet, sat, and waited, her gaze riveted on the toy as if there would be a prize for Most-Focused Dog.

"At least give me a chance to put my bike away." Dakota was cold despite the earlier warmth of the day. She should have taken the time to change out of her clammy suit, but she'd needed to escape. She put her bike into the shed, and Bella, who'd followed her, dropped her toy again. Dakota picked it up by the grungy rope, gave it a toss, and said, when Bella came back, "One more, and that's it until I change."

"She's going to have to wait, because dinner's ready," her stepfather said from the back porch.

"Hey." She tossed the toy once more, then ran lightly up the back stairs and gave him a kiss on the cheek. "How you feeling?"

"Oh, you know. Can't complain." He turned and hitched his way into the kitchen. "Stew in the crock pot for dinner, using up the meat from that roast. Came out pretty good, though."

"Five minutes," she promised. She took her bag into her bedroom, stripped off her tank and shorts, caught a look at herself in the mirror, and recoiled in horror.

There she'd been, looking like that, giving her "I wouldn't stoop so low" speech to Blake-Bigbucks-Orbison. Her hair looked like a five-year-old's after a long nap, her face was pale and nearly gaunt, and most horribly of all, she had a piece of water weed sticking out of the bottom of her suit like some kind of off-center green tail. Blake must have walked away from her and started laughing like a hyena. He'd had a girlfriend who was a *Sports Illustrated* swimsuit model, and Dakota looked like she belonged in a *Field & Stream* dog handler feature. Possibly as the dog.

She shook it off once again—she was getting plenty of practice today—took a lightning-quick shower, changed into warmer clothes, and went into the kitchen to have dinner with Russell.

He looked at her and said, "That's better," which pretty much confirmed her suspicions. When they were eating, he said, "I got that new storage unit finished and stained for you today. Tried to move it out of the garage, but it didn't work out. You'll have to do it on the weekend."

She shot a glance at him, but he was focusing on his stew. "Sure," she said easily. "Thanks for that." He was moving more stiffly than usual, and Bella had her nose practically against his leg, which meant he was hurting bad. Probably from overdoing it. He must know he didn't have to push himself that hard. She was perfectly capable of moving and hanging a storage unit. It wasn't like she hadn't told him so. She knew why he did it, and she didn't know how to stop it. "How did the physical therapy go?"

"Didn't show. Again."

"Those jerks. Workers' comp, right. Workers' *non*-comp. I'm going to call them."

"No, you aren't. I did it. Don't coddle me."

She shut her mouth, and they ate in silence for a minute before she said, "I did something stupid today myself. Went for a swim after work and had a run-in with Jerry Richards. I met Blake Orbison, too."

Russell had been reaching for a knife to butter a roll. Instead, he knocked it off the table, and it fell to the floor with a clatter. Dakota was out of her chair, but Bella was faster, chasing the knife over the slippery linoleum until she managed to grab it. She brought back over to Russell, sat by his leg, and presented it to him.

"Good girl," he said gruffly, taking it from her even as Dakota handed him her own knife.

"I know," Dakota said. "Like I said. Dumb. I went for a swim out there, probably because Jerry told us not to."

"Orbison doesn't own the water," Russell growled. "It's not his lake."

"It was his shoreline, though. I thought about Evan afterwards, and about you, too, and wondered why the heck I'd put both of you at risk just to jump off the rocks."

"You lose the job?"

"No. I don't think so. Blake didn't seem like he minded. Hopefully he told Jerry that. And I'm sure he doesn't know who I am other than one of his peons, no matter how many letters I wrote or how many phone calls I made. He obviously doesn't care how negligent his contractors are or how many workers get injured on his watch. We all know he's a bottom-line guy."

"Sounds like you've got no problem, then, other than all that mad you're still hanging on to like it's going to get you somewhere. What is there to feel so bad about?"

"I told you."

"Jumping off the rocks? Doesn't sound like that big a deal to me. You gotta be a rebel some way. It's in the blood. Look at me. I was ten times the outlaw you'll ever be, right up until seventeen years after I had a kid. What was I, fifty? You're fine."

"Do you really think it's in the blood?" She asked it quietly. That was the other thing that had nagged at her all the way home. "That I can't change?"

"Change what? Who's saying you need to change?"

"Nobody. But you know—Mom. My father. Sperm donor. Whatever. It's pretty clear that I don't come from the clean end of the gene pool." She looked him in the eye, finally, and he looked right back at her, his gaze, as always, as straight as his back wasn't. "I'm reckless, Dad," she admitted. "You know I am. I keep feeling like one push will send me off to the wild side, and I can't afford the wild side. How did you stop?"

"How do you think? When something mattered more. How you feel isn't who you are. What you *do* is who you are. Take it from an alcoholic."

"Oh." She swallowed. "Still?"

"Every damn day. I feel the urge, and I don't do it. Here's another way to look at it. Find somebody who likes your wild side. Somebody who wants a wild child. Why should you give up the best part of you, the free part? For who? For a bully like Jerry Richards, who pushes his wife around and probably took the belt to his kids? For that lawyer you were going out with? Screw him. Screw 'em all if they don't like it. Go find yourself somebody who wants to see that part of you. Go be Dakota someplace besides your glass."

"I can't afford even to be Dakota in my glass. You know that. That isn't what the people want."

"Then find different people."

♡♡♡

They finished dinner, and Dakota bit her tongue not to say anything at the way Russ hauled himself out of his chair and hobbled into the living room to watch TV, Bella shadowing him every step of the way. She tossed the Kong for the dog until Bella was—well, not satisfied, but panting—then washed the dishes, watched half an hour of a Mariners game with Russ to be companionable, gave him a kiss on the cheek, and headed to bed.

All right, to her workroom, but only because she had to look. She shoved her feet into flip-flops, stepped over the baby gate that kept Bella's paws safe from glass slivers, and entered her domain.

Twelve feet by fourteen, order in every inch of it, and passion in every breath she took here. This was where she came to life. With her glass.

Her new storage unit, a labyrinth of zigzagging supply cubbies as complex and pleasing to the eye as an Escher print, was in the garage waiting to make it even neater. Russell's hand was everywhere, from the frames setting off her most inspired pieces to the prosaic dividers along the wall that separated the precious panels of stained glass. Panels she bought on the occasional trek to Seattle, spending far too much money every time for a woman who was slowly, painstakingly paying down her stepfather's precariously balanced mortgage debt. But she had to have the glass or she couldn't breathe. And she always made back the cost of her materials, and more, too. Eventually.

She walked down the row of racks, arranged along the spectrum, ending up as always at the golds and, farther along, the roses and reds. The most expensive colors—and the most beautiful, especially when they swirled and bubbled with hue and texture. She crouched before her pink rack and carefully shifted pieces.

There. That was it. The palest pink, brushed with darker color. The outer shell of the conch that would reveal its heart of deep rose starting on Saturday. She had the vision in her mind, and she had to do it. She *had* to.

Customers sometimes asked to see her sketches, occasionally even for an autographed version, and looked skeptical when she tried to explain that she didn't sketch. She *saw*. The design happened only when she was ready to create, when she laid out the squares of glass on her work table and drew the pattern. Customers couldn't understand, because she couldn't explain. How could you describe the anxious minutes and hours beforehand, when you found yourself delaying the start because you feared not being able to transform the perfect vision in your head into the fragile medium of glass, always only one clumsy misstep away from not reaching your ideal? And how could you possibly explain the relief, the freedom of actually starting, of taking that leap no matter what?

They were her dream babies, so nebulous before she made them real with her tools, her patience, and the magic of the soldering iron so they could glow against the light. So they could come to life. Before she let them go to somebody who, she hoped, would love them half as much as she did.

Her fingers itched to create her piece now. *Right* now. But if she started, she'd be here all night. She knew herself. Her body ached with the fatigue of a day of physical labor, capped off by her swim and her ride home, and she had another day just like it tomorrow. She had responsibilities to more than herself, and always—*always*—to more than her vision.

There was more than one kind of love. Creation was one thing. People were another.

Saturday, she promised the glass before stepping over the gate again, kicking off her flip-flops, and heading to bed. This one project for love, and then the next in the line of simple, nonthreatening flowers and birds, of fan lights and cattail-bedecked sidelights that the public expected. The ones rich owners would snap up to adorn the front entries of their lakeside "cabins." The ones that paid for the most expansive panels of glass and let her excuse all the time and money she spent here.

But when she put her head on the pillow and closed her eyes, she saw a sliver of unstained background crackling with texture, and then a shell, so close-up you were almost dreaming it, its swirls and bands and spikes made up of pale and darker pinks... and that deep, secret swell of rose leading to the mysterious, pulsing life within. She saw a conch.

Famous in a Small Town

♡

Blake climbed down from the Explorer on Friday morning, ignoring the protest from his knee, and headed into Wild Horse Bait & Tackle. He'd spent most of the past couple days flying to various meetings for Sundays, his sports bar/restaurant chain—also known as "what he was supposed to be doing"—and he'd be in more meetings today for the stretch-goal project that had had him waking up at night wondering what the hell he'd been thinking. Today was lunch with the mayor and city council to talk about the plans for the resort's grand opening on the Fourth of July. If he was going to have to be charming again, he needed something to look forward to afterwards. A willing woman in his hot tub would do it, but he was working toward a goal here that took his wild side off the table. That pretty much left fishing.

An old-fashioned bell on the door chimed out a welcome when he walked into a space that was a bona fide throwback. Linoleum on the floor, a long wooden counter at the front, a whole wonderful section devoted to fly-tying, and what looked like a surprisingly good equipment selection.

A couple guys conferred over tackle, both outfitted by L.L. Bean and showing "tourist" like it was written on their backs.

The older man behind the counter, though, had been cut from different cloth. He'd been talking to a man of about his age in a plaid shirt and paint-splattered white cap, accompanied by a medium-sized brown dog that sat at his feet, ears pricked like it was taking in every word.

Both men shut up at Blake's entrance and looked him over. Probably the clothes, since he'd flown straight in from a franchisee get-together in Seattle. He'd left the suit coat in the truck after getting off the jet, but he was still a little bit designer for Wild Horse. He'd even shaved this morning.

"Hey," he said, and both men nodded. The dog just looked interested.

"Help you?" the man behind the counter asked.

"Sure hope so. I'm looking for whatever I'll need to go after salmon this weekend."

The two men looked at each other, and then the owner— he had to be the owner—scratched the back of his head and said, "Well, now, you can go *after* 'em all right. Whether you *get* 'em, though…"

"Yeah," Blake said. "That would be the idea."

"What kind of a boat you running?"

"Hatteras GT54."

He'd swear that the old-fashioned ceiling fan overhead stopped moving, such was the stillness in the air. "You'd be Blake Orbison, then," the owner said. Everybody looked tense. Including, Blake could swear, the dog.

"I would be," Blake said.

"I've seen that rig," the owner said. "Now, Hatteras makes a mighty fine boat, don't get me wrong, and I can't say I wouldn't pay cash money just to take one out and put her through her paces. But, all due respect—it takes more than a boat, and that thing's so new, she practically still has the stickers on. City guys—I usually suggest they go out with a guide, learn the lake before they go wild."

"Well, there you go," Blake said. "I'm not all that much of a city guy. That rig might be new, but she's not my first. My first—now, she was a bass boat, and that's being charitable. Only room for two, and one of 'em had better not be fat. It's been what you'd call a gradual upgrade."

"Thought you were from Portland," the owner said.

Everybody else, including the city guys, was still listening, and Blake *didn't* allow himself to feel a stab of annoyance. Par for the course. Attention was the price you paid for that twenty million a year. Put that way, it was a mighty small price.

"Nah," he said. "Virginia boy, by way of Mississippi. Did a few years in Georgia, too. I know lakes a little, and I know oceans a little more. But I sure don't know Idaho, and I don't know Chinook and kokanee, either, but I'd like to."

The owner looked at the guy in the paint cap, who was standing stiffly, canted to one side. Old injury, probably. "Nah," Paint-Cap Guy said to the owner. "You go on. It's over and done with." Which was cryptic.

"You sure?" the owner asked him, ignoring Blake.

Paint-Cap Guy didn't answer, just shoved off the counter, limped a couple steps forward, put out a hand, and said, "Russell Matthews." Nothing wrong with his handshake, whatever was messed up with the rest of him.

The owner hauled in a breath and said, "Larry Nagle here. This is my store."

"I figured," Blake said, staying patient.

He spent a half hour after that asking questions, listening, and amassing a collection of flies, flashers, herring to use as bait, and a whole lot more. The two city guys left, but Paint-Cap Guy—Matthews—stuck around for all of it, along with his dog. Moving slow and rough and not talking much, but what he did say seemed worth listening to.

"You want to troll slow out there," Matthews said. "Call it one-point-three, one-point-five a hour. And this time of year, the Chinook are maybe thirty, fifty feet deep, that's all, so you don't want to go too far down."

"Good to know," Blake said. "Now, here's the real question. Best spots?"

Larry and Russell looked at each other, and even the dog seemed to be holding her breath. Blake said into the silence, "I'm happy to pay for a guide, if you know somebody who wants to earn a couple hundred bucks tomorrow or Sunday to show me the ropes. Either day works for me, and anything he catches on his own line belongs to him. I've got rods and all out on the boat."

"You got a license?" Russell asked.

"Yes, sir. Sure do."

"Well, hell," Russell said. "For two hundred bucks, I'll go out with you. Bella comes too, though. My dog."

Blake cast an eye at her. Nobody could have called her noisy, and she'd moved about two feet this whole time. "Long as she doesn't scare the fish."

"Nah."

"You sure, Russ?" Larry asked quietly.

"For two hundred bucks, I'd strip naked and do a lap dance," Russell said. "I've got a mortgage."

"There you go, then," Larry told Blake. "You can't do better than that. Russell doesn't get out much anymore, but nobody knows the lake better."

"Can't get into those low boats, that's why," Russell said. "A Hatteras, though—I might be able to haul my ass on board her. Eight o'clock tomorrow morning," he told Blake. "Pick Bella and me up at my place."

Blake thought the timing over for a second. He had a date tonight, yeah. But he wasn't expecting it to last all night. He had a game plan, and for the marriage deal, he was pretty sure, it would involve going slow. He was going to have to be a gentleman. He hoped he still remembered how.

"Sure," he said. "Except I don't want the lap dance."

♡♡♡

When Dakota had arrived at the resort on Wednesday morning, they'd let her in. So there was that. She hadn't seen

Blake again during the next couple days, which was good. As long as she managed to behave herself, she could probably finish the job without getting herself, her partner, and their entire crew fired.

"Got any plans for the weekend?" she asked Evan as they were cleaning up on Friday afternoon. It was as hot as ever, but she'd save her longing for the lake until she got to City Beach. No place for the high jumps out there, but on the other hand, you weren't risking your livelihood.

"You know the answer to that," Evan said. "Why? You need some help?"

"Yeah, if you wouldn't mind coming over for an hour and giving me a hand to hang the storage unit Russ built me. I hate to ask, but otherwise, he'll insist on helping me, and you know how much that'd hurt."

"You got it. I'll do it tonight, if you want. My mom took Gracie up to Sandpoint to visit a friend. Not back till late."

"Oh, yeah?" He wasn't looking at her; just carefully folding dropcloths. "That's exciting for you, then. Been a while since you had an evening off dad duty, hasn't it?"

"Yeah."

"Good or bad?" she asked cautiously.

"Hard to say. I haven't really thought about it."

That was a soliloquy for Evan. He hadn't said as much as that when April had taken off four months ago, practically on their way home from the hospital. He'd just moved the crib into his bedroom and gotten on with it by himself. With his mom's help, but they'd always been going to need that. April hadn't exactly been mother material. "Fragile" was one word. "Needy" was another.

"You know," Dakota said, "I keep thinking I can't find a good guy. But there you are right next to me, and about the best guy I know. So why aren't we having wild monkey sex?"

He glanced at her, and she didn't need to be a psychologist to read the alarm in his eyes. "Uh…"

She sighed. "Never mind. Slow the heart rate down. I

know—we don't love each other that way. But how come?"

"Because you were Riley's sister. *Little* sister."

"Riley's been gone eight years." Even now, it hurt to say it. "But we were both involved with other people. At least at times."

"Yeah."

"And I'm not your type," she finished for him, since he'd never say it.

She was right. He just looked at her and shrugged.

"Huh," she said. "I should probably feel all defeated, but I don't. If I examine my feelings, I'm sort of relieved. I don't need to wonder if there'll be any weird awkwardness. I know we can stay comfortable."

"Maybe that's why," he said.

"What?"

"You're always examining your feelings."

"Evan. That's women. We do that."

"Kind of pointless. There they are anyway. Why look at them that hard? Just makes you feel worse if they're bad. And if they're good, you already know it, because you feel good."

She couldn't help smiling. "Well, that's true. And yet I persist in being female. So you know what? Since I know you won't do it on your own—let's go out. I'll buy you a beer at Heart of the Lake. We could check it out." The new wine bar-slash-restaurant was the hot ticket in town, opened in anticipation of the resort's higher-end customer base. "They're bound to have craft beer, since I know you won't drink wine. Or hey, you know what—we've both been strapped down so tight, and we're sending in that final bill next week. I'll buy you dinner. Call it Dad's First Night Out."

He glanced at her sidelong, then returned to hammering tops onto paint buckets. "I heard their food's weird."

"Kale pizza," she agreed. "I looked. Quinoa. Huckleberry sauce on the venison."

"See, that's just wrong. Fruit and meat don't go together."

"If I get you plain cheese pizza, instructing them to leave

31

off the kale and the strange mushrooms and any other suspect ingredients, will you come? Have a heart. I'm trying not to be pathetic and broadcast that I don't have a date for the weekend, and haven't had one for quite some time."

"You aren't going to get one if you're out with another guy."

"Maybe I'll find the competitive type, looking to take me away from another man. Alpha dog. Master of all he surveys. Gets all the hot women."

He shot another look at her, and she sighed and said, "Yes. My goggles are on my forehead, my respirator's around my neck, my glasses are on my sweaty face, and I'm wearing overalls. Leave me my illusions. Dress up and go out with me. We can at least look."

Worse than Kale Pizza
♡

Dakota's night out didn't start exactly perfectly.

When she came out of the bedroom at six-forty-five, practically midnight dining by Wild Horse standards, Russell looked her over from his spot in his easy chair and said, "Maybe you want to wear some pants that aren't ripped."

"They're supposed to be that way. They're distressed."

"Huh. See, now, I'd say they're ripped, but could be I'm not up on fashion. It probably doesn't matter anyway, since it's Evan. I guess you're not looking for attention."

She wasn't sure whether to laugh or sigh. "On that vote of confidence… I'll see you later. I won't be out late."

"Yeah," she heard as she left the house. "Probably not."

She picked up Evan along the way, and he didn't help much either. He just swung up into the pickup without a word. She drove the ten blocks or so into downtown, then said, "Russell said I shouldn't have worn these jeans."

"Oh," Evan said. "You looked OK to me. I mean, you cleaned up and everything."

Well, great.

He looked good himself. Dark Levi's, blue plaid shirt that showed off his broad shoulders, cowboy boots. His ruthlessly short reddish-brown hair was still damp from the shower, and he'd scrubbed all the paint off his hands. He looked like what he was. A strong, solid, hard-working guy. And she probably looked like what she was, too, she thought glumly. A working woman who'd taken a shower and changed her clothes to go out to dinner.

"Do I actually repel men?" she asked before she could stop herself.

"What? No. I don't think so. You're good-looking."

"Let me guess, though. More like the woman who's going to paint your ceiling or gut your fish than the one you promise to love and cherish."

He didn't say anything for a second, then said, "There's a space on the left."

She pulled a U-Turn in the middle of Main, parallel-parked the old truck with a bunch of hauling on the wheel, and said, "Well, thanks anyway. You may have to drive home, because I plan to have at least two glasses of wine. Looks like I'm going to need them. I wore my *contacts*. Doesn't that count for anything?"

"Oh," Evan said, sounding surprised. "I told you. You're good-looking. I'm just used to looking at you. I wasn't thinking about it. Get out of the truck so I can see, and I'll tell you."

She rolled the window down so she could grab the handle from the outside, since it was stuck from the inside, then cranked the window up again, put the keys under the floor mat, and climbed down.

Downtown Wild Horse wasn't exactly hopping, but the Tervan, the bar across the street where some prankster had switched the letters on the sign twenty years earlier and nobody had ever switched them back again, was satisfactorily noisy. Sheila's Steakhouse was doing a good business, too. Dakota stalked around the front of the old white pickup in her unaccustomed platform heels and told Evan, "Encourage me. Go."

"Your hair's nice," he said. "Sorry I didn't notice the

contacts."

"That's what you've got?"

"What do you want? Am I supposed to talk about your body? I'm not classy, but I'm not going to say 'Nice ass' or something."

"How about my outfit?"

"I already said you looked good."

She sighed. "All right. Never mind. Let's go."

She perked up on heading into Heart of the Lake. The historic building had been painted a soft gray—not by M & O, unfortunately—with darker gray accents, and inside, discreet lighting shone on clubby groups of black leather chairs, a back wall made of weathered brick, and a long, curved mahogany bar. It looked upscale, warm, and welcoming. Maybe this whole resort idea was going to work after all.

"Primo chairs over in the corner," she told Evan. "Let's grab them."

Even as she said it, two men detached themselves from the bar and converged on the inviting seating group. She was already turning away when she heard, "Well, well. Looks like you lose."

She could have walked away. She *should* have walked away. Instead, as always, her feet were taking her in the other direction. Jerry Richards and Steve Sawyer were planting themselves into that black leather and looking up at Evan and her with what could only be described as smirks. Two men separated by twenty years, but separated-at-birth twins in every other way that counted.

"You could say I pick my battles," she said. "Like the ones that come with a paycheck?"

Steve's good-looking face twisted beneath blonde hair that was cut short and neat, like the Homecoming King he'd been and the successful contractor he still was, thanks to stepping into the family business. "You bite the hand that feeds you," he said, "and you might just find that you're the one who gets bit."

"Your hand doesn't feed me, and I already got bit," she said, unable to keep the fury out of her voice. "And Russell stayed bit. I wish you could see him trying to get out of bed in the morning. I don't know how you sleep at night. I know I'm not losing any sleep over you."

"I knew somebody had to've run around behind my back." Steve's expression was hard now. Frightening. She remembered that face, and everything inside her wanted to cringe, but she wasn't going to let that show. "Somebody with a grudge. I guess I've figured out who that could be."

"I'm not the one who lost the job," she fired back. She wasn't sixteen anymore. She wasn't weak, and she was nobody's victim. "You did that all by yourself. I'm the one who cleaned up your mess. And when they told me they wanted somebody going along behind with a roller on every wall, I made sure we *did* it. It's called satisfying the client. You should try it sometime. I didn't need to rat you out. You cut a corner, and this time, *you* paid for it. Look at it this way. At least nobody fell. At least nobody broke his back."

"Because I don't hire old guys who are past it anymore," Steve said. "Or drunks or women, either. I hire guys who can handle the job."

She'd have lunged at him, except she couldn't, because Evan had her arm. "Don't," he said, his voice low and urgent. "Let's go. Not worth it."

"She carrying your balls in that purse of hers, O'Donnell?" That was Jerry. His heavy face was flushed, his voice slurred with what Dakota guessed were a good four beers already put away at the bar.

The tips of Evan's ears had reddened, his one telltale of emotion. "I heard you got canned, too, Richards," he said. "Both of you are looking to take it out on somebody. Pick somebody else. I'm not biting, and neither is Dakota."

"Maybe you'd better not answer for her," Steve said. "Maybe you don't know what she's doing when you aren't looking. Ask her *why* Jerry got canned. Ask her who twitched her tail for Blake Fuckin' Orbison the other night. Who did he strip down for and run off after when they were both still half-naked? How exactly did that go down, Dakota?"

She was going to kill him. Except she couldn't, not if Evan didn't let go of her.

"And then," Steve went on, "she probably told him how Jerry made her *uncomfortable*. How she felt *unsafe*. Ain't it just a damn shame that Jerry got his ass handed to him two days later? Now, why do you think that could be, O'Donnell? My guess is that whatever you're getting, Orbison's probably biting off a chunk for himself. But then, you're probably used to that by now. Where's your girlfriend again?"

Evan still had his hand clamped around Dakota's upper arm in a vice grip. A good thing, too, because the red mist had descended over her eyes, and she was straining against his hold. Her partner's voice was absolutely level when he said, "I'm not too bright, I guess, because I don't know what you're talking about. I only know a couple of things. One of them's that two of us here are drawing a paycheck out at the resort and two of us aren't, and I know which ones are which. And the other one's that guys who talk big in a bar do it because they're scared to say it in the parking lot. I'm not a big talker, but I'm real good in a parking lot. Maybe you remember that. You're welcome to try me again sometime. I'll be right here." With that, he all but hauled Dakota away.

"Let me go," she hissed.

"Nope," he said, still sounding as calm and cold as the lake in winter. "We're going to sit down and have a drink, and you're going to remind yourself that Steve Sawyer is a scumbag who doesn't have any power over you, and Jerry Richards is nothing but a mean drunk. And then I'm going to eat pizza that costs four times as much as Domino's and doesn't even have a stuffed crust, and I'm going to tell you again, as many times as you need to hear it."

He was dragging her over to the hostess stand now. "You pick the worst moments to be assertive," she complained.

"Why didn't you tell me Jerry got fired? How did you find out already? I could've helped you out in the parking lot, too. It wouldn't even have been two against one."

"Might've messed up your pretty see-through shirt, though. You wouldn't want some scumbucket's blood all over it."

"I thought you didn't notice what I was wearing."

"I noticed. You got dressed up, I'm about to pay way too much for a beer, and Wild Horse is about to find out that Jerry Richards got himself canned and the two of us are doing fine. So come on, Dakota. Let's do it."

She hated it when he was right.

♡♡♡

This date, Blake thought, was like wading in molasses.

The back patio of the Heart of the Lake winery and restaurant was probably what you'd call "enchanting," if you were writing it up for a newspaper. Plenty of plantings around the perimeter, patio heaters taking the not-quite-summer chill off the evening air, candlelight and roses on every table, and tiny white lights winding through tree branches, all of it shouting, "Romantic as hell! You're knocking her socks off, dude!"

Except he wasn't.

It wasn't her fault. Beth Schaefer was a pretty woman, and a very nice one, too. That was what had struck him when he'd met her at her parents' over-the-top lake house two nights ago. Her parents being the previously richest residents of Wild Horse, and seeming not at all unhappy to be supplanted, especially once Beth's mother had introduced Blake to her daughter.

The occasion had been a cocktail party and silent auction on behalf of the Friends of the Lake. A conservation organization Blake had figured he'd be wise to join, because there were plenty of people in town who'd fought the resort hard, some of them with the resources to make serious trouble.

He needed to get them on his side, or at least off his back. Jobs and tourist businesses and the tax base were one thing, but the environment was something else, and a golf course wasn't the kind of "green space" people wrote letters to the editor about. Besides, he liked the environment himself. That was the whole point.

He'd considered publicizing the amounts of his annual donations to the Sierra Club, but that could have put off as many people as it pleased in this north Idaho town. After some thought, he'd spent a very sizable chunk of money the previous autumn to buy a tract of land close to town containing a good-sized almost-mountain, with a promise to turn the whole thing into open space. As a tool to disarm at least some of the bad feeling, it hadn't been too bad, but he'd been at the party to seal the deal. He could be a charming guy if he worked at it, at least that was what they said.

The truth was, of course, that if you were rich enough and didn't actually have a personality disorder, somebody would call you "charming," especially if they wanted your money. In any case, he'd used the occasion to announce the start of the project to build a public trail to the top of his new mountain. That had gone over well, especially when he told them it would be named the Kalispel Trail after the local Indian tribe, and not the Orbison Trail as he was sure they'd expected. He'd even gone wild and bid high on a case of very pricey north Idaho Cabernet, which had turned out to be not half bad, and a huge stained-glass hanging that hadn't been so great.

It was of rainbow trout in the water, and it was stuck in his hall closet right now. He could hang it in a guest room window, maybe.

It wasn't that he didn't like trout. He liked them fine, on a plate and crispy-brown. Looking at their gaping mouths didn't do much for him from an artistic point of view, that was all. But it had been that or another piece of a boat whose sails looked rigged all wrong. Or a painting of the lake—he'd rather look at the lake—or, finally, a coffee table with legs made out of antlers, an object he hadn't wanted one bit. He didn't care for animal parts as furniture, although he'd keep that opinion to himself up here. He also didn't like tree trunk legs on beds or branches as headboards. He liked furniture to look like *furniture,* not like something that belonged in a kids' book. The wine and the glass piece had been as far as he'd been willing to go, but they'd seemed like enough, together with his new trail and the promise of a signed and framed jersey, guaranteed worn to the Super Bowl, for a future online fundraiser.

Of course, it wasn't a jersey in which he'd *won* the Super Bowl, but there was no need to get all crazy about it. Some things, there wasn't enough money in the world to buy.

All that hadn't been bad, not really. The evening had left him grumpy once again, though. Standing around wasn't his favorite thing, but with *running* around off the table, let alone running around with any purpose, like to win a football game… at least it beat sitting around.

Beth had been a surprise bonus. Her mother, Michelle Schaefer, was one of those women who'd adopted the platinum bob as their signature hairstyle twenty years ago and had never seen any reason to change it, and whose favorite brand of makeup was Botox. Blake's own mother was always telling him not to judge so fast, though, so he was doing his best to put off his final verdict, despite the calculation in Michelle's eyes when she'd introduced him to her daughter.

Beth, though—she'd been different. Caramel-colored hair with blonde streaks that looked natural, pulled up into a conservative twist. Blue eyes, a pretty smile, and class all the way. A law degree *and* family money, which meant she wasn't after a meal ticket. Not like Courtney.

Forget that.

Beth. She was a little reserved, but that wasn't bad. Sweet, he'd say. Wife material. The only problem was, his supposed charm wasn't proving all that charming so far. Beth might have worn her hair down tonight, but whatever it took to make her let it down in any other way, he hadn't found it. All that family pressure not letting her relax, maybe. Well, it was only the first date.

"Tell me more about the company," he soldiered on now. "Why aren't you working for it? I'd have thought that'd be a no-brainer."

"You really think so?" she said with a wry smile. "They make salad dressing. Maybe that's why I moved to Seattle and went into wills and trusts. That's not necessarily interesting either, but at least it's my kind of boring." Her voice was slightly breathy, which was sexy, and so was her sleeveless blue sheath dress, in a conservative sort of way. She had great legs, too. Everything was there except a spark.

"So you're just visiting," he pushed on. Nobody'd ever called him a quitter. She didn't live here, no, which wasn't ideal from the courtship standpoint. But then, he didn't live here, either. He was in Seattle as often as he was anywhere else except Portland, and a long-distance romance would be good. Keep it on the slow track, keep things from getting out of hand. "It sounded like your folks would love to have you back for good. Not even tempted? Your dad must be doing something right. It's got to be rare in packaged goods for a company to be so successful selling only one product line, as dominant as the multinationals are." He was putting himself to sleep here, and he didn't think he was doing Beth any favors, either.

Her eyes strayed from his face, and her hand stilled on her fork. Not that she'd been eating much. She was slim to the point of thinness, and it was easy to see why. She'd barely touched her salad plate, and she wasn't doing much better on her fish. It was a safe bet that the dessert menu would be passing them by.

When she kept looking away, he twisted in his chair to see... not much. A couple threading their way between tables behind the hostess, that was all. One of them was a guy with the build of a linebacker, and the other was a woman who had him taking a second glance. A whole lot of artfully tousled dark brown hair falling around her face like she'd just gotten out of bed, a pair of low-slung skinny jeans ripped strategically down the thighs, and platform sandals that made her legs look a hundred miles long. All of her looking like a red-flag warning of the very best kind.

When he recognized her, it was with a leap of excitement and—call it annoyance, neither of which he managed to suppress well enough. His swimming partner. Out with somebody else.

He turned his attention hastily back to Beth. How long had he been staring? "Pardon? You were saying?"

"Oh," she said, shifting her own gaze back to him. "Nothing. You were asking about the business."

"More wine?" he asked, picking up the bottle.

"Oh, no, thanks. I'm good."

Wonderful.

He kept talking to Beth as well as he could manage, but her mind didn't seem to be on the job, either, and it was hard going. If she'd been reserved before—now, she was stilted. His own attention might have divided, too, because there Dakota was in his peripheral vision. Shoving her hair back over one tanned shoulder, revealing a little more of a filmy white top that draped just low enough, plus a delicate silver necklace on a chain that caught the candlelight. Her hair was loose and wild in the very best way, and her eyes lit up with animation as she laughed and gestured at the guy with her.

". . . Now we're into this case, and it's pretty hectic," Beth was saying. She went on, but Blake wasn't listening. Opposite him, Dakota had pushed her chair back, stood up, and touched her date lightly on the arm as she bent to tell him something, her blouse dipping with the movement and revealing a flash of cleavage, her wonderful mouth curving into a sassy smile. And then she was walking toward Blake, and right past him. And totally ignoring him.

Her hips didn't sway, exactly. That wasn't it. It was the confidence. And that little bit of a blouse she had on. It fell asymmetrically over the waistband of her low-slung jeans, and she was showing a tiny bit of bare brown skin down there. When she got close, he could see that the jeans had a button fly. They sat so low on her hips that there was only room for three buttons, though. Those buttons were silver, and they were absolutely magnetic. Because above them was something else silver, he saw as she shifted her purse on her shoulder and her blouse rode up. The wink of a curved stud in the dimple of her belly button.

Lord have mercy. If there was one thing he was a sucker for, it was an innie belly button on a toned stomach. And if she pierced it... well, he was a dead man. His tongue wanted to go right there, and it wanted to stay there awhile before heading on south.

That honey-colored skin. That little curved barbell. *Damn.*

Some men loved breasts, and some loved legs. Those things were absolutely great, don't get him wrong, but let's just say he enjoyed a woman he could appreciate coming and going, and a girl with gorgeous skin made him stupid. He loved to look at it, he loved to touch it, and he loved to kiss it. And the softer and smoother it was, the more he wanted to do it.

He'd bet that chain was still in her ear, too. The problem was, there was so much there that needed to be kissed and licked and taken care of, and he wasn't the guy who'd be doing it.

It felt like forever, but it was over in a couple seconds. She was past him, leaving behind the barest whiff of her perfume. Spicy and warm, dangerously potent and seriously sexy. It wasn't the light, ladylike floral scent Beth was wearing. It was a whole lot more addictive than that.

Beth. Whoops. His manners had taken a hike, and she'd obviously noticed, because she'd stopped talking and was just looking at him.

He said, "Sorry. Long day," smiled at her, and thought, *Dial it back, horn dog.*

"They can be that way," she said, that dry note back in her

voice.

"Would you like a coffee?" he asked. "Dessert?"

"No, thank you. In fact, it's been a bit of a long day for me, too. Maybe we should get out of here."

In another woman, it might have been a discreet come-on. In her, it wasn't. He paid the check as Dakota walked by him again, and he *didn't* look up, because he was with another woman who deserved his attention, and Dakota's efforts were for the other guy anyway.

She wasn't even the one who'd invited him to come swimming, he reminded himself when his mind tried to go straight to "jealous." If she'd flirted with him… well, he'd flirted with her, too. Before she'd told him she didn't want any part of him.

That was the old you anyway, he told himself. *New life plan, remember? No more wild side. No more wild rides.*

Fifteen minutes later, he was turning down the Schaefers' driveway, with its discreet lighting buried in the greenery on either side, and ending up at the guest house beside the enormous pile of her parents' place. He hopped out and walked Beth to her door. Despite all evidence to the contrary, he *had* been raised right.

He wouldn't have had to be nearly as good at body language as he was to interpret the stiffness of her shoulders, though, and it didn't take any skill at all to hear the undercurrents when she said, "Thank you very much for dinner. I had a nice time."

He grinned at her ruefully and scratched his nose. "Well…"

She laughed, showing more animation than she had all night. "Yeah. You're right. That wasn't either of our best effort. But we can tell my mom I tried."

"She giving you a hard time?" he asked, liking her better than ever.

"Oh, not compared to, say, a football coach trying to get his team to the Super Bowl. But thank you anyway. You're a very nice man."

"I'm not that nice a man," he said. "But I think I'm with a

very nice woman." He bent, gave her a kiss on the cheek, and said, "Good night. Thanks for your company."

"You're very welcome," she said, then offered him a sweet smile and headed inside.

Why couldn't he go for a woman like that?

A Battle You Can't See
♡

When Blake pulled up the next morning outside a modest frame house painted a neat if unimaginative white, Russell was out the door with the brown dog before the SUV had even stopped. Cattle dog, Blake thought that was. She wasn't beautiful, but she sure seemed loyal.

He hopped down from the truck and went to take the bag from the older man's hand, but Russell jerked it away with an "I've got it."

Ah. Pride. "Right," Blake said, and didn't open the door for him, either.

Russell urged the dog into the back seat, where she immediately lay down, and then hauled himself into the front passenger seat. Blake could tell it hurt like hell, but he didn't say anything. He knew something about pride himself.

Russell didn't say much on the ten-minute drive to the resort, which meant Blake didn't have to chat. Fine by him. He liked guys who didn't yap at him, and he especially liked guys who didn't feel the need to yap about football. He liked talking just fine when there was a point to it. When he was talking about a game plan, say, or a business strategy.

Or when he was talking to a woman. That worked. Not like

last night with Beth, which had been too much like hard labor for both of them. Out at the rocks with Dakota, though? Now, if he'd been taking *her* home last night, if he'd been telling her exactly how much he appreciated her in that little white shirt and those jeans with their three silver buttons, and exactly what he wanted to do about it. How he wanted to touch her, and how he wanted to kiss her. If he'd been smelling her spicy-sexy perfume, watching her eyes darken, hearing her breath come faster, like his hand was already there, sliding inside that blouse, stroking over all that warm, smooth skin...

Yeah. That was the kind of talking he could get into.

Except that somebody else had been taking her home. Except for that.

Russell finally said something when Blake was unlocking the gate out at the new marina, although it was just, "The place is looking pretty good. Guess it'll change the town some."

Blake looked back at the staggered line of honey-stained wooden building that was the Wild Horse Resort. It *did* look good. Plenty of windows, including in the soaring lobby with its distinctive slabs of greenish-gray slate making up floors and counters, with the wood to warm it up. That had been the idea, and it worked.

It looked exactly like his vision, and pretty damn close to perfect. The resort followed the edge of the shoreline, its manmade contours softened by plantings and fronted by marina and beach, with eighteen holes of magnificent golf course off to one side. None of it too obtrusive. No gleaming towers of glass rising too many stories high. Rustic luxury, that was the idea, its beauty coming from, and blending into, the land and the lake around it.

He said, "Not everybody's happy about those changes, I know."

The older man shrugged lopsidedly and stumped his way along the wooden dock, surefooted despite his crooked body. "Tree-huggers. What good does it do to protect the environment if the town's dead? Who's going to be here to see it? When the mill went, half the jobs went with it. I didn't hear those folks from California worrying about that. Probably had a party."

"Well, to be fair," Blake said mildly, "they've got a point. Even from a business point of view—we're selling natural beauty up here. Can't do that if the lake's a mess, and the air's got to be clear, too, no bald spots on the mountains from clear-cutting. Nature in all her glory, that's what looks good to a guy who's been sitting in his car on the freeway for three hours a day the other fifty weeks of the year."

Russell didn't answer that. He was looking at the boat. That was a thing of beauty in itself. Gleaming white, her lines as sleek as a thoroughbred's. A Rolls-Royce in the convertible fishing boat world, to mix a metaphor, if a Rolls-Royce on the smaller side.

Russell was still looking, but all he said was, "A lot of boat for this lake."

"That's true. On the other hand, I haul her over to the coast, and she's ready for a cruise to Alaska. That was the other thing I had in mind." Blake had come out and got her ready to go before picking Russell up, and now, he did take the bag from the other man and set it in the stern before climbing aboard and offering a hand. To his relief, Russell accepted the grip on his forearm, because Blake couldn't see any way he'd have made it otherwise. The weathered face tightened, but the grunt that escaped him on swinging into the boat was quickly muffled. All the same, the sweat was standing out on his upper lip when he turned and ordered the dog, "Bella. Jump."

She leaped neatly into the boat, and in fifteen minutes, they were in the teak-lined cockpit, motoring out into the center of the lake and headed for a cove on the far side. The twin diesels purred, the sound discreetly muffled up here in their luxurious surroundings. Russell hadn't made a comment on the cabin as they'd passed other than to ask, "How many does she sleep?"

"Five. Two doubles, and a single for crew. Two heads."

"Huh. Like I said. A lot of boat for the lake. Open water,

though… yeah. You had her out in the ocean yet?"

"Nope." He didn't mention the boat's big sister, the GT 77 he kept out in Hawaii. He wasn't actually a pretentious asshole. At least he hoped not.

"Huh," Russell had said again, and that was all.

Now, Blake said, "Portside compartment over there's got a thermos and a couple cups in it. You could pour us a cup of coffee. I put a little whisky in there to take the morning edge off."

Russell pulled them out, but said, "I brought my own. Coffee."

"Plenty for two."

"I don't drink."

Blake shot a quick glance at him, but Russell's craggy, lined face was expressionless under the same white cap he'd had on when they'd met, daubed with what looked like years' worth of splatters. Blake accepted his cup of spiked coffee, watched Russell pour his, which was black and smelled strong enough to dissolve paint, and said, "I guess that's why you stay away from the painkillers, too. Good move if you can handle it, but it takes some doing. I went a few rounds with the Vikes myself, and they had me on the ropes for a while before I beat 'em. More than one way to drown your sorrows, but all of them turn out about the same, I guess "

"What was that?" Russell asked. "Ankle?"

"Knee. I've more or less got a peg leg there now. That thing's pretty much destroyed."

"Devils aren't my team," Russell said. "I didn't follow all of it. Hard on a man to retire before he's ready, though."

"You got that right. That what happened to you?"

A long pause, then Russell said, "Guess there's no reason you'd remember. You'll want to head on over to shore now." He pointed to a deep indentation in the shoreline. Not many houses out here on the far side of the lake, halfway to Montana and miles of winding lakeside road from the highway. Not developed, which gave Blake a curious divided feeling, the outdoorsman in him enjoying the hell out of that, and the businessman in him seeing the opportunity.

He turned the wheel, eased up on the throttle, and said, "No reason I'd remember what?"

"Broke my back. On a job about six months ago."

"I'm guessing there's more to it," Blake said slowly when Russell didn't go on. "What job?"

"Coeur d'Alene. That Sundays you built out there."

It was a shower of cold water right down Blake's own back. That had happened on his watch? He tried to remember if he'd heard anything about it, but he couldn't. Six months ago, he'd been thinking about other things. Like a knee destroyed in the final minutes of an otherwise uneventful win on Thanksgiving weekend, and another quarterback taking the Devils to the Super Bowl. Like the team losing that game, one they should have won. Like a ring Blake should have been adding to the one sitting in a box in his dresser drawer. The only one he'd ever win. As much as he'd thought about anything through the haze of a dozen Vicodin a day.

Suck it up, he told himself. *You blew out a knee. He broke his back. And you're the one with all the consolation prizes.* He cut the engine at a muttered word from Russell and said, "I'm sorry," knowing how lame it sounded. "I didn't remember. Tell me now."

"No point," Russell said. "It's over and gone." He'd said that to the tackle shop owner, too. *Over and gone.* He went on, "Everybody's got his own stuff to think about. Tends to drown out the other guy's. That's life. Let's fish."

Check it out, Blake thought. *See if there's something you should've known about, that you need to know now.*

It took a while for the constraint to lessen, but it did. Being out on the water helped, and so did the kind of male companionship Blake missed most, the brotherhood of doing a thing together. One person wasn't a team, but it helped. And so did Bella, oddly enough. Sitting still and absolutely attentive, her gaze fixed on Russell no matter what, until they put the rods away and he told her, "Go on, then. Go for a swim," and she sailed into the lake with a mighty leap. She paddled all the way around the boat, then did it again, the happiest dog in the world, before she came back on board and shook joyously all over that pristine Hatteras deck.

He should get one of those, Blake thought, and knew he wouldn't. A dog was ridiculous for somebody who spent his life flying from one place to another and one house to another, and his days in boardrooms, in restaurants, and on jobsites. He'd turn into one of those Hollywood stars who had a personal assistant to fetch his lattes and walk his dog. Ridiculous.

But a dog would sure be nice.

By the time they were motoring back again, past two in the afternoon, Russell had a twenty-pound salmon in the fish locker. Blake had nothing, but that was how it went. You didn't get your way in fishing. You gave it your best shot, and you got what you got. Kind of like football.

When they pulled up again outside the little frame house in a part of town that would never get fashionable, Blake peeled off ten twenties, and Russell stuck them into a battered leather wallet with a nod and said, "Come on in and have an iced tea. Stick around for supper if you want. I'm going to be firing up the barbecue, and that's way too much salmon for two."

"I don't mind if I do." Blake had no place to go, he was tired of his own company, and anyway—he liked Russell. "You married, then?"

"Nope. Never did get married. I'm dumb, but I'm not stupid. Got my stepdaughter living with me, though."

He swung on down from the SUV, another painful affair, and Bella jumped down after him. Blake hauled out the cooler with the fish, already cleaned at the marina's station, and said, "Wait, though. If you weren't married, how do you have a stepdaughter? If you don't mind my asking."

"Ex-girlfriend's daughter," Russell said. "My son's sister. Half-sister. Same mom, different dads."

"Oh. Gotcha." Blake followed Russell and Bella up the concrete walk and said, "Your boy's not around here, I guess, or he'd be fishing with you."

"He's gone," Russell said. "Iraq. Eight years ago."

"I'm sorry," Blake said, because what else did you say?

It was like his mom was right there in his ear. *Of course it's hard on you, sweetie. Of course it is, losing football, losing your knee, and both of them so sudden. You need to let yourself feel it. There's no weakness in that. Go on and grieve it. Go on and let go. Just remember not to lose sight of where you are in the scheme of things. Other people have it hard, too. Everybody you'll ever meet is fighting a battle you can't see.*

And some of them were a whole lot worse than a busted knee, a vanished girlfriend, and a career change.

Past Imperfect

♡

Dakota held the curved segment of pink glass against the wheel of the grinder, working patiently until the piece she'd cut matched the overlaid paper template perfectly. Then she turned to set the finished piece on her worktable, and a muscle spasmed in her neck. She stifled an exclamation, set the glass down—slicing her finger in the process— and rubbed her neck and shoulder with one hand while she sucked on her sore finger until that got boring.

It was probably time for a break. She checked her phone and blinked. Well, yeah. Two-thirty, and she'd been at her table for seven hours. She was starving, and she needed to pee. Time alone meant time in the zone, but it could also lead to what some people called "excess."

The conch tugged at her, but the fatigue and stiffness did, too. Plus, she really *did* have to pee. All of a sudden, that was an emergency. Her obsession screamed, "No!" But her body told her that a snack, a bike ride, and a swim to loosen everything up would make her more productive. Her conch would still be here when she got back. Ready and waiting.

Tearing herself away was always the hard part, but by the time she'd biked to City Beach and swum for twenty minutes along the farthest edge of the floating-log barrier, she felt refreshed and ready to go again. She maneuvered around a group of noisy, rambunctious boys, waded up to the beach, and did her usual squint-and-stumble effort to find her towel and bag.

Somebody said, "Dakota. Over here." Evan's voice.

She navigated by sound and fuzzy sight over to where he was sitting with Gracie and said, "Can't find my stuff."

"I figured," he said. "Come on." He guided her to her red bag, and she reached for her glasses and, as always, felt more secure when she had them on.

"Why don't you just wear your contacts when you swim?" he asked.

"Not worth it." She grabbed her towel and wrapped it around her waist. "I save them for when it matters how I look, and as contact-worthy occasions are sadly rare in my life, I still have plenty of pairs left. But if I'm wearing this suit, contacts wouldn't help. I know you were going to say it."

"Nah, I wasn't. Haven't said anything yet, have I?"

"Not that much. But you tend to be fairly restrained in general."

"Why'd you buy that, anyway? Since you brought it up."

"It was cheap."

"Well, yeah," he said doubtfully. Then he shut up, because somebody else was walking over to join them.

Beth Schaefer, who *didn't* have an ugly bathing suit. She was wearing a conservative but beautifully designed aqua bikini that showed off her slim figure and pale skin, and her blonde hair was in a French braid. She looked like what she was. Rich, classy, and poised, exactly the same way she'd looked last night when she'd been out with Blake Orbison.

"Hey, Beth," Dakota said. Jealousy was ugly, and she had nothing against Beth. Not really. Not anymore. "How're you doing?"

"Oh, I'm good," she said. "Really good. Fine. Just home to see my parents for a few days. Visit, you know. How are you?"

She glanced at Evan and Gracie, and Gracie did one of her big smiles, which made Beth smile back. Evan didn't smile, and he still wasn't saying anything, either.

"Great," Dakota said, then couldn't think of anything else.

"I need to get going," Evan said. "The baby."

"Oh," Dakota said. Clearly, they were done. "Hey, if you've got the van, can I shove my bike in the back and get a ride to my place with you? Maybe you'd help with that storage unit."

"Sure," he said.

"Well," Beth said, "nice to see you, anyway."

Dakota waited until she and Evan had left the beach and she was unlocking her bike to say, "So that wasn't awkward much."

Evan didn't answer, just went ahead to the van and opened it up, then started to buckle Gracie into her car seat. "If you hang on a minute," he said while Dakota wheeled her bike around to the back, "I'll put that inside for you."

"Nope." Dakota wedged it into the back of the van, careful to position it so it wouldn't fall on Gracie. When Evan finally shifted the big old Ford Econoline into gear and eased carefully out into the crowded parking lot, she said, "You know, when you didn't say anything last night about Beth being out with Blake, I thought you were being careful of my delicate sensibilities after my unfortunate encounter on the rocks. Guess not."

A muscle ticked in his hard jaw, and there was a long pause before he said, "No."

She sighed. "That's communicative. 'No' what? No, you weren't being careful? No, you don't want to talk about it?"

"No both."

"You know, many experts recommend talking out one's issues with a trusted friend. It's a concept."

Evan made the turn onto Cedar. "What's the point? It's not going to change how I feel. It's not going to change what I do."

Dakota hesitated, then probed the tender spot anyway. "It was a long time ago. None of us is the person we were then."

He glanced at her, then back at the road. "I am. I'm still the same guy. Exact same guy."

She considered that. It was true, pretty much. She tugged the elastic off the bottom of her braid, undid her hair, finger-combed through it, and did her best to squeeze it dry with the towel. She hadn't bothered with her clothes, and she was dripping wet again. "Except that you're a dad. You don't think that's changed you?"

"Yeah. Made me less likely to waste my time." He turned onto Seventh. Smoothly and quietly, the way Evan did everything. But that didn't mean there was nothing happening underneath.

"I should probably have been more sensitive back then," she said. "When all that happened. Sorry about that."

"What, probed my feelings some more? No, you shouldn't have. I felt crappy. There you go. Saved you the trouble. Besides, you had other things to think about."

"Yeah." She looked out the window at a sprinkler watering a front lawn, with a couple of shrieking kids running through it. Big brother, little sister. "I've been thinking about Riley a lot lately. It's being back here, because he's everywhere I look in this town. Every memory I have. Do you ever get that?"

"I told you, I don't think about sad stuff when there's no point."

"I do. All the time."

"I noticed."

Dakota looked out the window some more. Kids on bikes, kids sitting on front porch steps eating popsicles with their friends. Wild Horse in the summer.

It had never been her town, and never Riley's, either. All Riley had done was make it bearable. Her first memory and her fallback position, always, until he wasn't. Through everything that had happened to them, every single time their world had been uprooted, Riley had been there, telling her, "It's OK. We'll stick together, and it'll be OK."

"But what if we can't stay together?" she'd asked him once.

That last, scariest time after Grandma had died, when they'd come to Wild Horse. Riley had been coming home— sort of— and she'd been coming nowhere close.

The two of them had stood on the sidewalk outside Russell's house with their backpacks and a garbage bag full of clothes, watching their mother's red taillights disappearing into the darkness. They'd stared at the closed door of an unfamiliar house where a man lived who was Riley's father, but not hers. She'd known she couldn't ring that doorbell, but she wouldn't have to. Riley would do it.

"Of course we're going to stick together," he'd said, sounding absolutely sure. "Of course we can."

"He's not going to want me. I'm going to foster care. You know I am." It was the dark cloud that had hung over their heads so many times, the storm that had always threatened but never broken.

"If you do," Riley had said, his Adam's apple bobbing in his throat, tension in every line of his wiry seventeen-year-old frame, "I'll run away and come get you out. No matter what." He'd held up his fist until she'd raised her own. Then he'd bumped fists with her and said it. "This bud's for you."

She hadn't been able to stop the tears from welling in her eyes, but she'd repeated the silly phrase just as she always had, even though her voice had wobbled. "This bud's for you."

She'd gotten the call from Russell on a day like today. A warm summer Saturday. She'd been twenty-one and independent, a free spirit in a city full of free spirits, where nobody had known her name. Where "Dakota" sounded cool, and "Dakota Savage" sounded awesome.

She'd taken her bike up to Seaside, on the Oregon coast, and she was riding on the Lewis & Clark Mainline, almost at the steel bridge, when her phone rang in her pocket with the distinctive piano notes of "You Are the Sunshine of My Life." Russell. She'd hopped off her bike, grabbed her phone from her pocket, and said, "Hey, Dad. How're you doing? I was just thinking about you."

"Dakota."

That one word, and the darkness had come. The cloud that had threatened for so long had broken, and she'd stood there in the sun, staring at the hand holding her bike, at the worn blue paint and the electrical tape coming loose on the grip, listened to Russell talk, and gotten colder and colder. Until she was shivering. Until she was frozen.

Evan had come to drive her home. He hadn't said much. He'd just been there, exactly as he'd been with her, and with Russell, during the terrible visit to the funeral home, and then all the way until they were standing at the gravesite. On Russell's other side when the honor guard had taken the flag off Riley's coffin and folded it into that perfect triangle, then handed it to Riley's father, the gift nobody wanted. When the bugler had played "Taps," the last mournful note had died, and Dakota had thought her heart would die along with it. When they'd put her big brother in the ground, and for the last time, she'd whispered, "This bud's for you." When she'd known that from now on, she had to be her own hero.

She'd probably leaned on Evan too much that summer Riley had died—for herself, but especially for Russell. However bad her brother's death had been for her, it had been worse for Russell. Dakota had still been around, but she wasn't Russell's. She didn't have his name, and she didn't have his blood. She was just Riley's half-sister, the girl who'd showed up at fifteen and had no place else to go. Part of the package deal.

As much as she'd loved Russell, her love hadn't come close to making up for the hole Riley had left in his life. Fortunately, there'd been Evan. Riley's best friend had been able to do what Dakota hadn't. Because after the funeral, when other people had said their "Sorrys" and gone back to their lives, when Dakota had had to go back to Portland, and to work—Evan hadn't. He'd kept coming over for dinner after work, staying to watch baseball with Russell, going out fishing and hunting with him as he always had. He'd been more than Russell's business partner. He'd been a friend. They'd needed him, and he'd stepped up, just like he'd been stepping up ever since. He was right. He was still the same guy.

Sometime during that terrible summer, though, Beth and Evan had broken up, and Dakota hadn't even known anything about it for weeks. He'd never said. She still didn't know what had happened, or why.

They were almost home. If she were going to say this, she needed to say it now, so she did. "Beth came to see me, you know. Right before she went back to Seattle to start law school."

"You think that's going to matter to me. I don't care. It was a long time ago." For once, Evan's movements *weren't* smooth. He pulled in to the curb in front of the house—and hit it with a hard jolt. *"Damn."*

"Da da da," Gracie sang from the back seat, and Dakota could swear Evan flinched.

"She's not a parrot," Dakota said. "You're unlikely to have a one-year-old who curses like a sailor just because you slipped up once."

"Want to bet?" He had his hand on the door handle like he couldn't be in here another minute.

"For Pete's sake." Dakota would have sworn she knew guys, but they could still baffle and exasperate her like nothing else. "Just *wait* a second."

"Nothing to wait for. I'm fine." Evan climbed out of the van and slammed the door, then came around to her side for Gracie.

He was fine? Swearing in front of his daughter *and* slamming the door? Yeah, right.

It *was* a long time ago. They'd both looked so sad, though. She'd seen it in Beth, and she'd felt it in Evan. Well, she'd felt his mad. But "mad" was just a guy's version of "sad."

She gave it up and went to the rear of the van to get her bike. Her own love life wasn't setting any heat records, after all. She sure wasn't qualified to judge anybody else's.

She rolled her bike into the backyard and put it away. Bella tore out to meet her, which meant Russ was home from his fishing trip. Good. She'd started to wonder about him when he hadn't showed up by the time she'd left for the lake. She didn't even know who he'd gone with.

Gracie was starting to fuss a little in Evan's arms. "She needs her bottle," he said. "But I'll give her a quick bath first, if that's OK, get the sand off."

"Sure," Dakota said absently, going up the stairs to the back door. Now that she was here, her glass was pulling at her again. She'd hang the storage unit with Evan, and then she'd get back to her piece, and by the end of tomorrow, if she had another day like today, she'd be done with everything but the soldering.

She was opening the door from the back-porch laundry area on the thought, going on through into the kitchen, and hearing the voices. Russ's. And somebody else's. Somebody saying something, low and slow, in a voice like warm molasses.

No. Not possible.

She was hustling now, around the corner and to her workroom. *Her* space. Where Bella was sitting on one side of the gate with her tongue out, and Russell was inside, showing off the finished pieces in the corner.

Showing her best pieces, her *private* pieces. To Blake Orbison.

Surprise All the Way Around
♡

"Sorry I can't offer you a beer," Russell told Blake when they got inside the little house, which was neater and cleaner than Blake had imagined it would be.

"No problem," Blake said, accepting the glass of iced tea. "This is the taste of home to a Southern boy." He leaned against the kitchen counter to watch as Russell put cedar planks into a roasting pan to soak and begun to cut the fish into fillets. The cleanliness would be the stepdaughter, probably. Russell didn't seem like the homemaker type. Grilling the fish didn't count. Every guy could barbecue.

Blake didn't think much of adults who lived at home, even if they traded off doing the housework in exchange. Arrested development was what it always looked like to him.

Right. So he'd judged. He wouldn't be sharing his opinion with Russell. And sure, somebody could say that when you left college for the NFL, you weren't exactly in a normal young-adult situation, and you didn't have room to judge. He knew that no matter how much he loved his parents, he wouldn't have moved back in with them. He'd have slept in his car before he'd done that. He'd wanted to be on his own—he'd *longed* to be on his own—and he didn't get why anybody else wouldn't. Especially a guy. Maybe women were different, although his older sister hadn't moved back home, either.

He sipped at his iced tea and looked around. There was a stained-glass piece hanging in the window that he liked a lot better than his trout. Three scarlet flowers—poppies, he thought—in extreme close-up, glowing vibrant in the light, as cheerful as sunshine. That one wouldn't even have been a sacrifice to buy. He'd have to ask Russell where he'd gotten it. It was a surprise, though. Russell didn't seem like a man who'd be interested in art. Must be the stepdaughter's.

There was something else on the wall opposite, though, above the table—a couple framed photos that took his mind off the poppies. A man in a desert camo uniform and boots, crouching in the sand beside a vehicle and holding a map, with two other guys crouching beside him as he pointed something out to them. Another strangely compelling shot of the same guy lying on his bunk in a sand-colored T-shirt and camo pants, one hand behind his head, looking at the camera without a smile.

It was a serious face, an intense face, fined down and tanned desert-brown, intelligence showing in the bright blue eyes. A lean guy bulked up by the uniform, a wide receiver type made of muscle and sinew, all fast-twitch muscle fiber and quick reflexes.

Russell finished with the fish and made his halting way over to the table with his own iced tea. "My boy," he said, seeing the direction of Blake's gaze. "Riley."

"Looks like he'd earned some stripes." Blake indicated the map photo with his glass.

"Sergeant," Russell said, all his pride there to hear in that one word.

"How old was he?"

"Twenty-three when he died. Nineteen when he joined up. Those two pictures… his commander sent me those with the letter. That one with the map? That was his last day, right before they went out. He won a Silver Star that day. They sent me that, too. Not much of a trade for my son."

A Silver Star. That was for bravery. Blake looked again at the picture of the guy on the bunk, at the intensity in that steadfast gaze. He looked a lot older than twenty-three. "What happened?" he asked, because he got the feeling Russell wanted to tell him. Because he knew, like you did when your mother was a minister, that the dead didn't seem quite so gone if you could talk about them. And because Russell was that thing he admired most. Mentally strong, with the guts to look your life in the face and the kind of courage that came the toughest, the kind you had to summon afresh every day to take what you had to take without whining. The kind Blake was still working on acquiring. He'd thought he had it, before. Easy to think so when you were on top of the world.

Russell said, "Have a seat," and, when Blake did, got himself into his chair, which wasn't easy. He looked down at his glass, rattled the ice, and said, "His squad was on patrol, came under attack. Machine guns, rocket-propelled grenades. He told his gunner to fire, cover them, and then he left the lead vehicle along with his squad leader to take care of it. They crossed over a berm and into the trenches the bastards had dug, took 'em on with grenades and assault rifles. The squad leader made it, and so did the rest of them. Riley didn't. But that was my son. If it had to be done, he was on it. He'd never have asked anybody to do something he wasn't willing to do himself. He took that attitude into the Army with him. Got him killed."

"But he saved his squad," Blake said. "He died a hero."

People had called *him* a hero. They'd talked about mental toughness, about playing when you hurt, about staying strong when you were down on the scoreboard, about holding onto your belief and doing it for the guys around you. Blake knew better, though. That wasn't a hero. That was just a guy doing his job. The heroes… they didn't get paid millions of dollars. They ran into buildings everybody else was running out of. They ran toward the gunfire. They risked a whole lot more than a game, or a paycheck, or even a knee. They risked it all,

63

because it needed to be done and they could do it.

Russell said, "You think that makes it worth it? That he was a hero? It doesn't. But would I rather have had a different kind of boy, if it had meant he'd have come home? I've asked myself that, and damned if I know the answer. I know I had a son I was proud of. I had no part in the man he was, but I was sure as hell proud."

"You had to have had something to do with the man he was," Blake objected. "I know my dad does." Why was he thinking about his parents so much today? Being with Russell, he guessed, although there couldn't have been two men more superficially unlike than the crusty, battered man opposite him and Blake's courtly Virginia-gentleman professor father.

Russell said, "Bet your dad was around, though."

"Well, yeah. Him and my mom both. Working, but we've all got to work."

"You don't get it. I wasn't around. When he and his sister showed up here, Riley was seventeen. When my ex took off with him, he was two, and I wasn't much good those first couple years. What do I take credit for? A couple years there, when he was practically a grown man already? No."

"Oh." That was strange. Normally, when a guy had stepkids, it was because they'd come with the woman, a package deal. "So your stepdaughter is younger, from when you and your ex got back together? Sorry," he said when the other man looked at him sharply. "Just trying to get it straight. Bad habit. My mom's a Unitarian minister. She goes on and asks the questions, pretty direct, so she can understand the situation. That's where it comes from. There and in business. Could make me forget my manners."

"Nah," Russell said. "I like a man who speaks his mind. That's the trouble these days. Nobody's willing to talk straight. We didn't get back together, the ex and me. You're thinking, why's my stepdaughter here with me, then? There's more to family than blood."

"I know that. I'm adopted myself." It was no secret. The

media had loved that story.

"Oh. Huh." Russell finished off his iced tea, heaved himself to his feet, and said, "Come on. I'll show you something you'll like. Show you what my girl does. She's an artist."

Great. A woman who lived with her... not even her dad, *and* she was an "artist"? Russell was a lonely guy, that was obvious, but still. What a price to pay. Blake stood up, though. What could you do, say, "I'll pass?" No, you couldn't. He'd have to say nice things about the "art," too.

On the other hand, there'd be fresh-caught salmon. Grilled on cedar planks? Couldn't put a price on that.

♡♡♡

When Russell unlatched a wooden baby gate and stepped on through, though, and Blake followed him into a workroom, he had to amend his opinion.

"She did the piece in the kitchen," he guessed. "The flowers."

Russell put the gate back into place, and Bella lay down with a heavy sigh and put her muzzle on her paws on the other side, a martyred dog who'd been unfairly shut out. "Yep," Russell said. "One of my favorites, is why she let me keep it, because those poppies would've sold. Got one in my bedroom, too, of a snowy owl at twilight. About the prettiest thing you'll ever see."

Blake barely heard him, and he hardly took in the meticulously organized workroom, a space that said nothing like "hobby" and everything like "dedication." He noticed the paper pattern laid out on the big worktable with paper-covered, numbered pieces lying on top of each numbered section of pattern like some kind of paint-by-numbers project, and then he forgot it. He was looking at something else. Something hanging in a corner like an afterthought.

It was big. That was the first thing that struck him. Probably four feet across. A bald eagle skimming over the edge of a rippling blue lake, its wings and talons outstretched, the vague suggestion of snow-capped mountains in the background. He didn't know how you did something like that in glass. The perfect symmetry, the incredible grace. The sheer number of pieces of glass, their minute size.

It was meticulously done, but it wasn't the craftsmanship that had him standing mesmerized. It was that he *felt* the eagle. He understood the bird's total concentration as it stretched its yellow talons out for that fish. It was exactly what you felt just before you threw the pass you needed, the one in the final seconds when the clock was ticking down. When you waited, knowing the hit was coming and not caring, because the ball had to leave your hand right... now. Right... there. The moment before you won, and to hell with what happened next, with how hard that linebacker would hit you. It was all about this moment, about concentration and resolve, about getting it done.

"That's one hell of a piece," he managed to say. "That for sale?"

"Don't know," Russell said. "She does some stuff on commission, mostly for folks with lake houses, and other stuff for sale in the galleries. Coeur d'Alene, Seattle. I'm not sure which this one is."

"Well, I'd like to buy it if it isn't already spoken for. Or even if it is."

Russell ran a thumb over his jaw. "Going to be pricey. See, it's about how many pieces of glass are in it. Every piece... that's a half hour's work. Something like that, maybe two hundred pieces? You can do the math. She worked on that eagle every weekend for more than a month, right on through. Not really a good bet, tell you the truth, not that she thinks of that when she gets an idea in her head. Makes a lot more sense to do the easy ones. Most people can't tell the difference, just looking for something pretty for the front window. They're not going to pay a couple thousand bucks for a piece of stained glass, or give her more than minimum wage for her time. She could've done six easy ones in those six weeks, could've sold 'em and been way ahead."

"Weekends? She doesn't do it full time?"

"Oh, hell, no. Like you say. Everybody's got to work."

"I'd think this could pay the bills."

Russell looked away, and something changed. Something Blake didn't understand. Some darkness. And clearly, Blake had got his ideas all wrong.

Hasty, his dad would have said in his cultivated accent. *Slow down, son. Think before you move, before you talk, before you act. Slow down and be sure.*

Blake hadn't been too good at slowing down then, and he hadn't gotten a whole lot better since. He'd kept on running when the rest of the family had walked, jumping into the water when they were still unfolding their towels, asking the girl out while the other guy was still thinking about it, making three deals while another CEO was still weighing the pros and cons of the first one. It was his nature—fast-twitch fibers in the muscle and the brain, if the brain had been a muscle—and it served him well. Most of the time.

Now, he tore his gaze away from his eagle and studied the workroom. "Nice space. Organized."

"Yeah. That's my contribution, you could say. Doing the dividers, the frames and that."

Blake went to the opposite corner, where a compartment held a dozen pieces framed in the same light wood as the eagle, leaning up against each other. "All right if I look?"

"Sure. Just be careful with 'em. You break it, you buy it."

Blake started flipping through them, then paused. "Whoa."

"Yeah," Russell said. "Those ones are a little different. Those are the ones she hasn't sold. Waiting to take 'em over to Seattle. Not everybody gets 'em, don't want 'em in their living room, you know?"

Once again, Blake had stopped listening. He picked up a heavy piece, moved it against the storage dividers holding colored sheets of glass, propped it up, and stood back.

"Whoa," he said again. "That's… I've never seen anything quite like that. What is it?"

"Iris," Russell said. "The flower."

Blake guessed it could be that. Like the poppies, it was in a sort of extreme close-up. But *this* one…

He was standing here with the artist's stepfather. His heart was beating faster, but that wasn't the reaction that was concerning him. He was getting turned on by a *flower*.

But holy hell, that was some flower. He guessed irises did look like that if you got up real close, but he'd just say that the Methodist church wasn't going to be hanging this thing in their community hall.

Delicate, curving, ruffled-edged petals unfolded and unfurled above the flower's center, picked out in shades of pink from delicate pearl to more of an inside-of-a-shell deal. Below the center, the petals were in shadow, nearly lavender, gentle and open.

But that center. That secret heart, that deep-purple oval with its waving indentations around the edges. Your eye went right there, like the petals were all arranged for you, laid out there for you, inviting you to…

Yeah. Well. He wanted this one, too.

He got a better grip on himself looking at the others, not that they were much less imagination-worthy. More flowers, from morning glories to calla lilies to roses, all of them in that same close-up. Silken petals laid open, and a deep, secret heart.

They were erotic as hell, was what they were. No heterosexual man was going to look at them and not see it, surely. He glanced up from where he was crouching before the pieces and saw Russell watching him not quite impassively, a hint of amusement in his eyes.

When Bella let out a short, sharp bark and took off, her toenails skittering on the floor, Russell said, "That'll be her. The salmon'll be a good treat for her, too. I bet she was in here working all day."

Blake heard the sound of a door closing and moved to slide

the latest piece back into its spot. When he met Russell's stepdaughter, it might be better if he weren't literally sporting a hard-on from her art. Might be a little difficult to explain, although he had a feeling he wouldn't be the only guy ever to have that reaction.

"They're all that and then some, aren't they?" Russell asked, waving a hand at the flowers. "Some of the folks in Seattle go for those big-time. Hang them in their bedrooms, I guess. Kinda making a name for herself with those, but it's not a name she wants to make around here."

"Ah, no," Blake said. "I'm guessing not. Small town."

"You got that right."

Blake was turning, moving to stand when she came around the corner like an avenging fury. An avenging fury in an ugly navy-blue swimsuit. His girlfriend from the rocks. Dakota.

She skidded to a stop outside the gate and said, her voice vibrating with outrage, "What the hell are you doing here?"

Her dark eyes were flashing, she was practically panting, and her hair wasn't in a braid this time. It was down and messy and dark and wet. One of her straps was falling down her shoulder, revealing a stripe of tan line and, where the suit fell away, the swell of a pale breast.

She saw the direction of his gaze and yanked the strap up. It was only then that he registered the other guy. The big guy, the linebacker from last night. He was with Dakota again. And this time, he was holding a baby.

First Quarter, No Score
♡

The big guy muttered something and took the baby away, but everybody else just stood there. After a few seconds, Blake heard water running, but he wasn't paying much attention.

When he'd seen Dakota last night, he'd been willing to overlook her flirting with him earlier, even though she'd been out with somebody else. He'd been out with somebody else himself, after all. She hadn't been wearing a ring, and the way she'd walked past him, like she'd known what she was doing to him and had wanted to do it, had made him think that it might have been a first date for her, too. It had felt like they were both out with the wrong people, no matter how hostile she'd seemed earlier. That heat hadn't just come from him. A fire couldn't burn without oxygen. She hadn't just been giving it oxygen, though. She'd been pouring the gasoline on, and he'd known it.

But now? This put it in a whole different category. She had a baby with this guy, and she'd still looked at Blake like that, talked to him the way she had, flirted that hard? And she'd made those… those glass pieces? He wondered if Russell knew what she really was. And he still let her—them—live with him?

She didn't look one bit ashamed. She looked mad. No

mistaking that lifted chin, those cheekbones showing sharp as knives. "What's *he* doing here?" she demanded of Russell.

"Watch your mouth," Russell said. "He's here because we went fishing."

"*That's* whose boat you went out on? Why would you do that? I can't *believe* it. How could you?"

"It's not your business who I go fishing with," he said.

"I'll head on out," Blake said. He didn't want to stay anyway. He liked Russell, but he wasn't feeling like using up all his manners on this situation. Dakota's stepfather had been hurt on one of his jobs. That must be why she was mad. But how did she have any room to talk?

And, yes, part of him might have pointed out that she was mad about her stepfather's serious injury on his watch, whereas *he* was mad because... because she'd confused him, and that those two things weren't exactly comparable. But he didn't care. He was still mad.

"No," Russell told him, a definite snap in his voice. "You won't head on out. You'll come on outside with me and have some more iced tea, and then you'll help me grill that salmon, and you'll eat it."

Blake had to blink. Well, that didn't happen to him every day. He didn't tend to get ordered around much.

Russell didn't wait to hear his answer, just fumbled with the closure for the baby gate until Dakota reached down to unfasten it. She drew back, though, at another glare from Russell.

"And *you*," her stepfather informed her as he stepped out of the room, forcing her to back all the way up, "will dial it right back and behave yourself. Blake's a guest in my house."

Her lips were pressed into a thin line, and she looked like she was holding back as many truth-bombs as Blake was, like she had a right, but she didn't say anything. She turned around and stalked off, and if Blake watched her go despite himself, if he noticed her slim, tanned back in that suit, the length of her legs, and the way the suit was riding up again—well, she was right there, and it was a narrow hallway, and he didn't have to like her to notice what she looked like. He was an observant guy. It wasn't like he was going to do anything about it. He didn't go after other guys' women, and he sure as hell didn't go after the mothers of other guys' children.

She went into a room off the hall, and she didn't slam the door, but she closed it hard. Russell kept on going until he was in the kitchen again, refilling the glasses from the pitcher without asking Blake if he wanted any.

"Come out on the patio with me," Russell said. "We'll get the barbecue going."

"Sure," Blake said, since he couldn't figure out any way to leave without actually being rude.

He carried out Russell's tea glass while Russell followed with the cedar planks, Bella trotting along behind. Russell set the planks on an old-fashioned picnic table before beginning to fuss around with charcoal briquettes and a Weber grill. "The Mariners are playing in a little bit, if you want to hang around and watch," he said. "Down in Oakland. If you're an A's fan, don't tell me, or I'll probably have to kick you out without your salmon."

Blake smiled despite himself, leaned up against the table, and took a sip of his tea. "Nah. Except in football and basketball, I kind of have to support the Seattle team. It's a requirement." Or it had used to be.

"Well, good. They'll lose, most likely, but that's the breaks. Got to watch 'em lose if you're going to watch 'em win. If you're a fan, you can't bug out when the going gets tough."

"That's the code we like to hear," Blake agreed. Hang around to watch, though? He was going to be lucky if Dakota didn't poison his salmon, and he didn't need to look at her happy little family any more.

The back door opened and the big guy came out, still holding the baby. A girl baby, Blake realized. Before, she'd been wearing a yellow swimsuit with a ruffled bottom, and now, she had on a sort of white cotton sleeper thing with tiny hearts all over it. Definitely a girl. She had fine blonde hair in a cloud around her head, and she was making some noise that wasn't quite crying while she chewed on her fist.

"Hey, Evan," Russell said. "How's my Gracie-girl? Oh, this is Blake."

Blake shoved himself upright and said, "Blake Orbison," then realized the guy couldn't shake hands, because he had the baby in one arm and a bottle in the other hand.

He wasn't sure Evan would've shaken his hand anyway. He got a long, slow, measuring look from the other man before he said "Evan O'Donnell." Like he knew what Blake had been doing with his girlfriend—or more like what he'd been thinking—which wasn't uncomfortable much at all. Evan asked Russell, "Could you give Gracie her bottle while I help Dakota put up that storage unit?"

"I'd be glad to give you a hand," Blake said.

Evan looked at him levelly and said, "Thanks. I think we've got it." Yep, Blake was a popular man around here for sure.

Russell said, "Let me wash my hands first. Give her to Blake in the meantime and go on and help Dakota."

Blake didn't think Evan was going to hand the baby over. There was a long silence, then Russell said, "For God's sake. He's not going to drop her. You don't get to play for the NFL if you drop things."

"Well, to be fair," Blake said, "quarterbacks mostly throw. But I won't drop her," he assured the other man hastily. "I've held babies."

Wait a second. Had he? Probably not. He'd seen other people hold them, though. How hard could it be?

Russell headed back into the house. Evan hesitated again, then handed the baby over, and Blake tucked her into the crook of his arm. Not so different from holding a football, except that she was surprisingly solid for somebody so little. Wriggly, too. He sat down just to be on the safe side, and Evan nodded and went into the house.

The baby squirmed, and he wondered if he was supposed

to support her head. He'd read that, but she seemed to be holding it up OK. He put a hand there just in case. She let out a squawk, though, and he took it hastily away.

All right, then. Not. He said "Shh" in a reassuring tone and patted her gingerly on the back. She heaved in a breath, then let out a wail, and he was so startled, he jumped. Then she really set in to scream.

He started to sweat. What was he supposed to do? She was crying like he'd just insulted her pajamas or something, and her face was turning bright red. The only person he got along with in this house, he thought wildly, was Russell.

Wait. The bottle. Babies cried when they were hungry, and the bottle was right there. And her father had said she was hungry. He picked it up, hesitated, then stuck the nipple in her mouth.

That was it. Both her dimpled little hands came up to grab the plastic bottle, she started gulping the milk down as if she'd been moments from starvation, and Blake's tense muscles relaxed some.

Russell came through the back door fast, took in the sight of him, then hauled his way down the stairs with one hand on the rail, saying, "I thought the neighbors were going to call the cops. How long did that take you to figure out? Guess you've never had to feed a baby before."

"Ah… no," Blake said. "You could call it a new experience."

Russell grunted out something that could have been a laugh. "You might as well hang onto her, then, and I'll finish lighting the grill. Tip that bottle right up so she doesn't get any air, or she's liable to spit up that milk all over your shirt when you burp her."

Oh, great. He was burping her? Well, it wasn't her fault that her mother wasn't everything she could be. She was actually pretty cute, now that she wasn't screaming her head off. Her eyes were closed in blissful satisfaction, her cheeks were working hard to get every bit of that milk, and her tiny feet were pushing against the leg of his jeans like a cat kneading bread. If she'd been as miserable as a baby hopelessly lost in the desert before, right now she seemed as contented as a baby... well, as a baby who was getting what she needed.

He could hear the whine of an electric drill coming from the house. "Got to say," he told Russell, "I'm better at putting up shelves than I am at babies."

"Join the club," Russell said, busy at the grill. "Luckily, they teach you, just like Gracie's doing right there. They've got a pretty good signaling technique."

Russell got the fire going the way he wanted it, put the cover on the barbecue, and came over to sit down. Blake asked, "How old is she?" because that was a question people always asked about babies.

"About five months now, I guess," Russell said, which was a fairly casual answer about your—well, sort of your granddaughter.

"She seems strong," Blake said lamely.

"Oh, yeah, she's an active little thing. Got a killer smile, too, though I guess you haven't seen that, and a pair of dimples that'll just about take you out. Evan's got his hands full, but he's not complaining."

Evan? Not Dakota? Blake was confused again. He realized that the plastic bag inside the bottle was empty and the baby was sucking on air, and pulled the nipple hastily out of her mouth. He remembered the spitting-up thing. She made a protesting sound, and he worried he'd hurt her, yanking it away.

"You're wondering what you do now," Russell said, the amusement lurking in his blue eyes again.

"Well, yeah." Blake looked down at the now-cherubic face. Gracie smiled at him, wide and joyous, and damned if she *didn't* have dimples, plus a pair of great big blue eyes. And she didn't have any teeth. He couldn't have hurt her, then, yanking the bottle out like that. "And I've noticed that you're laughing at me, in case you were wondering."

"Nah," Russell said. "I was that guy myself once. Kinda funny to watch you do it, though, it's true. What you do now is, pick her up and rest her against your shoulder. Pat her back, help her get the bubble up."

Blake did it, feeling uncharacteristically clumsy, but the baby made a surprisingly snuggly little bundle. He could get the hang of this. But if there were any diapers to be changed, he was bowing out.

Russell said, "You're not going to get anywhere patting like that. A little harder. Don't whale away on her or nothing, just harder than that."

All right, Blake might have been sweating again. How hard was hard enough?

The next thing he knew, the baby made a choking noise, and Blake felt something wet and warm against his T-shirt. He lifted her a little bit away from him and looked down.

"I told you not to let her get too much air," Russell said, completely unhelpfully. "Well, she got the bubble up, anyway. Here, give her to me."

Oh, *now* he was taking her. Blake checked out the milky mess on his shirt and sighed. Good thing he went for Hanes. Some of his more fashionable teammates, who wore T-shirts that cost a boat payment, would've been in deep wardrobe trouble right now.

The noise of the drill had stopped some time ago, and this was the moment Dakota and Evan chose to head outside.

Dakota didn't look at Blake. She wasn't wearing any makeup, and she was still barefoot, but she'd fixed her hair and changed into a stretchy little orange knit skirt. It wasn't quite a mini, but it was coming mighty close. What was worse, she'd topped it off with a snug white T-shirt with a wide neckline, and the bra under it wasn't the thickest thing he'd ever seen. If he wasn't supposed to look at her, he wished she'd have worn something else.

Russell said, "Gracie's about asleep. Evan, why don't you go on and grill that salmon for me and stick around and eat with us? Dakota, you can set the table and make a salad real quick. But first, take Blake on back and get him one of my shirts to change into. Gracie spit up all over him."

Dakota muttered something that sounded like, "Good taste," and Evan said, "Sure. I'll put Gracie in the house, though."

"You can put her on my bed," Dakota said, and Blake thought, *Wait, what?*

"Well, decide and put her somewhere," Russell said. "Blake and I are hungry, and those coals are going to be ready soon. We caught the fish and cleaned it. I figure our part's done."

"Wait," Blake said. He was going to be direct again. "Whose baby is that?"

Everybody stared at him. "Mine," Evan said. "Of course she's mine. Whose did you think?"

"Oh," Blake said. Russell had on his amused look again. Blake was glad he was entertaining somebody, because he was feeling downright annoyed by now. He was covered with baby puke, he'd been beating himself up for lusting after somebody else's girlfriend, and now she wasn't?

Russell said, "Nah. She's not Dakota's. Evan's my partner. *Was* my partner. He's Dakota's partner now."

"Business partner," Dakota muttered. "Painting partner."

My partner has a baby. She'd said that, out at the rocks. "Oh," Blake said again. He practically had whiplash by now, he'd changed directions so many times this afternoon.

Evan took the drowsy baby from Russell, and she gave a contented little sigh and snuggled in close. *Obviously* she was his. He'd been the one holding her all along, and she was blonde with blue eyes, while Dakota was anything but. How could Blake have thought anything else? And maybe his radar wasn't that far off after all.

Except it was, because Dakota jerked her chin at him and said, "Come on. I'll find you a shirt if you're going to stick around." Which didn't sound very much like, "Take me out dancing, pull me up close, and whisper dirty things in my ear."

But then, nobody won the game in the first quarter.

Power Play

♡

Why, why, *why* was Blake Orbison in her house?

Or more like—why was he in Russell's house? If he'd been in *her* house, she could have kicked him out. Or never have let him in.

But, even worse, what was the first thing she'd thought? Well, the second thing. The first thing had been, "He's looking at my flowers," followed by a rush of heat that had been embarrassment and anger and awareness and... and something. The second thing had been, "I'm a mess again." The *third* thing had been, "What does that matter? What do I care whether Blake Orbison finds me sexually attractive?" The fourth thing had been, "Liar."

And then what had she done? Had she put on her comfy shorts and a loose T-shirt and stuck her hair on top of her head like she would have done on any other warm day? No, she'd waited for Evan to get out of the bathroom with Gracie, then had taken a fast shower, blow-dried her hair halfway, and put on an outfit that she'd never have worn otherwise. At least she'd drawn the line at makeup and her contacts. She'd told herself it was a simple matter of pride, and had known she was lying. She'd just look like she hung around the house in sexy outfits as a matter of course.

Except that Blake's girlfriend had been a supermodel. He wasn't going to think her outfit from Dress Barn was sexy.

Now, he was following her back into the house, and she thought, *Shirt. Salad. Self-control.* She couldn't kick him out, but she wasn't going to let him get to her, whatever he said. Instead, she led the way into Russell's room, opened his shirt drawer, and said, "Pick a color. You've got gray, navy blue, black, or white." Russell didn't exactly live on the cutting edge of fashion.

She turned to look at him and wished she hadn't, because he was pulling his gray T-shirt up his chest and yanking it over his head, and then he was standing there in a pair of red gym shorts with a devil insignia on one leg. They hung too low on his slim hips, displaying the eight-pack again, the start of a thin trail of dark hair leading down from his navel, and that other thing. That vee of abdominal muscle that was her downfall.

She didn't like gym boys, and she didn't like puffed-up muscle-bound freaks, but she sure had a hard time resisting a man with that abdominal vee. Not to mention the kind of arms where you could say, "Shoulder muscle, check. Biceps, check. Triceps... ." and move on down.

"White, please," he said, and she blinked at him.

There was that crooked edge of smile trying to get out. "The T-shirt. If I get puked on again, at least I'll match."

"Oh." She handed him the shirt and had to watch the whole over-the-head performance in reverse. It wasn't that he preened, because he didn't. It was just that some men could do a whole lot with putting on a T-shirt. He tugged it down over his broad chest and all those abs, ran a hand through his brown hair, smoothing it back and unfortunately displaying too much bicep for her entire comfort, and said, "Thanks." And then, instead of flirting with her the way he'd done at the rocks, the way she'd expected, he said, "Russell told me you'd made him an owl that was the prettiest thing he'd ever seen. I'd sure like to see that owl."

"Uh... OK." Well, *that* had thrown her off balance. She went over to the window and carefully opened the drapes to reveal the octagonal piece. What else could she do? She always got flustered and embarrassed talking about her work, but she had to get over it. She might as well practice on Blake, because surely nobody else would be harder.

He didn't say anything for a moment. He just sighed, and she forced herself not to wonder why. If it was, "Sorry I asked," or "That's nice." She *knew* she was good, but she had a hard time showing her work to gallery owners, let alone multimillionaire tycoons who must be used to the best. Even if they were football players who were more likely to see art in a sports car than a sculpture.

Finally, when she couldn't stand it anymore, he said, "I've got to admit, Russell was right. That *is* about the prettiest thing I've ever seen."

"Not fair," she said after a minute, when she had her composure back.

"Excuse me?" he asked, and she didn't have to look hard to see the mischief in his eyes.

"Forcing me to be gracious."

She got a barely-there smile. "Somehow, I think you'll recover. I'm preparing to be mortally wounded, but before you get there—how'd you get the idea for this? How'd you get that eagle? Do you go off pictures or what?"

"If I'm studying," she said, "figuring out the feather pattern—yes. But the idea? No. That's something I see."

Blake looked at the snowy white and black of the owl's wings, the head and breast glowing nearly pink as it soared across the twilight sky, its bands of blue shading to violet above the indistinct black outline of mountains. "You saw this?"

"Just for a moment. Just a flash." She let herself look back and remember that evening hike by the lake, that breathtaking moment. "It was a good flash."

"I'll bet."

"This was my first big bird piece," she found herself going

81

on, since he actually seemed interested. "I almost didn't do it, not just because I knew it was a bad idea economically, but because it'd be such a hard test. I didn't think I'd be up to it."

"I'd say you were wrong," he said quietly, and she felt a rush of... something. Of pride. Or pleasure that wasn't sexual at all, but was too close to attraction. "Why was it a bad idea economically?"

She traced her index finger with the lightest touch over the tiny pieces of white and black that made up the owl's wings, with their suggestion of speckles. "Too many pieces. Too much art glass—the expensive kind, because I needed these textures, these swirls—but mostly, it took too long to do."

"Why? Why was it too long?"

"You can't charge enough to make it worthwhile."

"Yes, you can." The intensity on his face, in his golden eyes... it was mesmerizing. "*You* can. You can charge whatever you want."

"Somebody actually has to pay it, though," she said dryly. "It's not fine art. It's stained glass."

"Now, sweetheart," he told her like it was obvious, like he was completely sure, "that's not believing. Damn straight this is fine art, and the more you charge, the more people will know it. You've got to make 'em believe, and that starts with you."

She was having trouble getting her breath. "Easy to say. I need... I need the money. And don't call me sweetheart."

He was standing so close. Nine inches away, maybe. She could practically feel the heat coming from his body. He took her hand, still resting lightly on the glass, and turned it gently over. His thumb brushed the pads of her fingers, and she shivered. She should pull her hand away. She should.

"You're cut here," he said.

"Glass," she said through a throat that had turned dry. "It happens."

"Mm." He let go of her hand, and she tried not to wish he hadn't. She didn't like him. He'd done Russell so much harm. He said, "How much would this cost if you could charge enough?"

"Um… I can't charge enough for this, not for the hours it took. It was my first one. It's not perfect."

"You're wrong. It's perfect. How much?"

"Two… thousand?" Her voice rose on the word. "Maybe fifteen hundred."

"Twenty-four hundred."

Her heart beat faster just hearing that number. "How do you know?"

"What I said. You get to declare your own value. You aren't the bargain bin. Don't put yourself on sale."

"Is that what all the quarterbacks say?" she asked, trying to rally.

There was something rueful in his smile. "That's what the agent says about his guys who are quarterbacks. I'm not a quarterback anymore. But it's the same deal with the resort. You can be mass-market, or you can be high-end. If you look high-end but you price mass-market, you're just confusing folks. Let 'em know you're there, and that you're the real deal. The girl who walked by me last night like she owned the room—where did she go?"

"I was…" She had to swallow. "Maybe faking a tiny bit."

"Maybe fake it a tiny bit more. Fake it until it's real. Don't give 'em room to doubt. And I want the eagle."

She blinked. "What?"

"The eagle in your workroom. I want it. How much?"

"Uh…" she began.

He held up a palm. "Stop right there. Don't move the number down. I can see you doing it. Don't think about what's wrong with your work, either, why you really can't charge that much. And if you say the number and I try to bargain you down, you say, 'This isn't a clearance sale. That's the price. If you can't pay it, I'll take it on over to the gallery.' Let me know that I'd better buy it now if I want it, because you know it'll get snapped up."

"Has anybody ever told you that you're annoying?"

He laughed this time, his eyes gleaming with what she could swear was appreciation. "Oh, maybe a couple hundred people. How in particular?"

"It's like you're in my head. And why would I move the number down? You've got more money than God."

There he was, smiling that crooked smile again, looking so damn good in that white T-shirt, all lean hips, biceps, and brown skin. "Well, that's true, darlin'. I do. And yet you were still moving that number on down." He beckoned with one hand, a come-to-me gesture that was way too compelling. "Come on, Dakota. Give me a number. And then give me one for that iris, and, no, there's no discount for two. And I don't care how many pieces are in the iris. I care that I want it."

Her knees were weak. "Maybe I don't want to sell them to you."

He smiled so slow, and she didn't want to analyze what that smile did to her. "Nah."

"Dakota." It was Evan's voice, and she whirled, as flustered as if he'd caught her in Blake's arms.

Evan's face was at its most expressionless. "Salmon's ready."

"Oh. Salad." She put a hand up to smooth her hair, then realized she was doing it and dropped it.

"I made it." Evan wasn't looking at her, though. He was looking at Blake, the tension stretching between the two of them like a rubber band. Evan didn't say anything else, just stood back and waited, and Dakota headed for the door. But before she got there, Blake touched her shoulder, and she turned.

"By the end of dinner," he told her, "I want that number. Be ready to give it to me."

♡♡♡

Not the life plan, Blake reminded himself as he followed that

84

orange almost-mini out the door. He tried to ignore the way the knit skirt showed off her absolutely gorgeous… curves. You weren't supposed to eat at a guy's table and think about his daughter's ass, and you sure weren't supposed to think about how much you wanted to take her skirt off and how you'd do it. When she was lying across your bed with her hair spread around her and breathing hard, because you'd been chasing her through the house in the best game of non-football a man could play.

But, see, this was why he needed a refined woman to rein him in. This was the exact *reason* for the new plan. He needed a woman to get him to where a thirty-five-year-old man ought to be once he didn't have the excuse of being a professional athlete anymore.

No more wild side. Marriage plan. Family time. Making a thought-out, rational choice. It had been so hard to remember, though, when he'd been looking at that silky skin above Dakota's neckline, at the hollow above her collarbones, and imagining how she'd shiver when he kissed her there. The same way she'd shivered when he'd held her hand. A woman who was responsive enough to shudder like that just from your thumb caressing her fingers, passionate enough to feel the colors in her owl piece all the way to her soul, and sensual enough to come up with those flowers? That spelled "wild side" all the way, and the push and pull he felt from her, the resistance and the response—that spelled "wild ride," too. She'd play that game of chase. He knew it. And he had a big house.

He shoved the thoughts aside as he sat down at the picnic table. First off, it was rude, and second, Evan was looking at him as if he knew what he was thinking and didn't like it one bit. Business partner? Maybe, and maybe he had ideas of his own, because that look was "hands off" all the way. And if that made Blake's own hand want to fist—well, that was just another example of the exact wrong kind of response.

"Dakota show you the owl?" Russell asked.

"Yeah," Blake said with relief. "You were right. That's a

beautiful thing."

Russell grunted and said, "This salmon's not looking bad, either."

It was true. The fish was so buttery and tender it was almost sinful, the pink flesh flaking under his fork and melting on Blake's tongue. The four of them sat under a sky slowly fading to dusk and ate in silence for a few minutes. Either the silence was normal for them, or they were constrained by Blake's presence. "Cedar planks worked," Blake finally said. "This came out perfect. Looks like you know how to man a grill."

Dakota had been digging in herself, he'd noticed. She looked up as if she'd felt his eyes on her and said, "Dad's a great cook."

"Got to do something around here," Russell said. "You were hungry, miss. You forget to eat lunch again?"

She smiled a little. "Maybe. I guess that's why I need you. I got wrapped up."

Russell shifted in his seat, a spasm crossing his face, and Dakota sat up straighter and asked, "Are you all right?"

"Of course I'm all right."

"You sat too long today, I'll bet," she said. "You were gone forever. Did you take an Advil out there, at least?"

"Don't coddle me." It was a growl, and she snapped her mouth shut.

Evan hadn't said anything, although Blake suspected that wasn't unusual. He spoke up now, though. "I'm surprised you'd go out fishing with him." He didn't look at Blake when he said it. "Want to explain that?"

"Why should I explain it?" Russell said. "I don't answer to you, or to Dakota, either."

Dakota had put her fork down. She said slowly, "I'd like to know too, though, Dad. And maybe it's better if you tell us while he's here. Maybe it's better if he knows. I'm not saying you're a terrible person," she said to Blake. "Personally."

Evan muttered something that sounded like, "You think?"

Dakota ignored him. "But you did a terrible thing," she said, "even if you didn't make every decision yourself. It's your company. You're responsible for Russell being hurt, and you ought to know that."

"The man's a guest in my home," Russell said. "Both of you need to shut up."

"It's my home, too," Dakota said.

"No," Russell said. "It's mine. My house. My rules."

Dakota flinched, and Evan said, "Russ."

Russell started to stand up, then had to grab the table. Dakota was up, too, uttering an exclamation, but Russell stared her down. "My back might be broke," he said. "The rest of me isn't. I'm still a man, and this is still my house. And if somebody wants to hire me as a fishing guide, I'll be a fishing guide. Just because I'm not able to paint anymore, that doesn't mean I can't still work. The check might say 'disability.' It doesn't say 'useless.'"

"Dad. I never said you were useless. And, wait. *Hire?*"

"I'm nobody's passenger." He was still hanging onto the table for support, and Bella was on her feet, too, pressed against his side as if to hold him up. "I'm not your responsibility. Now or ever."

Now, she was more than flinching. She was white. Evan said, "That's not fair."

Russell turned on him. "I'm not yours, either. I know you think so. Well, you can stop. I can't change what happened, and neither can you. Shit happens. It's over. Right here and now, I've got a mortgage that's one more goddamned missed payment away from foreclosure, and both of you know it. The man paid me two hundred dollars. I'm a working man who doesn't have a job and can't get one. I'm taking that two hundred bucks, and the hell with what either of you have to say about it." He looked at Blake. "I apologize for my daughter. Seems nobody ever taught her how to treat a guest."

"He's... not... a... *guest,*" Dakota said. She was still pale, but her teeth were nearly clenched, those cheekbones standing out again. "You took his *money?* I'm *handling* things, Dad. I've *got* it. You can't throw away your pride like that."

"Wait," Blake said. "I need to know what this is all about. I want the whole story, and I want it now."

"No," Russell said. "It's over. It's decided, and it's done. I'm no crybaby victim out to sue the world because I got hurt and it isn't fair. I'm going to watch baseball. Blake, you're welcome to come join me. Dakota, you can clean up."

An Offer You Can't Refuse
♡

It's mine. My house. My rules. I'm not your responsibility.

Russell might as well have said, "I'm not your father." Dakota knew that was what he'd meant. And she wasn't going to cry, because the man whose responsibility all of this was, the man who had caused it, was sitting next to her, and she wasn't going to show him that kind of weakness.

He'd flirted with her, had taken her hand like that would make her forget the whole thing, like she was just another woman to fall at his feet no matter what he'd done. Like being hot and rich could get him anything, including her.

Well, it didn't. It didn't get him her. She told Evan, hating that the words came out pinched, "You take Gracie and go on home. I'll clean up later. I'm going for a walk."

She didn't care about Blake. She wasn't going to say goodbye. It wasn't her house? Well, she wasn't his hostess. He was the cause of everything, and if she'd forgotten that for a few heady minutes, she wasn't forgetting it now.

Evan said, "I'm here anyway. I'll clean up. Go take your walk." He didn't look at Blake either, and Dakota figured Blake was smart enough to get the message. He was smart enough to make millions of dollars, or hundreds of millions of dollars, or some number that regular people with regular lives couldn't even dream of. He was smart enough to know how to manipulate people and towns and review boards and get his way. He could be smart enough to know when he wasn't wanted. She was out of here.

She was around the side of the house on the thought. She only realized she was barefoot when she hit the sidewalk. Too bad. She wasn't going back until he was gone.

"Dakota." Like a bad dream you couldn't shake, Blake was there beside her. "Hang on."

It wasn't an entreaty. It was a command. What right did he have to command her? "Go away," she said. "Go home."

"Sounds like you're talking to your dog."

She whirled on him. "Maybe I am. Maybe I'm talking to a dog who doesn't think it's enough to cripple my fa— my stepfather, who wants to rub salt in the wound."

She started walking again, and he stayed right with her. She was barefoot, and *he* was wearing boat shoes like some preppy from Maine with a sweater tied around his shoulders. Because he'd been out on his *yacht.*

"What kind of boat do you have?" she demanded.

He didn't answer for a moment, then said, "Hatteras."

"Of course you do. And you took Russell out on it and showed him the difference between the two of you. You paid him to guide you like he was your… Sherpa. Your native bearer."

"No," Blake said, and damn it, he didn't even sound rattled. "I paid him to guide me like he was my guide. Like he was a good fisherman who knew the lake. Which he was. I learned a lot, I enjoyed his company, and he earned his money. And I'm still waiting to hear the rest of it. Tell me how he got hurt."

She was walking faster, ignoring the chill settling into the evening air, the rough surface of the asphalt under her bare feet as she crossed the street. "You don't even know." It only made her angrier. "Does that happen on every job, then? That must be a pesky problem for you, but hey, that's what you pay workers' comp insurance for, right? So they can give the guy some pitiful amount that isn't going to let him pay his mortgage, so he'll lose his house, but you don't care about that, because you earned another million dollars? The job came in under budget! Yay, you!"

He said, "You don't know how much I want to grab you right now."

She turned on him. *"What?* What did you just say?"

He ran a hand though his dark hair and exhaled. "I don't mean 'grab you.' I mean grab your arm and make you shut *up* and talk to me."

"If I shut up," she said, "I won't be talking to you."

"You know exactly what I mean." She stepped off the curb again, stepped on a rock, cried out, and hopped, and he said, "Stop. Stop walking. You're killing me here."

"Ask me if I care."

"Now you're acting like a little girl. You've got something to tell me? Then sit down and tell me."

A little girl? A little *girl?* She stepped back onto the curb, but only because her heel still hurt, and said, her voice low and trembling, "I am not a little girl. I am a *woman* who's justifiably angry."

"Right, then." He sat his butt down on the curb and stuck his long legs out into the street. "Sit down and lay it on me."

Karen McCallister was across the street watering her window boxes and staring at them. Dakota didn't want to have this conversation here. On the other hand, she was the one who'd walked out of the privacy of her backyard. *Russell's* backyard. And it felt so much better to be mad at Blake than to think about what Russell had said. Thinking about that made her throat close up tight and her chest hurt.

She sat down a good foot away from him, which made her skirt ride up, which she tried not to care about, and said, "He got hurt on your job. Painting your Sundays over in Coeur d'Alene."

"He told me that." Blake still sounded so calm, she wanted

to hit him. "But that was all he'd say. I was going to check it out on Monday."

"Sure you were."

He exhaled. "I don't have to prove myself to you, you know. Think what you want. Why is that my fault? The project's fault? Didn't OSHA investigate it—an injury that bad?"

"Sure they did. And everybody lied up and down. Said Russell had changed the planned rigging of the scaffolding himself, because he wanted to get it done faster, because he was in a hurry."

"And that wasn't true, I'm guessing. Wasn't your... his... your company, whatever it is, the contractor on the job?"

"No. He and Evan were working that job for the company you hired instead."

"Which was..."

"Sawyer Contracting. Steve Sawyer." Even saying the name made her shoulders tense up.

"The guy who had the contract for the painting on the resort at first," Blake said. "I wondered if I'd been too much of a micromanager on that one. I don't usually supervise this close. I haven't been able to." It sounded like he was talking to himself. "You can't be a football player and a hands-on CEO."

"You can make decisions, though," Dakota said. "I know you can. Like that there's a bonus for on-time and under-budget, and never mind how that happens."

"I never said 'Never mind how that happens.' I don't say that."

"Well, that's nice for you." She was getting agitated again. He was so *calm*. But it wasn't *his* stepfather. It wasn't *his* life. "Nice to have your hands clean. Russell would never have taken that job. He knew what Steve was like to work for, but they needed the hours. Evan's girlfriend was pregnant, and the winter's always slow. So they took it, and Steve cut every corner he could, because that's the kind of contractor he is, but the client doesn't care if he's cheaper. And do you know what? Do you realize one thing?"

"Uh… no," he said. "Not until you tell me."

She stood up again. She couldn't stay sitting down. And he stood up with her like he was some kind of gentleman. Like your manners mattered if you ran a company that way. "Evan was supposed to be up there. Russell went up high himself *because* he didn't trust that scaffolding."

"Why didn't he say something at the time, then?"

"He did. Of course he did. And nobody cared, and they needed the work. So Russell went up there instead of Evan, because Evan's girlfriend was pregnant, and because Russell's that man. You must have seen that he's that man. And Russell was the one who fell. He's the one who's still hurting, and he'd still tell you that at least it was him and not Evan." The tears were standing in her eyes, but she didn't care. "He's lucky if the physical therapist even shows up. I keep thinking that there's something else they could do, because he hurts so much, but I can't get anyone to listen, because it's workers' comp, and everybody knows that everyone getting those payments is a scammer who doesn't want to work. They wouldn't even give him hundred-percent disability, because he can still walk. He can still use his hands. But what good does that do if he can't paint, and he can't sit, and he hurts that much, and he won't even take pain pills?"

Blake was silent for a long time. "But you weren't there."

"So what? So *what*? You mean Russell lied? And Evan lied, and Steve Sawyer told the truth? Like he's told the truth about everything else he's done, all the way back to high school? Like it didn't really happen, and the other person's lying anyway because she's out to get him?"

"Wait, what? What does high school have to do with it? Who's 'she?' You? I didn't say Russell lied. I meant, you weren't there. You weren't working with them."

She hauled herself back under control. Not all the way, because that was impossible, but closer. "No. I came home from Portland after Russ got hurt, and I took over for a while.

93

Until he was back on his feet, I thought it would be. Able to retire on that disability. And that's when I found out that he'd gotten behind on the mortgage, too, when I opened the letter from the bank. And I couldn't help with that if I had to pay my own rent, especially not in Portland. I couldn't just leave him here to… I don't even know what. What would he have done? Where would he have gone? And you can say he hadn't saved enough. You can say whatever rich people say who have no idea what it's like."

Blake was still just standing there frowning at her. "So you stayed. You moved back in and stayed. What did you do for work in Portland?"

She took a couple more breaths and tried to dial it back. When you raged, the other person stopped listening. The louder you talked, the less they could hear. She knew that, but it was so hard. "Same thing as here. I painted. I worked with Russ during the summers in high school and learned how, and after that, I moved. I didn't want to stay in town, because… because I didn't. I've got an eye for… for color. I moved where there was more money and more big old houses that people like to paint more creatively, where they'd pay more for what I did. And then, after my brother died…" She had to stop again.

"Riley," Blake said. The green in his eyes was showing now, his gaze as direct as it had been in Russell's bedroom, but the way she felt under that gaze was completely different.

"I stayed a while." The words came out too jerky. "And then I left again."

"Until he got hurt."

"That's it."

Blake wasn't looking at her now. He had a thumb hooked in his waistband and was gazing into the distance. Toward where, Dakota saw with a quick glance, Karen McCallister was still watering, probably drowning her plants.

"Right," he said. "I'll check it out on Monday."

Dakota sighed. What was the point in this? So she'd said it. How had it helped? Losing her temper felt strong at the time, but it always felt weak later. The self-controlled one—that was the one who won, who came out looking strongest, and that sure hadn't been her. "Nothing to check out. Russell's right. OSHA investigated. The case is closed. He's getting his workers' comp, and even you can't make anything else happen."

"If it's my responsibility," Blake said, "I'll take care of it."

"How?"

He shrugged. "I don't know. I'll check it out."

Her anger had drained away, and now, she just felt tired. The hours of work on her glass, her swim, what Russell had said... it was all trying to swamp her. And she didn't want to hope anymore if nothing was going to happen. She was right about one thing. There *had* been an investigation, and the case *was* closed. "Don't tell Russell whatever it is you're thinking. Don't make him hope that ..."

"I don't think Russell gets his hopes up. I think that's you."

She laughed, a ragged sound. "Could be."

"Come on. I'll walk you home."

"You don't have to do that. It's Wild Horse. It's not even dark." Not far off, though, with dusk closing around them.

"Well, yeah, I do. My truck's there."

"Oh. Right."

They walked back in silence for a couple blocks, and Dakota tried not to notice how sore her feet were getting. Finally, Blake said, "You've got maybe another week at the resort, right?"

"Four days. We'll be done by the end of the day Thursday. A day ahead of schedule, because we're going to earn that bonus. The difference is, we won't cut corners to do it."

"How about after that?"

"What, you want me to drag out all the details of my pitiful life for you?" Seemed she wasn't done with emotion after all.

"No. I want an answer to my question. I have a reason for asking."

Calm down. "We have a job lined up painting that empty block of storefronts next to the Heart of the Lake. The wine bar." Then she remembered that she'd seen him there. When he'd been out with Beth Schaefer. Another rich person. "And then a couple of houses."

"Doesn't sound like that's going to keep a crew busy all summer."

"No. Thanks for pointing that out."

"Want to paint my house?"

"*What?*"

"I bought this house on the lake. It's all right, but the colors inside are funky as hell. Somebody's going to have to paint it. How about you?"

"Uh…" She didn't want to do it. She didn't want to take his money. "I'd have to talk to Evan."

Blake jerked his head toward the house, where Evan's van still stood at the curb. "No time like the present."

♡♡♡

Why are you doing this? Blake asked himself. He was a decisive guy, but he was an analytical one, too. His former career had required lightning-quick judgments, and so did his present one. He was good at that by nature, and he'd gotten better with practice.

His decisions might be quick, but when he analyzed them afterwards, he could always figure out the path he'd taken to arrive at them, even if the neurons had fired too fast to follow at the time. So what was the reason for this decision?

There were a couple of possibilities. He decided to stick with "helping somebody else out at no cost to himself." Sounded good. Noble, even, when he didn't even know the full circumstances yet, whether Russell's accident had been any more than unfortunate, and one thing he didn't do was leap to conclusions.

Besides, his house *did* need painting. He wasn't the world's fussiest man, but he'd have gotten around to it sooner or later. M & O were doing a good job at the resort, and it sounded like they had the time. There you go—two reasons. He had a need, and he'd found the answer. Bingo.

Dakota didn't say anything else, just walked up the sidewalk and went into the house. He knew her feet were hurting, but she didn't show it. She knew a thing or two about pride. A thing or two about loyalty, too. And if those were qualities he admired—well, that was good, because that meant this wasn't about those other qualities she'd showed him. The passion and the temper, and a will that could stand up to his own. The set of her shoulders, the tigress-stalk that had set his heart pounding when she'd been walking out on him, then giving him a piece of her considerable mind. Not to mention when she'd jumped up from that curb with a powerful flash of thigh and turned on him like a wild thing.

She was full of fire, all right. But fire got you burned.

Inside the house, Russell was in his easy chair, and Evan was sitting on the couch watching the game with him.

Evan didn't look overjoyed to see Blake. He didn't look disgusted, either. Evan had "impassive" down pat. He picked up a plastic grocery bag from the floor beside him, held it out, and said, "I put your shirt in a bag."

Message received. *Now go home.*

Blake could play the body-language game too, though. He stood still, hooked a thumb in his waistband, and said, "I'd like to hire your company to paint my house on the lake as soon as you're done out at the resort."

Evan glanced at Dakota, then said, "We've got another job."

Blake said, "I know you do. You've got a crew, too. I want my job done now, and I'm willing to pay to move it to the head of the line." He knew why Evan wanted to turn the job down. The same reason Blake wanted to hire them. Dakota.

Evan locked eyes with Blake for a good ten seconds until Dakota sighed and said, "No need to do the staredown, Evan. We already talked about Dad."

"Not that I asked you to," Russell said. He reached for the

remote and muted the game. "Leave me out of it. We don't need charity," he told Blake. "If that's what you're offering, forget it."

"I'm not offering charity. I'm offering a job. And in my experience, figuring out how you can get the job done is a better technique than turning the job down, if you're looking to make money."

"Right," Evan said. "I'll do your house. Dakota can do Main Street and then start on the Lake Street house. Danny's the only guy still available," he told Dakota. "Least I think he still is. He can help you."

"Nope," Blake said. "She's the one who's good at color, right? Well, I want color. Besides, I find you hostile."

"That's because," Evan said, "I *am* hostile. But I don't like lots of people I paint for."

"You find *Evan* hostile?" Dakota demanded. "Did you hear a word I said?"

"Yeah. But like I said, I want color."

"If I don't have a helper, it's going to take a while."

"As I mentioned," Blake said, "turning down work probably isn't something you want to include in your business plan. Yeah, it's going to take a while. The house is five thousand square feet. Something like that, anyway. Big monster. I want it done in time for the resort's grand opening on the Fourth of July, because I'll be here for that, and I might have company."

Her expression turned thoughtful. "That's only a little more than a month away. I might be able to do it, though, if I have some help from Evan eventually. Is it furnished?"

"Yep. Bought it that way. Not saying it's beautifully furnished, but it's furnished."

"So you just walked into a new town," she said, "and bought a five-thousand-square-foot house for one person, *on* the lake, *with* furniture."

"It has a good view. And like you said, I can afford it. Which I'm telling you, even though I should be saying that I'm stretched right now so I can bargain you down."

"Somebody told me not to bargain." Her eyes weren't stormy anymore, and how could she look that sassy-good in those librarian glasses and not a speck of makeup? Dark, winged eyebrows, perfect golden skin, and killer bone structure, that was how, not to mention all that personality. "Somebody told me to say that was the price, and that he could go on and find someone else to do it if he didn't want to pay it. Plus—rush job. I think that's, oh, fifteen percent tacked on."

He rubbed a thumb along the side of his jaw and gave her a rueful smile. "Now how did I know that would come back to bite me?"

"You're probably very bright," she said sweetly.

He had to laugh. "Well, that's true, darlin', but you aren't so bad yourself. Right, then. You're done with the resort on Thursday. I'll see you out at my place on Friday morning at eight. I can tell you my color ideas, and you can tell me I'm wrong. And then you can tell me how much it'll cost, and I can tell you I'll be getting other estimates, and you can say 'fine' and know I won't."

"If you do business like that," Russell said, "you're a damn fool."

"I never do business like that," Blake said. "But then, a man's entitled to a little extravagance now and then. Twelve-twenty-one Arrowhead Drive," he told Dakota. "Eight o'clock Friday. See you then. Catch you later, Russell. I'll be in and out over the next couple weeks, but when I've got time to get out on the lake, I'll get in touch. I'd appreciate your guide service again if you want to sell it to me. Got to get a salmon of my own at some point here if I'm not going to hang my head in shame."

"You can buy the boat," Russell said. "You can buy all that fancy equipment, too. But you can't buy the salmon, and you can't buy Dakota."

"Somehow," Blake said, "I already figured that out. But then, as she pointed out, I'm a bright guy."

Except, he thought as he climbed back into the Explorer, that she'd never given him a price for his eagle. He didn't have that, and he didn't have his iris. Those ruffled petals, that dark, secret center...

He wanted that iris.

A Gene for Appreciation
♡

The old white pickup rattled around another curve on the tree-lined road. Dakota only realized she'd missed the house when she overshot it, despite the fact that she'd been watching for it. She saw 1225 on a low, discreetly carved wooden sign beside a driveway, hit the brakes, pulled in, turned the truck around, and went back to find Blake's place.

She could see why she'd missed the turn for 1221. It was just this side of the sharp curve, and there was no sign here, no indication that the narrow blacktopped drive disappearing into the cedars went anywhere special even once you were on it. You knew the real estate was expensive when you couldn't see the houses.

She rounded the final bend of the driveway, and there it was. A pile, but a good-looking one. All wood, glass, and stone, the house rising two stories on the uphill side, and certainly three stories on the other, where it overlooked the water, built to make the most of the view. She'd bet you couldn't see another house from here, either. Money might not buy happiness, but it sure could buy privacy.

She got out of the truck and headed for the front door. There was no reason to be intimidated. She was here to do a job, not to be Blake Orbison's buddy. She'd painted more than one big lake house. This was no different.

The door opened as she approached, and there he was, leaning against the doorjamb with a thumb in his belt loop, studying her like he was too cool for school. Black T-shirt and worn Wranglers, like that day on the shore.

His feet were bare, though. He had good feet. Strong, with high arches and long toes. Big.

"Morning," he said, and she realized why she could now inventory the charms of his feet. Because that was where she'd been looking.

"Morning," she said, pretending she'd been momentarily checking out the… flooring. To better protect them from paint splatters, perhaps. Not to mention pretending that she hadn't been up since six this morning figuring out what to wear.

Normally, it would have been jeans and a T-shirt, exactly like him. Customers didn't respond well to "feminine" when it came to their home-maintenance tasks. That, she'd long since discovered, made them discount M & O's expertise and ask *her* to discount her price. But she hadn't been able to stand the idea of showing up looking like that today, and never mind why. There was still that water-weed tail to get over. *That* was why. She needed to make a polished impression, especially if she were going to charge him extra. And she *was* going to charge him extra.

She'd tried on four dresses before she'd realized how *that* looked. "For Pete's sake," she'd muttered as she'd yanked a red dress over her head and tossed it on the bed, "it's not a friggin' date. He's not taking you to the senior prom. You're the *painter*."

She'd ended up with a pair of dark jeans, a green scoop-necked cotton top with an embroidered yoke, and cowboy boots, and had put her hair up in a knot. A little bit polished, but not like she was trying too hard. She'd worn some makeup, but she'd also worn her glasses. All so she could give an annoying ex-quarterback a painting estimate and talk about possible colors. She must be losing her mind.

"Still digging the glasses," that quarterback said now. He was looking at her face. *He* didn't have to check out her feet, and he hadn't checked out the rest of her, either, at least not too obviously. Of course he hadn't, because that wasn't what this was about, and anyway, she wasn't all that, and she knew it. And he wasn't a total jerk.

"Still not asking you," she answered.

He laughed. "Well, darlin', you got me there. Come on in and talk color to me." He held the door for her.

"Did we have a talk about not calling me 'darlin'?" she asked, stepping inside.

"Nope. We had a talk about not calling you 'sweetheart.' But I'll do my best to remember both of 'em. Could be tough."

She would have answered that, but she'd lost the plot a little. "Nice view."

He smiled, slow and sweet. "It's good, huh. Want to come see?"

She followed him out to the wall of windows, and beyond, to the deck that hung out over the floor below. It was an enormous semicircle stretching the width of living room, dining room, and more, furnished with two chaises and a full dining set, plus a fairly enormous hot tub in one corner behind a screen of bamboo, but that wasn't what she was looking at.

"Why I bought the house," he said, leaning back against the rail and gazing not out at the lake, but at the walls of glass and wood. "This deck, and the look of the thing."

"Angles and straight lines balanced by this curving line," she agreed, following his example and taking in the view of the house. "It's pleasing, and the proportions work, and they work with their surroundings, too. Symmetry, simplicity, the Golden Ratio, all of that. Big houses can be a challenge that way, to keep them looking harmonious and not clunky, but whoever designed this one did it well. "

"Now, see," he said, "that's why I need you. I just saw the look of it. You told me why."

She tried not to let herself be affected by that. "Walk me through it, if you don't mind, so I can see what needs doing and make some calculations."

"You trying to keep me on track?" There was his hint of a smile again.

"Could be."

"Come on, then." He still sounded amused, but he was listening. And he wasn't calling her 'darlin'.' Which was good.

When she stepped back into the living room and really took it in, she drew in a breath and said, "Well, I wouldn't say this color."

"I know," he said. "I keep thinking I'm in the hospital, and I've spent enough time in those. Who paints their living room green? Who buys this furniture?

"Whoever you bought this from, clearly. Congratulations for being able to look past the hideousness, I guess. They obviously thought they were matching the stone."

"Stone's nice, though."

That would be one way of describing it. Predominantly jade green, but with so much depth and richness to it.

An enormous fireplace and chimney surround dominated one wall, the band of stone rising the entire two-story height of the ceiling. Pale green, gold, cream, black, and gray ran through every thick-tiled piece in complex patterns full of life and texture. The floor was more of the same material, and it was gorgeous.

Those puke-green walls, though… at least the trim was painted a glossy white. But then there was the furniture. Couches and chairs in over-upholstered brown leather, with great rounded arms and tufted backs, like English club chairs on growth hormones. Coffee and side tables made of all sorts of terrible things, from reclaimed barrels banded in copper and covered with glass to barn-wood tabletops that looked like they'd give you splinters sitting on top of deer-antler bases. Drapery fabric in apple-green gingham falling in swags and pooling on the floor, and—to add a final touch of horror—

topped by bows at the corners. And since there were a lot of windows, there was a lot of that fabric.

All of it shouted "rustic retreat" in the most over-the-top way possible, like a stage set for "Annie Get Your Gun," as if a troupe of yelling cowboys and square-dancing maidens would be bursting onto the scene at any moment and starting a hoedown. It was horrible.

"Who the heck," Dakota asked, "*was* this guy? And who was his decorator, Buffalo Bill?" You'd think she'd know, but there were plenty of rich people tucked into acreage on north Idaho's scenic lake frontage. Either they flew in and out and took no part in the life of the town, or they descended on City Council meetings to offer the inbred backwoods dwellers the benefit of their insight. Those types were less popular.

"Some investment banker from New York," Blake said. "His wife wanted a cabin in the wilderness, but she decided it was a little too much wilderness after all, and they bought a place in Vail instead. I think they came out here about three times. So what do you think? Looking past the hideousness. You said color. You still sure about that? I don't think my eyeballs can take much more color."

She turned in a circle. The view—you had to account for that, whatever you did inside here. The scene was so vibrant, it nearly came inside. Deep green mountains reflected in silver-blue water across thirty feet of window. In the winter, it would be all grays, whites, and blacks, but the view would be just as dominant in this room.

The enormous kitchen at one end seemed to have counters and breakfast bar made of something more subtle than the flooring, which was good. A barely-veined cream-colored granite, she found when she went closer. Whoever had designed the house originally had had taste, even if the person painting and decorating it hadn't had one bit.

She crouched to study the flooring more carefully, running a hand along one of the veins of sand-colored rock that interrupted the predominant green. Blake, to his credit, didn't say anything, just waited.

"I think," she finally said, "you want a taupe. Do what they did here, pick up a color in the stone, but the *right* color that won't compete for your attention, so you keep the focus on the natural materials and not the décor, and then you choose harmonizing textures and colors in your furnishings. Taupe."

"I hear… words words words," Blake said. "And damned if I know what taupe is. Is that like tan? I don't want tan."

"No. It's taupe. And I know you can't be as much of a Philistine as that. You're building that resort. You liked this house. Clearly, you know what you want."

"Usually," he said, and she looked up at him standing over her and got a little… breathless.

She pulled a Pantene color deck from her bag and fanned it out for him against the stone floor. *Get it together. Color.* "Here. This."

"I can't tell." He crouched down beside her and touched first one tiny block of color, then the next, his hand brushing hers.

"It'll give you warmth," she went on desperately, "especially if we keep it light but do a touch of red in it, give it a slight rose undertone. Then you do some browns, some mushroom, some splashes of pale gold in your decorating, in your window treatments. You warm it all up, make this big space cozy just with color. Subtle, but warm. Restful and masculine. The opposite of what it is now."

"Rose undertone?" His eyes were amused. *Warmth* was the word, all right. "Are you paintin' my house pink, darlin'?"

She sighed. "All that, and that's what you heard?" She didn't mention the "darlin'." He couldn't help it, or he didn't want to. And maybe she didn't hate it. "I'm not painting it pink. Your testosterone levels will remain intact. Hey, you want the whole thing in Decorator's White, we'll do it. You could've just gotten Evan out here for that, though. No need for my talents. You'd be speaking each others' language. 'White,' you could grunt at each other with manly nods. You'd be getting Navajo white, max. That's about as frisky as Evan gets."

"Navajo White, huh? You know, that's exactly what you remind me of. How you look, how you act…"

He was looking at her, not the walls, and definitely not the fan deck. Crouching so close to her, she could smell the scent of him. Warm, clean cotton, and something else, too. Something faintly spicy. Soap or shaving cream, maybe, except he hadn't used shaving cream this morning. He still had that dark stubble going on, and he was all firm lips and square jaw, warm eyes and no smile. Broad shoulders and a forearm, thick with corded muscle, resting on a lean thigh.

It took a minute to realize what he'd said. When she did, the blood drained from her head. "Pardon?"

"You're part Indian, aren't you?"

She stood up fast. "Show me the rest of the house. Taupe's a good basic color, but if you want some variation, we can do that. Maybe in the bedrooms."

"Wait." He put a hand on her arm, and then, when she looked down at it, took it off. "What did I say?"

"How I *act?*" She wasn't doing very well on her customer management. Her professionalism was all over the place, and she couldn't help it. *"Part* Indian? Why don't you just call me a squaw and get it all out there?"

"What? Oh." He looked truly discomfited, and she tried not to let that bother her. "Sorry. I'm so used to the NFL, to being in such a…"

"A diverse environment," she finished. "So it's not possible for you to say a racist thing. You're just honest, that's all."

"Well, yeah." He wasn't as cool as usual, either. "I'm used to saying what I think, and to everybody else saying it back. Which you're doing, if I can point that out."

"You don't have to be politically correct, because it's stupid, and anyway, you're the boss. Just like you were the quarterback. You're in charge, and other people can just get over it if they're going to be that sensitive."

His eyes were hard now, his mouth set. "Right, it was rude

of me to ask you about your ethnic background. I apologize. But the way you see those birds and the flowers you make, the way you see this stone… it all fell into place. I wasn't judging you or calling you names. I was just trying to get at why you're the way you are. It was a *compliment*."

"You think you're doing better," she said, "and you're digging yourself in deeper. There's not actually an Indian gene for 'appreciation of nature.'"

"All right. I stand corrected. I stand pretty damn embarrassed, too."

She shot a quick look at him. He actually seemed like he meant it. He went on, "Maybe you could come sit down in my ugly green kitchen and have a cup of coffee with me and tell me why that stung so bad. And before you answer, I'll say one more thing. Maybe I said it because I've been thinking too much about how you look. It's different, and I like it, and I keep noticing it. You could say it's been at the forefront of my mind."

Annoying Blake

♡

He'd actually thought for a minute that she was going to turn around and walk out. Walk out on the job and the money, even though she needed it, and badly, and he knew why. What he'd said still didn't seem so terrible to him, but for some reason, it had been. It had hurt.

She didn't exactly leap into his arms at his apology. Instead, she stood for a second, hovering like a dragonfly poised over a pond, ready to dart away. She was solid, and she was quicksilver. Both things. And he was holding his breath.

"Nothing to talk about," she finally said. "Show me the upstairs, if you don't mind."

The ease, the responsiveness he'd felt while she'd been crouched beside him, his hand brushing hers—they were gone. She'd dressed for distance today, and he wanted the other Dakota again. The one in the ugly swimsuit and the messy hair, the one who laughed at him and teased him back. Even the one who faced him down and gave him a piece of her mind with all that passion he wasn't supposed to talk about.

He wasn't getting that Dakota, clearly. "Sure," he said, and led her up the staircase, down the hallway, railed off from the great room downstairs but with the same view that had made him buy. He opened the double doors at the end of the hall and said, "Master. This is the other room I really care about."

She walked into the middle of the enormous room, glanced at the California king bed—which, yes, had legs made of sections of tree trunk, and a headboard of intertwining branches that was uncomfortable as hell—and he could see when she noticed the huge mirror hung on the wall to one side of the bed. She moved on hastily to the wraparound windows with their lake view that took up most of two walls, and the deck outside. Everything about her body language now said "tense," as if she'd imagined that chase and tackle herself, as if she'd looked into that mirror and watched him taking her clothes off, had seen him behind her, kissing her neck as she'd knelt on the bed, and none of it had been a positive experience. And yet he'd swear…

"Bathroom," he said, indicating with his head. "Dressing room."

She went in and looked, and he didn't follow her, because he could tell it would make her even more uneasy. Anyway, he knew what she'd be seeing. More of the stonework in the bathroom and double shower. She came back out of the bathroom again and said, "A gray, but a taupe gray, is what I'd do. White trim. Very crisp, very masculine, very simple, and it would be fine with this gray carpeting. I'd probably keep that for all the bedrooms and other rooms up here, whereas the hallway would be the same color as downstairs. You'll harmonize, because you'll have the shades of taupe, but it's not all the same. Or we could do it all the same, if you'd rather."

"No," he said. "Gray's good."

She nodded. "Show me the rest of what's up here to make sure."

He did, and then they went down to the bottom level, to a second office, the media room, the game room, and a fourth small bedroom and bath, all of them opening onto the lake view.

"Taupe gray down here too," she said when she was

standing in the game room, which was dominated by a mahogany bar more suited to a drinking establishment and enough chairs and tables to set up your own sports bar, plus a pool table, another fireplace, and a TV that defined "big screen." "At least that's my suggestion."

"Go for it. Sounds good to me. Don't you wonder one thing, though?"

"What's that?" she asked cautiously.

"How much drinking do you really want to do?" He smiled at her, trying to get that ease back again. "That's what I always wonder when I see houses with this much bar."

"Well, yeah," she said. "It wouldn't be what I'd do with the space, but people want to fill it up, I suppose. And I thought athletes and drinking basically went together."

"Not if you want to perform. And I do tend to want to perform. So what would you do?" He leaned a hip against the mahogany bar and took her in. Waist and hips and long legs in those cowboy boots. And when she turned around... yeah. Call him a dog, but he was still going to be looking at that. He could mind his manners, but he couldn't mind his mind.

"Me?" she said. "Well, pretty obvious. I'd use it as a studio. All this natural light, all this window space where you could hang your pieces, all the wall area for storage. Since I don't have a teepee. And by the way? If you think that last thing was subtle, you're wrong."

"Ah." He rubbed his nose. "Yeah. Maybe I mentioned I was sorry about the Indian deal. And I'll just say... you're cutting me off at the knees here. All my best stuff, purely wasted."

"I'm keeping to the point. Which is to accept your apology." She took a second, then said, "Maybe I overreacted, too. It's just that around here, people say these things."

"To you."

"Yes. And my father was Lakota. At least so I hear. The reason for my name. It's my mother's fault that my last name is 'Savage,' but that didn't help. And if you don't mind, that's all I'm going to say about that. I can send you a written estimate for the painting, or I can tell you right now, or both."

That was a whole lot to think about. "Tell me now."

"Five thousand two hundred fifty. Plus paint and materials."

He blinked. It wasn't much, but it was a little on the high side for Idaho. "Yes," she said, "you can get another estimate. Go get it from Steve Sawyer, or anybody else. It might be cheaper. It won't be as good a job. Plus, there's that rush fee."

His smile started slow and grew, and finally, she smiled back, let out her breath, and asked, "How'd I do?"

"Darlin', you did awesome. That's what I'm talking about. And, yeah, I said the word again. Guess I'm a slow learner."

"Oh," she said, "I don't think so."

He was still grinning like a fool, and the planes and angles that made up her remarkable face had softened some, too. She looked great, though she'd look a whole lot better if he could take her hair down. He asked, "How about my flower and my eagle? Going to sell them to me?"

"Oh. I wasn't—" She cut herself off. "If you're willing to pay what I'm asking."

"Tell me the damage. Tell me what to give you to get you started on the paint, too." He pulled his checkbook and a pen out of his pocket. "Go."

"Twenty-four hundred for the eagle. Fifteen hundred for the iris. Thirty-nine hundred for both. No discount." The words spilled out fast.

"Now, how hard was that to say?" he asked, starting to write.

"You'll never know."

"Betcha I would." He signed his name, ripped the check out of the book, and handed it over. "Paint."

"Um… five hundred twenty-five to start. Ten percent." She was looking at the check, sounding breathless. "I'll bill weekly, and bill separately for the paint. Pay within ten days on the labor, and you get a two-percent discount."

"That's good business. That you, or Evan?"

"Me."

He nodded and wrote the second check. She took it, too, folded it up with the other one, stuck it in her bag, and said, "Wow. I would've taken half that for the stained glass. I would've been *thrilled* to take half."

He cocked an eyebrow at her. "Here's something to chew on. I would've paid double."

She was hanging onto her purse like the checks would blow away. "Don't tell me that. It annoys me."

He laughed. "I'll tell you this instead. I'm taking off this afternoon, and I won't be back until Monday night. So if you want to get started right away, go for it. If I've got to wait for you to finish your glass piece, don't tell me. It'll annoy me to know I don't come first with you."

She smiled sweetly at him. "But you know… I've decided I like annoying you. It's a very powerful feeling."

New Information

♡

Blake wished he could look at his watch. It was Monday. That much, he knew. He'd flown to Denver on Friday afternoon, then down to Dallas and on to Houston last night before returning to Wild Horse this afternoon. He'd come into the resort straight from the jet again, and he had restless feet. And restless hands.

He stood in the middle of the largest of the retail spaces at the resort, all blank white walls and echoing emptiness, frowned absently at Melody Farnsworth, and clicked the volume buttons on his phone up and down while his assistant Jennifer typed on her own phone beside him.

"We've got leases signed and ready to go on all but a couple of the retail spaces," Melody said. "And we've got a few companies on the fence for those. I'm confident they'll be rented and set up by the time the resort opens, even though the time frame's getting tight. To be honest, some of them have been a little hesitant about how much draw the resort will have in such an unknown area, although of course your celebrity and that NFL-studded opening weekend has helped to convince them."

Melody had a sheet of the straightest, shiniest dark hair you

114

could imagine, and now, she smiled at him and shoved it back over her shoulder, where it fell into place in a way that seemed too perfect to be real.

His ex-girlfriend Courtney had explained to him once in eye-glazing detail how you got your hair to do that. He'd zoned out, to be honest, as he did through most of Courtney's beauty and fashion critiques, but it had started out with, "I was out at the mall today, and I've decided to do a post dedicated to hair improvement. Not maintenance—*improvement*. It's an investment of an extra half-hour a day, a salon visit, and a couple hundred dollars a month, that's all. Women would be surprised how fast it would pay off, because good-looking people *always* make more money. If women *got* that, maybe they wouldn't let themselves go like they do. As it is, they let themselves go gray and gain weight and don't update their makeup for the new season, and then they wonder why they don't get ahead. It's just *grooming*."

She'd followed up with specifics, but that was when he'd stopped listening. He'd been too busy imagining his mom or sister spending an extra couple hundred dollars a month on their hair and going to some website to figure out how to update their makeup for Spring.

Unfortunately, he hadn't been quick enough—or been too blitzed on those pain pills—to catch that one when he and Courtney had gone to visit his folks over Christmas. And sure enough, his mother had skewered Courtney in the nicest possible way, starting with, "Is that the best use of a woman's time, though, do you think?" and "I wonder if we don't have to be careful about telling women that their best path to success is focusing on their looks." His sister had stared at Courtney as if she were analyzing her DNA and it was coming up lacking, and his dad had said, "You both make interesting points. Fascinating subject, grooming, all the way into prehistory. Now, the Egyptians…" And Courtney had cried in the bedroom later, telling him, "Your family hates me. I can tell." And then there'd been his mother the next day, saying,

"Honey, I don't like to interfere, and of course you'll choose your own partner, but…"

Fortunately, there wouldn't be another Christmas like that one, because Courtney was explaining her beauty secrets to another lucky guy now. But that was why he was on the new track. So much less aggravation in every way if he had the well-bred, ladylike type who'd pick up on social cues and steer the conversation onto safe ground and all that good stuff. So much calm, orderly structure at home, too. The way it was supposed to be when you were raising a family.

"How about interest in the possible expansion?" he asked Melody, getting back to the topic. If the resort went the way he was hoping, he was going to open up a destination mini-mall beside it, a pedestrian space full of the kind of upscale boutiques people enjoyed wasting their money in while they were on vacation. Some people, anyway. Courtney had cured him of any hidden shopping desires he'd ever possessed.

"Interest is strong," Melody said. "I can send you a summary."

"Do that." She should have done it already. "And then update it every week," he added. "Business name, what they do, website, revenues."

"Spreadsheet," Jennifer murmured beside him.

He glanced at her. Wasn't that obvious? "Yeah. Spreadsheet."

"Oh," Melody said. "Sure. I'll get right on that."

"Good," Blake said. "That's it, then."

Melody made a note, shoved her hair back again, crossed one foot over the other in her high-heeled ankle boots, revealing some extra leg in her short skirt, and asked, "Do you have everything else you need out at the house? Can we do anything for you?" She was taking care of the commercial leasing side, while her mom had handled his house and the much more complex business of acquiring all that lakefront. Small town; family business. The mom, Candy, was pretty good. Lots of experience, and she knew everybody. Melody, he wasn't so sure about.

"I'm good," he said. "Thanks for giving Dakota the key." Somehow, he'd forgotten about that on Friday when Dakota had come out to the house, and she hadn't asked for it, either. Maybe she'd been distracted. He knew he had been.

He'd remembered to give her his phone number, though. That hadn't escaped him. She'd called him that afternoon in Denver, and he didn't care to admit how his heart had leaped when she'd said, "This is Dakota Savage" in that low, slightly husky voice.

He'd kept pedaling the exercise bike that was his warmdown after the workout in the hotel gym, trying not to favor his right leg, pushing through the pain, and said, "Tell me you're missing me already, and you'll make my day."

"I don't think your ego needs supersizing," she'd answered, which had made him laugh.

"That was a good one," he'd said. "What can I do for you?"

It had only been, "Get me a key to your house," but he'd still been smiling when he'd hung up and made a quick call to Farnsworth Realty. He was almost smiling just thinking about it. Thinking how Dakota was there now, starting to make his house non-ugly. And just that she was there.

"Well," Melody said now, reaching a hand up to tuck her hair behind her ear like he might not have noticed the first three times, "if you do need anything—anything at all—let me know." She hesitated, catching her lower lip between her perfectly straight teeth, then added, "And if Dakota Savage doesn't work out, I have a couple other people I could recommend. We have a list of the most reliable tradespeople, and I'd be happy to help you with getting estimates or anything else you need. Another time, just call. You can leave it to me."

He looked her over. "Is there a reason you're expecting Dakota not to work out?"

She shrugged one blue-clad shoulder. She was wearing a snug royal-blue knit dress with a high neck, long sleeves, and a swingy, short skirt that looked exactly like a high-school cheerleading uniform, a type of outfit with which he'd once been intimately familiar. "Dakota doesn't have the… best reputation," she said delicately, as if she were picking her high-heeled way through a minefield. "There's her stepfather, and her brother, and then… well, I don't want to get into it, but let's say that they've both had issues, and there's been some talk about… well. Why she's home, why they have that…" She coughed. "Bond. I'll just say that they're not on our 'recommended' list."

"You got anything to say about her as a painter?" he asked, keeping his tone even.

"I don't know her work very well, although her stepfather had that accident on the job and tried to blame it on Steve Sawyer, and Dakota got into it, too, and made a huge stink when everybody knew it was Russell's own fault. So from a liability standpoint, I'd have some concerns. And for the rest… I suppose you could call it a character issue."

The way he was firing people in Wild Horse, pretty soon there'd be nobody left to work for him. He needed to let this go. "If I need recommendations from you," he said, not adding *when Hell freezes over,* "I'll ask. Thanks for coming over, and I'd like that spreadsheet tomorrow."

She nodded, and if she understood the snub, she didn't let it show, because she looked as polished and perky as ever when she said, "You've got it. Like I said. Whatever you need, we're here for you," smiled at him, and walked out.

Blake didn't look at Jennifer. He breathed a couple times, then said, "I can tell you're holding it in. Go ahead."

"I'm not unbiased," his assistant said.

"Now, why doesn't that surprise me?" He grinned at her, feeling better, and she grinned back. Another woman who, if he'd been a different man, he could've gone for. Funny and smart and pretty, and no baggage that he could see. The problem was, he never fell for cheerful redheads. It was that damn wild side. That side kept shouting "brunette! With a temper!" in his ear. "Go on," he said. Tell."

"Well, you know how you took Beth Schaefer out?"

"Yeah, I do remember that, but I didn't know *you* knew."

She shrugged impatiently. "Of course I knew. If that was because Beth's a sweet person, you don't want Melody. If it was because Beth's got the right family and always looks pretty, then maybe you do, because from what I hear, your date may not have gone that well."

Why did he have the feeling that Jennifer knew about his marriage-and-family plan? He'd always held his cards close to his chest, but then, he'd never had an assistant like her before. "I don't. Want Melody, that is. I don't like that kind of woman much anymore."

"You mean bitchy women?"

He was so surprised, he laughed out loud. "You said the word. I didn't. Was she a cheerleader in high school, by any chance?"

"Not *a* cheerleader. *Head* cheerleader. Had the cutest clothes from kindergarten on up, and she still does. But my great-grandma would have said, 'Pretty is as pretty does.'"

"Well, mine probably would've, too, so don't worry, she's not going to become your... boss-in-law."

Jennifer waited a second, then said, "You aren't asking me about Dakota."

"Nope. I've always kinda prided myself on my judgment, for some crazy reason."

"Maybe because it's made you an estimated six hundred twenty-five million dollars as of the end of last year?"

"That could be it. Must you be so crass?"

"Apparently I must." She looked at her phone. "Almost time for your four-thirty. You want me?"

"No." The humor was gone. "I've got this."

♡♡♡

He jumped down from the Explorer ten minutes later and headed into the office block in a handsome historic building on Main Street, then up the stairs and on into Suite 201. Sawyer must have been listening for him, because he came out of the back office before Blake had even checked in with the receptionist, a smile and a handshake at the ready.

"Good to see you," he told Blake. Come on back."

Blake had considered doing this at the resort. Home-field advantage was always best. But he wanted to get Sawyer's cooperation, and doing it here would make that more likely to happen.

"Now," Sawyer said when they were sitting in his office. He eased back in his oversized leather desk chair and asked, "What can I do for you? Glad to see that we've gotten over that misunderstanding out at the resort." When Blake didn't answer immediately, he laughed and said, "Hey, I'm a direct guy. Anyway, you can't hold grudges in business. You got another job you need my help with, I'm your man."

He looked like what he was—an ex-jock who'd kept himself in shape. He'd been his own high school's quarterback and gone on to play some college ball, a fact he'd shared with Blake pretty quickly. He had the confident, friendly small-town manner, too, but Blake was starting to wonder about what lay beneath.

"That's true," Blake said. "Glad to hear you say so. I'll be direct myself. Since I've been in town, I've been hearing about Russell Matthews's accident on my Sundays site. I have a few questions about that." He set the OSHA report on the desk— the one he'd been sent after last week's conversation with his Chief Operating Officer. "If you'll indulge me a minute here, go through a few of these spots with me."

Sawyer's blue eyes lost some of their warmth. "There was a full investigation. It's all in there, the case is closed, and I don't have anything else to say about it. Matthews got his payout, and he's still getting it. It's workers' comp, which means no-fault, no matter what lame-ass thing the 'worker' does to cause it."

"Uh-huh. He's pretty bad off. Who set up the scaffolding, exactly? Just run me through it."

"A few people. *Including* him. It's in there. Accidents happen. You want to talk about 'bad off,' maybe you'd like to compensate me for the major hike in my workers' comp insurance afterwards for something that was the guy's own fault. Where are you getting this?"

Blake rubbed the spot behind his ear with a thumb and stared thoughtfully at Sawyer. "Hmm. See, now, he says that wasn't true, that he didn't help rig that scaffolding. Says it in the report, and said it to me. His partner says the same thing. They both say Matthews questioned the scaffolding at the time, that he had concerns. Seems like he was a pretty experienced guy. Pretty competent, too. Thirty years painting, and never had an accident? Makes my nose twitch, and when my nose twitches, I check it out."

"When he was doing all that telling, did he tell you that he was a drunk?" Sawyer had lost the good-buddy ease.

"He told me he was an alcoholic, yes. If he'd never had an accident, I'd guess he did his drinking after work. Anyway, seems he's been sober for quite a while. Not even taking his pain pills, and trust me—if a guy's looking for a crutch, he's not going to turn that one down."

"Hey. I followed *every* one of your candyass regulations to the *letter* on that job." Sawyer's finger was jabbing at the report now, ratcheting straight up to "losing control" as soon as he was challenged, which was illuminating in itself. "You got the town drunk whining to you six months after the fact, and you're going to believe him over me? And then do what, smear my name some more, like what happened out at the resort wasn't enough? I've got a reputation in this town myself, and it's not for being a drunk. And don't tell me about Evan O'Donnell," he went on fast, even though Blake hadn't spoken, just folded his arms across his chest and leaned back in his chair. "Evan O'Donnell can't wipe his ass without asking for permission from Matthews or Dakota. About half retarded. He'd say anything they told him to."

"You done?" Blake asked.

"Hell, no, I'm not done." Sawyer stood up, bracing his fists on the desk and leaning forward, the threat posture familiar to every silverback gorilla. "If I hear you're telling people that I was at fault on that project, if I get a hint that you're trying to mess with me like that and damage my reputation, I'll sue you for slander so fast, it'll make your head spin."

"You know," Blake said, "I have a feeling you can damage your reputation all by yourself." He didn't move. Instead, he focused on relaxing, gathering his energy into himself. Partly because it was the best place from which to launch, and partly because it drove bullies like Sawyer crazy.

He was right. Sawyer was flushing now, a vein throbbing in his temple. "Let me guess. Dakota Savage. I heard you hadn't gotten enough of her out at the resort, and now she's painting your house. Can't believe nobody's explained to you yet that you don't have to go out of your way for Dakota. She knows where she stands around here. Her stepdad was the town drunk, and her mom was the town whore. Bet she didn't tell you *that*. And her dad? He was a *real* piece of work."

He paused like he expected Blake to say something, and when he didn't, went on, "Bet Dakota didn't give you the rundown on him, either. Full-blood Indian, and he let you know it, headband and all, according to my dad. Ex-con, prison tats, the whole nine yards. My dad gave him a chance as a roofer, and that's all he was good for, except he wasn't even good enough for that. Came to work high one too many times, got fired, and skipped town with Dakota's mom—knocked up, of course—and the other kid. And ol' Russell didn't even get up from his barstool to watch 'em go. That's your Dakota. She's got so much bad blood running through her, she bleeds black. I'm guessing she didn't tell you she was a half-breed, huh? Dakota *Savage,* and that's just about right."

He was on a roll now, his mouth running away with him.

Trash talking, but Blake was familiar with trash talking. "I hear you're taking out Beth Schaefer, too. One on your arm and one on the side. You're probably worried about that, small town like this. Well, don't be. Dakota's used to being that side piece. You could say it's her specialty. So don't be thinking you got to do something special to get some of that. There are girls you fuck and girls you marry, and she knows which one she is."

Blake stood up. He did it slowly, and Sawyer smirked and said, "Sorry if I got you all disappointed."

"You done?" Blake asked, his voice low and cold.

"Hell, yeah, I'm done. Done with this BS, and done with you."

Blake's hand shot out so fast, Sawyer didn't even have time to blink. His fist closed around the other man's collar, and he was hauling him across the desk, watching his sincere blue eyes bug out and his smug mouth gasp for breath.

"Say any of that again to anybody," Blake said, the words still measured, "and I'll personally come to your house and beat the shit out of you."

He let the other man go, and Sawyer shoved himself back, stumbled over his desk chair, and nearly fell. He regained his balance and hauled himself upright, his eyes blazing. "You try it. Just try it. You want to hit me, NFL?" He beckoned with both hands toward his face. "Go on. Hit me. I'd love you to do it. You've got a squeaky-clean reputation and a liquor license to lose. My uncle's the mayor. My second cousin's the chief of police. See how good you run your company when you're in a six by eight cell with a bunk and a toilet. This is *my* town."

"Maybe so," Blake said. "But you forget one thing."

He let the moment stretch out until Sawyer asked it, as he'd known he would. He was a bully, and bullies never had self-control worth a damn. "What's that?"

"One of us has a corporate lawyer. One of us has a PR department and a Super Bowl ring. One of us is a golden boy who's been on a Wheaties box. And one of us has the power to take a piece of shit down and keep him there. And that ain't you." He picked up his OSHA report. "It might be your town. It's *my* country."

He didn't let the adrenaline take over until he was back in the Explorer again and down the road. Once he hit the city limits sign, though, he had to pull over and do some deep-breathing exercises.

It's over, he told himself. *You went looking for information. You got it. It's over.*

But not for Dakota. For Dakota, it would never be over.

Working Woman's Paradise

♡

Dakota was on her hands and knees, painting trim like lightning, when she heard the front door opening. And then that dark-molasses voice. "Hi, honey. I'm home."

Shoot, shoot, shoot. Not fast enough.

She barely had time to shove up onto her knees before he was there in all his glory, dressed in dark-gray slacks, tooled black cowboy boots that made him even taller, and a black T-shirt, his suit coat slung over his shoulder, every bit of him looking like a working woman's paradise. Warm eyes, firm mouth, broad shoulders, and biceps to die for. A bona fide good time.

What she *wanted* to say was, "Cowboy, take me away." What she *actually* said was, "I'm just about done." She also tried to pretend that she wasn't wearing a painter's cap, overalls, and knee pads. "I wanted to finish these baseboards so you'd have your main living area done. You said you wouldn't be back until tonight."

"Keep talking like that," he said, "and I'm going to think you didn't want to see me." Something in the way he said it caught at her, and she looked at him more closely. The words and his pose were casual, but everything else about him, she realized through her own discomfort… wasn't.

"Is something wrong?" she asked. "Something not go well in your… meeting, or whatever it was? I can be out of your way in ten minutes. I can finish the baseboards tomorrow." She was still kneeling, which was awkward, with the way he was standing over her. She set her brush down in the paint pan, stood up, pushed her glasses up her nose with the back of her hand, then ran the hand in what she hoped was a casual fashion over her upper lip. She could tell she was sweating.

"Nope," he said. "Everything's fine. And sure, go ahead and finish up tonight. I can't believe you got this far already. Looking real good, Miss Dakota. Maybe you really are all that. Of course, that could just be because the furniture's covered up. Antler-free zone."

"You can't tell very well now," she said, trying to ignore the glow of satisfaction that gave her. He was charming; that was his deal. "It never looks good until you clean up. If you do want to see, just give me half an hour."

"I do want to see. And if I give you a hand, we can get it done faster."

"You don't want to give me a hand."

"And why would that be?" He still looked tense to her. Something in his shoulders. Like he was trying to be polite, but he wanted his house back. Exactly like that.

"For one thing," she said, knowing she should be professional and get out of his space, "you're paying *me* to do it. And for the other, you're dressed up like the Cowboy Angel of Death, and no piece of that outfit is going to look good with taupe paint all over it. Especially those boots."

Maybe not all *that* professional.

He didn't answer her. Instead, he stepped closer, and she caught her breath. And then he reached out and took her chin in his hand, and she forgot to breathe.

She thought for one crazy moment that he was going to kiss her. He didn't. Instead, he rubbed his thumb over her upper lip. And didn't let her go.

For a second, she just stood there, shocked into stillness. And then she realized what he'd been doing. She'd smeared *paint* all over herself, and he'd wiped it off.

Some of the tension seemed to have left him, because his smile looked real when he finally dropped his hand and said, "I don't know about that. And I think I like you with a little bit of a paint mustache. Pretty cute. The Cowboy Angel of Death, though? I'd be insulted, except that it sounds kinda hot."

Apparently she was abandoning any hope of "professional," because she said, "Yeah, I'm a class act with my paint mustache, and you're my dark, dangerous fantasy man. The gunslinger outfit's totally working. But do me a favor. If you're going to stand around here, go change your clothes. You're making me nervous that I'm going to mess you up. And do *not* tell me," she added while he was still opening his mouth, "that you'd be glad to get messed up with me. I can hear the thought forming, and it's beneath you. You can do better."

He actually stood there with his mouth half-open for a second, and then he clapped a hand to his chest and staggered. "You got me again. Straight to the heart. Be right back." He headed for the stairs, the heels of those boots ringing out on the stone floor once he was off the dropcloth, then turned around halfway there and asked, "So the black shirt works?"

"Go away," she said, sinking to her knees again and picking up her brush.

"I'm keeping it on," he said. "I think it works."

♡♡♡

Blake started to take the stairs two at a time, and his knee instantly told him what it thought of that idea. He switched to one at a time, trying to make it look nonchalant, and then tried to pretend he wasn't hurrying. Just like when he'd been driving here and wondering why he'd scheduled his afternoon so he wouldn't be home until after five, when he'd wanted to see

Dakota again ever since he'd left her. After that, he'd tried to tell himself that he hadn't had any spike in his pulse rate when he'd seen her old Ford pickup in his driveway. That hadn't worked, either.

She didn't fit into the life plan, and after what he'd heard today, messing around with her would be a purely lousy thing to do. So why was he changing into faded Levi's and applying a little extra Jack Black deodorant just to make sure he smelled all right for her? All she'd be able to smell was paint.

It was stupid, but he did it anyway. Story of his romantic life. He kept the black T-shirt on, too. That "gunslinger" comment had come from somewhere.

Because you were a quarterback, dude. Except he didn't think that was it.

He headed back down the stairs, and when he came around the corner from the landing and saw her taupe-painted walls… yeah, they looked better, blue painter's tape and all.

She was on her hands and knees painting the baseboard, her movements quick and neat. Her baggy white overalls weren't doing a thing for her, and the thick braid hanging over one shoulder had some paint at the end, like she'd dipped it in the pan sometime during the day. And he was glad she was there.

She looked up when he walked over, and he said, "Put me to work, boss. Painting's in my blood."

That made her smile. "Casual" had sure-enough been the way to go here, because she was relaxing. That was good. "I'm almost done with this," she said, "and besides, you have to be neat to do trim. I have a feeling you're the messy type. Exuberant painter, that'd be you."

"Exuberant? That sounds almost like an insult. Bet you're right, though. I tend to get into my work. You could say I put my whole self into it."

"Uh-huh," she said dryly. "Well, put your whole self into climbing that ladder and taking the tape off from around the windows, then. You're taller than me."

"I am that."

She looked at his bare feet. "Not exactly dressed for the jobsite. You're going to get yourself messed up."

"Us exuberant types," he said, "we don't mind rolling around in it. It'll wash off."

"Then go do it. My paint's drying out."

After that, she had him taking the dropcloths off everything and folding them up, but when he finished, she was still painting. He sat on the edge of his uncovered coffee table— still unfortunately antler-intensive—and asked her, "How long did all this take?"

"The weekend and today. It's a huge room, especially when you add the entry, and a high one. Major ladder time. I haven't gotten to the kitchen, you probably noticed, but I'll do that tomorrow."

"Weekend, huh? What about that stained glass piece you were working on?"

She smiled, and as always, it gave her a whole different look. Still strong, but—shining.

Whoa, boy, he told himself, and promptly forgot it.

"My conch," she said.

"That what it is? The thing you were working on last week?"

"Oh, yeah." She forgot to paint for a moment, and her eyes went dreamy. "I didn't get to finish it. It's going to be so good." She turned away, gave a few last careful swipes to the end of the baseboard, then set her brush down and started to gather her things. "I'll take this stuff out to the truck, and you can enjoy looking at your living room in *almost* all its glory. I'll take the tape off from around the baseboards tomorrow, once they're dry."

"Mm," he said. "I've got another idea. I help you load up your truck, and you come back in and help me admire your work, maybe have a beer, and tell me about your conch."

She sighed. "I've got to say, a beer sounds good. I've been here a while. I don't drink at Russell's, for obvious reasons."

He got up and picked up the paint can and a stack of dropcloths. "Happy to be your designated drinking spot. Come on, wild thing. Let's drink a beer. We could even jump off my dock if we wanted. Did you see I've got one? Got your name on it, too."

"Let me guess," she said. "Your meeting, or whatever you went off to do in your private jet? It got boring."

"You got that right. Besides—badasses gotta badass."

A beer was fine, he told himself. A beer was absolutely no big deal. He liked her, that was all. She was interesting. Also an artist. He needed more people like that in his life.

Hanging out with her was fun, and if they flirted a little— well, that would be fun, too, for both of them. They could be… friends.

Yeah. Friends would be good.

A Beer With Blake

♡

Go home, Dakota told herself. *Right now.*

Instead, she gathered the rest of her supplies and asked, "So did you see it?"

"Uh… see what?" He headed after her into the soaring entryway, then rocked to a stop. "Oh."

She couldn't tell. What did "Oh" mean?

"If you don't like it there," she said quickly, "we can move it. I just thought, since I'd painted, I'd show you how it looked, and…" She shut her mouth on the rest. He was standing there, holding the paint can, staring at her eagle. *His* eagle. Which was hanging in the big window above the front door, looking like it would swoop down on them.

The seconds ticked away. He was going to say he didn't want it after all. Now that he saw it in the house, he was realizing everything that was wrong with it. That part at the bottom of the left wing, the awkward place where she hadn't gotten the shadow just right. And she'd already sent the money from his check to the mortgage company. It was *gone.*

He said slowly, "I don't know. I'm wondering, now…"

"Oh." She thought she was going to throw up. "Uh, I can… I could switch it for the owl, if you want." He'd liked the owl.

He'd stood there in Russell's room and studied it. She couldn't have mistaken the look in his eyes that day. "Or make you another piece, maybe, if you…" It had been so much money. She'd known it. Way too much for two pieces. What had she been *thinking?*

"Dakota. No."

The blood had left her head. She swallowed hard and said, "I'm going to… put these things in the truck." There would be an answer, some answer. But she couldn't, she *wouldn't* let him see her cry.

She headed fast into the circular drive and shoved her supplies into the back of the truck. She could tell he was still behind her, and sure enough, he set down the paint can and the dropcloths.

Get it together. She took a breath that was unfortunately unsteady, but even as she was doing it, his hands were on her shoulders, turning her around. "What the hell is going on?" he demanded. "What could you be thinking I was going to say?"

There was nothing but concern in his eyes. And she'd gotten it wrong. How was she going to explain this? "Oh," she said weakly. "Huh. I thought you were saying you didn't like it."

"If I hadn't liked it, I wouldn't have bought it. But I did buy it. It's mine, and I'm not giving it back. There's no way I'm letting it go." He must have realized he was holding her, because he dropped his hands from her shoulders. "Come on back inside with me, and let's look at it together. Your room, and my eagle. And whatever you were thinking—it's not true. We've got to work on your confidence, darlin'."

She didn't answer that, maybe because he was right. She went back into the house with him, the smell of paint hitting her hard, like always. Blake didn't seem to notice it. He turned in the middle of the entryway to study the eagle again, and this time, she concentrated on breathing and not making assumptions, and waited.

"It looks good there," he finally said. "It looks *great* there, and if I didn't like it so much… but I don't think you can see it well enough up that high. I want to see his wings. I want to see his eyes, and the way he's grabbing for that fish. I want to feel him doing it."

"If we put him in one of the living-room windows, though," she said, "he'll be smack dab in the middle of your lake view. I don't think that works. That's why I put him here. Maybe the dining room?"

He. Blake thought of his eagle as a "he"? Like it was a real bird, the same way it seemed to her? And he wanted it. It was as good as he'd thought at first. He wasn't going to change his mind. The thought was making her lightheaded.

"That's a point about the lake," he said. "But I've got an idea. Come with me." He took her hand and headed for the stairs, then stopped and said, "Are you comfortable?"

"Uh… what?"

"Aren't you hot? Don't you want to change?"

"I'm looking forward to it, yeah, but I'm always hot while I work. Nothing new there."

"Baby, you're the artist here. You're doing me a favor right now. So why don't you say, 'Blake, honey, quit pushin' me around. I'm off the clock.'"

"I don't know." Suddenly, she was feeling a whole lot better, and not just because she wasn't going to have to somehow figure out how to pay back twenty-four hundred dollars she didn't have. "Maybe because I'm never going to call you 'honey,' just like I'm never going to let you call me 'baby'? And you might have caught me off guard there."

His eyes were smiling again, even though his mouth wasn't. "I must've, the way you lost all your badass like that. Good to see it coming back. You've wounded me again, too, but I'm ignoring it. So what do you think? Tell me to quit wasting your time and to go get you that beer? Tell me to quit wasting your time, period, because you've had a long day and you're heading on home? Or take off those clothes and come help me figure out where to hang my bird? Which sounds dirty. Why is that?"

She was laughing. "Let's go for 'combination.' Let's go for 'my choice.' I'm taking off these clothes. I'm washing my hands. I'm telling you to get me my beer first, and then, if you ask me nicely, I'm helping you figure out where to hang your bird. In a non-dirty way."

He grinned. "See, I knew you had it in you."

She was still smiling when she headed into the bathroom. Until she had another of those moments of truth.

This house had way, *way* too many mirrors. Painter's cap, check. Overalls, check. Knee pads and paint-smeared tennis shoes, double-check. And she still had a smear of paint on the corner of her mouth. That was extra attractive. When she took off her cap and took her hair out of the braid, she found she had paint in there, too.

It was a while before she headed back out the door carrying a handful of clothes and shoes, but by the time she did, she looked a little better, and more importantly, had given herself a much-needed reality check.

The woman who's going to paint your ceiling or gut your fish, she'd told Evan, and she'd been right. And maybe, horribly, something else. *The woman who's going to be your short-term good time, because you're bored, she's in your house already, and you've heard she's good for it.*

Blake was waiting for her in the kitchen. "That's better," he said, taking in her shorts, white T-shirt, and bare feet, then handing her a wonderfully cold bottle of beer. "Dump those somewhere, and I'll show you my idea."

It sounded casual, and in the right way, too. It was "paint your ceiling," then, not "swipe right for tonight."

He took her upstairs to his office, next to the master suite. A huge black walnut desk sat in the middle of a room dominated by five panes of bay windows, with an upholstered window seat made for reading, for sketching, for dreaming.

"I do like your house," she said.

"It's not too bad at all. It'll look better once you're done with it, of course. And I was thinking the same as you, that the eagle should be downstairs. But I've decided I want it in here. I'm a greedy guy, I guess. I want to keep the best for myself. Besides, it'll get me in the right frame of mind while I work."

"Mm. Put it in the middle window, right here? It'd sure make a statement." She took a sip from her beer and glanced at him. He was leaning up against the desk, the bottle held negligently in one big hand, one ankle crossed over the other, and he wasn't looking out the windows. He was looking at her. "So the right frame of mind is 'predatory'?"

"So often," he said. "At least the way I do it."

Was it warm in here? Or was it his eyes? "Sounds a little scary," she said, going for breezy. Going for confident. "Do I really want to be doing business with you?"

His eyes were shining gold. His eyes made her weak in the knees. He said, "Oh, I think so. 'Predatory' might just mean that I know what I want, and then I go after it."

"And do you always get it?"

"Usually. The secret is—you got to want it enough. And I do want it."

She took another sip of beer, and he didn't. He was just watching her. She said, "Well, I'll hang the eagle here, then."

"Dakota…" He said it like he liked saying it, and all she could do was look at him. He shoved off the desk, took a step closer, then reached out and brushed the back of his hand over her cheek. She was swaying into him, and just like that, his hand was holding her head, his eyes drinking her in. He took one more step, and she could barely breathe. And then he kissed her.

It was a bare brush of his lips over hers, but it sent a tingle of pleasure right down her body. His thumb was stroking her cheek, his lips returning to hers as if he needed them. Gentle, but so sure. And in another second, it wasn't going to be gentle, because she could feel his urgency.

She realized she was dropping her beer bottle the second it happened. She grabbed for it, but she was too late. She jumped back as it hit the carpet, the frothy liquid spilling out in a soaking mess, splattering on her bare feet.

He was down before she even had a chance to react, scooping the bottle up, then standing and setting it on the desk.

"Sorry," she said, trying to laugh it off. "That was smooth of me. I'll just... ah, the eagle. I'll wait to move it until after I paint in here."

"Dakota..."

She didn't listen to whatever he would have said. She was already talking. "I should get home. Russ will have dinner going. I need to go."

He looked at her without saying anything. Two seconds, three, and she forced herself to shut up and meet his gaze. Finally, he asked, "Is it Evan, or is it me?"

"*Evan?* No. What? No. I just need to go. I'll do your kitchen tomorrow. I'll be here around eight, unless you'd rather I started later. Tell me when."

She thought he was going to say something else, but all he said was, "Eight's good. I'll be gone."

♡♡♡

Blake stood in the front doorway and watched her haul on the steering wheel, turn that battered old truck around, and head up the drive.

Too much. Too fast. You pushed too hard. And in no possible universe was that "friends."

The worst thing was, when he'd been looking into her eyes, feeling the pull in her, feeling her wanting to come to him, knowing how much he wanted that—no, how much he *needed* that... he'd known something else, too. That she knew what Steve Sawyer had said about her. And that she knew Blake had heard it.

And that she thought he believed it.

This wasn't what he'd wanted to do. This wasn't it at all.

Then why did you do it?

Because he was a damn fool with no discipline, which was the whole entire problem. Next time, though, it was going to be different. Next time, he was going to do things right. Next time, he wasn't going to be making her run away.

Damn Straight
♡

Stupid, Dakota told herself, punching the steering wheel with one hand and doing nothing but hurting her fist. *Stupid, stupid, stupid.*

She'd known she should pack up and leave, that there was nothing there for her. Instead, she'd stuck around, and sure enough, Blake had made a move on her, and she'd stood there and waited for him—*wanted* him—to do it. It had been perfectly clear what it was all about, and it wasn't true love.

He wasn't the boy next door. He was an NFL player, a multimillionaire working his way up to the "billion" mark while he dated women like Beth Schaefer, women who met his standards, women with graduate degrees and family money and *class.* And this was Wild Horse. She was no Beth Schaefer, and everybody in this town knew it. Blake wasn't her hero riding in to save the day. He was another rich guy used to taking what he wanted. That's exactly what he'd said. *I know what I want, and then I go after it.*

Predatory. It wasn't on anybody's list of love words.

The disappointment was right there, tightening her chest, constricting her breathing. Or maybe that was the shame.

You have nothing to be ashamed of. Nothing. Maybe if she said it

138

enough times, she would actually believe it.

She didn't go straight home, even though she was already late. Instead, she pulled into the lot at City Beach, sent Russell a quick text, and went for a swim.

No hesitation. Not here. Not anymore. She ran into the cold water, then dove under and swam for her life. For her self-respect. For her dignity, and most of all, for her courage. If it didn't come easily—well, nothing did. It came hard, always, but she wasn't getting out until she had it back.

When she walked into the kitchen at last with Bella following her inside, disappointed out of a session with her dog toy, the table was set, but Russell wasn't there. She followed the sound of the TV into the living room.

"Hey," she said, her tongue sticking on the "Dad" as it had all week, ever since that dinner with Evan and Blake. "Sorry I'm late. I hope dinner isn't ruined."

Russell turned the set off and struggled to stand. "No problem. You told me. Not like I've got someplace else to get to. Go clean up. I'll get the burgers started."

Even after her shower, though, which usually made her feel better, the food didn't go down easily. She should be hungry— she *was* hungry—but she was having trouble anyway.

She'd look at her glass after dinner, that was what. She wouldn't work on it—she'd mess up if she tried, and she knew it—but she'd look at it, and she'd believe in herself a little again. She'd feel better.

Russell had been nearly silent since they'd sat down. She hadn't seen much of him lately anyway, between the work, her glass, and the excuses she'd made to be somewhere else. Now, though, he spoke. "I was checking the bills today. I looked at the mortgage balance, and it said it was almost out of the red. Looked to me like about four thousand bucks too much in there. That a mistake? If it is, I'll take it."

Dakota glanced up at him, then back at her burger. "Blake Orbison bought two of my glass pieces on Friday. The eagle and one of the flowers. He paid me thirty-nine hundred dollars for them, too. Once we get the last payment for the resort, you'll be all the way out of the red. Then it'll just be keeping up with the payments."

Russell had stopped eating. "That's a hell of a lot of money. It's a whole lot more than you've ever charged. He paid that? Why? And you shouldn't be putting that money into the mortgage anyway. That's yours, for your own start someday."

"It's my debt, too. Mine to help with."

"It's not your debt."

She wasn't even pretending to eat anymore. "I know. It's not my house. You told me so. I got it. It's still my debt. You took me in when I had no place else to go, and then you kept me. That's my debt, and I pay my debts."

"You stop that right now." Russell shoved away from the table, and she saw the spasm of pain that crossed his face. Sudden movements always hurt. "Kids don't owe parents. That's not how it works."

"Except that I'm not your kid."

The words hung there. Her throat was tight, her breathing shallow as Russell stared at her, pale blue eyes in a face creased beyond its years. The face she loved. The man who wasn't her father.

He said, "Of course you're my kid."

"You forget." It was hard to say. She said it anyway. "I heard you. This isn't my house, and you're not my responsibility. But I still owe you."

His palm came down on the table, rattling the silverware, but she didn't jump, and she didn't flinch when he raised his voice, either. "God *damn* it! That wasn't what that meant! You telling me you've spent all this week thinking I was saying you're not my daughter? That's why you've been so messed up? I thought it was Orbison, and you having to paint his house. Why would you think something that crazy? Just because I don't want to be reminded that I'm useless, and that you're carrying all the weight for me like nobody's daughter should have to do? That you have to work for him like you never wanted to do? What the hell does that have to do with whether you're mine?"

Her voice was shaking, her hands gripping the paper napkin in her lap. "I thought…"

"Well, stop thinking." He was glaring at her, barking the words out. "Maybe I had some payback of my own to do, you ever think of that? Man stays drunk the whole first two years of his son's life, lets his girlfriend go off with somebody else without even putting up a fight, never tries to get those kids back? And then they finally come back to him through nothing he's done, and he still barely manages to hang onto them? What kind of payback do you think he needs to do for that?"

"But you did," she managed to get out. "You held onto us. You stopped drinking so they let you keep me."

"And how much good did it do? Riley still had to join the Army, didn't he? You still left town. And now you've had to come back."

"I'll survive." She took a gulp of iced tea, then choked on it and coughed helplessly for a minute, the tears she'd held back earlier coming to her eyes with the force of the spasms.

"If you're taking favors from Blake Orbison," Russell said when her coughing had subsided, "that's too high a price. I'm not letting you do that for me."

It was her glass hitting the table this time, its force surprising both of them. Russell jerked back, and Bella, who'd been standing up leaning against his leg, barked twice, the sound unexpected and sharp.

Dakota jumped, but she went on anyway. "I am not prostituting myself for Blake Orbison. I wouldn't be worth that kind of price to him, so there'd be no point even if I wanted to. I'd be fifty bucks on the nightstand and 'That was great, honey. See you next time.' That isn't paying any mortgages, and I'm not doing it."

"You bite your tongue." The leathery skin on Russell's cheeks had darkened. "Don't you ever think that. Don't you dare. You've got more in you than any ten models Orbison ever dated. You ought to know it. And if he's pressured you… you'd better be telling me, and telling Evan, too. You switch jobs with Evan, and if Orbison doesn't like it, he can talk to me about it, and I'll tell him how it's going to be."

Dakota shrugged, suddenly so tired. "I don't need to do that. It doesn't matter. I asked that price for my glass, and he paid me. Maybe he's a fool. Could be. He has too much money, that's for sure. But I didn't trade anything for thirty-nine hundred other than my glass, and I'm not going to."

She saw the fight go out of Russell like a balloon leaking air. He slumped in his chair, and Bella shoved her nose into his palm. "Good," he said. "That's good. Eat your dinner."

She had to laugh. "Really? All that, and that's what you've got?"

He smiled, a painful twist of his mouth. "No. Guess I need to say more than that. Guess I need to tell you that of course you're my daughter. What else could you ever be? What else have you ever been?"

She couldn't say anything. The lump in her throat was too big for any words to come out. The heat was rising in her chest, and if she didn't stop herself, she was going to cry. "But I was… I'm not yours. I was just… Riley's sister. I know that's why you took me. Because Riley wouldn't let me go. I know. That's OK. You did it anyway."

He was still glaring, the words still sharp. "Of course you're mine. Maybe that was why I did it at first. But just because I don't go around talking like some Hallmark card doesn't mean you're not my daughter. It sure doesn't mean I'm not your dad."

Her mouth worked, but no words came, and his voice was gruff and not a bit steady when he said, "You better come over here and give me a hug. I'm too damn crippled to do it, and I can't stand to watch you cry."

She was out of her chair in an instant. In the next moment, she was on her knees with her arms around his waist. Russell's arm had gone around her shoulders, and Bella was right there, too. It was a family hug. A family that was two people and a dog with no trace of blood to hold them together. But they had love. That, they had.

Dakota's shoulders shook with the effort not to cry, and Russell's hand stroked awkwardly over her hair. He said, "I'm lousy at this. This is what I'm talking about. I should've been saying it. I never had any practice, I guess. Too much in love with the bottle. Maybe if you give me a grandbaby someday, I can start at the beginning. Maybe I can do better at being a dad then."

"You're already doing better," she whispered. "You're already my dad."

"Damn straight I am." He sounded absolutely sure, and now she *was* crying. "Damn straight."

Sprouts and Kale
♡

Blake said, "OK. Thanks," hung up the phone, sat back in the desk chair in the office he'd temporarily allocated himself at the resort, and tapped the phone absently against his leg. Then he stood up and headed for the door.

If he was going to take care of this, he needed to get started. It was Thursday, he was leaving this evening for a swing through the Midwest, and besides… he needed to get started. That was all.

He hadn't seen Dakota since that evening three days earlier. He came home every night to find another room painted, the mess cleaned up, and only the pungent, lingering smell of paint telling him she'd been there. She didn't hang around to see him, which would have been the easiest thing in the world for her to do, and that told its own story. But then, she'd already given him the message.

He walked into the house ten minutes later and didn't see her. She wouldn't be on the main floor, though, because she'd finished it yesterday. He ran upstairs, and sure enough, dropcloths covered the desk in his office, and two of the walls were pale gray. But she wasn't there.

He called out, "Dakota?" and didn't get an answer. Her

144

truck was outside, though, so she must be around. He headed downstairs, then to the bottom floor, but didn't find her there, either.

Well, huh.

It was lunchtime. Maybe she was swimming? It was another warm day. He headed out to the deck to look for her, calling her name as he went.

He found her at last, sitting up hastily in a chaise in the shade at one side of the wooden expanse of the deck. She started to climb out of her chair at his approach, a messy sandwich in one hand.

"Oh," she said, looking flustered and self-conscious. "Were you looking for me? Sorry. I was just taking my lunch break. Half an hour."

"Am I allowed to interrupt your lunch break?" he asked. She was wearing her overalls as usual, but she'd taken off her cap and unhooked the straps so the bib hung down around her waist. Another white V-necked tee, the same thick, dark braid, delicate collarbones, and smooth skin. And paint, of course, tiny drops of it speckling her arms.

"Of course," she said. "It's your house. It's your job. And I assume it's OK that I'm using the deck. I like to get out of the paint for a little while."

"Sure. Use whatever you want. Go on and sit down, though, and eat your lunch. Or better yet—I'll go get mine, too, and join you. What are you having?"

He tried his best to send the message. *Just lunch.*

She held up her sandwich. "Turkey and Swiss, plus an apple. Pretty exciting. Russell makes it for me, so I'm not going to complain."

Her words were casual, but her face had that somber thing going on big-time. She wasn't smiling today. She was the very last thing from "cute," and she was very nearly beautiful, in the way a piece of polished hardwood was beautiful. Nothing superficial, but something born in the texture of the wood.

What was he, a poet? He was losing it. That wasn't what he

145

was here for. "Give me three minutes," he said. "I've got this idea I want to talk about with you."

"Uh…" she said.

"It's not personal. Or rather, it is, but it's not about you and me."

"Oh. All right." She was shoving her sandwich back into its plastic bag, her movements quick, her tension obvious. "I wasn't going to hang around out here for long, though. I want to finish that room today."

It didn't sound much like, "Kiss me now. Touch me, love me, hold me tight," but it was what he'd expected.

When he came back out again, she was sitting sideways on the chaise, her feet planted neatly on the ground, still looking the opposite of relaxed. She'd fastened the straps of her overalls, too. He wanted to say something about that, but instead, he just handed her a plate, knife, and fork and said, "In case you wanted a little change from the turkey and Swiss." He set down his own plate, tugged a chair over, and sat down at an angle to her. "And I wish you'd get comfortable again. You're making me nervous."

She was looking at the plate in her lap. "Oh. Thanks. That's nice of you. This isn't exactly what I imagined an NFL star would eat for lunch, though."

"No? But then, I'm not an NFL star anymore. And this isn't too far from what I've always eaten. Leftovers from last night, to tell you the truth. Which I didn't cook, I feel I have to mention. Takeout from the Heart of the Lake."

"Russ is going to be disappointed," she said, a little sparkle showing in her eyes at last. "Chicken pieces, kale salad, and roasted Brussels sprouts? I'm sure he envisioned enormous slabs of filet mignon and maybe some manly potatoes. And I'm not even going to *tell* Evan. He thinks kale is a cruel joke foisted on the men of America for their sins."

"I've been known to eat a steak or two, but you've got to lower the calorie count when you're not burning it anymore. We going to talk about nutrition or eat lunch?"

He got a little smile for that, and she started to eat, too. "So you had an idea?"

"I guess if I said I wanted to see you, that wouldn't be a good thing."

She lost the smile. "Probably not."

"Right, then. I came to talk to you about Russell."

Now, she lost the ease. "Russell what?"

"I can't get any definitive answers on his accident. Sawyer's employees aren't talking, I can't force them to, and there's no way to reopen the investigation. I went all the way up the ladder, but you know—OSHA. Government agency."

"Oh." She shook her head. Shaking it off. "Well, I never thought you could."

"Or that I would," he guessed.

"That too. Like you said. It was investigated."

"Yeah. It was. So that's where we are with that. I can't change the investigation, so I started looking into what I *could* do. That's where you come in. I called around and found the best guy to deal with a broken back. In orthopedics, now—there, I *can* throw my weight around a little, or if I can't, an NFL trainer sure can. They practically have those docs on retainer. I got Russell an appointment to see this guy down at Cedars-Sinai next month. But I thought I'd tell you first, because I'm guessing Russ could raise a couple objections."

"But…" She looked at her plate as if she'd forgotten it was there, then speared a tiny Brussels sprout. "They said they'd done everything they could."

"And do you think that's true?"

"No. I've always thought, maybe… workers' comp won't cover it, though. I know they won't, because I've checked. I've called and called. It would have to be preapproved, and they won't. As far as they're concerned, he was treated, he's fixed as well as he can be, and they're done."

"I know that, too. I had my head of HR checking into all this stuff. Big ol' brick wall. I'm not talking about workers' comp, or maybe I am. My version, because if it was wrong, and it happened on my watch, it's my job to fix it."

She looked at him, a frown drawing her winged brows together. "I can't believe you'd do that. I can't believe any HR person would let you, or your attorney, either. I know you must have one."

"Ah." He rubbed his nose. "Let's say they aren't happy about it. And would you please eat that lunch? If you don't, I can't, and I'm hungry."

She did, finally, but after a minute, she said, "So your attorney said no."

"Yep. Told me I'd be as much as admitting liability. I pointed out that it was workers' comp, the investigation is over, and that's that, no liability possible, but she still didn't like it."

"And you said…" She cut a piece of chicken and studied him like she was a human lie-detector test.

"And I said the same thing I told my HR director. Thanks for her advice, and I was doing it anyway. I'm the boss, you see. I get to do that."

"Oh." He thought she might be breathing a little faster. "So… what?"

"So in about a month here, you and Russ go down to LA and talk to Dr. Fischer, see what he can do. And then, assuming that's 'anything at all,' Russ goes down there again and gets it done."

"And you're going to *pay* for it? How could you do that?"

"I sure am. With a check, probably. And before you ask— yeah, that means your time off and a place to stay and all that. If it's my fault, it's on me to fix, and that's it."

She was definitely having difficulty with her breathing now, and she'd stopped eating again, too. "You make it so hard to hate you," she said, sounding truly sad about it.

This time, he laughed. "Well, darlin', let me keep working on it, and I'm sure you'll find yourself moving past that obstacle and finding yourself some reason. But it's not going to be this one. I'm guessing Russ isn't going to want to be beholden, so I'm going to need your help. Or could be he's going to worry about my motives, so I thought I'd better go right to the source on that."

"Uh-huh." She was eating again, and he thought she was smiling. "He's going to ask you about your intentions like some kind of old movie, and you don't want to squirm. Let me put your mind at rest. I already told him I wasn't prostituting myself for him. I told him fifty bucks a shot doesn't go that far. I'd never pay it off."

He realized that his mouth was open and snapped it shut. She was still eating, and she didn't look one bit vulnerable now. This was all badass. "What am I supposed to say to that?" he complained. "That it'd be a whole lot more than fifty? That's what we call a no-win conversation. That's a big ol' pit that a man would never climb out of."

"I know." She was trying not to smile, but she wasn't succeeding. "Sorry. I couldn't help it. You reminded me, that's all. But you'd really do that? What if they can't fix it with surgery?"

"Then we tried, and I get a physical therapist for him, get him a better doctor, get him to the pain clinic to see what they can do for him without narcotics. I do what I can, is what. I do what I ought to do."

She'd stopped smiling. She was holding her plate on one knee, but she took the other hand and set it on his forearm, and her expression was completely serious, and somehow... shining. That golden glow he'd only seen when she'd been talking about her art—that was what he was getting now. That glow was something special. Something beautiful.

"I shouldn't have joked," she said. "I guess I was trying to make it less... to feel less about it. I don't know what to say. I don't know anybody who'd do something like this. This is... you don't know what it'll mean to Russ. You don't know how hard he's had to fight."

"Yeah," he said quietly. She hadn't let go of him, and he wanted her right there. "I do. You think I don't see him, the man he is, and you're wrong. He's a hell of a guy."

149

"He took me in, you know." Her eyes were bright, and their legs were so close, they were almost touching. He could feel every bit of her spirit, the shining core of her, and it was pulling him closer as if he were magnetized. "Before our mom dumped us on him—Riley and me—Russ went to the tavern every day after work. He didn't go to work drunk, but he spent every night drunk. I bet that's not news to you. I bet you heard that already."

"I did. But people don't have to stay stuck in what they used to be."

"No. Maybe not. He was what they call a functional alcoholic, but he's not one now. Or rather—he'd say he still is, but he fights that fight and wins it every single day. And you know why? Because they said he couldn't keep me. He could keep Riley. He was Riley's dad. But I was a girl, I was fifteen, and I wasn't his, and that's a recipe for risk. He had to go to court to be my guardian, and they said no. I was in foster care for months until he could prove he was able to stay sober, and if it hadn't been for Riley…" She stopped, maybe because her voice wasn't steady anymore. "Russell did that, and I know it was the hardest thing he ever did. He did it for Riley, and he did it for me. Do you know how much that means to me?"

Somehow, her legs *were* touching his now, or his were touching hers. She still had her hand on him, too. She was right there, and he was going to drown in her eyes, in her passion.

"I know how much," he said. "I'm adopted."

Her eyes widened. "Oh. I didn't… I didn't know that. I thought—"

"That everything had been easy. You aren't wrong. Everything *has* been easy. It's just that I know how lucky I am that it has been."

"It can't have been. You must have worked so hard."

"I'd have told you I did. But when you can see the rewards right there, when you can see it all falling in your lap if you just keep pushing… that's not the same as working for it when there's nothing falling in your lap, when those rewards aren't coming, when you're fighting just to keep your head above water. It's not the same at all. Not the same as what Russell's doing. Or what you're doing for him."

She didn't say anything for a moment. "Wow," was what she finally came up with. "Uh... I'm doing a serious re-think here."

He smiled. "Nah. I'm still that guy you thought. But maybe I know I'm that guy."

"No. You're not the guy I thought." She seemed to realize for the first time that she was pressed up close to him, holding him, because she sat back, tried to laugh, and said, "And thanks. For Russell... thanks. Even if it doesn't work out, even if he can't get better, thank you for being willing to try."

He could see her pulling back into her shell again, and he couldn't stand it. "Know what I've got upstairs?" he asked.

"Oh, geez. I can't wait. The mind boggles. You know, you don't *have* to convince me that you're not a great guy. I could preserve my illusions."

He laughed out loud. "I've got a swimsuit, that's what. I'll bet you do, too. If you didn't have to look at my undershorts, maybe you'd put on that truly terrible swimsuit of yours and jump off my dock with me. I got all tired there, all that scary emotion. I need something to perk me up and somebody to break the rules with, or else I need a beer."

"What rules?"

"Sign right there on the dock. No diving."

"There is not."

"There is. There purely is."

"You can't break the rules in your own *house,*" she protested, but she was laughing. "Speaking of which, I still have two-thirds of that house to go, and I've got this ruthless employer. You should see him crack the whip."

There she was, teasing, and she still had those two little rings and that chain in her ear. She still had that mouth, too. And he wanted to go swimming with her. "Well," he said, "you're in luck, because I'm heading out again tonight and not coming back until Tuesday morning. You can finish your shell *and* paint my house this weekend, get all caught up. You've just got to promise me that you'll show me the shell when you're done. I get first dibs."

"It's pink." She was looking at him from under her lashes, and wasn't that a beautiful sight? "It could be a little sexy, too. It's sort of looking into the… interior. It's, ah… smooth. And pink. Like I said."

His smile started slow, and that glow was more of a spark now, moving right up toward "flame." He said, "That does sound mighty unappealing, darlin'. But I still get dibs."

Passion Project

♡

The nagging little voice in Dakota's ear tried to buzz at her while she changed into her suit, but she shut it out. She didn't care what that voice said. It was just a swim. The lake was out there beckoning, she was hot, and Blake hadn't done one thing to try to make her stay on Monday. He'd let her choose, and he was letting her choose now. He was a guy who could hear "no." And he was going to take care of Russ.

Plus, he was fun. She was allowed to have fun.

She didn't see him when she came out of the bathroom, but when she headed down to the first floor of the house and out to the lake, there he was, already in the water. She headed down there, relishing the cool grass under her toes, moving more cautiously over the sun-heated boards of the dock. And when she dropped her swim bag and took off her glasses, he called out, "Come on, Dakota. Show me how it's done."

Forget caution. She backed up, got a running start, leaped out as far as she could, hit the cold water and felt every bit of the shock of it, came up laughing, and told Blake, "Whoa. That'll wake you up."

She didn't hang around and talk to him, though. The water was still cold, after all, or maybe she just needed the release.

She swam hard all the way around the point that separated Blake's house from the next one along the lakefront, and then back again. She didn't bother to check whether he was coming, but she saw him powering past her, moving smoothly, swimming the same way she was. Like he wasn't messing around. Except that he was faster.

When she got back to the dock again and turned in a circle, he was still with her. She swam over to the dock and pulled herself up, then grabbed for her glasses. Which was why she was able to watch him getting out. He put two palms on the wood of the dock, shoved up with a flash of ridged muscle in arms and shoulders, and was out of the water with a grace she could only envy.

"Whoa," she said, rubbing a towel over her hair, then wrapping it around her waist. "You're pretty good at that."

"What, swimming? So are you." He slicked his wet hair back with one hand, but didn't go for a towel. He just stood there, tall and lean, his swim trunks riding low on his hips, showing her that vee of muscle again. Maybe he could tell she was looking, because he smiled at her, sweet and slow, and just like that, she was heating up.

She said, "I was mostly talking about the way you got out." She was teasing. She knew it, and she didn't care.

"Well, now, darlin'," he said, his voice and accent both deepening, that dark-molasses sound that made her knees weak, "I could say the same thing, except that my mama raised me to be a gentleman."

"Oh. That's *very* smooth." She was tingling from the way he looked, and how he looked at *her,* but she was laughing, too. "That supposed to be a comment about what? My legs? My butt? Let's say that I know it's a view. You could call it a panorama. Probably too much of one."

"Oh, no." He was still smiling, but the smile had changed some. "That's not too much. That's a Southern boy's hello-baby. That's biscuits and gravy you got going on there. That's a long, slow good time, sweet tea in the porch swing and your

sweetheart in a pretty little dress, shoving off with her bare foot
and giving you that come-on-boy smile. That's bourbon and
Coke and Friday night, is what that is."

Wow. She held onto her cool, but it wasn't easy. "Huh. That
was pretty good. That's your Southern-gentleman description
of my… assets?"

"Oh, yeah. I can do a whole lot better, though. Want to hear
it?"

"Ah… we'll call that a 'no.'"

He sighed. "That's mighty disappointing, but I'll get over it
in a second. Come on, wild thing. Let's go up and get some
iced tea, now that you got me all thirsty for it, sit for a couple
minutes."

"I should get back to work."

"So should I. Fifteen minutes."

She did it, too. He didn't change out of his suit, and neither
did she. He leaned back in the same chair where he'd eaten
lunch, and she put her towel on the chaise, but this time, she
lay back in it. She pushed a knee up like a bathing beauty, then
had to laugh at herself. She so was not.

"You know," she said, putting her arm up over her head
and letting the sun bake her a little, "you've got quite the way
of making a woman feel good."

He turned his head to grin at her. His hands were laced
behind his head, his ankles crossed. Biceps and abs and chest,
all right there on display, but he didn't look like he was posing.
He just had it all to show, like he couldn't help it. And then
there was the long red line of a healing scar down the middle
of his right knee. That was a show, too. A different kind of
show. "Well, Miss Dakota," he said, "we aim to please."

She tried not to shiver. "So what do you think of your
house?" she asked, going for safer territory.

"I think it looks real good. Can't wait to see my eagle
hanging up in that window."

"Mm. That'll be today, if you don't waste too much of my
time here. If you're leaving tonight, I'll do your bedroom and

bathroom, all that, before you get back. They'll take a while."

"You can hang my flower, too. I do want my flower."

"You want to show me where?" she asked. "Lots of people put them in the master bath. A little more… private."

"Oh, no. I want my flower in the bedroom. Maybe I'll put my shell in the bathroom, though."

"You're pretty confident you want it." Her voice was languid. The exercise, the sun's rays, Blake's voice… they were all doing their best to melt her bones.

"I do tend to run that way," he said. "Confident. And, ah… I tend to know what I want. But I already told you that."

She fought the shiver again, and he went on. "If you do my bedroom over the weekend, though, you won't be able to finish your shell. That's what we call a dilemma, because I want both."

"You can have both," she found herself promising. "If you're not back until Tuesday? I'll make sure you get both. If you can meet my price on the shell, of course."

"I'll meet your price."

"Sight unseen?"

"Yeah. Sight unseen. Because I know what that'll do for you. It won't make you slack off. It'll make you even more determined to make it your best. That shell's a passion project all the way around, and I've seen your passion projects. It's going to be something special, and I want it."

She hummed, because he was right, and because she was getting sleepy. He asked, "Is that what you'd do if you could do anything you wanted? Glass?"

"Sure."

"So tell me," he said. "What's your perfect life?"

She looked out on the lake, the cedars, the mountains, drifted a little on the warmth, and finally said, "I guess it would be spending it in beautiful places. Traveling, seeing things. I've been to Seattle. I've lived in Portland, and a few other places when I was a kid. Nowhere I'd ever want to visit again. Now I want to see all the beautiful spots. Snorkeling from the beach in Tahiti. Walking through Paris in the rain. Flying over the Rift Valley in Africa with flocks of flamingos in the sky. Hiking through the jungle in Costa Rica, in the middle of the rainforest trees and the vines, the birds and monkeys and insects, where the air's so warm and humid and filled with sound, it's like you can touch it. I want to see all that, I want to explore it all, and I want to make glass from what I've seen. That's my dream life. Emphasis on 'dream.'"

"Scenes?" he asked. "Like painting? Or birds, or what?"

"Maybe those things. And maybe something else, because I don't think you can capture all that in glass, not literally. It might be more abstract, but still with that representational element. Using texture and colors to create something that *feels* like the place, like the feeling it gave me. Pushing my own limits. Trying, and being scared I can't do it. Failing, sometimes, and then, other times—creating something that makes me catch my breath. Where I can say, 'I did that. I went out that limb, and it worked.'"

"Doesn't sound like much of that dream is about money," he said after a minute. "Or being famous."

She felt a stab of impatience. "Sure it is. It's all about money. The luxury of doing what I want, going where I want? That's money, because there's Russ, and there's life. And it's not about *famous*, but is it about people loving what I do? Yeah, it's that. Loving it enough to pay for it, loving to have it hanging in their houses. It's hard, because it's not 'art.' It's craft. And nobody does craft to get rich. But it's what I love."

He didn't say anything, and she turned her head and looked at him. He still had his hands behind his head, but his expression was serious. Thoughtful. She asked, "So what about you? What's your dream life?"

He shifted position and looked away from her, out to the lake. "I had it."

The words hung there, a cold dash of water on this hot day. She said, "Football."

"Yeah."

She didn't know everything in the world, but she knew something about men. She knew Evan, and she knew Russ. Sometimes, a man needed to talk it out, and he couldn't talk to another man. He needed a woman for that, so he didn't have to worry about being strong, about being tough. He needed to let down his guard, and for that? He needed a woman. "What was special about it?" she asked quietly, not looking at him. Trying her best to show him that she was safe ground, the same way he'd just been for her.

"Oh, I don't know. How about everything? You don't really get it until you don't have it. Being part of a team, I guess. That's the big one. You can say it's the same in business, but it's not."

"Quarterback," she said. "That's a little bit the same, I'd think."

"No. It isn't. I wasn't the boss, I was just one of the leaders. There's a big difference. When you're on a football team, you—everybody—you're not trying to win for your paycheck, for your ego. You're doing it for the guy next to you, and the guy next to him. You know all you can do is your job, but you know that offensive lineman is doing his, too, that he's putting his body between you and the sack. He's got your back, and you've got his. Even if it's a defensive player, a special teams player. You're in it together, doing it for each other, winning or losing together. You can't get that in business. Not possible."

It was as if she could feel his heart beating, and the rift in it, too. The pain of losing family. "Like being a soldier. My brother would say that. 'My buddy.' It wasn't just a buddy, though. It was a brother."

Blake was still looking at the lake, but she didn't think he was seeing it. "That's a whole different level, what he did. Putting his life on the line. But—yeah. That's the deal, and I miss the hell out of it. They're still my buddies, but it's not the same."

"And it's wasn't just about the money for you, either. Not

just being a star.”

"Oh, the money's nice. Sure it is. But you know—I've got money. I'm making more. It's about the rest of it. Using your body that hard, emptying the tank all the way. That level of commitment… it's not what your brother did, but it's something special. Hard to find. I've had it since I was eight. I don't have it anymore.”

She waited a few more seconds, but he didn't say anything. Finally, she asked, "How long ago did it happen? Your injury?”

"Six months. Day after Thanksgiving. But—" He sat up straight. "Here I am whining, with nothing in the wide world to whine about. I was lucky for a long, long time, and I'm still lucky.”

"You're not whining," she said, but she sat up, too. "You're explaining.”

"Nah, darlin'. I'm whining.” He stood up. "I'll change and get back to work, let you get on with your day. If you work here over the weekend, go on and use anything you want. That'll make me nothing but happy to think about. Watch TV, drink up my beer, use the hot tub, whatever. That thing feels good after a swim in the lake, tell you that. I'd have suggested it already, but I'm minding my manners. It gets a little intimate, maybe, sitting in those bubbles.”

He so clearly wanted to pull back, so she smiled and said, "Well, maybe I will,” got up herself, and picked up her towel. "Thanks for the swim, and the lunch. And thanks for Russell.”

♡♡♡

She did finish Blake's office that day. She didn't wrap it up until after five, but he didn't come back. Which was definitely for the best. She pulled off all the tape she could, then got her ladder and carefully hung his eagle exactly in the center of those bay windows. She hoped he'd see it before his trip, but if he didn't, he'd see it afterwards. When she asked him where he wanted to hang the flower. And her shell.

The flutter she felt low in her belly was for the shell. It had to be. She'd make it be. Or if it wasn't—well, a person didn't have to act on every feeling they had. Good thing, or she'd be in big trouble by now.

And then she went home for dinner and Evan came by with Gracie, which made her life just a little bit more complicated. She couldn't talk about Blake's offer with Evan there. It would get too… awkward.

As it turned out, she didn't have to. Russell brought it up himself.

"Orbison came to see me today," he said. "Had a proposition for me."

Evan froze, and then his eyes went to Dakota, and she dropped her gaze. And Evan was the one who asked, "Yeah?"

"Said he's going to send me to some back doctor down in LA," Russell said. "See if they can fix me. Surgery, maybe."

"Why?" Evan said.

"Well," Russell said slowly, "that's kind of what I was wondering."

They were both looking at Dakota now. "He told me about it," she said. "He came out to the house today to talk to me." She met both men's gazes with what she hoped was steadiness. "He said that what happened to you was his responsibility, Dad, and that it was up to him to make it right. Isn't that what he told you?"

"Of course it's what he told me. What do you expect him to say? He wasn't going to tell me any other part of it. That's not what any dad wants to hear. You might not know how I feel about you, but you can bet he does. He's not stupid."

"Wait," Evan said. And then *he* waited, clearly marshaling his thoughts before he said, "If he's going to get your back fixed, Russell—well, that's good, obviously. But what's been happening out there at Orbison's house? I knew I should be painting it instead."

"You know," Dakota said, "I'm turning thirty in a few months here. Last I checked, I was officially an adult."

"Nobody's saying you're not," Russell said. "We're saying you don't always know what's in some guys' heads. We do."

"We sure know what's in his," Evan muttered. "Pretty obvious."

"And he needs to spend, what? A hundred thousand dollars? Two hundred thousand? To buy *me?*" Dakota said in exasperation. "Sorry, guys, that's stupid. He went out with a supermodel. He can get any woman he wants, and a whole lot cheaper than that."

"Can't get you," Evan said.

"*Thank* you," Dakota answered. "Because that's exactly my point. I'm not for sale, and he's a decent guy."

"Since when?" Evan asked.

"Since now. Since he's done this. Since I've gotten to know him better."

"He hasn't *done* a single thing," Evan said. "He's *said* he'll do something. Promising's cheap. Guy like that, he's all about promising. All about that sweet talk."

"Silver-tongued devil," Russell said. "That's what I thought at first, too. But I got to say, Evan—I'm not so sure. I wouldn't have said he'd go back on his word. Not from what I saw. Sounded like he had good folks and all that. A man who's got good folks, who tells you what his mom says—you don't bring up your mom like that and then, bam, do the wrong thing. Not unless you're an all-the-way bad guy, and he's not that. Anyway, so what? If it doesn't happen, I haven't lost anything."

"Just hope," Dakota said.

"No," Russ answered. "That'd be you. I just wait and see. Most things you hope for don't happen, and most things you worry about don't, either. Usually, life just bites you in the butt or hands you something better than you deserve with no warning at all. It'd be nice to think you get what you deserve, sure it would. Only problem is, it's not true. Either way. I'll wait and see which one this is, but I won't sit back and wait and see about you."

She sighed. "I'm fine, all right? I'm *fine.*" Smart enough to resist her impulses, for sure. Hadn't she done just that today, and Monday, and… every time she'd been in Blake's vicinity? "This isn't some novel, and I'm not selling my virginity to Blake Orbison because my beloved grandmother needs surgery. I appreciate your protective impulses. You know I do. But I don't need them this time."

"You sure?" Evan asked. "I think you could get stupid. And Orbison isn't looking to marry you."

"How do you know?" Her pride was stung now, even though she'd told herself the same thing.

"Maybe because he was out with Beth Schaefer?" Evan suggested. "He met you. He went swimming with you all right. But who did he take out?"

Gracie started to fuss in her seat at Evan's feet. "See," Dakota said, "now you've upset both us girls. I get it, Evan. I always got it."

He reached down, picked up his daughter, and cradled her in his arm. "Just so you do. Just so you remember it."

"You're way over the line," she informed him. She was getting more than annoyed now. "If I wanted to do the wild thing with Blake, that wouldn't be your business. Women can have recreational sex too, you know. It's a thing. It's the twenty-first century, even in Wild Horse."

"Some women can," he said. "You can't."

All right. Now she was mad. "Excuse me? I *can't?* Did somebody die and make you my keeper?"

Evan's ice-blue eyes were perfectly calm, and so was his face. Infuriatingly. "I didn't say you couldn't have sex. I said that if you had it with him, it wouldn't be recreational."

"And you know this how? Because you're in my head? You are not in my head."

"No. I know it because I know you. You're romantic."

She felt, she really felt, as if the anger were going to blow straight out of her ears. She didn't even know what to say. *Yes, I can so have recreational sex,* wasn't the response she was going for, and neither was *none of your business.* Unfortunately, *shut up* wasn't, either, though that was the one she was longing for right now.

Fortunately, Russell stepped in. "Evan's not telling you what to do."

"You think?" she muttered, and stabbed at her pasta, since stabbing Evan with her fork while he was holding Gracie was out of the question. He was eating again himself, looking about as emotional as a boulder.

"He's just trying to tell you how men are," Russell said. "Don't get me wrong, Orbison's a pretty good guy. Rich guy, though. Guy who's used to getting what he wants."

"Thanks," she said. "I think I'm clued in on that." *And how.* She should tell him that Blake had come right out and said it, except that it would only show that Evan was right. "If you're going to LA, that's the main thing. Let's just focus on that, OK? You'll focus on that, I'll focus on that, and maybe even Evan will focus on that, once he gets himself out of big-brother mode, or dad mode, or whatever that's supposed to be."

"Just watch it," Evan said. "And if you need to switch jobs, tell me."

She sighed. "Thanks. I think I got it. I appreciate your concern. Now back off."

Water Damage
♡

Blake switched the garment bag and duffel to his left hand and stuck the key in the door with his right. He tried to turn the key, but it didn't go anywhere.

Huh. Dakota had left the door unlocked? It *was* Wild Horse, but still. He pulled out the key, turned the knob, and stepped inside.

She'd left lights on downstairs, too. She wouldn't have left the house unlocked *and* lit up, surely. She must still be here, even though it was six-thirty Monday night. But if she was, where was her truck?

His heart was pounding, which was annoying. Also stupid. His dinner meeting had canceled, he'd come home early, and she was still here. So what? It wasn't like she was waiting for him. He hadn't let her know he was coming back. He'd figured she'd be long gone.

"Dakota?" he called out, and got no answer. He headed upstairs, and his pulse rate went up a little more.

The lights were off in his bedroom, though, and he hit the switch and tried to ignore the depth of his disappointment. It was pointless. He'd already been through all this, and he'd made his decision. Dakota wasn't the right woman. Look at her

164

dream life: adventuring around the world. The exact opposite of the life plan he'd laid out for himself. He was already doing enough running around, and it was time to settle down anyway. If he was going to have that life, an adult life, he needed a home-loving woman, a settled woman who'd cure his restlessness. Somebody like Holly Samuels, the twenty-seven-year-old whom he'd been set up with last night in Chicago. A warm, pretty brunette with kind blue eyes and a good sense of humor, Holly worked for a children's charity, and her parents donated to the symphony and the ballet. See? Perfect.

All right, not *Holly,* exactly, but somebody like that. She'd checked all the boxes, including the ones Beth Schaefer hadn't: she was brunette, and she'd actually seemed to be attracted to him. He'd liked her, too. He'd liked her fine. She hadn't been quite the right match—for one thing, he might actually have to *go* to the symphony and the ballet—but then, he was picky. He was getting warmer, though. He just had to keep working at it, and he'd get there. He hadn't failed to hit a major life goal yet.

A relationship with Dakota, a woman who was all wrong for that life goal, would be nothing but a distraction and a waste of time, and he didn't do distractions or waste time. As for anything else—that wasn't going to work out well for her, and he might be arrogant, but he wasn't an asshole. He hoped. So that was enough of that idea. Period. Case closed.

If he needed somebody to help him with that wild side—well, he knew how to get that, too. Random sex with a pretty stranger had lost its appeal quite a ways back—seemed a man actually *could* get too much of a good thing—but he wasn't blind to the possibility. He just didn't want it that much. Getting old, maybe. His testosterone levels dropping. *That* was a horrifying thought. It had better not be that.

His bedroom looked good, though. *Really* good. The walls were the same warm gray she'd painted his office, the trim a crisp white, and it looked clean and masculine, the way she'd promised.

And then there was the iris. She'd hung it in the window

closest to the bed, next to the mirror. His flower, the ruffled petals opening to reveal that dark, secret heart. It was his, and it was here.

He did his usual lightning job of unpacking—anybody who'd been on the road as much as he'd been for the past twelve years knew how to pack and unpack—and changed into comfortable old Levi's and a faded Devils T-shirt. He'd stick around tomorrow morning until Dakota showed up, he decided. Maybe she'd have suggestions about what else to do in his bedroom. Curtains. Things like that.

He headed barefoot down to the kitchen, where the light *was* on, opened a bottle of Laughing Dog IPA—Idaho did beer pretty well, that was one thing—and went out onto the deck. The slanting rays of the evening sun were shining through the trees and making the lake glow a rich blue, and it all looked great. He'd kick back, drink his beer, and look at it, and tomorrow, he'd do an extra-long workout that would take care of the urge to pace.

The sliding door was unlocked, too, and he was just suppressing a pang of irritation when he registered the noise. The sound of a running motor. He knew that sound.

He headed over to the nook where the hot tub sat, screened by a row of bamboo growing in pots. He went around the bamboo, and… whoa.

She didn't even have the jets on. She was stretched out in the middle of the huge six-person hot tub, facing him. Her eyes were closed, her lips were parted, and she had earbuds in her ears, the cord plugged into the phone sitting safely on the edge. Dark hair streaming down around her and floating on the water, skin like amber honey, curves like… like exactly what a man wanted to see when he came home after a long day.

She was naked, but that wasn't the main thing. One hand was drifting lazily over a perfectly small, perfectly shaped erect brown nipple that was giving him heart palpitations. The other hand was…

Lord have mercy. Dakota Savage was giving herself what

looked like some very nice slow, sweet pleasure in his hot tub. She looked terrific doing it, too. And there was nothing at all wrong with his testosterone levels.

She opened her eyes, and that was when everything went south.

He jumped, and so did she. She leaped up, scrambled to cover herself, and the cord of her earphones pulled her phone straight into the water.

She was yelping, yanking at the cord, going underwater and grabbing for her phone, and he was saying, "Oh. Sorry. Let me..." He skirted the hot tub to get closer and reached for the phone.

"What are you *doing?*" She was holding her drowned phone and backing away in the water, crouching down. "You weren't supposed to be home!"

She didn't seem to know what to do, so he said, "Here. Give me the phone. Let me see."

"Get *out,*" she said. "I'm naked! Oh, my God. What did you see?"

"Sorry," he said again. He decided it would be prudent not to answer that. "Give me the phone, and I'll..." What? Give it the kiss of life? Too late. That phone was going to be fried. Kind of like his brain cells.

Her discarded painting clothes were on a chair, he saw now, together with a towel. "Tell you what," he said, carefully looking beyond her. "Hand me the phone, I'll get you a robe, and we'll figure out what to do."

"Could you please just go *away?*" she said, but she handed over the phone, then dropped her hands to cover herself.

"Right now," he said. "Going. Bringing you a robe."

He ran upstairs and found what he was looking for in the back of his closet, brought it down, and called out from the other side of the bamboo, "I'm setting this right here. Come on inside when you're ready. I'm checking about the phone."

"You'd better," he heard. "I can't believe you stood there and *looked* at me. Oh, man. I can't believe this."

"I didn't mean to. You just surprised me. I didn't know you were here."

"You were looking."

"Well, yeah. For a second. I was about to leave, I swear." A lie for which he'd probably be struck by lightning. There was no way he'd been about to leave.

He was still talking through the screen of bamboo, and now, her arm came around it and started groping on the ground. He picked up the robe and put it in her hand, and she whisked it around the corner. "I'm leaving now," he told her.

"You keep saying that," she said. "Except that you don't go."

He went.

Silver-Tongued Devil

♡

Dakota didn't want to take Blake's robe. She didn't even want to come out. But what was she going to do, cower in the hot tub all night? Dash through the house and out the front door like the world's biggest drama queen? She hadn't done anything wrong. So he'd seen her naked. And maybe… all right, she needed to face it. He'd probably seen just about everything. That couldn't have shocked him, though. He was a big, big boy.

And—her *phone*. She wasn't sure which thing was worse. No, she *knew* which thing was worse. And it wasn't her phone.

She dried herself off hastily, pulled on the robe, yanked the sash tight, and grabbed her clothes. This whole thing had been one impulse leading to another, and it had been stupid. Story of her life.

Blake was in the living room, sitting on one of his gigantic too-many-cows-died-for-this leather couches, tapping at his laptop with a frown on his face. A single lamp cast a pool of light, but the rest of the room was lit only by the soft glow of the sun, sinking quickly behind the mountains. She *was* plainly able to see a rolled-up towel on the coffee table beside him, presumably shrouding the corpse of her phone.

"Congratulations," she said, deciding "breezy" was her best tack. "Phone killer. And now you're going to say that I shouldn't have electronics near water, and *I'm* going to say that I wasn't expecting a Peeping Tom, and *you're* going to ask me why I was here this late, in your house like it was mine, and, ah… making myself way too much at home. I also parked my truck in your garage. Go ahead and say something about that, too, while you're at it."

"I'm not going to say that," he said. "Any of it. Come over here and tell me which phone you want."

He didn't even look up, and she started to feel a little stupid. She'd been right. It wasn't that big a deal to him. She dumped her clothes by the couch and sat down beside him. "Shouldn't we try to dry it out first?"

"I looked it up," he said, still clicking and scrolling. "It's not likely to work. Besides, that phone's old. Here's the latest version. Unlocked. That way, you can use any carrier you want. Will that do? We'll put on the protection plan, in case some other bozo throws it in the lake or something."

She leaned closer. "That is over a thousand *dollars*. Are you kidding me? My phone is three years old."

"Yeah. And we killed it. So—is this good? Or do you want to change brands? And do you have a backup for your data?"

"Uh…" She was having some trouble here. "Everything's on my laptop, I think. Mostly, anyway. But if you're buying things, buy me new headphones. I'm sure they're just as drowned."

"Gotcha." Some more clicking. "Cord, or no cord?"

"Oh, whatever's most expensive. I want to make you hurt."

He looked at her at last and started to smile. "I'm sure I shouldn't say this, darlin', but you already made me hurt."

"Oh, way to keep it classy. You've seen that before." Fortunately, she never blushed. That was one benefit of her Indian side. He didn't have to know how she'd felt when she'd seen him standing there. Other than the hissy fit she'd already thrown, of course.

"Could be," he said, "but I've never seen you doing it. And no, that wasn't a real subtle comment, either. Hang on a sec." He did the kind of one-clicking she could never have dreamed of, then sat back and said, "There you go. Tomorrow, you'll have a new phone. You'll even be here to get the package. Problem solved."

She sat still for a moment. "I'm trying to decide whether to be huffy and flounce off like this was all your fault, sit here and be gracious and ask you about your trip like none of it happened, or slink off and show you how embarrassed I am. I'm really struggling with it, to tell you the truth."

"Tell you what," he said. "I'll get you a beer while you decide. Or better yet—I'll get out a bottle of wine from this case I had to buy. Long story, but I ended up with way too much fancy wine. You were drinking wine that night at the restaurant, so I'm pretty sure you'll like it."

He'd noticed what she'd been drinking? "But you already have a beer," she said.

"Yep. Happy to pour it down the sink, too. And I'll give you something to chew on while I'm gone. I was pretty happy to think you were still here, and then I was pretty bummed to think you were gone. I was thinking about sitting here, having a beer, and watching the light change on the lake, and I'd sure rather do that in your company. And if you want to ask about my trip and tell me how my shell's coming along—well, that'll be good, too."

"Which makes me look stupid if I'm huffy and flouncing off."

"Let's hope so. Hang on. I'll get that wine."

He was back within two minutes, handing her a glass of deep ruby liquid and setting the bottle on the table. "I've got to say," he told her as he sat down with his own wine glass, "you look a whole lot better in that robe than I ever did."

She plucked at the delicate fabric. "Brown and black paisley silk? Blake Orbison, you secret cosmopolitan, you. It's like I'm sitting here with Hugh Hefner." She took a sniff of the wine, then a sip, and had to sigh, because that was *good*. Black cherry and black pepper, tobacco and black licorice. Exactly like sitting around in a gorgeous house in a silk robe, possibly with a man who was smoking a pipe. "No," she decided, "it's more like Dinner With My Billionaire. Serious class overload."

"There we go," he said, sitting back down beside her. "The badass returns. I shouldn't tell you that my old girlfriend bought me that robe, and that I don't even know why I brought it up here and stuck it in my closet. Or that I bought all that wine and only cracked one bottle. Thinking I was turning into a different guy, maybe. But I *will* tell you that I've only worn that thing a couple times, because I hate it. Well, I *did* hate it. It's growing on me. And right now, the wine's looking like a real good idea, too." He touched his glass gently to hers. "Here's to all that badass," he said with his slow smile, and took a sip.

"Mm." She gave him a quick sideways glance and drank some more of her wine just to hold the dark flavors in her mouth and let the pleasure fill her. She tried not to remember that she'd been about thirty seconds from reaching that mountaintop when she'd opened her eyes to see Blake, and that she still had the lingering tingles to remind her of it. She looked out at the lake, because the alternative was looking at Blake and watching him watch her. "Did you see your bedroom?"

"I sure did. Saw my flower, too. I do like that flower, darlin'. Kinda reminds me of this wine, wouldn't you say? Seductive, I think that's the word. All that darkness pulling you in, like when you see the sin coming a mile away and you know you're going to be taking the fall. Or maybe that's just me."

His voice was as deep and rich as the wine on her tongue. She tried to haul herself back from the edge, and failed completely. Those tingles were back again, and they'd brought their friends.

Somehow, she'd stopped looking at the lake and was looking at Blake from over the rim of her glass. She shouldn't flirt. She *wouldn't* flirt. He might be doing it, but nothing said she had to return the favor. But what came out of her mouth was, "Does that mean you had a good time on your trip? Or does it mean you didn't?"

"Not good enough," he said. "Not nearly good enough."

This was getting out of control. Time to pull it right on back. She sat up straight. Somehow, she'd ended up with her feet curled under her. "Do you want to see the shell? Or have you had enough stained glass?"

He looked confused for a second, like he hadn't quite shifted gears. "What, it's here?"

"Yeah. In your hall closet. I was going to show it to you tomorrow. I'll go get it."

She started to get up, but he was faster, and he had a hand on her shoulder, pushing her back to sit. A casual gesture, or... maybe not. "Nah," he said, giving her a look that made her pulse flutter despite everything. "I've got it."

Whoa. Alpha much?

Yes, and you knew it.

She'd leave as soon as she showed him. Or as soon as she finished her wine, anyway. It was a customer meeting, that was all. Maybe it had had an unorthodox start, and maybe she was unusually dressed for it, but he didn't seem to mind. He hadn't made a move on her since he'd kissed her and she'd taken off. He'd flirted, sure, but flirting came as easily to Blake as breathing. It was *fine*. She just had to be casual about it, the same way he was.

It was fine.

She was still working on that thought when Blake came back holding the framed piece of glass. He was frowning at it, and she forgot to be casual.

He didn't like it. Despite everything he'd just said, it was too suggestive. It was another step beyond her flowers, and she knew it.

His next words confirmed it. "How the hell," he asked her, looking at her at last, still with that frown, "do you do that?"

173

"What?" She'd jumped up and was pulling the robe more tightly around her.

He came to sit on the couch, holding the framed piece in front of him. He was still frowning, too. She sat down again, because she couldn't think what else to do. Snatch her shell away from him and make her escape?

Customer meeting, she told herself. *Professional.* "You're under no obligation." She heard the stiffness in her voice, but that was all right, too. "You asked me to show it to you, and I am. I'm aware that it's experimental, a different direction for me."

He frowned at her some more, and then his expression cleared. "You think I don't like it. I like it. I want it. If you've shown it to somebody else, I'll outbid him. I'm just saying… how did you get the idea? No shells like this in Idaho, and none in Oregon, either."

"Oh. No." Once again, she was off balance. "I just… it was the flowers, I guess. First. And there are some shells in Oregon, even if they're not conches. I have a few in my workshop, in a jar. I was looking at them, studying them, close up, sort of… unfocusing. Seeing the roughness outside, the edges, then all that smoothness, you know, inside, where they're polished like that. And I wanted to show that. The contrast. Different from a flower."

She looked at the piece, which Blake was still holding up, and couldn't help that same sense of *rightness* that had driven her as soon as she'd started working on it. Now, she tried to explain it better to Blake. He could see the fluttering edges, the deepening pink, the gorgeous, secret shine, but he couldn't know this. "As soon as I started," she told him haltingly, "it was there. That happens sometimes. My brain doesn't even seem to be telling my hands, or it's not the neat front part of my brain, the part that plans. It's the messy, dark, unorganized back part, and it wants what it wants. The shell's right. It might not be right to sell, but it's right for me."

That wasn't flirtation in his eyes now. It was intensity, a nearly ferocious need to connect, to understand. She understood it in the same way she'd seen her conch. From someplace deeper than her conscious mind.

"I want it," he said. "And not just because it's the sexiest damn piece of art I've ever seen. It's a piece of your soul. And I want it."

Her scalp prickled, and the fine hair on her arms rose. The shudder came from someplace deep inside, and he sat there and watched it happen.

"How much?" he asked.

"Ah…" Her mouth was dry, and she took another heady sip of wine, which didn't do anything to still the electricity that was sending sharp little shocks straight to her core like some kind of devilish sex toy. She tried to think through it, but it wasn't easy. "A thousand dollars." She'd thought of asking more. She'd chickened out. This *didn't* have a million tiny pieces. It was good, but it hadn't been complex, not once she'd gotten it right.

Blake sighed. "Now, darlin', we had a talk about this. This isn't some pattern you found in a book. Come on. Give me a price that lets me know what I've got here, what it ought to be worth to me and how I ought to treat it. Give me a price that tells me it's precious."

She was losing herself in his intensity, his focus. "Fifteen… hundred," she whispered.

"Now say it like you mean it. Like you know it."

She took a deep breath. "Fifteen hundred."

A slow grin spread over his face. "That's what I'm talking about, baby. That's telling me you mean it." He stood up and carried the glass across the room, where he set it against the wall. "Going to put this bad girl in my bathroom for me tomorrow?"

"Oh, so this one's a girl, huh?" she said, trying to rally. She went to take another sip of wine, then realized it was gone.

He saw it too, because he came back to the couch and filled her glass again, then topped up his own. "Yeah. My eagle's male all the way, but that shell? That's sure-enough a beautiful woman. All the secret spaces of her, the ones she's holding back until she knows you're worth showing them to."

"I think you might be reading between the lines there," she said, trying with all her might to keep some dryness in her tone.

His mouth curved in a smile, and he sat down again, not seeming in any hurry to get anything going. "I might be," he said, "or could be I'm getting to know you a little bit. And that isn't easy, because you're all sorts of things."

"What sorts of things?" She shouldn't ask, but what woman would have been able to resist an opening like that?

"Oh, let's see. Smart, and she doesn't know it. Creative, though that's not a good enough word, and she doesn't quite believe in it yet. Loyal. Honest. Brave. How's that?"

"I sound like the Boy Scout Oath, is how that is. I thought this was going to be some sexy list that was going to send me into your arms. So much for that. Same old story. The woman who'll gut your fish for you. I have bigger hands than any man I've ever dated, and I could probably have beat most of them at arm wrestling, too."

She didn't look down at his feet. They were bigger than hers. A *lot* bigger. She was turning into some sort of foot fetishist, the way she kept looking at his bare feet. It was that high arch, those long toes.

Definitely a foot fetishist.

"I noticed Evan doesn't seem to mind," he said.

She blinked. *What?* Evan? "That's because he knows he'd win."

He put up his hand, palm out. "Let's see."

She put her right hand up to meet his left. Their palms touched, and it was an effort not to jump.

And, yes. His hand had to be two inches bigger than hers. Big palms. Long fingers.

"And that other thing?" he said. "I'd win at that, too."

"How big are your feet?" She could hear how breathless she sounded, and she couldn't help it. She couldn't stop looking at their hands, either. She couldn't seem to take her hand away.

He didn't smile. "Thirteen."

She swallowed. "Oh. Big."

"Yeah." He was looking into her eyes, and so slowly, he pushed his fingers through hers and held her hand there. "You didn't like my list. I'm ready to make a better effort, because I'm watching you drink that wine, the way you're tasting every bit of it. I'm seeing the way you're looking at your shell. I'm remembering the way your perfume smelled when you walked by me at that restaurant. And I'm sure as hell thinking about the way you looked in my hot tub. So if you want the rest of my list, I'm waiting to give it to you."

"I think you just did," she managed to say. She realized that her body was turned toward him on the couch, and that the material of the robe had parted over her legs, so she was flashing some thigh, and she didn't care. The sky was glowing pink, reflected in the water, and she was floating on a pink cloud herself made of warm water, rich wine, and hard man.

He reached out at last, but he didn't touch her. He took off her glasses and set them on the coffee table, and she forgot to breathe. Then his hand came down on her shoulder, and she sighed as if she'd been waiting for it and it was finally here. And still he didn't grab her. Instead, his fingers rubbed along the edge of the silk, and his voice was low and deep and absolutely mesmerizing. "I'll give you some more, then. Your art turns me on like nothing I've ever seen. Your face changes every time I look at it, and it makes me want to keep looking. Your mouth makes me want to do dirty things to you. And your skin makes me want to lay you down and love you all night long. I'm looking at your legs right now, and I want to take this robe off you and touch you everywhere. And damn, girl, but I want to kiss you."

Silver-tongued devil. She heard Russell's words, but all she could think was, *Oh, yeah. Tell me some more.* His fingers were still stroking, her eyes were trying to drift shut, and he was taking her wine glass from her hand. And she let him do it.

When his lips brushed over hers, all she thought was *Yes,*

and all she felt was fire. And when the back of his other hand traced the edge of that silk robe down the vee between her breasts, all she wanted was more. He'd let go of her hand and taken hold of the back of her neck, his fingers so strong there, and somehow, she was going back, sliding along the edge of all that leather until her head came to rest on the arm of the couch. And he came right along with her.

His mouth tasted like wine, and like man. One hand still held her head, and she wanted it there. Her mouth had long since opened under his, and his tongue was exploring, tasting.

She heard a humming in her head and realized she was moaning, and she couldn't help it. His hand had parted her robe and was on a bare breast. His thumb flicked over the nipple, then did it again, and the shock went straight to her center as if he'd licked her there.

His mouth left hers, and her lips tingled and wanted his back. And then she forgot that, because his mouth was trailing over her cheek, kissing its way down her neck, lingering every time he felt her squirm or heard her moan.

"I want to kiss you everywhere," he said, his breath warm in her ear, and she shuddered. "Everywhere you were touching tonight. It's going to be me this time. All mine."

He was biting the lobe of her ear, his lips moving up around the edge, sucking the chain in her ear into his mouth, and somehow, that felt better than anything else. Or maybe it was his hand on her breast, exploring, pinching, then circling, not letting her get used to anything, not letting her settle.

"Dakota," he said, and now, he'd moved down her body, brushing the robe entirely aside. She was lying there, sprawled naked against the leather of his couch, and he was propped on an arm, looking at her like she was all he wanted to see.

"I'm going to have to fuck you, baby," he told her, and his finger was there, painting her, probing, parting the slick folds and pushing inside, where she was already so wet. Exploring her like there was no such thing as embarrassment, no such thing as a second thought. "But I'm going to eat every bit of this first. I'm going to open this shell and eat it all up. I'm going to watch you come, and then I'm going to do it again. And after that, we're going to do the rest. I'm going to do it slow, and then I'm going to do it so hard and so deep. I'm going to make you know you're mine."

She was burning up. His fingers... oh, that felt *good*. His tongue was in her belly button, swirling around the barbell, licking into the holes of her piercing. One of her hands was in his hair already, and she was halfway to losing her mind.

Bam. Bam. Bam. She jerked upright like somebody had pulled her strings. Somebody was pounding on the door. And then they were ringing the doorbell. And she was naked.

What was she *doing?*

Showdown at the O.K. Corral

♡

It took Blake a moment for the noise to register, but the doorbell finally got through.

Whoever it was, they could forget it. He shoved himself up so he could kiss Dakota, took her lower lip between both his own, and sucked on it. *Go away,* he told whoever was at the door. *I'm busy.*

The doorbell rang again, and this wasn't working. Dakota was stiffening under him.

"Ignore it," he murmured. "They'll go away."

"Orbison!" He heard the bellow, and she heard it, too, because she was pushing off, struggling to sit.

Damn it to *hell.*

She was pulling the robe back on, tying the sash, trying to smooth out her hair, not looking at him. "Aren't you going to answer the door?" she asked when he didn't move. "It's Evan."

"Yeah," he said. "I already figured that out." He got up, reached into his jeans, and gave himself a quick, not-so discreet adjustment. His body was screaming at him, but Dakota was about to do the same thing, so his body was losing this one.

He went to the front door and opened it, and Evan had to spin to pull his punch. "You might want to watch it," Blake

180

said, not bothering to hide his disgust. "Not beat the door down."

Evan didn't answer that. His face was hard. And he had his baby daughter in one big arm, which made this Showdown at the OK Corral faintly ridiculous. "Is Dakota here?" he asked. "Or do you know where she is?"

Blake sighed, stood back, and swept out an arm. "Come on in."

Evan walked into the living room, and Dakota was already up. Her hasty attempts to put herself to rights hadn't worked too well, though, because she still looked decidedly rumpled. Lips swollen, hair tousled, feet bare, and with the silk of the robe clinging to her. She looked like what she was—a woman who'd just been getting kissed hard and loved up good.

Blake was a fan. He didn't think Evan would be.

He was right. Evan looked her over and asked, "Just what are you doing?"

She crossed her arms. "Just what do you think? And why is it your business?"

"I came," Evan said, "because Russell was worried. You said Orbison would be gone tonight, and you were going to finish up here and would be home for dinner by seven. When you weren't home by seven-thirty, Russ called you, and it went straight to voicemail. Then he kept calling, and same thing. That's when he called me."

"Oh." She looked discomfited, pulling on the sash of the robe as if that would make her more dressed. "I sort of wrecked my phone. I didn't think to use Blake's to call."

"Obviously." Evan was getting worked up, which was another way to say that he was finally registering an expression other than "frozen." "You keep saying that you're an adult. How are we supposed to treat you that way when you're acting this dumb? Russell thought the truck had gone into the lake or something. He kept saying, 'It's not like Dakota. She'd know I'd be worried. She'd call.' And instead, you lie about being with him"—he jerked his head at Blake—"and get Russ that

181

worked up? Just because you don't have the guts to tell him the truth?"

"I wasn't *lying*," she said. "Blake wasn't supposed to be home. I finished up, and he... surprised me."

"Uh-huh." Evan's voice was flat as he looked at the wine on the coffee table. "Surprised the clothes right off you, too. Haven't you learned one single thing in all this time? Riley told you. Russell told you. I told you. You think we were kidding? Messing with you? How many times has somebody asked you to marry him? How long does it take before you stop putting yourself out there like this? Letting some guy laugh at you, laugh *about* you? How many damn times do you have to get hurt?"

The baby had started to fuss, and Evan put her onto his shoulder and started to pat her back and sway back and forth. It was so incongruous with the tension he was showing, it was almost ridiculous. Except it wasn't.

"Hang on," Blake started to say just as Dakota said, "You don't know anything. You sure don't know Blake."

"I don't know him, huh?" Evan said over his daughter's whimpers. "Tell me this. How many times has he taken you out? Sure, he's happy to screw you on his couch. Let me tell you something, since you don't seem to get it. That doesn't take a whole lot of effort. You asked me if you repulsed guys. You don't repulse anybody. You go lie down half-dressed on any guy's couch in this town, and he'll take that invitation. It doesn't mean he likes you. Is Orbison picking you up at the house and taking you to dinner, though? Talking to Russ? You can bet he's taking out other women. You saw him do it. But you? He doesn't even have to make an effort. All he has to do is tell you to, and you're taking off your clothes for him. That's not the way any guy who cares about a woman does it. Wise up, Dakota."

Dakota's chin was up, her eyes sparking. "Why don't you ask him?" she said. "He's right here. Go on and ask him."

"I'm not asking him," Evan said. "I'm not looking at him.

I'm trying not to hit him."

"Quit holding back," Blake said, goaded past anything his temper could bear. "Go ahead and try it."

"If I wasn't holding my baby," Evan said, "you bet I would. Dakota's worth more than that, and you're a piece of—" He broke off and breathed a couple times. The baby was really starting to fuss now, and he spoke over her cries. "Tell me this. When was the last time you took a woman out?"

Blake hesitated, then looked at Dakota. She stared right back at him. Challenging him to tell the truth, and he wasn't a liar anyway. He finally said, "Last night."

He left it there. Anything else would sound like the excuse it was.

Dakota closed her eyes and swallowed, and Evan told her, "Get your stuff. Let's go."

"Now hang on," Blake said. "You don't need to leave, Dakota. Stay here and talk about this. Or better yet, go to dinner with me and talk about it. He says I haven't taken you out? Here I am asking you."

"You forget." Her lips were compressed, her dark eyes blazing. "I'm not dressed to go out. I'm dressed for the couch."

"That's—" He always had an answer. He was famous for it. The quick, dry quip after the game, the quote that always got printed. But he didn't have an answer for this. He couldn't think of anything to say.

She didn't even get dressed. She grabbed her pile of clothes and said, "I'll bring your robe back later. You can leave me a check for the shell, if you still want it, or let me know if you don't. And if you want it? The price is a thousand dollars."

"I told you I'd pay fifteen hundred," he said. "I said it was worth it. I meant it."

"And I know what I think that fifteen hundred was for," she said. "I asked for a thousand. That's the number I'll take." She told Evan, "The truck's in Blake's garage. Wait for me, will you?" As if Blake would stop her from going. As if Evan needed to protect her.

She walked straight out of his house. And Evan looked hard at him, then followed her.

No Pressure

♡

Russell didn't say much. But the way he looked when Dakota walked through the front door... it hit every single guilt receptor she had.

He struggled to his feet from where he'd been sitting on a side chair, holding his phone, and Bella didn't move from his side. And his face...

She dropped the pile of clothes and walked straight over to him, then wrapped her arms around him and said, "Sorry, Dad. I'm so sorry."

His arms closed around her and held her tight, and she blinked back the tears. Because she'd worried him. Because she felt like something had been ripped away from her. Because everything.

"Come eat," he said.

"It's probably wrecked, though," she got out through a throat that was trying to close.

"Nah. Chili. Probably be better for the extra time." He took in the robe. "Go change first, though. Take a shower, too." As if he knew she needed to wash all of this away.

When they finally sat down, though, she had trouble eating, even though it was nearly nine o'clock. She kept stirring her

185

chili until Russell asked, "Want to tell me?"

She looked up and tried to smile. "Do you want to hear?"

"No," he said. "But it hurts more when you hold it inside. Better to get some air on it."

Her eyes filled with tears despite every attempt to hold them back. "Why am I so dumb, Dad?"

"I don't know. Why do you think?"

She shrugged helplessly. "You're going to say something like, 'Looking for love.' 'Feeling unworthy.' It doesn't *feel* like that. At least this didn't this time. It felt like... hope. Like he saw me, and he liked what he saw. You know? And I thought I saw him, too. I thought he was letting me see him."

Russell didn't answer for a moment, then said, "This is Orbison we're talking about, right?"

She laughed, even though it wasn't funny. "Like I've been able to look at anybody else since he showed up."

He waited a minute. Thinking, apparently, because when he did speak again, he said, "You sure you're wrong? You sure you're stupid? Who said you were?"

"Evan. Me. Every bit of common sense I have."

"Hmm. Not sure Evan's a big winner in the love stakes himself. I don't exactly see him taking over the *Dear Abby* column anytime soon."

That was the moment the doorbell rang, and the *exact* moment Bella barked. Dakota jumped so hard, she dropped her spoon into the chili bowl and splashed red sauce all over her green-striped white pajama top.

She was exclaiming, grabbing a napkin, trying to wipe it off, and Bella was already headed for the door, tail wagging. Russell started to haul himself up, but Dakota said, "I'll go."

"No. You're hardly wearing anything."

"Shorts."

"Pj's. I'm going."

He headed out into the living room, and Dakota went over to the sink, wet a dishrag and started to scrub out the spots, and hoped with no confidence at all that it wouldn't be Evan.

And knew it couldn't be anybody else. Evan, coming over to yell at her some more, like she was still sixteen. Like she was still stupid, and he was still protecting her. This time, though, she was ready for him. She was going to set him straight.

Her hand stopped moving, until the water soaking through her top made her drop the rag in haste. That wasn't Evan's voice.

Oh, man.

She was out of the kitchen on the thought. There was Russell, standing in the middle of the living room. And there was Blake, standing with him. Hands in his back pockets, frowning down at the floor, looking less confident than she'd ever seen him.

Both of them turned as she came in. Blake's eyes widened a little, and she looked down at herself and realized why. She hadn't gotten rid of all the chili stains, but that wasn't it. Her top was wet on one side and clinging to a breast, and it was just about transparent. She was wearing some very short boxers underneath it that were slung low and cut high. She was, in fact, way too close to naked.

Well, tough. He'd already seen her naked tonight. Twice.

"Hi," he said, and didn't smile.

"Hi," she said back, and stopped.

"I was just telling Russ," he said, "that we had a... misunderstanding, and that I'm here to make it right."

She glanced at Russell. He said, "Don't look at me. You're two grown people. You work it out."

Something was happening in her chest again, and she forgot all about Blake for a moment. She went over to Russell, kissed his cheek, and said, "Thanks, Dad. I love you."

He cleared his throat. "The man's waiting. You got this. You don't need me. I'm going to do the dishes and go to bed. I'll put your chili in the fridge." He limped toward the kitchen with Bella following him, then turned to Blake and said, "Got no reason not to trust you with my girl. Don't give me one."

"No, sir," Blake said, and Russell nodded and left, shutting the door to the kitchen behind him.

"Uh…" Blake said. He still had his hands in his back pockets, and he was still frowning. "I don't exactly know what to do here. I tried to think it over, but it's just a big ol' confused mess. I thought I'd know once I got here."

"I'm guessing that's a new feeling." Suddenly, Dakota felt a whole lot better.

He smiled, just a twitch at one corner of his mouth. "You could say that."

"So sit down and start." She sank down on the couch, he sat down beside her, and she glanced at him out of the corner of her eye and said, "I feel like we've done this before."

He smiled for real this time. "It does, a little bit. I've got to say—it's easier with wine. But here goes. I get that O'Donnell wants you for himself, and I don't care. He had his chance, and I'm not stepping aside for anybody. You're not stupid, and you're the very last thing from easy. Even though 'easy'—that's a crappy thing for a man to say about a woman, or to think. But it was what he meant, so I'm telling you. You're not it. If you asked me what *I* think, it's that you shouldn't let him talk about you like you're fifteen. Your dad's right. You're a grown woman. Decide for yourself. One way or the other. I'm a grown man. I can take whatever you throw at me."

"Wow." She blinked. "Are you done?"

"Yeah. More or less. Go."

"First of all, Evan doesn't want me for himself. That's ridiculous."

"Not how it looks to me. I'd say that's exactly what he wants."

"He was my brother's best friend."

"Hate to tell you, but that doesn't stop a guy."

"I don't know how to convince you, but I'll just say—no. Evan's like my brother. He's said so."

"As long as you aren't in love with him, I don't really care what he wants. What I want to know is what *you* want."

He was looking at her so hard, like her answer really

mattered. "No," she said. "I'm not in love with him." She'd been having trouble with her heart rate since she'd heard his voice. Now, she was half-worried that she was going to have to ask for a paper bag to breathe into.

Some of the tension seemed to leave him. "Good. That's good, then." He ran a hand through his hair. "So… I guess I should ask you out."

She wasn't going to need the paper bag. "I guess you should."

"Right, then. I'm invited to this thing on Friday night. This dinner party at the Schaefers'. She—Michelle—invited me to bring a date. I think I'd better do that, if you'll go with me. That seems public enough even for Evan. Even for you."

She was looking at him sideways again. "You realize that Michelle's probably going to poison me if you take me along."

"Nah. Beth and I… we didn't click. She's a nice woman. She's just not *my* nice woman."

"You know why, don't you?"

"Uh… my personality disorder? What?"

"Nope. Because *that's* who Evan's still in love with, I think. Or still hung up on. It's not me. It was never me."

"Oh." He seemed to be digesting that. "Huh. So that night…"

"Yeah." She was smiling now. She couldn't possibly have helped it. "Wrong partner."

"Mm." His eyes were doing that golden gleam thing again. "All the way around, because, baby—I sure wanted you that night. When you walked by me like that, I about half lost my mind. If you want to take care of the other half, you could wear that perfume on Friday."

"Did I say I'd go?"

"Nope. You surely didn't. I'm sitting here waiting."

It was more than a daunting prospect. It was throwing herself right smack into a part of Wild Horse that had never accepted her and never would. But she'd never have better insulation.

It was that reckless streak again. It was her wild side, the side that refused to cower, that raised her head and her fists and fought back. And the side that wanted Blake Orbison with a ferocity beyond reason.

"Yes," she said. "I'll go with you." What was the worst that could happen?

He smiled, then, and that smile did the same things to her it always did. And then he pulled a folded piece of paper out of his back pocket and put it in her hand. "That's for your shell. I meant what I said. That thing—it's mine."

She unfolded it, but she didn't have to. "I said a thousand."

"And I said fifteen hundred. I told you, darlin'. You've got to tell me you're worth it. You've got to believe it. I'm telling you that I do."

He stood up before she could say anything else, and she got up, too. What else could she do?

At the door, though, he turned to her. "So you know. Everything else I said tonight? That was true, too."

"Uh… what would that be?"

He put a hand out, brushed her hair back from her face, and let his fingers drift down her cheek, and it was an effort to keep from leaning into that hand. He said, "Tell you the truth, I can only remember some of it. But I remember I meant it."

She fought to keep her eyes from closing. "I'm going to have to think about that."

She was falling into his eyes, drowning in his heat, and he wasn't smiling now. "You do that," he said. "You go to bed tonight and think about me. You can know that I'll be thinking about you, too. And when I do… we aren't stopping. You can think about me imagining how you'd look when you're lying back on my bed with your arms up over your head, with your eyes closed and your mouth open, making all those little noises for me. You can think about how good your legs are going to look when I've got my hands on your thighs. You can think about many times I'm going to make you come, and how many ways I'm going to wear you out."

There wasn't enough air in this room. She needed to say something. Anything. "You're kind of pushing your luck, aren't you?" she finally managed.

It was more than a smile this time. He laughed. "Always, baby. Always. I just can't help it. And you make me want to do it. You make me want to stand over there on that wild side and say, 'Come on over, Dakota. Come on over here, darlin', and let me show you how.' I want to go there, and I want to take you with me."

Did he kiss her, then? He did not. He walked right out the door and left her with that.

She stood there looking at the closed door for a full minute before she turned around and headed for bed like a sleepwalker.

Friday night.

No pressure.

Surprise Package

♡

Dakota spent all day Tuesday thinking about what to do.

Did she plan out her next glass piece? No, she did not. Did she think about which galleries she might approach, now that she had not only her collection of flowers, but the image of the shell to show them? Nope. Did she work through Russell's budget in her head, now that she had another sizable check in the bank, and consider M & O's schedule for the rest of the summer? Not even once.

Did she even reconsider the wisdom of going out with Blake?

No. She didn't. Instead, she spent nearly nine hours painting his walls and thinking about clothes. And makeup. And manicures. And waxing. And hair. She told herself that the check should go to the mortgage company even as she wondered how much it would cost if you did absolutely *everything*, beauty-regime-wise, and then tried to calculate how much it would be if you did the minimum. She ran through a mental inventory of her closet and her bathroom drawers, thought about Michelle Schaefer and her probable subscription to *Vogue*, and got a mental image of Michelle and every other female dinner guest mentally going, "Dress Barn.

$49.99." And then told herself that didn't matter, that she was more than her external appearance, and knew even as she gave herself the talk that "inner beauty" was one thing, and Michelle Schaefer's living room was another.

And what did she do in the end? Did she put a thousand toward the mortgage and five hundred toward reinvestment in glass supplies, like any prudent woman would do? Did she go for that bare minimum, buy a new dress on sale, give herself a pedicure, and figure the shoes she had were good enough? Not a hope. She took off Thursday at one o'clock and drove to Spokane—spending money *and* not earning it, double whammy—spent three full hours shopping and nearly three more getting beautiful, didn't get home until nine-thirty at night, and took off even more time on Friday afternoon to finish the job.

No, not finish the *job*. She'd set the job back, in fact. She wasn't even done with the upstairs, and she still had the whole downstairs to go. On the other hand, whatever Michelle Schaefer or the other plucked, painted, coiffed women at Blake's dinner party thought of her, she'd know she looked good.

♡♡♡

Blake drove back to the little white house in the shabbier part of town at six-thirty Friday night, questioning himself the whole way.

He'd been planning another trip this week. Instead, he'd put it off.

Why?

So he could take Dakota out.

Why?

Because he wanted to.

Got no reason not to trust you with my girl, Russell had said. *Don't give me one.* Blake had a feeling Russell wouldn't approve of the life plan. But the fact was, Blake wasn't going to get anywhere with it until he got over this… obsession.

He wasn't just looking for some kind of conquest. It wasn't like one night was going to do it anyway, at least it sure wouldn't for him. It would be a relationship like any other one. It would just be higher octane. He and Dakota needed to ride that wild side until they burned out.

She'd probably be the one to call a halt, in the end. Blake wasn't all that easy to live with, or even to be in a relationship with. He seemed laid-back to a woman at first, until she found out the guy he really was. Too intense. Too focused on his work, and on being the best. Not interested enough in the things women liked. Too interested in sex, and never around to pay attention to her otherwise.

He was a bad boyfriend, and he knew it. He ought to, as many women as had said it. It was going to take him a while to be a good husband, if he ever made it. He'd need somebody patient, and probably someone who didn't expect too much, and that sure wasn't Dakota. Dakota would expect everything. Look at what she was already doing. Sneaking into his mind, tormenting his body, messing up his plans even when he never saw her. *Especially* when he never saw her. She'd gone straight back to ghost mode this week, coming in and doing her painting after he'd left for work, then disappearing before he got home.

If anything, Dakota should recognize that this deal would probably turn out the opposite of what she'd been thinking. She thought he was just looking for a short-time good time. The truth was, *she'd* be the one realizing that was as much as *he* was good for, and that she deserved more.

She needed somebody who was going to stick around here, somebody to go fishing with Russell and then barbecue that fish, to sit and watch the Mariners afterwards and wonder aloud when the team was going to trade for a leadoff hitter who could put his bat on the ball in any kind of reliable way. She needed somebody who liked her art as much as it deserved and would encourage her to push it harder, somebody willing to save up for a trip hiking through the rainforest and snorkeling over the coral just to make her happy. Somebody to appreciate her and give her what she needed.

And if the thought of it made his hands tighten on the steering wheel and the muscles of his thighs seize up... well, that was that obsession again. Especially when he remembered that whatever Dakota said, he knew who that guy was. It was Evan. But Dakota didn't belong with Evan.

So who does she belong with, dude? You?

Yeah. Me.

Which started the whole thing up again. It was a relief to pull up outside the house and head up the walk. And there his stupid heart was, racing like he was sixteen and borrowing his dad's car to take a girl out. All he needed was a bad rental tux and a corsage in a plastic box, and he'd be going to the prom.

He knocked on the door, and Russell showed up to answer it. "Come on in," he said. Sure enough, he was watching baseball. "Dakota's not quite ready, I don't think. Sit down a minute."

"Sure." Blake sat on the couch, then gave Bella a pat or two before she settled down again at Russell's feet.

On the screen, a Mariners batter was taking some practice swings, and the Red Sox pitcher was pivoting, then throwing fast to try to catch the guy on first. The runner dove for the bag, and the practice swings started up again.

"Training camp must be coming up pretty soon," Russell said. "NFL, I mean."

"Another month or so."

A quick glance from Russell. "Yeah. You don't want to talk about that. Guess I know how you feel. Watching everybody else go to work when you ought to be there and you won't ever be there again—that's no good at all."

"Nope." If Russell knew Blake didn't want to talk about it, why was he talking about it?

"Seems like you still run around a hell of a lot, though," Russell said. He was still watching the TV, where the guy's count was two and two.

"I do my share," Blake said cautiously. Where was this going?

"Huh, now," Russell said. "Course, I don't know exactly how it all works, but I don't see how you could've been doing that kind of thing while you were playing." The pitcher threw an inside ball, the batter leaned back out of it, and the count was three and two.

"I didn't," Blake said. "I'm just the CEO, not the president. I'm the idea guy. I make the appearances, court the investors, make the big calls. You can't run a company hands-on and quarterback an NFL team at the same time. I've always had an executive team to execute." The pitcher threw to first again, the runner dove for the bag again, the first baseman tossed it back to the pitcher, and they were back at Square One.

"Guess you're doing it different now," Russell said. "Doing it how you said. Hands on."

"Well, a man's got to do something," Blake said. "When one door closes, a window opens, and all that."

"That helping, then?" Russell asked. "Business-wise? Making you more money? Making the stock rise, or however you count it?" The batter was taking yet more practice swings, and the catcher had come out from the mound to confer with the pitcher.

Playing sports always felt fast. Football time went by before you could blink your eyes. Watching sports on TV always felt too long. Too slow. Made you too impatient, when you couldn't do it yourself.

Blake actually had to stop to think about Russell's question. "Hard to say. People seem not to scream and run when they see my face, so I guess it's doing some good. It's how business works, I guess you'd say. Airports and hotels."

"Huh," Russell said. "See, I'd think, if you didn't have to do it, why do it? But then, I never did like moving around all that much. If I wasn't getting some big payoff from it, I'd probably just stay home."

The pitcher wound up again and threw a blazing fastball. The batter swung mightily. And missed.

"Three and out again," Russell said. "You know, sometimes you got to wonder why you keep watching, when a team just seems bound and determined to do it wrong."

Blake had stopped listening, though, and he was rising to his feet. His date was here.

He wasn't sure what he'd expected. The only time he'd even seen Dakota without her glasses was that night at the Heart of the Lake. She'd been hot then. Tonight, though, she was something else.

Her dress wasn't anything like he'd expected. It wasn't red, and it wasn't black. It was a yellow floral print with wide-set straps and a halter top, cut close to her body. It wasn't too tight, it wasn't low-cut, and it wasn't too short. It was the way it showed off the smooth skin of her upper chest and arms, though, not to mention the length of her legs and the curve of her waist. And as for the way it hugged that gorgeous ass... Lord have mercy.

Or maybe it was the shoes. They had a little platform and a high heel that made her even taller, a strap that tied below her perfect red toenails, and another one that tied around her ankles. Those shoes were hot in the most accidental way possible.

Or her hair. It could have been that. She'd cut it, maybe, and it tumbled around her bare shoulders and down her back. He missed seeing that chain in her ear. On the other hand, if he brushed her hair back behind her ear, he'd be able to uncover it just for him, so he could kiss her there again. She had a silver heart on a chain around her neck, and that was all. No other ornamentation. Nothing but soft skin and all that personality.

She was made up, though, and he loved it, even though he liked her face just fine naked. The eyes that were normally hidden behind her glasses were almond-shaped and tilted up at the corners under her black-winged brows, her cheekbones sliced across her face like she was daring you to take her on, and her mouth was painted rose, the lips looking richer and fuller than ever.

She still wasn't cute. He wasn't sure she was even pretty. She was beautiful.

He realized, all of a sudden, that she was just standing there and looking at him, a hand on her cocked hip and a sexy tilt to her head, while a smile played over that rose-red mouth.

"Uh…" he said, then shook his head to try to clear it. "I'm trying to think what to say. What happened to my painter? And darlin', I'm not even going to try to kiss you hello, because I'm scared to mess that up. You look great. I'm going to say that and shut up."

Dakota's smile was the tiniest bit smug. "Russell says you're a silver-tongued devil. I don't call that your best effort."

Blake laughed out loud. "What do you think, Russ? Think I'm good enough for her?"

Russell settled back into his chair with a sigh. "Nope. Guess you'll just have to do your best. Game's back. You two should go on and go out."

Dakota bent and brushed her lips over his cheek. "Bye. I'll text if I'm going to be late."

He reached for her hand and gripped it. "You remember," he said, his voice low. "You're just as good as everybody else there."

She straightened up fast, blinked, and asked Blake, "You ready?"

"Yeah," he said, breathing in the rich, exotic scent of her. "I'm ready."

Cocktail Hour

♡

You look great, Dakota told herself. *You're going to do fine. Just be quiet and let Blake do the talking. He's good at it. Meanwhile, you are poised. Classy. Mysterious.*

Well, no. She was a house painter, and everybody knew it. But she'd pretend.

Everybody would be looking at Blake and not her anyway, because (a) he was the one with hundreds of millions of dollars, and (b) he looked fantastic. He was wearing the Cowboy Angel of Death clothes again. Black T-shirt, dark-gray pants, tooled black cowboy boots. He'd shaved, too, which was flattering, although as far as she was concerned, he needn't have bothered. That dark stubble of his looked nothing but hot. She might have spent some time imagining how it would feel against her skin the next time he was kissing her neck. Maybe.

He shut her car door, hopped in himself, and took off, and she said, "So how's it—" at the exact same moment he said, "So how is—"

They both stopped talking, and Dakota said, "You go on."

Blake shook his head. "Can't believe I'm nervous. I was just thinking, walking to your door, that this feels exactly like picking up my date for the senior prom. Except that I didn't bring you a corsage and I'm dressed better."

"Now, why in the world would you have been nervous about your prom?" she asked, feeling better already. This was a big deal to him? Really? "Don't tell me you weren't homecoming king."

He glanced at her, that little grin starting to form, and she sighed and said, "It's too depressing. So, what? Did you do a little dance with the queen, like the bride and groom at a wedding? Did you save your crown?"

"Yeah, to the dance thing. It meant a lot to my date. She was a cheerleader. Man, she loved that night. And that's a big nope on the crown. Tossed that thing the next day. A guy who keeps his homecoming crown is a guy who wears his Super Bowl ring."

"I bow to the knowledge of the master. So wearing your Super Bowl ring isn't done?"

"If you're a tool, it is. Or if you're going to be in a fight, maybe. They're big suckers."

"How many do you have?"

He glanced at her again, then sighed. "Crushed once more. One."

"What, I was supposed to memorize your stats? Sorry."

She was smiling, he was, too, and her tension of the past hours was gone.

"So how about *your* prom?" he asked. "Who'd you go with? Anybody I'm going to have to punch tonight because he kissed you first?"

That wiped the smile off her face. "I didn't go."

He turned onto the lake road and started around the first of its curves. "Let me guess. You were one of those artistic types who thought prom was juvenile. Wore dark eyeliner and a lot of black. The kind of girl the jocks always had a secret thing for. Or maybe that was just me."

It took her a moment to answer. "I didn't have a great time in high school."

"Oh."

He seemed to be thinking about how much to pursue that, so she asked, "Who's going to be at this thing tonight?"

"I don't know, really. Michelle said something about 'putting together some people you'll want to know socially, going forward,' which I translated as 'People guaranteed to be boring.' You see why I invited you."

"Oh, is *that* why?"

He grinned. "Maybe it's one reason." He turned off the road and headed down the winding drive. "You been out here?"

"Oh, no." Her tone was dry again, and he shot another glance across the car, then parked in an enormous circular driveway that already held ten or twelve other cars.

"Well, whoever it is," Dakota said, "it's a lot of them. It won't be too concentrated."

She hopped out and reminded herself, *Classy. Mysterious.*

That idea deteriorated as soon as the door swung open to reveal Don Schaefer. Balding, glasses, golf shirt and slacks, as genial and casual as his wife tended to be cool and scary.

"Blake!" Don said, pumping his hand and clapping him on the back for good measure. "Glad you could make it." He turned to Dakota, put out his hand, and said, "Don Schaefer."

The dryness was all the way back as she put her hand coolly into his and said, "Hello. But you know me. Dakota Savage."

He stood still for a moment, and then he laughed, a jolly *ho-ho-ho* that actually made Dakota relax some. "Well, how about that? Didn't even recognize you. That's how women are, though, isn't it, Blake? They get so glamorous, it's like they're living in some different world, whereas us poor slobs just go on looking exactly the same no matter how they try to shine us up." He rubbed a rueful hand over his scalp. "Or not. I swear, Michelle looks prettier every year, and I lose a little more hair and gain another couple pounds. But why am I talking to you out here? Come on in and say hello to everybody. Some folks you'll know, Blake, and some you won't. Way it should be. Get you settled down and feeling at home, now you're part of the community. Dakota can help you there, too. She'll know just about everybody."

He was ushering them into a living room even bigger than Blake's. A fairly astonishing room, in fact. All three sides were walled with windows, opening the room to the outdoors in spectacular fashion. One entire wall opened onto a wraparound deck, creating an indoor/outdoor space that doubled the room's already substantial size. A grand piano sat in a corner, looking no larger than an upright under a peaked ceiling that rose twenty feet above it, while three separate cozy seating areas invited guests to settle in.

Their hostess, Michelle Schaefer, detached herself from a group standing near that opening to the deck. A group that included not only Steve Sawyer and his parents, but his wife Ingrid, too. And Ingrid's best friend and fellow cheerleader, Melody Farnsworth, with *her* mother, Candy, and her father, Rob.

The contractors, the realtors, and the banker. Of course they were all here, and more of them, too, out on the deck. The mayor would be out there, Dakota was willing to bet. Steve's uncle. Plus everybody else who was anybody in Wild Horse. It was no surprise that they socialized, but it didn't matter. Dakota wasn't the hired help, she wasn't in high school, and she was Blake's date. She was a guest.

She saw the exact moment when Michelle recognized her. The pause in her step, the falter in her smile. "Blake," she said, coming up to him and reaching out a hand. "I'm so glad you could make it. And Dakota." Another warm handshake, a less sincere smile. "What a nice surprise. Don't you look beautiful. Doesn't she, Don?"

"She sure does," her husband said, and *he* actually sounded like he meant it. "I made a fool of myself back there, didn't even recognize her. Happens to me all the time with you younger folks, friends of Beth's. I keep expecting all of you to still have your hair in pigtails."

"Well, I'm not in overalls now," Dakota said, liking him

better all the time. "You're forgiven."

"That's right," he said. "Taken over your dad's painting business, haven't you?"

"With Evan O'Donnell," she said, and saw Michelle's smile slip again. She'd always wondered whether Beth's parents had been behind her breakup with Evan. Looked like it was true.

"How's your dad doing these days?" Don asked.

"Her stepfather, honey," Michelle said.

"He's not doing so great," Blake said, saving Dakota from the minefield that this whole conversation had become. "Hurting a lot. That was a bad accident. I hate to say that I only just found out it happened on one of my jobs."

"Well, anybody who's got any kind of business knows that accidents happen, no matter how careful everybody is," Don said. "But hey. Come on over and say hi to some people. And here's the liquor, finally." A young woman, who'd been circulating with a tray filled with glasses of red and white wine, was approaching. "Or there's beer in the fridge if you'd rather."

Dakota took a glass of white wine, since the one way this evening could get trickier would be if she spilled red wine all over herself. Blake grabbed a red, and Don was ushering them across the room and straight into the shark tank. She whispered to Blake, "You didn't tell them you were bringing me."

"She said to bring somebody if I liked," he murmured back. "And I said I'd do that."

That was all they had time for, because they'd reached the others. Don was making jovial introductions, saying, "But you all know Dakota Savage, of course."

Blake was shaking hands all around, and Melody and Ingrid were smiling those insincere mean-girl smiles. Melody said, "You look *fantastic*, Dakota. I almost didn't recognize you. What a gorgeous dress. It really shows off your figure."

"Thank you," Dakota said, feeling as fake as a three-dollar bill and about as welcome. "Yours is beautiful, too." It was a deep blue jersey knit with a low, draped front, and Melody was wearing a gold necklace and small diamond studs in her ears.

All of her, in fact, looked rich and gorgeous and like the real thing.

"I wish I had your skin," Ingrid said, giving a flick to her perfectly straight, naturally platinum hair, then taking a ladylike sip at her wine. "I bet you hardly have to wear makeup. You're so exotic, you can get away with it."

"That's all the Indian in her, honey," Steve said. He reached out a hand for Dakota's, and before she realized what he was doing, leaned in and kissed her on the cheek. She stiffened, and then she felt Blake's arm coming around her waist, pulling her back even as Steve stepped back himself. Steve went on, "You gotta love the melting pot, don't you, Orbison, when it turns out like that?"

Blake's arm tightened around Dakota. "Not sure what you're talking about," he said levelly. "If you're saying that Dakota's beautiful, I've already noticed that and told her so. But then, that's because she's my date. Where I come from, you don't talk about a lady's looks in front of her. That's not how we do it down South. Guess I'm not used to Idaho manners yet."

The very air seemed to still, like the moments before a summer cloudburst. Then Bill Sawyer, Steve's father, said, with a smile on his lips but his eyes cold as chips of blue ice, "You got one thing right. You don't know everything about Idaho yet. Or maybe you just don't know everything about Wild Horse. You might want to look around before you leap. I'm sure a man who's done that well in business knows to do his research before he makes an investment."

Dakota could feel Blake stiffen even through her own tension. She'd never know what he would have said, though, because Don got there first. "Isn't that the truth, Bill. And I'm sure glad Blake *did* do all that research. The resort's looking better than anything Coeur d'Alene has to offer, far as I'm concerned, and it isn't even open yet. Exclusive, and that's what you want. Everything's more valuable when it's harder to get. Candy found Blake about the best house on the lake, too, and he was smart enough to snap that sucker up. Because that whistling sound you hear?" He spiraled a dramatic finger skyward. "That's the air resistance from all our property values shooting straight through the roof. Before you know it, I'm going to be losing my head from the excitement and getting wild and crazy with Beth's inheritance. Good thing I've got Michelle to keep me from getting too carried away."

"How *is* Beth?" Melody asked. "I've always looked up to her so much. So pretty, and so smart, too. She was always such a lady even in high school, wasn't she, Ingrid? That's the kind of person I admire."

"She's great," Don said. "Just great. Up for partner at her firm next year, in fact. Works too hard, of course, but then, don't we all? I'm going to steal Blake and Dakota away, though. Got some more people out here I want him to meet."

With that, he slapped a hand on Blake's shoulder and was ushering them outside onto the deck. Dakota wanted to make an excuse and run to the bathroom, check her appearance, and maybe hide out for a few minutes. Or the entire evening. On the other hand, she didn't want to give Melody and Ingrid the satisfaction. She wasn't even going to think about Steve.

For the next fifteen minutes, she smiled and sipped her wine and answered when somebody addressed her, and Blake's hand barely left her waist. He talked about the Devils' chances for next season, listened to a long critique of the team's offensive line as if he were getting new information, and generally acted like he was having a good time. And eventually, when Dakota felt like her face had frozen solid, Blake said, "I'm going to check out the view. I see a fishing spot that's calling my name. Come on, Dakota." And she went with him with a gratitude she wouldn't have though possible.

When they were standing, elbows on the deck railing, looking out across the water toward Blake's house on the opposite shoreline, he asked quietly, "You OK?"

"Oh. Sure." Her wine was gone, unfortunately. It hadn't helped much anyway. "I hope dinner's not too much longer, though."

"Yeah. Cocktail hour can be a killer." Michelle was heading their way, and Blake took Dakota's elbow and said, "Come on. Over here." He led her around the corner, to an alcove in the jigsaw pattern that was the Schaefer deck, and said, "I really *should* have done more research about where I invested, except that I suppose you get rotten apples in every barrel."

"Even in football teams, I hear," she said. "This isn't anything new. Don't worry about me."

"You're plenty tough. Not the first time I've noticed that."

He was looking at her too closely, and she wished she could be confident that her expression wasn't slipping. She lifted her chin and said, "Maybe so. It's all that Indian in me."

He smiled, but he didn't look happy. Which was when they heard the voices.

"Oh. My. *God.* I can't *believe* he brought her. It's like a slap in your face." The voice belonged to a young woman, and Dakota could already guess who.

"I *know,*" another voice said. "I'm so mad at Steve right now, too. He knows how much I hate to even see her face. And to see him kissing her like that, it's like it's happening all over again. Did you see how she looked when he said that about the Indian, though?"

Ingrid's giggle was answered by Melody, who said, "I *warned* Blake about her. That's what gets me. Men can be so stupid. I guess it's like Bill said, right? You do your research before making an investment, except sometimes, when you have money to throw away. You know, you go to Nordstrom for the investment pieces, but you buy the trashy stuff at Target. You'll use it once and toss it, but it was cute, and who cares if it gets stained?"

Ingrid gasped, then giggled again. "You are so *bad,* Melody. I swear. And I know I should just get over it, but when I see her dressing up like that, sticking her butt out like she does, and I see Steve ready to go after it again…"

"Well," Melody said, "if you won't give it up… some girls

do."

Another gasp, and Dakota realized her fists were clenched, her nails digging into her palms. Nails she'd had manicured just for tonight in nude polish that she'd hoped would send the same tasteful message as her dress. A message she was never, ever going to get across in Wild Horse. The hot blood had risen to her head, and she was breathing hard. Wanting to be anywhere but here. Wanting to erase the past twenty minutes, to rewind the clock and have told Blake instead, "Oh, sorry, I'm busy Friday. How about Saturday?" It would have been the easiest thing in the world. A thing that Melody Farnsworth and Ingrid Sawyer had been born knowing, and that Dakota never seemed to learn.

She hadn't dared to look at Blake. Now, though, he was moving. Not away from the homecoming queen and her princess, the head cheerleader and her minion, but toward them. Straight around the corner of the building.

Dakota followed him. Well, she had to. He was holding her hand.

The expressions on Melody and Ingrid's faces as Blake nearly charged into them were nearly comical to behold. Identical O's of surprise on painted mouths, false eyelashes making their eyes look even rounder.

"Oh, excuse me," Blake said. "I was looking for some ladies." His voice didn't have one bit of its usual warmth, and when Dakota looked at his face, it was cold. Hard. *Game face,* she thought, and shivered. Out of embarrassment, and anger, and too many other things.

"For who?" Melody asked, clearly confused.

"Somebody told me," Blake said, "that there'd be ladies here. But I seem to have brought the only one. Do you kiss your mama with that mouth?"

She gasped. "You wish."

"I wish what? I've got what I wished for. You know, in football, we call that thing you do trash talk. I don't talk much trash myself, because it's always seemed to me that the person who looks trashy is the one doing the talking."

"What?" There were two spots of red on Ingrid's porcelain cheeks. *"I'm* trash? Melody and me? Ask Dakota who's trashy. Ask your *girlfriend* if she remembers who tried to steal my boyfriend. Ask her who else she got, or who got her. I have a feeling you might be surprised."

Half of Dakota wanted to run. The other half, though, had cowered for way too long in this town. She was done. "I didn't steal your boyfriend," she told Ingrid. "And if we're asking here, why don't you ask yourself why you married a rapist, and why you're still making excuses for him? Ask yourself what that makes you."

Ingrid's mouth was opening, then closing, but Melody had no such problem. "You little *bitch,"* she hissed at Dakota. "You were trash then. You're trash now, and everybody in this house knows it. Everybody's laughing at you. Why don't you get the hint?"

Blake's arm was around Dakota again. "There's that word again," he said. "You know what? I wanted to take my lady out someplace special tonight, show her something as beautiful as she is. I thought this was it, but it turns out not. This is what I call a downright ugly view."

To Dakota's horror, Michelle Schaefer, alerted by some hostess-vibe to the catastrophe on her deck, had somehow come to join them. "Dinner's almost ready," she said. "Does everybody have a drink?"

Blake addressed himself to her. "It's real rude of me to show up and then take off, ma'am, but to tell you the truth, my stomach's upset. Something not sitting right, making me sick. I'm afraid Dakota and I can't stick around for dinner after all."

"Oh, no." Michelle looked rattled for once, her gaze darting among the four of them. No doubt seeing Dakota's blazing eyes and the steam coming out of her ears, Melody all but hopping up and down on her toes, and Ingrid with her hand over her mouth. "I'm so sorry."

Blake was already shepherding Dakota back into the house.

"I sure don't want to cause a scene," he said over his shoulder. "We'll try it again sometime. Small group, so my stomach can handle it. It's a little sensitive."

He didn't stop, either. He took Dakota right out of the house, strode around to the passenger side of the car, pulled the door open for her, and slammed it after her. Then he jockeyed forward and back to get out of the tight spot, swung around the drive, and was on the road. All without another word.

Alternate Plans

♡

Blake controlled himself. That was the guy he was. Which was why he had to get out. Right now. Watching Dakota standing so tall, refusing to let anybody take her down, when he was the one who'd taken her into that lion's den... it was killing him.

He pulled out of the Schaefers' driveway, watched for the next turnoff, and took it. He put the SUV into Park, rolled his shoulders once, and told Dakota, "Right. Two choices. I'll take you out to Heart of the Lake for dinner, or we can pick something up and go out on the boat, let the lake carry the ugly away. It's up to you."

She said, "Boat, please." Still holding it together.

"You sure? Because you're beautiful, and I'd purely love to show the rest of this godforsaken town that I'm the guy with you."

"Ah," she said, all her dryness back again. "But would we actually get to eat, or would you call somebody out again?"

"Well," he admitted, "there's that." His hand was fisting right now, in fact. He relaxed it with a deliberate effort.

"If it's my choice," she said, "I choose the boat. I need some... peace."

"Right." He pulled out his phone, dialed, and waited.

"Hey," he told the woman who answered. "This is Blake Orbison. I'd like to pick up some food. Uh... hang on." He held the phone away from his ear and asked Dakota, "Fish? Or what?"

"Fish is good," she said.

Blake put the phone to his ear again. "Thanks for waiting." He closed his eyes and recalled the menu. Advantage of all those years memorizing a playbook. "I'd like a couple orders of salmon, an order of scallops, and asparagus for two people. And a bottle of the best white wine you've got, whatever goes with that food. Chardonnay, I guess. And there's a hundred dollars for you and another hundred for the cook if that's ready for me in fifteen minutes."

He hung up, and Dakota said, "Whoa."

"Money works for some things." He put the car back in gear and headed toward town. "I'm going to wait to ask until you get into some of that peace, but I'll just say—what a snake pit."

"I was thinking a shark tank," she said. He looked across at her, and she smiled. He'd have sworn she'd felt sliced into little pieces back there, but she was smiling now.

He tried to think of something else to talk about, but his patented line of charm seemed to have deserted him, and Dakota didn't seem to mind, so he shut up. When he got to Main Street, he pulled into the bank lot and said, "Hold on. ATM."

"Oh, man," she said. "You mean you don't carry a wad of large bills at all times? I'm strangely disappointed."

He laughed. "Yeah, well, so am I. Just close your eyes for a minute so you don't notice me doing this. We'll pretend I'm suave."

That helped, and when he got to the Heart of the Lake, his food *was* waiting, even though the place was jumping. He told the hostess, "You're saving my life here. You don't know how much," handed over his credit card, and peeled off ten twenties.

"Happy to help," the woman said. "And the cook says, 'Any time.'"

Finally, he was walking down the pier, unlocking the gate to the marina, stepping onto the boat, and putting a hand out for Dakota, who was carrying the wine. She asked, "Should I take my shoes off? For the deck?"

"Only if you want to. They look real good, but you look just as good barefoot. Whatever you want. This one's for you."

She looked at him for a long moment, her eyes dark and searching, then said, "You mean that."

Something twisted hard in his chest. "Yeah, baby. I do."

"I'm going to take my shoes off, then," she said. "Because my feet hurt." She smiled at him, which lit up her face in that way her smile always did, and there was that twist again. It might have been his heart.

He took her through the salon and dumped the food on the galley island, and she looked around at the mushroom-colored leather of banquettes and couch, the profusion of rich, polished teak, and said, "I'm seriously impressed."

"Bring that wine up to the flying bridge," he said, pulling out a couple wineglasses and a corkscrew, "and we'll get out of here." He took off his own boots and socks. "Barefoot style."

The summer sun was setting as he sat in the captain's chair, maneuvered out of the slip, and headed across the lake with Dakota on the banquette beside him. "Open up that wine, darlin'," he said over the purr of the big engines, "and we'll start this evening off the way it ought to have been."

She got the cork out, poured him a glass and handed it to him, and sat back with her own, her back against the banquette, her pretty ankles crossed, and one arm behind her head. Her skin glowed amber in the fading light, as beautiful as that day on his deck, and she'd been right. This was the right choice.

He drove the boat out, leaving the lights of Wild Horse behind. The white prow sliced through the water, as graceful as a dolphin, and the rose tint of alpenglow was settling over the mountains ahead of them. And Blake didn't try to talk. He just drove, looked at Dakota's red toenails and bare legs, and wondered why he'd planned his night any other way.

He was almost sorry when they reached the quiet cove, cut the engine, and dropped the anchor while the last remnants of twilight glowed purple and indigo. Dakota might have felt the same, because she sighed and said, "That was good, and this wine's better. I guess you've schooled me on what 'the best you've got' really means."

He looked at her, lying there looking so lazy and peaceful, and had to smile. She said, "Yeah, I just got it. Don't say it. It'll be cheesy, and it'll spoil the mood."

"Tell you what," he said. "Let's go below and warm up that dinner. I'll do my best not to be cheesy, we can drink some more wine, get ourselves relaxed and a little bit drunk, and you'll be giving this ol' boy a damn good Friday night all by yourself."

She stayed quiet, though, when they were sitting at the dinette, sipping oak-aged Chardonnay as rich and buttery as the fish, with a tart lemon finish that was pure delight. They speared bites of grass-green asparagus and tiny, perfect white scallops, and finally, Dakota put a hand up, pushed her hair back, and turned to look at him.

Her face was at its most solemn again. Beautiful in a different way now, in the way the high mountains were beautiful, snow-capped and austere. "This is exactly the evening I'd ask for," she said. "You've made me feel special. Thank you. But if you're going to live here, you're going to hear about me, if you haven't already. And I want you to hear it from me."

His heart picked up, and not in a good way. "All right. I'm listening."

She looked across the cabin, though there wasn't much to see, because it was full night outside the big windows. The boat rocked gently in a breath of evening breeze, the water slapped against the hull, and Dakota rubbed a hand down the stem of her wineglass and said, "I told you that my brother and I came to live with Russell when I was fifteen. Riley was seventeen. I was in foster care for a few months until we got it all sorted out, but I told you that, too. I came into the middle of sophomore year that way, and in a town as small as Wild Horse, the fact that you're in foster care isn't exactly a secret. I was… not so accepted, but that wasn't new. We'd moved a lot, Riley and me, before we'd settled down with our grandmother. Before she took us for good."

"What happened to her?" Blake asked. "Your mom?"

"She died." Dakota took another sip of wine, ate another bite of fish. "And after a couple months, our mother took us to Russell's and dropped us outside his door. Which sounds harsh, but trust me, she did us a favor. Being with her was never any kind of stability."

"Is she still around?"

"Oh, from time to time. But I don't have any money, so I'm not too interesting. Plus she doesn't like women. And Russ won't let her in the door."

"Whoa," Blake said. "She doesn't like *women?* You're not 'women.' You're her daughter."

"Yeah, well, not everybody's cut out for motherhood. It doesn't matter."

"Of course it does."

"No. It doesn't. In the scheme of things that matter, it doesn't."

Blake tried to imagine what your life would have been like if your mom abandoning you was the least of it, and failed. And Dakota went on, "So anyway, I got out of foster care, eventually, and I could move back in with Russell. And with my brother."

"Riley."

"You remember. Yeah. Riley." She took a breath. "Anyway, I was with him again, and I got to know Russ some, even though I was still being… careful, the way you are at first, when you're new. But I made some friends at school, and things got better. I even went out, girls and boys. I turned sixteen, and I didn't have good clothes, but I wasn't too awkward, like some girls are when they're teenagers. I had good skin, you know. Good teeth, good hair, good bones. A pretty good figure. I was doing all right, because for girls, looks help. And the captain of the football team had a locker right next to mine. Savage. Sawyer. Alphabetical."

"Ah." He was gripping his own wineglass pretty tightly. He relaxed his hold and took a sip.

"Yeah. He was dating Ingrid already, of course. You heard that. They were both seniors. She was a cheerleader, very pretty. Both of them were blonde. You know the type. You *were* the type."

"I was never that type."

"No, I guess you wouldn't be. Sorry. Wrong comparison. You've got a sister yourself."

"A sister, and a mother, and a dad, none of whom let me get away with too much entitlement, believe it or not. 'For unto whomsoever much is given, of him shall be much required.' Ask me how I know. My mom's a minister. But not everybody gets that message at home, and some guys are just plain assholes. Like Sawyer. Who had a girlfriend, but also had that locker next to yours."

"Yes. And when she wasn't around, Steve used to flirt with me. Called me 'Indian maiden,' and even though that's bad, it still felt flattering. That he noticed me, a sophomore like I was, even though I wore glasses and hadn't started school with the rest of them, and I wasn't even Russell's daughter. And one day, you see, he had a fight with Ingrid, and they broke up. Everybody knew about it. It was big school news. So when he asked me to go to a party with him on Saturday night, I said yes. I thought he wanted to be my boyfriend. I told myself he'd broken up because he liked me. I told myself stupid things. I was romantic. I was looking for true love to ride into my life, or maybe I was just looking for excitement. I was dumb, but then, girls can be dumb."

Heroes and Villains

♡

She'd been more than dumb. She'd been downright delusional, changing clothes over and over on that April night before she'd settled on the shortest skirt she dared, a little sweater that buttoned up the front, and the only shoes she owned with a decent heel. She'd put on extra lipstick and blow-dried her hair, then bent over and run through it with her hands before flipping back up, so it looked tousled and sexy. And then she'd sat on the bed and waited until she heard the sound of the car horn.

She put the hood of her jacket up, then, and called to Russell, "Bye. I'm going to Monica's." Riley had already gone out. Dakota had made sure of that, because he'd have seen right through the hood, and he'd have noticed that she wasn't wearing her glasses. Russell, on the other hand, didn't even know about things like, "Be home by eleven." Not like her grandma, who'd always done curfews and bedtimes.

She headed out to the curb and hopped into Steve's brand-new black Chevy Silverado. "Hi," she said, trying not to sound breathless. Trying to sound cool.

"Well, hey, good-looking," he said. "Totally awesome without the glasses."

She smiled and twirled her hair around her finger and tried to pretend she did this all the time. Dated the coolest guy in school, even though she was only a sophomore.

He headed out of town and onto the lake road, and she asked, "So where's this party?"

"Conner Fitzpatrick's house," he said, and Dakota gave a little sigh. Conner was on the football team, too. The *second* most popular guy in school.

The party was loud, and crowded, and dark, and exciting, and Conner's parents were nowhere to be seen. Music blared from speakers set into the walls of the lake house's downstairs game room, and somebody had rigged a disco ball. She danced with Steve, and she drank punch and danced with him some more. She couldn't see too well, but that only made it more glamorous. People said, "Hey, Dakota," to her like she was one of the cool girls, and she said "Hey" back and thought that on Monday, she'd be walking the halls and they'd be saying it again.

She danced until she got hot and it got late, and when Steve filled her punch glass for the fourth time, she didn't drink it. Instead, she poured it into a plant near the window when he wasn't looking. She could feel herself getting fuzzy, and she knew Russ would notice, but she didn't want to be uncool and turn down the drink, either.

"I should get home," she finally yelled at Steve over the music.

"Aw, come on," he said. "We're just getting started."

"No, I really should. My stepfather…"

When they left, they had Rowan Williams with them. "Giving him a ride home," Steve said. So Dakota sat in the middle, so close to Steve, and got a little breathless. Maybe he'd kiss her goodnight. Should she let him? She wanted to. She'd been kissed before, a couple times, but he was so much more adult than the boys she'd gone out with. So much more exciting and confident.

They didn't turn back toward Wild Horse, but instead drove

on the lake road some more. Steve had the radio on loud again, but Dakota was getting sleepy despite the noise, and despite throwing away her last cup of punch. She couldn't see anyway, so she closed her eyes and let herself drift on the throbbing waves of sound until the pickup slowed and the sound under the tires changed to the *crunch* of gravel. She sat up and blinked, but she couldn't see anything, just the hypnotic white headlights picking up the rough road.

"We almost there?" she asked. "R-rowan's?" She was so sleepy.

"Yeah," Steve said, and something in his voice cut through the fog in her head. "Right here." He pulled off the road and killed the engine, but left the radio going. "Going to have another drink. After-party."

"I need to get home," Dakota said. Something was flickering in her chest, rising to her head, buzzing between her ears. Alarm.

"Just a little drink," Steve said. Rowan laughed from her other side, and she suddenly realized that she was hemmed in between them. Steve pulled a bottle out from under the seat, unscrewed the top, and held it to her lips. "Ladies first."

She shoved the bottle away. "No, I really have to go." The alarm was shrieking as loudly as the music now. "Please take me home."

"You want a little drink," Steve said. Before she could react, he gripped her hair at the nape of her neck, pulled her head back, and tipped the bottle up. She pressed her lips together as hard as she could, and the acrid liquid splashed over her chin and ran down her sweater, soaking it.

Steve didn't seem to realize that she hadn't drunk. "That's it," he said. "Bottoms up." He took a long swig himself, then handed the bottle across Dakota to Rowan, his arm brushing across her breasts when he did. She jumped, but he didn't pull away. Instead, he grabbed her by the breast and said, "They're little, but they're tight. Huh, Rowan? You think the rest of her's that tight? Or do you think somebody's already popped the little girl's cherry? I still bet we could show her something new."

"Don't," Dakota said, her voice coming out too high and too scared. "Let me go. Now."

"Give me a kiss, Indian maiden," Steve said. He was over her, his hands gripping her shoulders, his tongue in her mouth, choking her. The smell of whiskey was in her nostrils, and one hand was on her thigh now, then diving under her skirt.

She tried to twist out of his grip, but she couldn't. He was groping, finding the edge of her panties, shoving his fingers under them, inside her. It was rough, and it hurt, and she wanted to scream, but she couldn't. Her head was being yanked the other way. Toward Rowan, who had her by the hair now, and had his tongue halfway down her throat. He was shoving her sweater up, too, pulling at her bra, freeing her breast, squeezing it hard. She was trying to kick, but she couldn't, because Steve was halfway over her, his fingers thrusting. Hurting.

The panic was coming in waves, trying to drown her. She was going backwards, somehow. Being pushed. "Back you go," Steve said. "Indians ride in the back."

Rowan giggled, a high-pitched, excited sound, and what felt like eight hands were shoving her. Her torso was in midair, her legs kicking. Kicking hard. Her foot connected with something solid, she heard a gasped curse, and she kicked some more. She kicked so hard, she went over backwards, her shoulders landing on the edge of the seat.

Back seat. She had no sooner registered it than she was scrambling up, grabbing for the rear door, tumbling out of the car, hitting the ground, and running.

She heard the shouts behind her, but she didn't look back. She ran blindly into the darkness that was the woods, expecting the hands to grab her at any moment. Expecting to be pulled back into the truck.

Run. She heard them calling, shouting, swearing, and she was still running, stumbling. Her hands out in front of her, scraped on knuckles and palms by the rough bark. She stumbled on a tree root, hit her knee hard on a rock, and got up again, limping into the darkness, the shriek of music from the truck still too close. She ran uphill, away from the sound. Away from the cries and the crashing of heavy bodies through trees. She ran, already feeling the hands pulling at her hair, dragging her. *Faster,* she thought. *Go.* And ran some more.

When she heard the truck's motor start again, the music fading, she thought it must be a trick. She stopped moving and dropped to the ground, hugging her knees, trying to quiet her sobbing breaths. If one of them was driving and the other one was still here, listening... If she came out, he'd get her. And he wouldn't let her go.

It must have been ten minutes, but it felt like an hour before the silence nearly convinced her they were gone. She walked cautiously in the direction from which the music had come, ready to bolt at any noise, a new fear making her heart pound even harder.

She didn't know where she was, and it was the middle of the night. Her glasses were at home, and her purse was in Steve's truck.

She found the road eventually, once she made herself think. *Downhill. I ran uphill to get away.* So she went downhill, her arms in front of her, bouncing off the trees, stumbling and swerving, until she found the road. After that, she followed it, shivering in the cold, her footing difficult over the gravel. When she made it to the pavement, she followed that. She didn't know where she was, except that it had to be a lake road. She just had to keep going around the lake, and she'd get home. Sometime. Eventually.

Every time she heard a car, she dove off the road, into the trees, and waited, trembling, until it had passed. They knew she was out here. They knew she was helpless. They would come back, and they would get her.

In the end, she had to take off her shoes, because her feet blistered in her heels to the point where she couldn't walk. Her bare feet were bruised on rocks, sliced on rough edges. They hurt so much, and she was crying now, her shoulders hunched against the cold. And still she walked, because she couldn't think of anything else to do. She walked because she was scared to stop.

And all she could think was, *Don't let them tell. Don't let them tell.*

♡♡♡

She told Blake as little as possible, but it was enough. What she'd said was true. He'd hear it from her, or he'd hear it from somebody else. This was Wild Horse. And she didn't have to look at him to see the rigidity in his posture, the fury in his eyes.

"It must have taken me hours to walk home," she said. "When I got there, it was after three. I sneaked in the back door, and all I could think to do was get in the shower. I turned the water as hot as I could stand it and tried to wash it all away. I scrubbed and scrubbed. But what I really remember is how much my feet hurt. I cried because my feet hurt. I couldn't stand to cry for anything else. I couldn't stand to think."

"And something else happened," Blake said.

Even now, the memory of the next few days—of that whole first week—made her tense and sick. "I told Russell and Riley that I didn't feel good, and I stayed under the covers all day on Sunday. On Monday, I didn't go to school. I couldn't stand to."

"You didn't tell anybody," Blake said. "You didn't go to the police."

"I didn't even think of it. I just wanted it to go *away*. I wanted it not to be true. I was so ashamed. I felt so dirty. I felt like *I* was the one who'd done something wrong. And what would the police have done? You know what. He-said, she-said. I was nobody, and Steve's family is a big deal, and I'd been drinking, and everybody would say that I'd wanted it. I'd have been dragged through the mud for nothing, and Russell would have known. That was the worst. I couldn't stand for Russell to know. I thought he'd kick me out. I was already only there because of Riley. And if he knew…"

She forced herself to stop, then went on more calmly. "Anyway. On Monday afternoon, after school, Russ got a call. Riley'd been suspended. He'd beaten Steve up. He'd broken his nose, split his lip, among other things. He beat him good."

"What about the other guy?"

"The other guy? Oh, Rowan. Surely you can guess. Evan took care of him. He and Riley jumped them in the parking lot, right beside that truck of Steve's. And after Riley punched Steve out…" She smiled. That memory was a good one. "He kicked a dent into the door of Steve's brand-new truck. They were suspended for a week for fighting. All four of them, actually, because none of them said why they'd been doing it. How could Rowan and Steve say why Riley did it? And there was no way Riley was going to. But all the kids knew. They said… Steve and Rowan told everybody. They said I'd had sex with both of them, and that they'd done everything to me. They… described it. I heard." Even now, the memory could make her burn. The shame, and the humiliation. "Riley heard, too, and he and Evan took care of it the best they could, but that didn't stop everybody from talking. It didn't make the next couple years much fun, either. That reputation… well, you saw. It never really goes away. Whenever anybody asked me out… well, usually, there was one reason. They didn't want to take me to the movies or go for a walk. They wanted to take me to a 'party.' So I didn't go out."

Blake swore under his breath, and Dakota said, "Yeah. It was bad, and you see why I moved to Portland. But it was half a lifetime ago, and I'm not that scared girl anymore. And anyway, I still have Evan. He's still right here, ready to do it all again. Ready to be my protector. The trick is convincing him he doesn't have to be. As you saw."

"Evan. Yeah," Blake said.

"He's a good friend. A good friend to Riley, and a good friend to me. But you know—here's the takeaway from the whole thing. You know what Riley told me, when he got the story out of me?"

"No," Blake said. "Tell me."

"We were sitting on the edge of my bed, Monday night, after he made me tell him what happened. We were both kind of a mess. My hands, my knees, my feet, even my face from crying. I was hurt inside, too. Bruised. That was the worst. Every time I peed, it hurt so much, and I remembered why and felt dirty all over again. And Riley—he had ice on his knuckles."

"His knuckles? Not his face?"

"No. Riley was tough, and Steve went down easy. Both of them did. And that night, Riley sat with me and made me tell him, and then he told me, 'You think you lost. You didn't lose. It wouldn't have mattered what they did. You're tougher than either of those assholes. The winner's the one who gets up the most times, and we'll always get up. We're always going to be the last two standing. That means we'll always win.'"

Blake exhaled. "Smart guy."

Dakota took a final bite of salmon. She'd thought telling him would be awful. It wasn't awful. The story was out there now—*her* story—and that was better. Riley had been right. She wasn't a victim. She was a survivor. "He *was* smart. He was the best brother. He's the only part of that night that can still make me cry to think about. Otherwise? He was right. I got up. Steve Sawyer is a pathetic piece of human garbage who's going to get what's coming to him someday, because he's stuck being his miserable self for the rest of his life. And Ingrid's stuck with him. Rowan's living somewhere else. I don't know and I don't care, but I'm betting his life isn't turning out great either. And Riley died a hero. His life might have been too short, but he'll be remembered forever by everybody who knew him. And me? I got up. Every time. I'll always get up. That means I win."

Both Sides Now

♡

Blake sat there and tried to force the adrenaline back. When he'd managed it, he said, "Two things. That's what I've got going on. They're kind of fighting it out right now."

"What two things?" Dakota asked. She was stirred up, but she was more under control than he was. That was the crazy part of it.

"I know I need to tell you how beautiful you are, and how brave you were to come back to this town and to face what you did tonight, to hold your head that high. I want to hold you and say all that, and try to make it better. You can call that my good side. Unfortunately, all my regrettable side wants to do is drive this boat back into town, hunt that bastard down, and kick his ass."

She managed a smile. "I may have mentioned that Riley already did that, and that if you want to do it again, you'll have to line up behind Evan."

"Now, see, darlin'," he said with a sigh, "that's a problem. I'm not good at lining up behind anybody. Afraid I'm going to have to take that first spot."

"Mm. But then…" She laughed, although it was still a little shaky. "Who's going to hold me and make it better? I could really use that right now. I never told anybody all of that. Nobody but Riley. Evan doesn't even know it all, I don't think. I never talked about it with him, and I'll bet Riley didn't either. I was ashamed for so long."

She turned that sculpted face to him, and it was like he was seeing her for the first time. His hand went to her cheek as if it had been pulled there, because it had. He stroked her cheek, and this time, she leaned her face into his palm. And still, she looked into his eyes. And then she raised her own hand to him, ran her fingers over his jaw, and said, her voice so soft, "You shaved for me tonight."

"Yeah. I did."

"Thank you."

"For what?"

Their hands were still on each other, and the moment stretched out until she said, "For making my night so special."

"Aw, baby," he said helplessly. "You rip my heart out."

"You know what the worst part is?" Her voice was barely a murmur, but he heard her. That was how close they were.

"No, what?"

"That now you won't kiss me."

"I'll kiss you." He wasn't going to be able to stop himself. Except that was the whole point. "Here's the deal," he said, while his thumb stroked over that carved cheekbone and he watched her eyes soften. "Anytime you want me to pull up the anchor and take you home, you tell me so. Anytime. You tell me, and I'll do it. That's a promise."

"Thank you." She leaned in, pulled his head down, and brushed her lips over his. Then she was kissing his neck, under his ear, and murmuring against his skin, "Message received. Could you go on and let your regrettable side loose now, though? Because that's what I dressed up for. Something else, too. Here's a secret just for you. You shaved, but I waxed."

Talk about a change of focus.

And then she bit him. Yes, she did. She took a nip out of his neck that made him jump, then kissed him there some more, her lips stirring that regrettable side into action. No hope at all.

His hand tightened on her cheek. "You know what? I think we'd better take our wine on over to the couch."

"Mm. What a good idea." She was still kissing his neck, and if he didn't stand up now, he wasn't going to be able to.

"Come on, wild thing." He collected the bottle in one hand and the glasses in another and slid on out of there. A couple of steps, and he set them down on the coffee table, then turned around and took her hand as she was getting to her feet. He took her over to the light switch, turned the dimmers on down, hit another button or two over there, and got some music going. That was better. That was *good*.

"We're not going to do it in the dark, huh?" she asked, still going for that badass. Some tease in her voice now, her hair falling over one eye, her body swaying to the soft pump of the music.

"Oh, no. No way. I've waited all this time to look at you again. I'm not missing my chance. In fact..." He put a hand on her shoulder and urged her gently around, then pushed her hair over one shoulder.

He had to sigh. Oh, that was nice. Her halter top was tied with a bow, and the back of the dress was cut low beneath that. Shoulder blades like angel wings, a slim, toned back, and all that smooth skin. He put a hand on one tie of that yellow bow and pulled. Unwrapping his Christmas present. She was sighing herself, melting back into him, so he found the zipper and slowly lowered it all the way down. Past the curve of her waist, down to the wonderful swell of her ass.

The two sides of the dress parted, and there was nothing underneath it but Dakota and two thin strips of lacy black thong. No bra, just all that wonderful body. He shoved the dress down, and when it hit the floor... oh, man. He had to get both hands on those firm, round cheeks, and then he had to run a hand down the center of that thong. And when he did, she shuddered.

He could have stood there and felt her for an hour, but on the other hand... there she was, reflected in the darkness of the window opposite him. Her eyes half-closed, her head thrown back, her high breasts bare, and that flat belly. Only that last secret bit of her hidden from his view, covered with a tiny triangle of black lace.

So much to do. So much to touch, and to kiss, and she wasn't telling him to take her home. She was going to be his, all night long.

He told her, "Step out of the dress, baby," watched her do it, then put his hands on her again. One of them on her hip, pulling her back against him, and the other one stroking slowly down her arm, all the way from shoulder to wrist, then up her body. Palming her belly, sending a finger stroking over that tiny silver barbell in her navel.

"Prettiest thing I ever saw," he said in her ear. "When we were at that restaurant and you walked by me? I thought I was going to go up in a puff of smoke just looking at you."

"You... noticed?" Her voice was breathy, and she was watching him in the window. Watching herself, and as turned on by it as he was, if that were possible.

"Oh, yeah." He stroked over her belly some more. Her ribs. He had her ass cradled in his thighs, and he was aching.

"Blake," she said when he slowed down, his palm over her middle, his thumb drifting in the valley between her breasts. "Please. Keep going."

"Mm. I'm going to do that, don't worry. I'm just enjoying looking at you so much." He watched in the window as his hand moved up, his palm settling over the firm curve of her breast. She sighed, pushed back into him, and whispered, "Yes. Please," and he wondered if he was going to be able to make this last.

"I think I need to lay you down," he said. "I need to have some room to kiss you and love you right. But we're going to leave this thong on for a while, because that's just too pretty."

"You know," she said breathlessly, her eyes nearly closed

now as his fingers worked her breast, swirling and plucking at that firm little brown nipple, "you talk a lot."

He was so startled, he laughed out loud. "Yeah. It's been mentioned. And you know what—I just changed my mind." He had both hands cupping her breasts now, was running his thumbs over the tips, and she was absolutely squirming. His mouth needed to be there. He needed to make her squirm some more, and he needed to do it for a long, long time.

"Wh-what? No. Don't change—" He gave her a gentle pinch, and she gasped. "Don't change your mind."

"Need a bed," he whispered in her ear. That chain was right there again, and he had to suck it into his mouth and bite her there. And when she moaned, he had to bite some more, didn't he? It was necessary.

But while he did it, he was walking her ahead of him through the galley and into his cabin. He spun her around, her thighs hit the mattress, and down she went. Right onto her back.

He switched on the lamp, and there she was, the gold and black of her laid out on his white comforter like his very best present. He was over her, levering himself on an elbow, and she was pulling at his T-shirt.

"No fair," she said. "I need you naked."

He got it up over his head, and she was rising up, helping him pull it off, her hands greedy on his chest, down his sides, like she needed to touch him, too.

"Come on," she said. "Please. Come on."

He'd get to his pants later, he decided, because he needed to kiss her. Needed to wrap his hands in her hair, hold her head, and give that full, soft mouth all the loving it deserved. Her mouth opened under his, and his tongue was inside, tasting her, and when she joined the party... Oh, hell, yeah. That was *good*. The desire was licking down inside him, all jabs and silver streaks, and he was so hard, he ached. She was making those noises again, too, because she was feeling the same thing. She had her hand around his head, her fingers digging into his hair, and he could feel the little shudders in her, the electricity of his kiss, as if her body were his own.

He needed her to be grabbing him harder, though. He needed to get her noisy. He needed to drive her crazy.

He was at her neck, sucking at her, biting her, moving over her, learning what she liked, and what made her crazy. The spicy scent of her perfume was in his head, her silken skin under his hand, and his palm was on her breast again. No choice. He had to. Her hips were moving already, and he was half gone.

And when his mouth moved over her shoulder and settled on her breast... her head went back, just like that. Her mouth opened, her back arched, and she was making some "ah... ah... ah" noises that were going to kill him. He used his tongue and his lips and his teeth on her, and he found out she loved to be bitten there, too. Gently. That was very good news, so he did it some more.

He didn't want to leave, and he had to leave. His hand was stroking up her thigh, her legs were parting, and the silk of her in those secret spaces at the tops of her thighs... he had to kiss that. He *had* to.

A detour for that barbell, licking into her navel, and then he was taking the two sides of that black thong in each hand and dragging it down her body, exposing her, watching her thighs part for him.

That was pretty as hell. That was Christmas and his birthday and the Fourth of July. She lay there across his bed, her arms flung over her head, her dark hair around her, breathing hard, and he felt a hundred feet tall. He stood up and rid of the rest of his clothes in one big hurry, barely remembering to grab the condom out of his pocket and toss it on the bed.

She opened her eyes, looked at him, gave him a slow, languorous smile with that pretty mouth, and sighed. "Blake."

"Yeah, baby." He wanted to say something else, but his words were gone.

"You're so beautiful," she said. "And you're really, really

good at this."

He laughed. He couldn't help it. "I get better. Just wait."

"Mm." She was on an elbow for him, reaching for him, stroking the length of him, and—damn. If she kept doing that, he wasn't going to make it. "Could you please hurry up, though?"

Now he was really laughing. "You're going to make me lose all my mojo. And, no, I can't hurry up. I'm going to go slow."

"Oh." She sighed. "Am I going to like it?"

"Oh, yeah. You're going to love it."

$$\heartsuit\heartsuit\heartsuit$$

Everything in Dakota's body was tingling. Every single cell in her wanted him to get there, wanted this to get *going*.

She'd never been a patient person. Now, she was about to scream. Because he didn't start up where he'd left off, where she needed him to be. He came down over her and kissed her again, long and slow and deep, and it felt so good, but she needed more. She shifted under him, grabbed his wonderfully muscular butt, and tried to move him over her, and he… stopped kissing her.

"Dakota," he said sternly, his hand wrapped in her hair, "you're being a little bit forceful here, darlin'. I think I'm going to have to insist on a little more cooperation."

She narrowed her eyes at him. "Did I ask for a quarterback?"

"Well, now, baby, I'd say you just about did. And I tell you what." He kissed his way around to her neck and sank his teeth into her skin until she moaned, then murmured in her ear, "How about this? You grab onto that headboard and hold on for me."

A surge of heat like molten liquid. "What?"

"You heard me. Go on and do it."

Slowly, she reached overhead, her hands closing over the top of the padded leather headboard.

Blake sighed. "Now, that's better. You hold on, darlin'. Because I'm going to love you."

And then he did. She might not be a patient woman, but Blake was a very, very patient man. He moved down her body, kissing his way, and finally, he settled in.

Except he didn't. He teased her, and he tormented her. He sped up, and he slowed down. He got her hips pumping, her body rocking, and then he shifted his focus. Again and again, until she was panting. Until she was begging.

"Blake," she moaned. "Please. Please. Let me…"

"Almost," he said. "Not quite yet." He was shoving something under her hips. A pillow, and that was good. That was better. His fingers were inside her, beginning to press, and she was rocking against them. Then he took them out, and she cried out in protest again. His hands were on the backs of her thighs, shoving them up high, all the way until her knees hit the bed.

That was when he set his mouth to her for real, and shoved her straight up the mountain and over the edge. Her hands were gripping the edge of the headboard, his hands were hard on the backs of her thighs, her legs were caught, and she was wailing. Screaming. And he didn't stop. He kept on, and she was going over again, harder this time. Again and again, until she was shaking. Until all she could do was moan.

When he let go of her legs at last, they were trembling so badly, she almost couldn't put them down. She let go of the headboard, and instantly, his hands were over hers, putting them back in place.

"No," he said, not sounding steady at all. "Don't. Hang on. Please. Hang on for me."

He was grabbing the packet, putting the condom on. And she was watching him. There was no way she couldn't.

Oh, my God. He was *big*. His hands and feet hadn't lied one bit.

Her breath was coming in panting gasps, her hands shaking on the headboard. And when his hands went back to her thighs and he shoved her legs up again… she let him do it.

He entered her in one hard thrust, and she cried out at the sudden stretch, the shock of it. He stopped, holding himself rigid over her. "Hurts?"

"No. Don't stop. Please, Blake." If he teased again, she couldn't stand it. "Please. Go."

A hard thrust, a slow withdrawal. His hands holding her legs, his face so intent over her, his eyes glowing golden. Finding the same spot he'd found with his fingers, the place she hadn't realized you could really touch. Winding her up higher, until she was making noise again, until his harsh breaths filled her ears. Higher and higher, and not quite there, and she needed more. She needed… she needed…

He stopped. He let her legs go and pulled out of her, and she opened her eyes in dismay. That was all? She'd been so *close*.

"Turn over," he said. "Hands and knees. Oh, God, Dakota. Turn over."

The dark fire leaped inside her, and she did it. She turned over, and he entered her again, and now, there was nothing slow about it. Hard and fast, taking her over, and his hand was on her, stroking.

No escape. Nowhere to go but here, nothing to feel but this. Her head was down, her hair in her face, and she was on her elbows now, her face buried in her hands, all of her reduced to him inside her, to his hand on her. To the need that was pulling her up, twisting her tight. She was biting her hand, and all she could hear was Blake's breath. And he was making some noise, too. She heard it, but dimly, because the concentric circles of pleasure were closing in on her, focusing more and more, and then the waves began to hit.

He seemed to have grown inside her, and he was gasping now, both his hands going to her hips, his fingers digging in, pulling her back into him as if he couldn't get close enough.

More and more. Deeper and harder, until he was groaning out her name, jerking against her, yanking her back so hard. And she knew he was as lost as she was. He was all the way gone.

Negotiation

♡

Blake got rid of the condom as fast as he could, hating that he had to move at all. Dakota hadn't, or barely. She was still on her knees, her face buried in her hands, and he felt a sickening lurch of fear straight to the gut.

He moved over her again, propping himself on an elbow, pulling her hair back from her face with a hand that insisted on shaking. Maybe from one of the most intense orgasms he'd ever experienced, and maybe from something else.

"Hey, baby." He kissed her cheek, then rolled her with him so she was on her side and he was wrapped around her. "How about talking to me? You all right? Was I too rough?"

Idiot, he was yelling at himself. *Insensitive jerk.* She'd told him about one of the most horrific things that could happen to a woman, and what had he done? Had he laid her down and loved her with the kind of tenderness she needed, the kind she deserved? Not hardly. He'd started out OK. But after that? He'd gotten carried away.

She rolled over to face him, and he put a hand out and stroked it over her shoulder, her arm. Smooth as silk, warm as honey. But her eyes were huge, her face somber, and his heart was going a mile a minute.

And then she smiled. Slow, with a teasing edge to it. "You're going to do all that to me, and then make me *talk?* Next time, boy, it's going to be happening to you. You see if you can talk to *me* after you lose that many brain cells."

"Oh." The relief punched into his chest, and he was grinning like a fool. He was running his hand up and down her back now, just because he could. Because she was here in his bed, naked, and he'd loved her right after all. "Well, good. You could say I had some stored-up frustration to work out. You could say that."

"Mm." She had her hand on his shoulder, on his arm, like she wanted to feel him, too. "Because I was so attractive the first, oh, five or six times we were together. In my navy-blue swimsuit and my overalls."

"Doesn't matter what wrapping you put on it. All that does is make me want to unwrap it more. Especially now that I know what's underneath, because, darlin', you have got about the most—ah—" He caught himself just in time. "... lovable body I've ever had the pleasure of taking over. And I did love taking it over."

She was smiling some more. "Oh, don't wimp out on me now. That wasn't the word you had in mind."

"I am a Southern gentleman," he protested.

"Oh, come on, Mr. Perfect. Let me hear it."

"Right." He scowled. "You want me to tell you that you're the most fuckable thing I've ever seen? There, I said it. Sounds bad. I told you."

She was laughing. "I'll tell you a secret. When *you* say it, it works. Mr. Irresistible."

He was stroking the curve of her bottom now. It felt too good, so he did it again. "I'll tell you something else, then, while I'm down here digging this hole for myself. You've got an ass like a Georgia peach, and I've been looking at since the first day I met you. Made my palms itch, and it still does. Know why I made you turn over?"

"Because you like to do it that way? Because it gets you all excited to see me do what you tell me?" She was still teasing, still smug.

He gave her a slap there. That was because he could, too. "You just keep talking, wild thing. Because I wanted to look at it, that's why. And by the way—when you were wearing that little orange skirt at Russell's that night?" He sighed. "Man, that about drove me wild."

"Mm. Very nice. You aren't so bad yourself. I could catalogue a few body parts of yours that I enjoy, but I'm not going to. You're conceited enough."

He touched the two small designs inked into her side. First one, then the other. He hadn't suspected those, hidden away as they were just below her shoulder blade. "What are these, darlin'? These tattoos? That was a pretty little surprise."

Her smile vanished. "They're doves. One for my grandma, and one for Riley. We did them at Riley's funeral, and I just... I got them after that."

He could swear his heart actually throbbed. "Tell me." She hesitated, and he said, "Please."

Silence for a few long seconds, then she said, "It was this... moment. When the bugler played 'Taps,' and the guy let them out of the cage. They flew up into the sky and away. Like Riley was still there, and he was free. I remember I lifted my arm. I couldn't help it. Sending him on his way. Waving goodbye. I wanted to remember that moment."

That thing in his chest twisted again, and he touched the tattoos once more. Gently. Tiny birds in flight, less than an inch across. A talisman, and a promise. "That's what these are, then. Letting them know you remember."

She looked into his eyes, there on the bed, their hands on each other, their hearts beating together, and said, "There's a poem they read at a military funeral." She took a moment while he waited, then said, her voice so soft, 'They shall grow not old, as we that are left grow old. Age shall not weary them, nor the years condemn. At the going down of the sun and in the morning, we will remember them.'"

"You are a beautiful woman," he managed to get out through a throat tight with emotion. "And I'm crazy about you."

She got still, and then she pushed herself up to sit. "What time is it?"

"What?" That had been her reaction? Why? "Uh…" He groped for his phone in his pants pocket. "Almost eleven."

"I should go home."

Somehow, she was slipping away. He was losing her. "You could stay," he suggested. "Stay on the boat and sleep with me. It's kinda nice, you know. Rocked on the waves."

"A shower. Brushing my teeth."

"Got some toothbrushes in a drawer. Got a shower, too. Tiny, but it's there. And I'd dearly love you to stay."

She was looking at him so closely, but she wasn't going to see anything there he didn't want her to. There was nothing bad to see. "Go on," he said. "Whatever it is. Say it."

"You don't have to be a gentleman now," she said. "I wanted to do this. I've wanted to do it since the first day I met you. I know you're not a bad person. I trust you not to hurt me. I know you won't talk about me."

All right. He was getting mad. "You know I'm not a bad *person?* Thank you very much. I tell you I'm crazy about you, and you say, thanks for the hookup?"

She sighed. "Come on, Blake. I'm not stupid. Your life is completely different from mine. You're dating other people. You told Evan so. No, I *saw* you doing it. I'm sure I don't figure into your plans, and you don't figure into mine, either. I've hurt enough in my life. I don't need to go sticking my hand in the fire, searching for something that isn't there."

She was groping around, looking for her thong, probably, and he was lost for words. "Wait. Dakota. Let's… wait."

She turned to look at him, all her wariness back. "I'm waiting."

"Why can't we have a… a relationship? Why the hell not?"

She laughed. *Laughed,* and he was burning up. "You don't

want to have a relationship with me."

"I don't?" He'd sat up now, too. "Maybe you should let me say what I want and don't want. Maybe I know a little better than you do." It wasn't true, of course. He had no clue. But it sounded good.

She crossed her arms under her pretty breasts, and that might have distracted him for a minute. Her hair was wild and tumbled, she was wearing nothing but that tiny silver heart, her legs were tucked to one side, and she was... well. She was something to look at.

She said, "My eyes are up here."

"Oh. Sorry. Uh... what were we saying?"

"You were telling me that you knew what you wanted."

"Oh. Right. Yeah. I do. I want you to spend the night with me. I want to go to sleep holding you, because it would feel so good. I want to wake up and make love to you again. I want to go to breakfast with you. I want to tell Russell that I'm dating his daughter, because she's pretty damn special and I like her a whole lot. I want this whole town to know it, too. How's that?"

She seemed to be considering, and that was good. What she said next, though, wasn't. "So you know. I have a life plan."

This time, he didn't have any problem looking at her face. *What?* Did she know about *his* life plan? How? Why was she using that word, otherwise? For that matter—wait. What did *he* think about his life plan?

She didn't seem to notice that he was grappling in the weeds. She said, "So you know where I am—it's this. Russell has about forty thousand left on the mortgage. If I can keep selling my glass all right, I can pay that off in three years. An extra thousand every month, and I can do it. If you can get him fixed up better, so he can... so he's not hurting so much..." That one stopped her for a minute, but she went on. "I'll appreciate it more than I've ever appreciated anything. After that, though, I'm paying off his mortgage, and I'm going. I'm going back to Portland, and I'm going to work on getting that life I want. I'm going to save for myself this time. I'm going to go to Costa Rica, even if I have to work my way there somehow. I'm going to hike in the rainforest and snorkel from the beach. I'm going to see dolphins. I'm going to see birds and animals and colors, and I'm going to make glass out of what I've seen. I'm going to have a *life*. And when I come back to Wild Horse…" That one hung her up for another moment. "When I come back to see Russell, I'm going to come back knowing I don't have to stay. I'm going to have a name, even if it's a little name. I'm going to come back knowing I've built my own life, and that it's good. That I don't need anybody here, and I don't care what they think of me. Nobody but Russell and Evan."

His throat was dry. *Wow.* "And you can't go out with me why?"

"Oh. Huh." She considered. "I guess I can. As long as I'm not stupid. As long as I'm not romantic."

Why didn't that sound one bit good to him? "Sure you can. Besides, just think how it'll stick in Melody's craw."

She started to smile, and the hard moment passed. "Yeah. That's a good one. Oh, yeah. Let me guess. She let you know she'd entertain your advances."

He laughed. He was completely confused, but still, she made him laugh. "Darlin', you were born to be a Southern girl. Yes, she did. Just imagine when I take you to breakfast tomorrow, and when I can't help but buy you some pretty new earrings, because your ears are so sexy. When I put diamonds in there, and she has to look at those diamonds and know they aren't hers. Even if she *was* the head cheerleader and she has shiny hair."

"Blake Orbison," she said, her arms crossed again, "are you offering to buy my honor?"

"Nah, baby. I'm asking you to give me your time and your company. And I'm sure hoping you say yes. I'm hoping you say it quick, too, so I can crawl in this bed with you and hold you some more. There's this place my hand wants to be while I fall asleep. I've waited this long for you. I don't want to let you go."

She hesitated, and he said with a sigh, "We're bargaining again. I knew it. Tell me."

"You're not dating anybody else," she said. "Nobody in Wild Horse, I mean. I'm not going to find out I was your…"

Steve's smug voice was right there in his head. *Dakota's used to being that side piece. There are girls you fuck and girls you marry, and she knows which one she is.* He said, "No, I'm not dating anybody else, in Wild Horse or anywhere. And you'd better not be doing it either. I'm the jealous kind. It's exclusive, or it's nothing. And I've had quicker negotiations to buy a million-dollar property. I'm just saying."

"Well," she said sweetly, "Melody's probably still available."

He slapped a hand over his heart, fell onto his back, and groaned. "You got me. Come on, wild thing. I'll find you a toothbrush. Anything. I want you in my bed, and I don't care what I have to do to get it."

Morning Refreshment

♡

How was Dakota supposed to resist that? She couldn't. And it didn't matter anyway. She'd told him her plan. She'd laid it out as much for herself as for him. They were all clear.

So she sent Russell a quick text and took her shower. And when she climbed into bed, Blake pulled her back against him, his arm came around her, his hand settled gently over her breast, and he sighed and said, "Yeah. Exactly what I had in mind. That's just about perfect."

He was asleep in minutes, but she lay awake. The boat rocked gently in the water, lulling her into peace, and Blake was warm and solid behind her. Like a security... not even a blanket. A security *wall*. Which was nuts.

He'd said he was crazy about her. That was nice. And her body was still humming, ticking over, letting her know that as well as he'd satisfied it, it wouldn't mind doing it all again. It couldn't *wait* to do it all again.

That had just been talk about the diamonds, of course, but it was sure a satisfying image. She'd have given a lot to see Melody's face. Not to mention Ingrid's.

It was all going to be fine. Good sex with a good man was something worth having, and if that man made you laugh and wanted to hold you close afterwards? That was even better. There was nothing wrong with taking something special when it offered itself to you, she told herself just before the lake and the darkness and Blake's warm body soothed her into sleep. Not if you kept your mind and your priorities clear.

She woke once in the night, and so did he. He made love to her again, soft and slow, and she let herself drift with it. And if she got some tears in her eyes at the gentleness of his hands, the tenderness of his kisses, the sweet words he whispered in her ear, telling her she was beautiful? That was all right. It was dark.

When she woke again, he wasn't there, and the boat was moving, the big engines rumbling soft and deep. She could have lain there and slept the whole way back. That noise was so soothing, and it was so dark and peaceful in the cabin. But she got up instead. It was Saturday morning, and she had work to do.

Breakfast with Blake first, which was fine. But after that, work. She couldn't paint his house this weekend, not with him there, and anyway, she was due to start a new glass piece. A poppy, all vibrant orangey-red petals and black center, bursting with color and life. Still sexy, but cheerfully sexy, if that was a thing. Sexy fun, like jumping off the rocks with Blake.

And if being with him made her want to laze the day away instead? That was why she wasn't going to do it, even if he wanted to. Bad habits. Dangerous patterns.

Self-discipline. It was a thing.

So she sat up and looked around, and found that her dress and thong were neatly folded on the narrow top of the teak storage unit along one wall, but there was something else there as well. A red Portland Devils T-shirt and a pair of his swim trunks. Navy blue.

She had to laugh. He'd read her mind. She wouldn't be glamorous, but that was nothing new. She put them on, pulled her hair back into a rough braid, and thought, *How do you like me now?*

When she went up the ladder to the flying bridge, Blake was in his captain's chair, dressed in his T-shirt and slacks from the night before, his feet propped up on a ledge, his ankles crossed, with one hand on the wheel and the other holding a coffee mug.

"Well, good morning, baby," he said. Dark morning stubble, white teeth, satisfied smile. He set down the mug, reached an arm out, and tugged her to him by the edge of her T-shirt, then pulled her into his lap. "Now, that's what I'm talking about," he said, wrapping his arm around her waist and giving her a slow, sweet kiss that got her tingling all the way to her toes.

"You're going to crash the boat," she murmured against his mouth.

"Nah. We're idling, see? I pushed the button. I'm talented that way."

Oh. He was right. He went on, "You casting aspersions on my boat handling? You cut me to the bone, darlin'. That's my manhood right there. Might as well tell me I'm not big enough where it counts, or say I slide to avoid the tackle. Them's fightin' words." He had a sneaky hand up under the T-shirt, and when his hand settled over her breast, he sighed. "I'm just going to put in my vote here for the no-bra deal all the time, by the way. No bra, no underwear—that'd make my life a whole lot more interesting."

"Did I mention you talk a lot?" she said, and he laughed. "And if I should decide to dress solely for your pleasure, I'll keep that in mind. Don't count on it. That wouldn't be too comfortable with overalls." It wasn't easy to be severe when you were leaning back against a man's shoulder with your shirt pulled all the way up and his hand on your breast, but she did her best. "Oh." She sucked in a breath as he got bolder. "That feels good."

"Mm." He kissed her again, tasting hot and dark, like coffee and Blake. "Maybe I should drop that anchor again and take you below," he murmured in her ear. "I can wait for my breakfast. Or I can start it with you."

"I should get home soon," she said, her resolve weakening by the moment. "Get to... um... work. I'm way behind. Can anybody... ah..." She couldn't help a moan as he lifted her with one arm, and his mouth went to her breast. "See us?"

He didn't answer. He was busy. She managed to open her eyes enough to look around. They were almost at the resort, near the swimming beach. And there was somebody walking along the shore near the building. A ways away, but still, he was there. She said, "Blake. Stop."

He sat up right away. "What?"

She tugged her shirt down and hissed, "Somebody's there."

He glanced toward the shore. "Security, that's all. We're ramping up the patrols with less than two weeks to go till the opening. But unless he's got binoculars, he's not thinking that I'm the luckiest guy in the world and he isn't. He's seeing my boat in the water. That's it."

She squirmed off his lap, and he let her go. If she didn't change their direction, Blake was perfectly capable of persuading her to waste her entire day. He was a convincing man. She said, "I tell you what. You take me out to dinner again tonight, *after* I put in my workday, and I'll have *you* for dessert. I think I've got a debt to pay, and I'll bet you're just delicious. Consider that an IOU." She put her lips up to his ear and whispered, "And I won't stop until you're done. All the way, baby," then danced back out of reach and said, "Right now, though, I need to cool off."

He wanted to tease her, work her up? Well, two could play that game. She didn't wait for his answer, just ran lightly down the ladder from the flying bridge and then down to the mezzanine, climbed onto the edge, and leaped far out into the water.

As always, the cold water shocked even in June, a tingling, jolting wake-up call, and she laughed out loud as she surfaced. That had been awesome. Blake's T-shirt ballooned out around her, but who cared? He'd turned the boat, and the look on his face made her laugh some more. She treaded water and called up to him, "I'm going to trespass again. I'll meet you at the marina." And then she swam for the floating logs.

It wasn't even a hundred yards. Not nearly far enough to qualify as exercise, but it felt good all the same.

She was still smiling when she dove and swam all the way to the bottom beneath the barrier, just for the heck of it.

At first, she didn't understand what had happened. She was swimming, and then she wasn't moving. Something was brushing against her face, one of her arms. *Water weed,* she thought, suppressing the flash of instinctive panic at the age-old threat of an unseen presence in the water. Her monkey brain screamed *Shark,* her logical brain answered *Lake,* and she moved her arm to brush the weed away.

Except that she couldn't. She wasn't going forward, either. Something had her. Something was *grabbing* her, and she couldn't see what it was. It was dark under here, ten feet beneath the surface. Deep green water, and a filmy something at the edge of her vision.

The thoughts processed in seconds that felt so much longer, like time had slowed.

Focus. Calm. Figure it out. She forced herself to stop kicking forward, which was only getting her more stuck, and felt around her head and arm with her free hand. Fine filaments tried to cut at her, and there were so many of them.

Some kind of web. A web that was torn, because her head was through, and one arm to the shoulder. The other hand was free, behind whatever it was.

Pull out your arm and swim backwards. She was still holding her breath. Of course she was. But it was getting harder, the panic starting to rise, trying to get loose and racket around her brain. Because there was nothing to push off of. Every time she tried, her hand went through a hole, and she had to tug it out. She tried to grab whatever was holding her arm, but something was caught. Stuck.

Net. A torn net. She reached above her head, grasped the

filaments, and tried to wrench them off, but something was stuck there, too. She couldn't get them off her hair. And Blake's shirt was trapping her.

She was kicking hard to stay horizontal, not to have her legs float upward. Trying with one hand to wrench the sodden, flapping shirt off her body, twisting in the water. On her back now, still far down in the green, the lighter water above her taunting her, the air much too far away. And it was getting so hard to hold her breath. Her fingers clawed at the wet cotton, but she could barely see now. Her lungs were bursting, and the water was darker. Her hand groped, fell away.

The water flickered, blurred around the edges. Then it went black.

Emergency Measures

♡

Blake watched Dakota swimming away and had to laugh even as his body protested her defection. Seemed like all she ever did was turn the tables on him.

Tonight, though? Dinner sounded good, and that promise of hers sounded better. Dakota naked, on her knees, and not stopping until he was done? Oh, yeah. That would be just fine.

He was still thinking about it when she disappeared from sight under the log, and he sighed, killed the idle, and started to turn the boat. It wasn't even eight o'clock in the morning. Breakfast, and then he could be taking her home by nine. Nine-thirty at the latest. And he'd tell her it was going to be an *early* dinner.

Early and quick. He'd waited a long time for this. He was done waiting.

He glanced toward shore again, maybe just because he liked looking at her.

She wasn't there.

Half of him was thinking, *She swam that fast?* The other half was turning the boat, his pulse racing, his muscles tensing, his body saying *Wrong* before his conscious mind caught up.

He got closer and realized why. A disturbance in the water

on this side of the logs. Ripples that shouldn't have been there. He was pushing that slow-idle button again on the thought, and then he was nearly sliding down the ladder, leaping over the side of the boat, and swimming hard.

Precious seconds wasted, twice, to surface and orient himself. And he still didn't see her. He was swimming along the edge of the logs where the water had been disturbed, turning his head, peering beneath him through water that wasn't clear enough.

He was on top of her before he recognized her. At least, he saw something far below, like a giant fish. Something pale.

Legs. Kicking feebly. And then not.

He was diving deep, touching her back, her arms, and she wasn't responding. She was stuck, caught somehow, and at first, he couldn't figure out how. He was groping around the billowing cotton of her shirt, the floating seaweed of her hair, and he felt it. Something catching her there.

He felt around some more. Her head, her face. Whatever it was, it wasn't around her neck.

Pull. He grabbed her by the shoulders and yanked her straight backward with all his might. A moment of resistance, then she came free, and he was dragging her to the surface, kicking hard.

Her body was limp, her eyes closed. He said, "Dakota!" and got nothing. No response at all.

Rescue breathing. Now. It wasn't easy to do it in the water, but he managed. Pinching her nose closed with one hand, holding her in place with the other while his legs worked hard to keep him afloat.

Two breaths. Still nothing.

Get to shore. You can't do the rest of it here. He grabbed her across the chest, his hand tucked in her armpit, and swam harder than he ever had. The shortest route around the logs, and then to the beach, using every bit of his strength and his will.

It was fast. It seemed like forever. He stopped once along the way to give her a couple more breaths. Still nothing. Finally, he got his feet on the sandy bottom, and then he was hauling her, striding against the resistance of the water like it wasn't there. Straight out of the lake and onto the beach, where he laid her down and dropped to his knees beside her.

Try again with the breathing. Then move on. The long-ago lifesaving lessons in the community pool had come back to him in force. Three more breaths, done right this time, here on land, watching her chest rise as he filled her lungs with air.

Check for a pulse first. Then chest compressions. If there wasn't a pulse, her heart would have stopped. He could start it again, though. He had to. First, though, he got a hand under her ear and focused.

It wasn't easy. He was trembling himself, and she was so cold. He was about to give up and start working on her chest when he thought he felt a faint movement under his fingers. Then he felt her jerk under him, heard the choking sound.

He rolled her fast, and even as he did, she gave a convulsive heave and was expelling what was in her stomach. A trickle of water came out, that was all. But she was breathing. Huge, sobbing gasps, only her chest moving, her arms and legs still limp.

Get help. He looked around. The guy who'd been on shore was nowhere in sight. He reached for his pocket, for his phone, and even as he pulled it out, realized it was drowned, as dead as Dakota's had been.

He couldn't leave her. She was breathing now, but what if she stopped? He didn't know if that could happen. He couldn't risk it. He left the useless phone where it lay, got her under the shoulders and knees, and was running with her through the deep sand. His knee protested hard and threatened to buckle, and he wouldn't let it.

Off the beach, onto the boardwalk, then the sidewalk. Far too long a distance, and still, nobody was there.

He was at the front doors of the resort now, a blank expanse of glass. Dark inside, nobody in sight, but somebody would be here. He had full-time security. Where the hell were they? He was kicking at the glass, hitting it with his bare foot. Over and over.

Above him, the burglar alarm started an insistent clangor, the noise harsh and unrelenting. Good. That would bring someone. Dakota moaned in his arms, a protesting sound, but that was good, too. If she was hearing that racket, she was conscious.

The man came running. Not from inside. From outside. Around the corner of the resort, coming fast, young and fit, shouting. "Hey! Hey! Get out!"

Blake whirled and roared at him. "911! Ambulance! Now! Ambulance! Now!" His quarterback voice, the one that could reach the entire offense even over the din of sixty-seven thousand in Seahawks stadium.

He was shouting like fourth and goal, and the guy heard, even over the alarm. He slowed, and his hand went to his belt. He had his phone out, and he was punching buttons, making the call. A few words, and then he asked Blake, "What happened? What do I tell them?"

"Drowning. Tell them to run. Tell them *now.*" Dakota was still breathing, he thought, but her eyes were closed, her face white.

The guy finished talking, then hung up, shoved the phone back in his pocket, unlocked the front door of the resort, stripped his shirt over his head, and made a quick pad of it. "Put it under her head," he said. "I'll get a blanket."

He took off, his footsteps echoing against the stone, and Blake laid Dakota gently down on the iron-hard floor. He was shaking himself, but she wasn't, and her skin was so cold. He stripped his swim trunks off her, then the Devils T-shirt. It was torn, a huge triangular rip where she'd been caught and he'd pulled her free.

By the time he had her clothes off, the security guard was running back again, a white down comforter in his arms. He threw it over Dakota and asked, "What else?"

Blake was shoving his soaking dress pants over his hips,

pulling off his briefs along with them, then yanking off his T-shirt. He climbed under the comforter and lay on the cold stone, then pulled Dakota over him. "Come on, baby," he told her. "Climb on. Hold onto me. Come on."

She heard him, because she was trying, and her eyes had opened. Her movements were sluggish, but she was moving. Blake told the security guard, "Help me get her on top of me."

The guard did it, his movements decisive, unhesitating, not seeming to notice or care that they were both naked, and Blake thought vaguely, *Probably ex-military.* After that, the guy pulled the comforter over them both, straight over Dakota's head, and said, "I'll go out front and watch for the ambulance."

Blake said, "Yeah." Dakota's body was so cold over his, and he began to rub his hands over her back, up and down, chafing warmth back into her. He felt her begin to shiver, and he thought, *Yes. Come on. Shiver, baby. Shiver hard.*

The ambulance didn't take long. It just felt that way. The two paramedics put Dakota on a gurney, covered her with a blanket, and strapped her down, and Blake got to his feet, holding the comforter around his naked body.

Dakota was shuddering now, her teeth chattering. She looked up at him as he walked beside the gurney toward the waiting ambulance and said, "B-b-blake. Your b-b-boat."

"What?"

"It's in the l-l-lake."

The security guard had been locking the door behind them, but now he was beside Blake again. He said, "Where?"

"By the logs," Blake said. What did it matter?

"I'm on it." The guy took off.

"You n-n-need to give him a r-r-raise," Dakota said.

The paramedics were putting her into the back of the ambulance now, and Blake climbed up behind them. He smiled at her, though it felt shaky as hell, and said, "Good thought, darlin'. I'm on it."

♡♡♡

At the hospital, a low brick building on the highway, Dakota was whisked out of sight into the ER. Blake stood on the sidewalk with the paramedics, and one of them looked him over and asked, "What about you?"

"I'm good," he said. "I'm fine." His body was still trying to shake from the adrenaline, but he was used to that. If Dakota was fine, he was fine. She hadn't looked all that wonderfully fine chalk-white, with her eyes closed and an oxygen mask on her face, but that was treatment, that was all. He'd had plenty of treatment himself in his time. Somehow, though, he was discovering that it was a whole lot different to be beside the gurney instead of on it. A whole lot *worse.*

The paramedics looked at each other, then the older one said, "You can probably get them to help you out in the ER."

"I don't need help," Blake said. "I'm fine. I got wet, that's all." And had aggravated his knee, he'd found when he'd climbed down from the ambulance and felt it buckle under him, but that would settle down once he got some ice on it.

"Dude," the younger paramedic said, "you're a little bit naked."

"Oh." Blake hitched the comforter more securely around himself. He'd forgotten about that. "I'll go see if they can help me out with that. Thanks, guys." He hobbled along the sidewalk toward the main emergency entrance and headed inside.

It wasn't the big city, that was for sure. A woman was holding a toddler who clung to her and looked miserable, and an older guy was sitting with a reddening towel wadded over his hand with his wife beside him. That was it. They both looked up at his entrance. Blake nodded and made his uneven way to the nurse's desk at the rear of the room while the woman behind it, a middle-aged woman dressed in plain blue scrubs, watched his progress.

"Hi," Blake said when he got there. "My…" He had to stop a minute and think how to put it. "My girlfriend just got brought in. Dakota Savage."

"The drowning," the nurse said. She started to write something down, and Blake's heart just about stopped.

"What?" he managed to get out.

She looked up. "Near-drowning. Sorry. That's the word."

"Oh." He did his best to get hold of himself. "Uh... I'm waiting for her. Letting you know I'm here."

"Name? Phone number? And I'll need some information on her. Address, date of birth, insurance carrier."

None of which he knew. He indicated the comforter. "Seems I came here in my birthday suit. No phone. No wallet." That was still on the bedside table, back on the boat. "If somebody can loan me a pair of pants and a phone, I'll get Dakota's dad out here, and he can give you all her information. But—wait. I don't have his number. If you'll look it up for me, I'll be much obliged. Russell Matthews."

"You'll want to get somebody to look at whatever's wrong with that leg, too," she said.

"I'm fine."

She gave him the hairy eyeball. She had those half-glasses that made older ladies look scary. "You're not fine," she said flatly. "You think you're fine. It's adrenaline."

"Thanks. I'm familiar with adrenaline. Look, I'm about half crazy here. How about a pair of pants and a phone? I've got to call her dad. He needs to know. He needs to get here." He added, any momentary vestige of humor deserting him, "And I also need you to call the sheriff and get him out here, too, right now. I don't mean a deputy. I mean the sheriff."

She eyed him over the glasses some more. "Why would that be? Is there some crime here?"

"Yeah," he said. "I'd say so."

What and Who

♡

You could say that calling Russell was bad.

Not that the man said much. He just said, "I'm on my way," and hung up. But Blake stood there at the pay phone in his borrowed blue scrubs and had to lay his forehead and hands against the wall for a minute. Just for a minute. He knew what that call could have been.

After that, he made a call to his assistant—another number he'd had to ask the long-suffering nurse at the desk to look up for him.

Jennifer didn't ask him why he was calling her at nine o'clock on Saturday morning. As soon as he said her name, she asked, "What's wrong?"

"Long story. Here's what I need you to do. Find out where my boat is—should be at the resort marina somewhere, but it was loose on the lake, and security's been running it down, I hope—and get my wallet and keys from the master cabin. Bedside table. My truck's down there at the marina, too. Take it to my house and get me some clothes and shoes, all the way down to the skin, and bring everything to the hospital. I don't know where I'll be exactly, and my phone's dead, so you'll have to ask. Ask them what room Dakota Savage is in. I'll figure out a ride home for you." He gave her a couple more instructions, then added, "And, Jennifer—right now."

"I'm out the door already. Dakota? How bad? Did you get hold of her stepdad? You need me to call him?"

That wrenched him out of taking-care-of-business mode once again. He had to take a deep breath before he said, "She's going to be all right. I hope. I already called Russell."

"I'm hanging up," she said. "Driving."

Blake hung up himself, then made his stiff-legged way back to Emergency. The nurse said, "Good. You're back. The doctor wants to talk to you," and pushed a button on her phone. "Go take a seat," she told Blake as she dialed.

Another lurch of fear, another fierce effort to shove it back down. The guy with the cut hand was gone, and only his wife and the mother and toddler were still in the room. Blake didn't sit—bending his knee was going to hurt—but leaned against the wall instead and tried not to think.

It was a long ten minutes before the doctor, a youngish guy in scrubs and a stethoscope, came out of the back. "Who's with Dakota Savage?" he asked.

"Me," Blake said.

"We've admitted her," the doctor said.

Blake was about to answer, about to ask, but the automatic doors at the entrance were opening, and Russell came in. Evan was behind him, holding Gracie in a car seat. Both men's faces were set, the way a man looked when he was trying not to show the fear. Blake said, "Wait one" to the doctor and motioned the others over.

The doctor looked between the three of them and asked, "Who am I talking to?"

"Me," Blake and Russell said at once. After a second, Blake said, "Him."

"Dakota's my daughter," Russell said.

"We've admitted her," the doctor told Russ. "She's doing well, but we'll keep watching for respiratory distress for a while. If she still looks good later this afternoon, we'll discharge her.

She's on oxygen, and we've got warm IV fluids going into her, but that's standard, so not to worry. It's good the water was on the cold side, actually. That will have diverted oxygen to her organs. Her heart's sounding good, and she's breathing all right. She's coughing, but that's normal. Tell me what happened as far as the drowning. How long was she under?"

Everybody looked at Blake. He said, "She got trapped on the bottom of the lake. I saw her dive down and not come up, so I went after her. She stopped kicking right when I got there. I saw it. That must have been when she lost consciousness, but it didn't take me too long to get her out, I don't think." He explained the rest of it as quickly as he could, tried not to relive those minutes, and failed.

"Sounds like you moved fast," the doctor said. "Explains why she isn't worse off. She was lucky."

No, she wasn't, Blake thought.

The doctor left, and Evan and Russell took off to find Dakota's room. First, though, Russell asked Blake, "You OK?"

"Yeah."

Russell looked at him hard, and Blake didn't allow his gaze to shift away. Finally, Russell put a hand onto his shoulder and said, "Thanks."

"You can't say that, Russ," Evan said. "You don't know if it was an accident."

"I don't think it was," Blake said.

Evan's eyes were hard, and his face was harder. He said, "You were on the boat with her. Alone. She almost drowned. How could that happen? Dakota's a great swimmer."

"He pulled her out," Russell said. "You heard him."

"I don't get it," Evan said. "I don't buy it."

Somebody else was coming through the front door. A woman in a khaki uniform. And it wasn't the sheriff. It was a deputy.

"I don't have time for this," Blake said. "Something was wrong out there, yeah. I'm going to find out what, and I'm going to find out who. Right now, somebody needs to go sit with Dakota. That was a bad time. She needs her dad." He saw the woman at the desk beckoning them over, her crooked finger imperious, and told Russell, "The nurse over there wants Dakota's info, but whatever her insurance doesn't pay, I'm covering."

"Why's that?" Evan shot back.

"Because it was on my property," Blake said. "Because it's my responsibility."

Which meant he had things to do before he saw Dakota. He went to meet the deputy.

♡♡♡

It took him a while to get the sheriff. He was still going around with the deputy when Jennifer showed up, dressed in shorts and a T-shirt, her hair in a ponytail, a paper bag in her arms. When she came over to where Blake was still leaning against the wall, the deputy said, "Excuse me. We're not done here."

Blake said, "Sorry, but as I've mentioned, I'm not talking to you. Please call your boss."

Jennifer said, "Hi, Shari. Sorry. He's really pigheaded. You'd better just do what he says."

Shari—the deputy—said, "That's not how it works."

Jennifer said, "I know. I'm just telling you. He's polite, so you think he'll come around, but he won't. You're talking to a brick wall. Save yourself the time and trouble."

Blake wasn't sure whether to be insulted or grateful. He decided on "grateful" when the deputy said stiffly, "I'll be back in a minute," moved a ways away, and started to make a call.

"Thanks," Blake told Jennifer. He stood up straight, because it looked weak, leaning against the wall like that.

"No problem," she said. "Everything's in here. I threw in some toiletries, plus a flannel jacket and a towel once I heard what happened out at the resort. Hospitals are always cold, and shock makes you colder."

"Oh. Thanks." He hadn't realized it, but he *was* cold. He'd been cold since he'd jumped in the lake, and he'd never warmed up.

She dug in the bag, handed him a cellphone, and said, "Temporary solution. I'll order you a legit replacement once I get home, and you'll have it tomorrow. The security guard who found your boat for you—Logan—also found your phone on the beach. It was dead. You said 'dead,' but it was *really* dead."

"Did you ask him to do the other thing?"

"Yep. I did."

"Good." Blake palmed the phone and immediately felt better, less unmoored. "Dakota said I needed to give him a raise."

"You probably should. He's better than most of them you've got out there. Just out of the service."

"How do you know everything?"

"It's a gift." She handed him the paper bag. "I put a few numbers on your phone already. Mine, mainly. If you need anything else, or to reach anyone else, call me."

"Thanks." He tried to think, to focus. "About you getting home. I said I'd fix that."

He started over to the nurse's desk, but Jennifer said, "I've got it. My mom's waiting for me. One second, though." She went over to talk to the nurse herself, engaged in some lively conversation, and two minutes later, came back with an icepack and handed it to him. "Go get changed before the sheriff gets here. You're freezing. And put this on your knee and sit down, for Pete's sake. You look like you're about to collapse. Call me and tell me what the sheriff says. Otherwise, I'll be going nuts finding out from my sources."

Despite everything, Blake had to smile. "I can tell I'm going to have to give you a raise, too."

"Don't get carried away. You're already overpaying me. I don't want you to regret it."

She left, Blake got himself changed, and he felt better, or at least warmer. When he came out to the waiting room again, Milo Sawyer, the sheriff himself, was sitting in one of the uncomfortable plastic chairs beside his deputy, tapping a pen against his knee in a *rat-a-a-tat-tat* that said he was already wasting his time.

Same blonde hair, same athletic build as his relatives. Probably the same arrogance, too. Blake's antagonism flared up a notch, and he hadn't even talked to the guy yet. He was ready to take this out on somebody, though, and it could start now.

No, it couldn't. *Dial it back, or you'll get nowhere.* "Hi, Sheriff," he said, limping across the room—Jennifer was right again, damn it—and putting out a hand. "Thanks for coming. We've got a problem."

Sawyer shook hands, but he didn't look happy about it. "That's what you said. My deputies are fully empowered to act, and around here, we don't treat people different just because they have a few dollars."

Yeah, right, Blake *didn't* say. *Tell that to Dakota.*

"Maybe you'll tell me what went on out there," Sawyer said. "All I heard was, Dakota Savage was on your boat, and she ended up half-drowned. Which is what Deputy Johnson is here to talk to you about."

Blake stared at him, for once lost for words. It seemed Evan wasn't the only one who could put a different spin on this. "Maybe you'd better ask Dakota what happened," he finally said.

"Uh-huh. Could be we've thought of that already. Could be we're doing it, too. This is law enforcement, and it's our job."

"You've got somebody up there with her, harassing her. She was *drowning.*"

Blake went to stand, and his stupid leg wouldn't do it. He grabbed hold of it to haul it up, but Sawyer snapped, "Sit down. You got me out here because you had something to say. That's good, because I've got something to ask. If Dakota's story matches yours, you've got nothing to worry about."

Blake sank back down and held the ice pack onto his knee, forcing himself not to grit his teeth. It wasn't from the pain. It was from the frustration, but Sawyer wouldn't know that. "Good," he said. "Go."

Sawyer asked, and he answered. The sheriff ran him through the sequence of events one way, and then he did it another. Over and over, trying to trip him up. The deputy took notes, and Blake knew it was to check his version against Dakota's. None of it was welcome. This wasn't what he needed the sheriff to be focusing on.

Sawyer finally said, "I'll get back to you if I have any more questions. That's it for now."

Blake said, "No. It's not. I did it your way, and now I need you to listen. Dakota got caught on something under those logs that shouldn't have been there. I need to know what it was. I need it out of there, obviously, but I also need to know how it got there."

"That's why you brought me out here?" the sheriff asked. "Because there's something on the lakebed that hung her up, and that's a criminal act?"

"Those logs were only put in place a month ago," Blake said, holding onto his temper. "There was nothing on the lakebed then. Nothing that could grab somebody the way she was grabbed. I had to pull hard to get her out of there. How would that happen, right under the logs at the edge of my swimming area? That's too big a coincidence."

"Uh-huh." Sawyer didn't sound convinced. "We'll take a look."

Blake wasn't going to be able to stifle his impatience much longer. "I'd appreciate it mightily if you'd take that look right now. As in *right* now. I've got a resort opening up in about ten days. It's going to bring a whole lot of money to this town, and we've already hired a whole lot of folks, too. If somebody gets hurt, they're going to sue. If it's bad enough, it could even close us down, and that's a lot of households losing their jobs. A lot of voters."

Sawyer's stare was hard. "So this is about you not getting your ass sued. I should've known. I'm surprised you haven't taken it on yourself to find out what happened, since you're so ready to think it's a conspiracy."

"I hear there's a thing called chain of evidence," Blake said. "Whoever did this—I don't want anything getting in the way of sending his ass to jail. Excuse my language," he added belatedly to the deputy.

She said, "I've heard the word."

"But that's why," Blake continued, "I've had a guy watching that shoreline since it happened. Making sure nobody tampers with whatever's out there. I've noticed news spreads fast around here."

"Or covering *your* ass," Sawyer said as if Blake hadn't spoken. "Making sure we'll think something out there *did* catch Dakota up, and you didn't try to drown her yourself."

Blake breathed out the steam. "You go on and think that if you want. Dakota's up there telling your guy what happened to her. Not sure how you'll get around that. Meanwhile, I want somebody out there investigating, and I want them now. I want video. I want analysis. If I don't get it, I'll do my own investigating, and I'll spread it around that it's because you wouldn't. I don't think that'll go over big."

"You don't threaten me," Sawyer said. "I've been sheriff here for seven years. I've got a reputation. I've got history. You've got nothing but a big mouth and too much money."

"Yep." Blake didn't try to stand up this time. Falling over wouldn't look good. "But I do have those."

♡♡♡

When the sheriff and deputy finally left, taking his brand-new phone number with them along with a reluctant agreement to call him with an update, Blake thought, *Dakota,* and hauled on his knee again to stand. He was the only one in the waiting room now, the lady with the toddler having disappeared sometime during his clothing change.

He went over to the nurse behind the desk again, said, "I

want to guarantee that payment for Dakota's bills," and pulled his wallet out of his back pocket.

She took his credit card and said, "The doctor will see you now."

"Huh? I don't need to see the doctor."

She inclined her head toward the back of the room. Blake turned around, and there the guy was, his arms folded across his chest. Same guy, with no customers. Dangerous.

"Yeah," the doctor said, "I know. It's just a flesh wound. Come back here and let me take a look at it anyway."

Blake said, "I know this knee. It's my knee."

The doctor said, "You're not making a whole lot of sense right now. Get back here before I decide I need to MRI your brain."

Blake went, which didn't turn out to be any more fun than he'd expected, and ended up the way he'd expected, too. After a whole lot of prodding and manipulation that upped the pain quotient way too much, he'd been told it was his MCL, which he could already tell, and that he probably needed another MRI "to be on the safe side," which he already knew. He'd answered, "Yeah, I figured you'd say that," with only a moderate amount of sarcasm.

He came out with some pain meds—carefully non-narcotic—his knee wrapped in an elastic bandage, and a couple more ice packs. He'd thought about refusing the meds, but on the way over to the main wing of the hospital, he stopped at a drinking fountain and swallowed the first pill, because damn, that hurt.

He was going to be crashing soon. But first, he needed to see Dakota. He needed to see her bad.

Security. Or Not.

♡

When she saw Blake walking through the door like a peg-legged sailor, all Dakota could say was, "Oh, no. Blake."

He stopped. "What?"

"Your leg. What happened?"

"Nothing happened."

"What do you mean, nothing happened? I can *see* that something happened. How?"

She was trying to yell at him, but her chest hurt, and she couldn't. She was all over the place, and it was scaring her. When she'd been lying here, trying to figure it out, and the deputy had come in and sent Russ and Evan away, and she'd realized what he was asking her, if Blake had tried to *drown* her... she'd wanted to shout then, too. She'd wanted to demand to see Blake.

Had she done that, though? No. Instead, she'd cried. She'd started sobbing so hard, in fact, that Russell had come bursting in like the posse, with Evan right behind him, still holding Gracie. Savior with a baby carrier. After that, the deputy had taken her over it again and again, and she'd nearly cried again, remembering her terror. She'd wanted to be strong, and she hadn't been able to be strong enough.

The deputy hadn't sounded like he believed her, no matter how many times she told him. Now, Blake was here, but he was hurt? She lay in the bed, immobilized by the IV in her hand, the clip on her finger, and the stupid oxygen tube in her nose, and tried to explain it to him. "You didn't come, and they said… and now your *leg*…"

"She's going off again, Russ," Evan muttered from her left side.

"Yep." Russell heaved himself to his feet on her right. "Come on. Let's go get breakfast. We'll bring back some coffee for you all. Maybe a cinnamon roll. Cinnamon roll sound good, Blake?"

"Dakota, though," Evan said. He'd stood, too, with Gracie, who was still in her carrier. Three men hovering around, and nobody was even giving her a friggin' *hug*? Couldn't they *tell* that was what she needed?

Russell said, "I guess Blake can take over for a little while. He needs the chair anyway."

Dakota wiped her face with a tissue. She couldn't even be a drama queen when she'd almost drowned, apparently. Not if there was nobody to listen. The thought was making her tear up again, stupid as it was, or maybe that was Blake. Why was he just standing there?

Because she had a plastic tube in her nose, which was also running. Her hair was like seaweed, and she'd gotten stuck in his lake, somehow, diving too deep, had nearly drowned herself, and had practically gotten him arrested for attempted murder. Those could be a few powerful reasons.

It had been such a wonderful night, and it had turned into a nightmare. Blake had hurt his leg again getting her out, and his beautiful boat…

He came to sit beside her, ignoring the others, took her hand, and said, his voice so tender, "Come on, baby. Don't cry. It's all right. It's all over."

That was all it took. She was weeping for good. Russ was practically hauling Evan out the door, and she was crying all over Blake. "Sorry," she got out through the tears, then started to cough and couldn't stop. Blake was on the bed, his arm behind her, looking panicked.

She stopped coughing at last, picked up the water glass from her table, and took some sips. "It's just… it's… sorry. It's so *stupid*." She put the glass down. "I can't… seem to keep it together." She tried to laugh, and blew her nose again. "They kept asking me these questions. They thought you *drowned* me. I kept saying, no, I got tangled up. But I couldn't explain it well enough, because I still can't figure out what happened. And your leg. What's wrong with your leg?"

"Aw, baby," Blake said. He got another tissue out and did some more mopping up on her face. She was lovely, obviously. "No. I'm all good, and you didn't do anything stupid. My knee sure is feelin' it, though. Seems to me you could scoot over a little and let a guy hold you for a minute. Then I could put ice on this knee, and I could pretend I wasn't resting too."

He didn't seem to care about the state of her hair, because he was smoothing his hand down it, kissing the top of her head. And she might have cried some more.

"Yeah," he said when her head was on his chest and his fingers were threaded through hers, holding tight. "That was a bad deal. You must've fought so hard, though. When I found you, you were still kicking. Still trying. Man, I was… it was bad."

There were the tears, welling again. She said, "I thought…" She had to breathe the terror back, because it kept rising, panicking her as if it were all happening right now. Her chest was raw, her throat like sandpaper. "I thought I was going to die. I would have died. I was too far down. They keep saying I was lucky, but I wasn't lucky. It was you. But the deputy wouldn't tell me what happened. He kept asking, 'And what did Blake do then?' How should I know what you did? I said, 'He carried me.' That's all I knew. I was stuck, and I couldn't hold my breath anymore, and the next thing I knew, you were carrying me. But *why?* It felt like a net, but how could a net trap me like that? Why would it be there anyway?"

"I don't know," Blake said. "I'm going to find out."

"And the part about you... I couldn't *believe* he was asking me that. I kept saying, no, I was *stuck*, and it was like he didn't believe me. He kept asking things like, 'How long had you two been swimming?' 'Whose idea was it?' and 'Where was he holding you when you went under?'"

"Shh." Blake was still smoothing her hair.

"You think I'm exaggerating. I'm not. They thought you were trying to *kill* me. I'm not *imagining* it."

"Dakota. Stop." His voice was so commanding, she jumped. He blew out a breath. "Sorry. I'm trying not to get you any more agitated, but I'm all out of ideas. Look. They asked. We answered. That part's done."

"Oh." She swallowed, and it hurt. "OK." He was right. She was crying all over him. Way too much emotion. She should... she could...

He ran a hand through his hair, which was sticking up already. He wasn't groomed either, she realized. He was as tired as she was, and he felt just as bad.

"Oh," she said. "You were scared, too."

"Yeah. I was. And I guess you need to—I don't know, work it out, cry it out—but I hate it. I hate that it happened to you, and that I can't fix it. I hate that I didn't get to you faster."

"Oh." It took her a minute to process that. "I felt the same thing, I think. Russell said you rescued me, and then I saw your leg, and all those questions... I was so worried."

"Well, we can stop now. We're both here to tell the tale." His arm was so firm around her, and he'd brought the other arm around her front, too, and that was even better, being held that close. She settled her head against his chest, and his hand was there again, stroking over her hair. They were quiet for a while, and then he said, "It was kinda hard, though, you know, because there I was, trying to explain why I wouldn't have drowned you, and I couldn't say the biggest reason. You could say I was hamstrung. Yep, that's exactly what I was.

Hamstrung."

Somehow, she was smiling. "How come?"

"How could I say that I couldn't possibly have drowned you after I'd had the best sex since... well, for a mighty long time?"

She opened her eyes, which had somehow closed. "Hey."

"Well. Come on. My first time, when I couldn't imagine how anything in this world could possibly feel that good, and all I wanted was to do it again?" He sighed. "Yeah. And then there was last night. Nope, not drowning you."

She was smiling again. "Except now we're both wounded." Then she stopped smiling. "And your beautiful boat. I forgot about that."

"Boat's all good." He yawned hugely. "Rescued, just like us. Yep. Luckily, we're both tough. Except I might need to take a little nap here, darlin'. I took this pill. Maybe you could snuggle up, get me comfortable. Be my security blanket."

He did sound sleepy, and she could feel the rumble of his voice from deep in his chest, right there under her cheek. It was all very... soothing. "Mm. Maybe." She'd been cold for so long, but the heated blankets, the warmed fluid dripping into her veins, and Blake's body against hers... Yeah. She was warmer.

His arm twitched around her, his breathing deepened, and he'd dropped off, just like the night before. Because she was his security blanket, the way he'd been hers last night, the way he was now.

She knew it couldn't actually feel the same to him as it did to her, but she didn't need to think about it right now. She could go to sleep.

Unfamiliar Territory

♡

Blake was underwater, and he couldn't see. He was groping in the dark, feeling wispy strands under his hands. It was hair, he realized with a surge of terror. Dakota's hair. But he couldn't see her, and he couldn't grab her.

She was drowning, and he had to get her out. She was dying. He couldn't find her. Every time his hands touched something—her hair, her shirt—it drifted away before he could grab it. He was lunging in the water, frantic, his lungs bursting. He needed to breathe. He couldn't find Dakota. He couldn't get her.

Then he saw her. Her face, white in the dark-green water, her dark hair streaming around it. Her eyes open. Staring.

Her mouth was gaping open. Because she was dead.

"Huh!" He woke up with a start and sat up straight, his heart galloping like it would burst through his chest.

The shout had come from him. He wasn't underwater, he was in a hospital bed. And Dakota was beside him, sitting up herself, looking sleepy and confused but absolutely alive, pushing her hair out of her face.

She was here. Right here. She was fine.

"What?" she asked. "What's wrong? Your... your knee?"

Her voice was raspy, and she coughed a few times. See? More life.

"Oh." Blake felt stupid and fuzzy. It was the drugs. "No. Bad dream, that's all."

"Do you want a drink of water?" she asked.

He almost laughed, it was so prosaic after the horror of his nightmare. "Sure. Thanks."

She reached over for it and handed it to him, and when he'd drunk from the straw, she took the cup from him and drank herself. It was so unexpectedly intimate, and something in that sharing, and in seeing how pale her face was, the tubes and wires, the mess of her hair, was making his chest tighten.

"Sorry, baby," he said. "Wrecked your nap."

"No," she said. "That's all right. Bad dreams are the worst."

He lay down with her again. She came right back into his arms, and it was so much better. "Except maybe good dreams," he said. "You ever have those?"

"Like when you're talking to somebody you love, and you wake up smiling, and then you realize they're gone? Yeah." She sighed. "Those can be even worse. They feel so good, and they're not true."

"Oh. Well, yeah, that *would* be worse. I was more thinking like you're playing football, and you wake up and you're not."

"I suppose that would be bad, too," she said. "Maybe not quite the same, though."

Eventually, he fell asleep again, and when he woke the next time, it was to the sound of voices. A nurse, he found when he blinked awake, who was switching the IV bag on Dakota's stand.

"Oh," Blake said. "Sorry. I'll just…" He got his good leg on the floor and himself in the chair.

"No problem," the nurse said. She had a thermometer in Dakota's ear now. "We're usually one to a customer, but we make exceptions."

Dakota asked, "What time is it?"

"Almost two," the nurse said, and Blake blinked again.

Dakota said, "That was a while. Our nap."

"It was," the nurse said. "I've been in here twice. That's good, though. You might as well sleep. Sleep is healing, and being in the hospital's boring otherwise."

"Do you know where my stepdad is?" Dakota asked. "Russell? I don't have my phone, or… or anything."

"He went home to get you some clothes, since you're likely to be released soon." The nurse wrote something on Dakota's chart. "Do you need to use the bathroom?"

"Uh…" Dakota glanced at Blake again. "Yes. Please."

"Good. That's what we like to hear. I'll give you a hand. It can be a little bit of a production."

Dakota hesitated. "Uh… Blake?"

"Yeah?" he asked.

"This hospital gown is sort of, uh… do you think you could wait for me? Outside?"

"Oh." He considered pointing out that she'd been naked, or close to it, during most of the time they'd spent together in the past eighteen hours or so, but decided it wouldn't be too helpful. Women were weird about things like this. "Sure," he said instead. "I'll go down and grab some coffee and something to eat, and get you something, too, if you want. You must be hungry."

"All right," she said. "Or you could go home. I'm all right."

That one rocked him back. "Do you want me to go home? Want to be alone?" The nurse was still waiting, but too bad. He needed to know.

"Oh. No," she said, looking flustered. "I'd rather you stayed. But you don't have to."

"Yep. I do." He reached over, took her cheek in his hand, gave her a kiss on the mouth, and said, "I definitely do. Back in half an hour. Don't leave without me."

When he got back up there with a cup of coffee and a sandwich for her, Russell was there, and Dakota was dressed. Baggy T-shirt and shorts, which he'd bet wouldn't have been what she'd have chosen.

"You hear anything?" Russ asked him when they'd settled in again. "About what happened?"

"Nope. Blake sipped at his own coffee. "Called the sheriff, though, and he said he'd come by later. Said they're working on it."

"Milo Sawyer. He's got a my-way-or-the-highway streak in him."

"I noticed."

"No mean streak, though. Not like some of the Sawyers. Come on back with Dakota and me if you want. Stay for dinner, watch the ball game. It's no good going home alone after a day like this, when you're shook up. Better to be with friends."

Blake did that, because it sounded good to him, too. That was why he was eating meatloaf and mashed potatoes in Russell's kitchen, his leg propped on a chair, when the sheriff finally showed up.

"Offer you some meatloaf, Sawyer?" Russell asked as he brought the sheriff into the kitchen.

"This is an official visit," Sawyer said.

"It's also dinnertime," Russell said, "and these two have had kind of a rough day. Besides, mashed potatoes don't heat up good. There's a whole bunch more in the pot. You're welcome to it."

Sawyer looked like he wanted to refuse, but also like he wanted meatloaf. "Thanks," he said. "If you've got enough. My wife's got us on this diet. Mediterranean. You don't eat red meat."

"Huh." Russell dished up a hefty plate of meat and potatoes, added a healthy spoonful of green-bean casserole with fried onions, and put it in front of the sheriff. "Can't say I'd care for that."

Sawyer took a bite of meatloaf, potatoes, and gravy, then sighed with the contentment of a man deprived. "When I get hungry, she tells me to eat a handful of nuts. I don't want a handful of nuts. I want a steak."

"Well, yeah," Russell said.

There was silence for a while as everybody concentrated on Russell's cooking, but finally, Sawyer pushed back his chair and said, "So—we found something out there."

Blake's neck muscles, which had been tense ever since Sawyer walked in, tightened some more, and he looked over at Dakota and saw the same thing. He put a hand on hers and said, "Shoot."

Sawyer opened the manila folder he'd set beside him on the table, which Blake had been trying not to eye as they ate, and pulled out some color pictures. "Gill net," he said. "Caught up in those logs, some holes ripped in it, nothing bigger than a human head, weights at the bottom like you'd have. It was a mess. Some fish hooks caught in it, too." He slid a close-up along the table to Blake. "Take a look at this."

Blake said, "Treble hook." The three-pronged hook was laid alongside a ruler. "What size is that?"

Russell reached a hand for the picture, frowned at it, and said, "That's a No. 1. Got to be. Rolled-in point. Could be a salmon hook, yeah. That's for a good-sized catch, and one that puts up a fight. What's that in it? Feather dress, or what's left of it?"

"Hair," Sawyer said. "Torn out at the roots."

Dakota put a hand to her head. "Oh," she said faintly, looking white again. "That's why… my scalp hurts at the front here."

A catch that puts up a fight. A woman, caught in a net made of nylon fishing line, hard to see, impossible to tear. A woman hooked by the hair, by the shirt, every twist and turn of her body catching her more securely, like a salmon set on the hook.

Russell's mouth twisted as if he were imagining the same thing. "How many of those in the net?"

"Almost ten hooks," Sawyer said. "Most of them trebles. About six feet of ripped-up gill net, caught between the chain and the log in a couple spots, weighted at the bottom."

"That's not an accident," Blake said. He kept his voice level, because his hand was still on Dakota's, and Dakota didn't need to see his rage. She needed to know this was getting taken care of. She also needed to see whoever had done it caught.

Or maybe that was him.

"No," Sawyer said. "Of course, gill nets aren't legal in the lake, or anywhere around here except on the reservation. The Indians… they make their own rules."

"Doesn't mean nobody uses 'em," Russell said. "And all those hooks in there? No. Were those tied with knots?"

"Yep," Sawyer said, and Dakota shuddered.

"How do we find out who did it?" Blake asked.

Sawyer looked at him, impassive. "You got cameras on that area?"

"No." Something Blake would remedy tomorrow.

"You'd do it from a boat," Russell said. "At night, maybe."

"Not at night," Blake said. "You'd need lights to do it, and we have security patrols walking the property. They'd see lights. No. It'd be somebody in a fishing boat, a small one. Outboard motor, and you stop for a minute when nobody's around and wedge that net in. A rowboat, even. A kayak. Could be anything. Sunday, early in the morning. Who's going to see that?"

"We can ask," Sawyer said. "We'll be interviewing everybody on your security team."

"You've got it," Blake said. "Whatever you need."

"More likely to get to it a different way, though," Sawyer said. "Who'd want to mess with the resort, or with you? Obvious place to start is the no-resort pukes who put up a fight early on. The Earth Firsters who spike trees so the logger's chainsaw skips and he cuts off his hand. They care more about trees than people. A pig is a dog is a boy, and killing a frog is murder. We'll be talking to them."

Blake scratched his cheek. This was a whole lot more cooperative than he'd expected Sawyer to be, but he needed to go easy. "Maybe. But I made a big donation, jumped through a lot of hoops to defuse that kind of protest. I donated that mountain, too, and I'm building that trail."

Sawyer snorted. "Think that's going to convince them? They're fanatics. They don't want a trail. They want wilderness. The only good land use is *no* land use. Any other names for me?"

"I fired Jerry Richards as my head of security a few weeks back," Blake said. "He didn't take it well, and I hear he hasn't found a job since, and that he blames me for it."

Sawyer nodded. "I heard that. And, yeah, it didn't look good for him. I heard not everybody on his team was happy about it, either."

"Tough," Blake said.

"Of course," Sawyer said, "Jerry's an ex-cop."

Russell muttered, "Which means what," which earned him a stare from Sawyer.

"And," Blake said, tightening his hold on Dakota's hand, "there's your nephew Steve. I fired him, too, or the next best thing. I've had a couple run-ins with him since, and a lot more recently than Richards. Hostilities haven't ebbed, let's say." Dakota's hand jerked under his, but he didn't look at her.

If Milo knew about Dakota and his nephew, he didn't show it. "Like what?"

"Took his team off the job painting the resort," Blake said. He'd bet Sawyer knew that. "I gave that job to Dakota and her partner." He'd bet he knew that, too.

"Uh-huh." Now, Milo *was* looking at Dakota.

"A couple weeks ago, I questioned him about Russell's accident last year," Blake said. "That happened on my job, but he was the contractor. He didn't like the question. And then, the other night—last night, I guess—he was nasty to Dakota at a party out at the Schaefers', and I called him out on it. Him and his wife."

"Nasty how? Called them out how?" Milo asked.

"They made personal comments. I made personal comments back."

"Steve's a good man," Milo said, not sounding nearly as

relaxed as he had been. "And last night? There's no time in there for something like this. Somebody thought this out. Anyway, Steve? He's always done well, kept his nose pretty clean. High school, quarterback of the football team. College, fraternity and all that. Business, too. He's got a clean record, other than a traffic ticket or two when he was a kid. I've known him his whole life, obviously."

"Uh-huh," Blake said. "Football players can do some bad stuff. I should know."

Milo shrugged. "He did the usual dumb things, sure. Some parties, some drinking, some wildcatting around like every young guy does, but nothing since then. He's still with his high-school girlfriend, and that says something. I don't see him setting a mantrap, no matter how pissed he was."

Dakota's hand was rigid under Blake's now. He didn't look at her. He said, "You asked who'd want to do it. Those two are at the top of my list. I'd appreciate it if you'd check them out."

Dakota spoke at last, and now, Blake was the one who was tensing. But all she said was, "I think you should ask yourself something else, Blake. If somebody did this, what else might they have done? What might they do?"

"Obviously," he said, "I'll increase security and add cameras. I've already thought of that."

"No," she said. "I mean, those are good ideas, but what else could they have set up for when the resort opens? This might have looked accidental, especially after a couple more months. If somebody had been caught by that net, or been snagged by a hook, maybe gotten scratched—who knows how raggedy and accidental that net might have looked by then? If the point was to have accidents happen at your site, though, what else?"

Blake started to speak, then caught himself and asked, "Do you have any ideas?" Sawyer shifted restlessly, but Blake didn't pay any attention to that.

"Yes," Dakota said. "Usually, people have one sort of... one kind of focus, when they're planning something. I mean..." She was looking agitated again, and Blake squeezed her hand to encourage her. "If you get an idea to mess with people's swimming experience, you aren't going to go put… I don't know, triplines across hiking trails. Bombs. Whatever. It's not the same thing. Those wouldn't look accidental, ever, and they're too extreme. Plus, with swimming, it's hidden. That's what happened to me, right? The danger was hidden. And it would be hard to booby-trap the resort itself, or someplace where you have security walking, anyplace on the grounds. I worked out there for weeks. You have housekeepers in and out of the rooms. Maintenance people. Waiters. A security focus. They'd notice, or they'd trip the booby-trap before you even opened. So what I'd look for would be what else they could do around the beach. What could they hide? What would look like an accident?"

"Like what?" Blake asked. Dakota hesitated, and he said, "Come on. Brainstorm. You're the one here who does all the swimming. You'd know."

"Two things," she said, "that occur to me. Besides something in some other spot on the logs, of course. One's nastier, but they're both bad."

"Tell us," Blake said.

"All right. First: the rocks. The ones that I jumped off, when you saw me. You have those posted 'No Trespassing,' because of course it isn't exactly safe, but people are still going to jump. To some people, that sign will mean 'Come on in.' What if somebody dumped—oh, say, an old, ripped-up set of box springs out there, with some of the springs broken? Or something else metal, something spiky? A person could jump in that wrong spot and be caught, stuck on a spike. They could be hurt badly, could even die, and you'd never find out who did it in a million years. It would look like an accident, too."

Blake felt sick. Sawyer whispered something that sounded like "Jesus," but he made a note.

"The other thing," Dakota said. "Not as bad, but more likely, maybe. Easier to do, too. You *could* do it at night, because it's easy as can be, even without a light. What if you broke a beer bottle and buried the pieces in the sand of the beach? Especially if it was in the shallow water? You put it just under the surface. What are the chances that somebody steps on that on your opening weekend? Every swimmer knows that's your most likely injury, stepping on something sharp. You have that happen to a couple guests, their feet sliced open? Kids? Babies, even? You wouldn't kill anybody. It's not a shark attack. It's not a drowning. But everybody sees it. Everybody knows it."

Sawyer was staring at her, but Dakota said, "Somebody who was willing to put that net up with those hooks—that's what they're going for. Who sits on those logs at the edges? Kids. Ten, eleven years old. Adults aren't messing around out there. They're swimming laps, or they're holding their toddlers in the water. It'd be kids. And it's teenagers who jump off the rocks, too. It's always worse when things happen to kids."

Blake said, "I'll get on it. I've got nine days." He was sick to his stomach. Teenagers? *Babies?*

"Heavy equipment," Russell said. "Get a couple front-end loaders to turn up that sand on the beach. Have some guys watching for broken glass, raking the sand. It'll take a while, but if it's there, you'll find it."

"And do it in the water, too," Dakota said. "They'd do it close in, not far out. The other one's easier. Hire a couple people with SCUBA gear to go around by the rocks, and anywhere else people might jump."

"Got it," Blake said. "And I'm asking myself why I didn't stick with sports bars."

"Oh, I don't know," Dakota said, her tone dry as dust. "I hear people can have accidents in those, too."

Sawyer inhaled, a sharp sound, and Blake said, "You're right again." He looked at Sawyer. "What else?"

"Nothing. I've got what I need." He stood up, collecting his printouts and shoving them back into the folder. "Thanks for the meatloaf, Russell. Orbison, I'd like a word with you."

"Sure." Blake shoved himself out of the chair and made his stiff-legged way to the door. Sawyer looked at him measuringly and said, "Front porch, I think," so they did that.

Blake started it. "I realize I came on a little strong this morning. Maybe too strong."

"Yeah. You did. But then, men can get that way when it comes to women."

Just like that, the tension was back. "You're right," Blake said. "I'm sensitive about Dakota. Especially when somebody tries to kill her."

"Seems to me that you could have some prejudices. But there are two sides to every story, and Dakota and Russell—they've got an agenda. Dakota might have said something about Steve, but plenty of people have said something about *her*. She didn't have a good reputation when she was younger. Sexually. Of course, it's not a crime for a girl to get around. The boys are happy enough about it at the time, but they do tend to talk. And, yeah, Steve might have talked, but that's not a crime either, or I'd have closed down the locker room at the high school a long time ago. And he's got no record at all. No safety record, no police record."

"No," Blake said. "There aren't two sides to every story. Sometimes, there's one side. I'm asking you, man to man. If you can't tell your department to question your nephew, say so. He sure-enough hates my guts. There's nobody who hates them more, and that's saying something."

"I'll do my job," Sawyer said, and if Blake was stiff, so was he. "I'm still putting my money on the tree huggers. If you find something else out there, let me know."

He left. Not an enemy, and not a friend. But at least a sheriff. At least that.

Spectator Sports

♡

Dakota watched as Blake limped back into the kitchen. He didn't sit down, though, just leaned up against the wall of the breakfast nook. Trying to make it look casual, like admitting his knee hurt would destroy his manhood. She knew all about that. She lived with Russell.

"Let me guess," she said, getting up and starting to clear the table. "The sheriff's concerned that you're getting yourself into bad company."

"Now, why would you think that?" Blake asked.

"Yeah, right." She began to scrape plates. It was no surprise, and it shouldn't bother her. Blake wouldn't have heard anything new. He'd already heard it all from her. And if knowing that he'd probably been out there hearing Steve Sawyer's version of it, what he'd probably said about her, hurt all the way down in her chest? Her chest already hurt.

"You know what I'm realizing?" Blake asked after a moment. "How somebody can turn the tables just by saying it's so. Somebody does wrong by you the way Sawyer has, and he flips it all the way around, so you're the one with a grudge and he's the victim."

"You just realizing that?" Russell asked, even as Dakota

turned to face Blake. She made a cutting-off motion with her hand, trying to signal to him. *Stop.*

Maybe Blake got it, because he said, "I'm a slow learner, I guess. I should take off. It's been a long day."

Dakota said, "There are stairs to your bedroom. A lot of them."

"Yep."

She hesitated, looking at Russ. He said, "I thought you were sticking around to watch the ball game, Blake."

"And if you go home, you'll have to get your own ice," Dakota said, then thought, *Well, that was lame.*

Blake scratched his cheek. "That's true."

Russell pulled himself up from the table. "Game's on right now. And if all this dancing around is because Dakota doesn't want to ask you to spend the night in front of me and you don't want to say it either, you can both stop. Last I checked, everybody here was full-grown, and everybody had a real bad day, too. I suggest you quit pussyfooting around, Dakota, and ask the man to stay with you. He needs to be sitting down with that leg up, and putting some ice on it, too. He might as well do it watching baseball with me, and then he might as well go to bed with you. He's going to want to make sure you're feeling OK, and you're going to want him to, so just go on and ask him."

Blake was laughing, and if Dakota had been the blushing kind, she'd have been doing it. "You're invited," she said, knowing she sounded stiff but unable to change it. "No obligation. If you'd rather go home, that's fine."

"Now, darlin'," Blake said, "why ever would I rather go home, especially when I've got my toothbrush and everything, thanks to Jennifer? I'll be out in one minute, Russ," he added.

Russell nodded and took off with Bella, as always, right behind. Blake waited until the door shut, then said, "Ground rules."

"What?" All the warm fuzzies she'd felt with him since the night before vanished. "You don't get to set rules."

"Sure I do. Sure *we* do. Every game needs rules. Here's my Rule One. Tell me the truth. I'm a lousy guesser. If you want me to go home, say, 'Blake, honey, I'm real tired. I almost drowned today, and I don't feel like spending my night helping you out with your bad knee and bad dreams. Come back when you've got something to offer.' And I'll say 'OK' and go. I'm not what you'd call sensitive. I can take it."

"I'm not going to say that." She'd started on the dishes again, and she'd started to smile, too. "What, I only want you if you can perform? And who says you're not sensitive? Who was that guy holding me today so I wouldn't be scared?"

"Nah. The holding was for me. And what do you mean, 'if I can perform?' I can perform fine. Just because I don't do it when a woman's in a hospital bed coughing her lungs out, that doesn't mean I can't."

She was laughing. "I take back the 'not sensitive' thing. Your knee hurts, though."

"In case you didn't notice, that isn't the essential equipment."

"All right. Now I know. I probably do feel too bad tonight, though. I just want to lie down again, but I'd rather lie down with you."

"See, now? How hard was that? Now tell me what I wasn't supposed to say to Russ."

She started to wipe the counters. It was too hard to look at him, even now, and say this. "He doesn't know about Steve. About what he did to me. I don't want him to."

"I'm going to ask why not," Blake said, "You can tell me it's none of my business if you want. If it's because you think Russ would think differently about you, I think you're wrong."

"I don't think so. At least I hope I don't. But I think he could try to kill Steve. And I mean that."

"I think you're right. I know I want to."

"So don't say anything."

"I've got it." He reached into the freezer and pulled out a new ice pack. "You going to come lie on the couch with me?"

"I'll be reading a book if I do. I'm not a baseball fan. Not a football fan, either, I hate to admit."

"There won't be a quiz," he said.

♡♡♡

Blake didn't make it through the whole game. Maybe because he could tell Dakota was tired.

All right, that wasn't it. It was because he watched it lying on the couch with her basically on top of him, and how could a man take that for very long?

He'd started out all right, lying down, his bad leg propped on a pillow on the coffee table, and Dakota sitting up beside him, resting against his good knee. But then she seemed to get tired, because she was sliding on down so her back was against his front and her head was on his chest. He had to do something with his hand, so he rested it on her belly.

Unfortunately, she'd changed before she'd come out to join him and Russ, and she had her hair loose and was wearing this soft little black cotton dress that he guessed was a nightgown. He could feel that belly button ring right through it, and it was riding up enough that he could see a whole lot of toned brown thigh, too. She was reading her book, because she was turning pages, and Blake had to watch the game, and even comment on it to Russell.

That is, until Dakota sighed and shifted position one too many times, managing to rub up against him once again while she did it. He put his hand on her thigh, and the dress rode up a little more, and…

Enough was enough. He gave her a shove. "Come on, wild thing. Time for me to get to bed."

"Oh. Sure." She got to her feet, flashing a whole lot more leg, and he wondered how the sight of a woman's skirt sliding up her thigh could be so damn sexy.

"Night, Dad," she said, leaning over to give Russell a kiss, which showed Blake a little more.

"Night," Russell said, his eyes on the screen. "Now go on. Count's three and two."

Blake stopped at the bathroom and said, "Ten minutes. I need a shower. And, darlin', I don't want to be telling you what to do, being as how you hate it and all, but seems I just can't help it. You'd better be in that bed when I get there, and you get bonus points if there's nothing underneath that little dress."

"Bonus points?" she asked, her hand on her hip, frowning at him from behind those hot-librarian glasses. "Do you give out the points? And do you get to order me around?"

He grinned, because that was just what she did to him. And then he gave her a hard little slap on the butt that felt too good, watched her jump, said, "Oh, yeah. I do. Ten minutes," and shut the bathroom door.

He took a pill first off, because he didn't want to be thinking about pain, and then he took a shower. Jennifer hadn't packed his razor, so Dakota was going to get a little beard burn tonight, but he was guessing she might not hate that, either.

When he opened the door of the bedroom, she was there. Glasses off, hair loose, and under the covers. Her cheek was resting on her folded hands, her eyes on the door. And when he shut it, she pushed the covers back, walked across the bed on her knees to him, and said, "I think you might need a little help tonight. Being incapacitated and all."

"Uh… sure," he said. "Help would be good."

She smiled, slow and wicked, and his heart was already starting to beat harder, even before she got her hands under his T-shirt and pulled it up his body, touching him more than was strictly necessary along the way. She got it to his shoulders, then said, "On the other hand… you can probably take it from there." She was stroking her palms over his chest, down his sides, and leaning forward and beginning to kiss his chest while he wrenched his shirt over his head in one big hurry.

Soft, feathery kisses, soft female hands lighting him up everywhere they touched, and then she was licking over his nipple and closing in on it, and he went all the way to hard, just like that.

He said, "Ah…" and then had to suck in a breath, because she was going to work on him for real with hands and tongue and teeth. "I have some… jeans on, too. Got a… bad knee."

"Mm," she said, licking down his midsection, then back up again to his chest, like he was her ice-cream cone and she was going to eat him up. "You taste too good, though. You might have to wait awhile."

"Dakota…" he groaned. "No. I need it… ah… faster."

She didn't even answer. "Standing up's good for you. I noticed that."

She was on her feet, then, pushing him against the wall. She wasn't going to have it all her own way, though, whatever she thought. He had his hands in that soft black material and was pulling her nightgown right up, and he was enjoying what was under it a whole lot.

"Baby," he said with a sigh, "you have got the prettiest body."

Points for her. She wasn't wearing anything underneath. Just sweet curves and soft skin, and once he had her nightgown off, he had his hands on all of it.

"Not your turn," she whispered against his neck before she bit him. "Mine." Her hands were still stroking, but they were moving right down his body, and she was dropping to her knees.

His heart was knocking against his chest wall, and all he wanted was whatever would come next. But he wanted to see her, too. He wanted to see her *bad.*

That was when he realized that she had a mirror on the back of her door, and that all he had to do was turn his head.

Holy hell. There they both were, and if he'd thought she'd look good on her knees? His imagination hadn't been nearly good enough.

"Oh, yeah," he said. "Oh, hell, yeah." He wrapped his hands in her hair and watched himself do it. And then he watched her unbuckle his belt and unbutton his Levi's.

His mouth was already dry, because she was going so slowly. Too slowly. She looked up at him, saw where he was looking, and turned her head herself.

"Oh," she said. "You like to watch?"

"Oh, yeah, baby." He barely knew what he was saying, not with her inching his zipper down. She had her hands on his waist, underneath the elastic of his briefs, and was kissing him just above them, her tongue licking into his navel, then sliding down. And still, she wasn't quite there.

By the time she finally got her palms down into his briefs and started easing them over his hips, he was breathing hard. And when she was on her hands and knees pulling everything gently over his feet, being so careful of his knee… well, he was grateful, but he was also looking at her in the mirror, and… damn. Dakota's ass…

"Darlin'," he said, his voice coming out hoarse, as she got him free of his clothes, "just stay like that one second. Just let me look for one minute."

She looked up at him, startled, and he should be looking at her or saying something nice, but he had to watch the mirror.

Did she look shocked? No, she didn't. She smiled at him, and then she gave him that wild side. She leaned slowly forward, put her elbows on the carpet and her forehead on her hands, and showed herself to him.

That was just about it right there. If his knee hadn't been so messed up, he knew exactly what he'd have been doing. As it was, his hand went down to touch himself. Somebody had to do it.

She was straightening up, though, and taking his hand away. "Oh, no," she told him. "This is my job. You get yourself fixed up, and you'll get that. You'll get it any way you want it. But tonight… I get you."

She did, too. She showed him what she could do, and then she showed him some more, and he watched every sweet, slow minute of it.

The sight of Dakota, naked and beautiful, on her knees,

taking him in, her hands working on him… if she hadn't teased as much as she did, it would have been over too soon. She made it last, though. She drew it out. She got him moaning, panting, and then she slowed down until he was groaning, "Dakota, please. Please do it. Please finish it."

And when she did? When he was sliding all the way down her throat, and he was watching it all happen? One moment, he was sweating, shaking. The next, that magic button had been pushed, and there was no stopping it. He was groaning, and then he was swearing. He was pumping into her, his head and fists were banging against the wall, and Dakota…

Dakota drank him down.

A Little Help From My Friends
♡

Dakota slept well that night. And she didn't think Blake had any nightmares.

When she'd helped him into bed, gotten him a new ice pack and put a pillow under his foot, pulled the covers up around them, turned out the bedside lights, and snuggled up close, he'd said, "You know, sometimes 'Thanks' doesn't quite cut it."

She'd smiled in the dark. "Just because I've got a thing for the wild side."

His hand, which had been running slowly over her side, stopped. "What?"

"Oh, like that's news to you?" She'd kissed his shoulder gently. "You show me your wild side, and I'll show you mine."

"Darlin'," he'd said with a sigh, "I think you already did. That thing you did in the mirror… I thought my heart would stop. Though on the other hand, that's pure torture, with my knee all messed up like this. Here you are, too, and I haven't done a single solitary thing for you."

"Is your knee going to be messed up forever?"

His soft laugh had made her smile in the dark. "Nope."

She'd kissed his shoulder again. "Shut up and go to sleep, then. Get better."

He wasn't in bed when she woke the next morning. She could hear the faint rumble of male voices, though, and it was a comforting sound. She sat up, did some coughing, drank some water, got dressed, and went to find those voices. Two men, sitting at the kitchen table, perfectly comfortable together, like they'd done it dozens of times.

It was a nice sight.

"Hi," she said, pouring herself a cup of coffee and sitting down beside Blake. "Let me guess. You handicapping the football season?"

"Nope," Blake said. "Talking fishing."

Russell got to his feet. "Breakfast."

"How you feeling?" Blake asked. "You did some coughing in the night."

"Not too bad. Still a little tired. How's your knee?"

"Aw, still tender." He had it up on a chair again. "I'll baby it today, and it'll be better tomorrow. This is a sprain."

"How can you tell?"

"Hurts too much to be anything bad."

"That makes no sense, but all right. You aren't even going to get it checked?"

"I will if it isn't better in a couple days. You could say I'm a veteran. But this is a boring conversation. Let's have a better one. The doctor said you're supposed to be taking it easy."

She eyed him sidelong from over her coffee cup. "I can't wait to hear what comes next. Has anybody told you that you're overly authoritative?"

"Maybe a hundred times. But with you? Only because I know you'll push back, and I do enjoy a contest. You ready to hear my idea?"

"Shoot."

"I need to take a couple days Monday and Tuesday and check in over in Portland. I think you should come with me. You've got a stack of flowers done in that workroom of yours, and Russell says you haven't figured out what to do with them. Now, Portland... it's got a pretty sweet art scene, and they surely do like Western artists."

"You know this how?"

He put a hand over his heart. "You wound me. I've got houses, darlin'. Houses need stuff on the walls. Why do you think I bought all those pieces from you?"

She eyed him, and he grinned and said, "Yeah. That too. But that wasn't the only reason."

"I think you should go," Russ said. He put a pan of scrambled eggs in the middle of the table and tossed a piece of toast each onto three plates. Plating, Russell-style. "Blake thinks you ought to be in higher-end galleries. I think so too. If he thinks Portland's a good spot for it, I don't see why you shouldn't try."

"I already did," Dakota said. It wasn't fun to admit, but it was the truth. "I know which galleries would be best, but they don't want stained glass. It's not considered art."

"Who says?" Blake asked.

"Well, let's see. The owners?"

"Uh-huh. What did you show them? How long ago?"

"Is this an inquisition?"

"Nope." Blake spread jam on his toast. "It's a temporary obstacle, and the way to get over it is to figure out why it didn't work, fix that, and try again. So I'm going to ask the next question. Did you show them those flowers?"

"Well, no. I hadn't done the flowers yet."

"How about the shells?"

"I told you. The shell was experimental."

"That's right. Experimental." He took a bite of toast, then said, "You should eat your breakfast. Most important meal of the day."

"I am." She dished herself up some scrambled eggs. "But not because you say so."

He grinned, and she had to laugh. "All right," she admitted, "that was fairly childish."

"Starting over," Blake said. "What's the best gallery? What's your dream?"

"In Portland? Elizabeth Fischer. That's the big one for Western artists."

"You tried them?"

"Of course. She said no. Very scary lady." She didn't want to talk about that anymore, so she asked, " How can you leave, though? Don't you have to do... things... at the resort? Especially checking into all those possibilities we talked about last night?"

Blake's jaw was covered with dark stubble now, after two mornings of not shaving. She got sidetracked for a moment by that. He hadn't even kissed her this morning, and that stubble would feel... interesting.

He said, "CEO, baby," and she had to think to remember what they'd been talking about. "That means you don't have to get down in the weeds. You'd just get in the way. I've got a resort manager. He gets to sweat it. I already passed it all along to Jennifer. And not that this isn't fascinating, but we were talking about you."

"I have a job. I have a deadline, and I'm already behind."

"Deadline just got extended."

"I thought you said you'd have guests before the opening. When is that, in ten days? I haven't even started the downstairs."

"Yep. My mom and dad. They're finicky, it's true, but I think they can put up with my whole house not being painted. Good thing I paid you that rush fee, too," he added when she'd have said something else. "And that I *heard* that doctor say, 'Take it easy for the next few days, especially with your lungs.' Climbing up and down ladders and breathing those fumes isn't taking it easy in any way, shape, or form."

He shut up, then, and looked at her.

She was rattled. It was true that she needed to try again with the galleries. And if everything in her shrank from the idea of rejection—well, she had to get over that. She could at least try.

"I got to say," Russell said, working his way through his breakfast, "if somebody told *me,* 'Come get on my fancy private jet and take a vacation, and let's see if we can get your career moving,' I wouldn't be putting up a great big fight."

"Whose side are you on?" Dakota asked.

"Yours," he said. "That's the point. So," he asked Blake, "what does she need to do?"

Dakota lifted both hands in resignation, then dropped them as Blake said, "She needs to decide if that's what she wants to do."

All right, that was fairly sensitive, she had to admit. He went on to say, "If she does, she makes a list of the places she wants to try and gives it to me so I can get her there. She packs up a couple pieces to show them what she's got. If I'm buying, I want to see the real deal. I don't want to see a picture. Her two very best flowers, that's what I'd say. Then she comes over to my house and gets my eagle and my shell and my iris, because I've got a damn good eye, and I got the best. That makes five, and five's plenty. She leaves all those with me, and she packs her suitcase and waits for me to come get her in the morning, and I take her to Portland and show her a good time and let her lungs heal up. And we sell us some glass."

♡♡♡

"I'm trying my best to be cool here and pretend this is my norm," Dakota said the next morning, when she was walking up a set of steps onto a sleek white business jet of a type she'd only seen in the movies.

No security checks, just Blake driving right up to the plane and being met by a couple of his security guys from the resort, who'd taken care of the transfer of the glass pieces she'd packed up yesterday. The guys had taken care of the luggage, too, and then Blake had tossed them the car keys and said, "Let's go, wild thing."

Now, he made his own stiff-legged way up the stairs, said, "Hey, Joe," to somebody who must be the pilot, and told Dakota, "Have a seat."

"No safety video?" She was going for casual here, even as she sat in something that would have qualified as "luxury leather recliner" in her world. "No explanation of where I'll find my life vest?"

"We're flying over the Canyonlands, darlin'. I don't think your life vest is going to do you a lot of good. And don't ask Joe. You'll hurt his feelings. For the record, though, it's under your seat."

She spent the extremely brief flight, while Blake worked at his laptop, looking out the window and trying to calm herself down. She'd decided on "artist" for her look, and now, she was second-guessing it. Jeans, her best cowboy boots, a tangerine top, and a silk chocolate-brown tapestry jacket she'd found in a consignment shop. Her hair was loose and artfully mussed, and she was wearing her most daring, dangly earrings, an Indian design intricately beaded in shades of orange and brown. Now, though, she wondered if she should've tried to look more upscale. Of course, she didn't really *have* "upscale," but maybe she should have worn a dress, or…

Blake looked across at her. "All right?"

"What? Sure."

"Uh-huh. Now, see, if I was guessing, I'd say you were worrying. Stop worrying, baby. You've got this."

"Right. I'm just going to walk in, unwrap a couple pieces, and blow them away."

"Yep. You're doing them a favor. You're giving them the first shot. *If* they can meet your terms. Just like we talked over yesterday."

She took a breath. "OK. I'm trying. Positive thoughts."

"That's my girl," he said, and went back to his laptop.

Another airport, then, another big, dark SUV, and another guy loading her glass carefully into the back. Blake climbed into the back of the SUV with her and said, "We'll drop you off at the Fischer place with the hand truck, and then Conrad here will take me to the office and come back for you when you call. He'll take you on to the next one, too." He sat back as the driver made his way onto the main road. "So what else do you want to do while you're out here? Want to buy some more glass or anything? I'm guessing that'd be your first choice. There are some good places around, I hear."

"Well, yeah," she said. "I'd love to do that, if you can loan me the car. How would you know whether Portland has glass supplies?"

"I've got my sources. Which is a mysterious way of saying that Jennifer did some research for me. How about tomorrow? I've got some meetings. You can go on and do that shopping, and whatever else you feel like. For today, do your visits, and then have Conrad take you back to the house if you get tired. Go to lunch. I won't be home until after five, but we can go out to dinner, do it up good."

"This must be what it's like to be rich."

He laughed. "Pretty much. It's not too horrible."

"So how come you're so... normal, relatively speaking, in Wild Horse? You have a nice boat and a nice house, sure, but why aren't you... I don't know, relaxing in a yacht on the French Riviera?"

"Because I'd expire of boredom?"

"Well," she admitted, "there's that."

She got quiet again, because she was nervous. But when they'd pulled up near the expanse of sleek storefront that was the Elizabeth Fischer Gallery and she had her hand truck loaded, she stopped outside the car door where he was still sitting, his leg stretched out in front of him, and said, "This is nuts. You realize this is nuts."

"Nope. And by the way. If I show up, act natural."

And then he shut the car door, Conrad drove away, and Dakota snapped her mouth shut and thought, *What?* But after that, she took a breath of Portland air and refocused.

She wasn't in Wild Horse. She was in Portland, people her age were walking by in skinny pants and hipster sneakers and funky haircuts and piercings that made hers look tame, and there was an energy in the air she could nearly touch.

She was here. She was home. And she had a shot. She wheeled her hand truck around and headed right through the door. Elizabeth Fischer, here she came.

The confidence lasted about two minutes. As long as it took for an assistant to ask her, "May I help you?" for Dakota to say, "I'd like to see Ms. Fischer, please," and for the assistant to eye her dubiously.

How about faking it a little more, darlin'? It was like she heard Blake's voice, right there in her head. She raised her chin, put her shoulders back, stared the assistant down, and said, "She's expecting me. Dakota Savage." Sure, it was a lie, but it might get her two more minutes, and walking out the door wouldn't.

"One minute, please," the assistant said, and left her to cool her heels.

It wasn't one minute. It was more like ten. At first, Dakota stood at the discreetly situated desk and looked around her. In one corner of the room, a fairly amazing silver mobile stretched from floor to ceiling and made her wonder how big a house you'd have to have to display it. On the opposite wall, three enormous wooden kayaks hung lengthwise, side by side, all inlaid wood and geometric designs. Now, *that* was wall art. Not exactly a painting over the couch.

She had a moment of wanting to run. And then she had a different moment.

Twenty-four hours ago, she'd almost drowned. If Blake hadn't found her, she'd have died at the bottom of the lake. All it would have taken was another few minutes, and she'd have been gone. All her problems would have been over, and Russell would have been planning another funeral.

Except she hadn't died. She'd lived. And that made every single day, every single *minute* from here on out a gift. It meant there was nothing left to lose. She was still here living her one and only life, so she'd better start doing it like she meant it. It could end at any time, but it hadn't ended yet. She was still standing.

The winner's the one who gets up the most times, and we'll always get up. We're always going to be the last two standing. That means we'll always win.

She could have sworn that the dove tattooed on her back throbbed. *Stand up,* her brother told her. *Stand up now.*

Which was why, when Elizabeth Fischer walked down the enormous spiral staircase from the second floor, all black turtleneck, gray trousers, black glasses, and coal-black hair, Dakota wasn't running. She was standing.

She'd also unpacked her five pieces of glass and set them against the wall, right under the wooden kayaks. Her eagle and her iris. Blake's shell, and two flower pieces from her stash. Her best.

She didn't say what she'd said the last time, either. She didn't say, "I know I don't have an appointment, but…" She turned around and said, "I'm Dakota Savage. This is my glass."

"Hmm." Elizabeth was eyeing it, walking along the row of framed pieces, then crouching down to study it more closely. Looking at the shell, and then the eagle.

Dakota didn't say anything. This time, it was Blake she heard. *Don't think about what's wrong with your work, why you really can't charge that much.*

Elizabeth stood up, looked Dakota over from earrings to boots, and asked, "Are you Native American?"

"Why? Does that matter?"

Elizabeth smiled, the barest movement of her thin lips. "Darling, in marketing, everything matters. Every piece has to tell a story. Like it or not, the artist is part of the story."

"I am Lakota."

The words hung there. And they had power.

Elizabeth looked at her for another long moment, then at the glass. "It's good. But it's stained glass."

"And those things hanging on the wall are kayaks," Dakota said. "Which is an Inuit design. They have exactly the kind of patterning in the inlay that you'd see in an Indian basket, too. They're not paintings, and they're not sculptures. And yet they sell."

"How do you know they sell?"

"Because they're beautifully crafted. Because they're unique. And because you chose them."

Another barely-there smile. "You don't lack confidence, do you?"

You'll never know.

The seconds stretched out, and Elizabeth said, "Your work is exceptional." And Dakota heard the *but*.

Which was when an older couple, two of the five or six customers who'd been wandering around the gallery on this Monday morning, came forward. The woman said, "Excuse me. Can you answer a question?" and Dakota knew her moment had passed.

That was why, though, she was watching when the front door opened and somebody made his stiff-legged way into the building. Somebody in a white button-down dress shirt of an Egyptian cotton so silky-soft you wanted to stroke it, a black suit coat that had probably cost as much as Dakota's pickup, dark Levi's, cowboy boots, and a whole extra person's worth of magnetism. Somebody a whole lot like Blake Orbison.

He didn't make any kind of beeline for her. He wandered around, looking at various pieces, like an art gallery was exactly where an ex-quarterback tycoon with a banged-up knee wanted to be on Monday morning, and worked his way closer to where she stood. A man on a mission, if a sneaky one.

The male half of the couple talking to Elizabeth said, "I like this, honey." He was looking at her frilled orchid. Fuchsia, with a nub of yellow in the middle of the pink.

"A flower?" his wife, a well-preserved woman in silk trousers and a platinum bob, asked doubtfully. "Are you sure? Flowers are so… decorative."

A certain quarterback was standing near the couple now, asking, "Anybody know who's in charge here? I can't find anybody with a name tag."

Elizabeth said, "I'm the owner. We don't wear name tags here."

"Huh," Blake said, scratching at his stubbled cheek and looking doubtful. "Excuse my saying it, but how does anybody know who the clerks are, then? When you go to Home Depot, they've got an apron on, so you can spot 'em." He asked the older man, "Know what I mean?"

"You're right about that," the man said. "Come to think of it."

"May I help you with something?" Elizabeth asked, her tone icier by the moment.

"Yes, ma'am," Blake said. "I was wondering if this bird's for sale." He pointed to the eagle. The one he'd already bought. "That's right nice. Saw it all the way across the room."

"I'm in the process of deciding on this piece," Elizabeth said. "If you'd like to leave your name..." She looked at his jeans and the dark stubble on his jaw, and then she looked at his jacket, as if she weren't sure which to believe.

"Now, that's just inefficient, if you'll pardon my saying so." Blake reached into his jacket pocket and pulled out his leather-bound checkbook. "Here I am, here it is, and I'm a busy man. I need something to hang up in my living room, and this looks good to me. I'm ready to buy it off of somebody."

"Actually,' Dakota said, "I'm the artist. I'd be happy to sell it to you."

Elizabeth's expression cracked just a fraction. Her mouth opened, then closed.

"That so?" Blake asked. "Well, this is my lucky day, darlin'. What's the damage?"

He lifted a dark brow at her as if he were telling her, *Don't move the number down. I can hear you doing it.* "Three thousand dollars," she said, and about fainted dead away saying it.

"Hmm," he said. "On the other hand, you're not payin' any overhead here, are you, if this lady isn't getting her cut? You could call it wholesale."

"Or you could call it the price," she said sweetly, and saw the gleam in his eye, the twitch at the corner of his mouth. "The *wholesale* price. If you wait until it's hung in a gallery, you'll have to pay the markup. If you get it at all. My pieces are all one of a kind."

"Guess I'd better buy it, then, else I'll be stuck with a hummingbird."

"I don't do hummingbirds."

"Wait a minute." That was the male half of the couple, who were still standing around listening. "Aren't you Blake Orbison?"

"Afraid so," Blake said.

"The Devils quarterback," the man told his wife.

"Ex-quarterback," Blake said. "How you doin'. Now, this thing here…" He took a couple more awkward steps over to the iris. "Usually, I'm not much of a flower guy, if you know what I mean," he told his new fan. "Doesn't quite send the image you're going for when you invite a lady over, if you catch my drift. But this thing here… yeah, I think I'm going to need to buy this one, too. And… whoa, Nellie." He was looking at the orchid, then at Dakota. "Darlin', I think you took some liberties. I know what that's a picture of, and it's not a flower. I need one of these for sure. Hang that sucker right in the bedroom, and I just got luckier."

"I was interested in this piece myself," the man said.

"That so? Did you buy it?"

"Not yet, no. I was about to make an offer, though."

Blake shook his head. "Now, see, that's where you went wrong. Got to make your move. You stand in the pocket too long, you're just asking to take the sack. How about this one?" he asked Dakota.

"Two thousand," she said. "For each of the flowers."

He sighed. "You drive a hard bargain, darlin'. Tell you what. I'm just going to go wild and buy the bird and that… what's the other flower there?"

"That's an iris," Dakota said.

"I'll buy that, leave the pus— ah, the other flower for my buddy here, 'cause I can tell he's got his heart set on it, and I know why. Gotta help a brother out. I'll take that pink shell there, too. Now, that is one sexy shell, and I've got this new place in Hawaii. Real nice place, great view, but the walls are still bare-naked. Kinda like a beautiful woman late at night, if you know what I mean. Of course, bare's *good*, but sometimes you want to dress her up, you know? How about if I write you a check for six thousand right now, sweetheart?" he asked Dakota.

"How about if you write me a check for seven?" she asked.

Blake shook his head. "Now, see," he told the man, "this is why I'm not married. Women are just too expensive."

"John," the man's wife said, "I think you should buy me this one. What is this?" she asked Dakota.

"A sego lily," she said. "It's a mountain wildflower."

"Yes," the woman said. "I thought I recognized it. It would be perfect up at the cabin, John, and it's not as... explicit."

"As long as I can get this other thing," John said stubbornly. "We could put it in that big window in the master bath. Nobody else would see it then." And Dakota bit her lip and ignored the sardonic gleam in Blake's eye.

Three minutes later, Dakota somehow had two checks in her purse for eleven thousand dollars. Of course, seven thousand of that she'd have to give back, but still. Blake pulled his phone out of the pocket of his snug-fitting Levi's, which John's wife, Dakota couldn't help but notice, had checked out, and said to Dakota, "I tell you what, darlin'. I've got a bunch of guys sitting around a boardroom looking at their watches right now. I'm going to hope that I can leave my bird and those other two things with this lady here and come back for 'em this afternoon. What do you say?" he asked Elizabeth.

She looked a little stiff at being called "this lady," but she said, "Of course."

"Good enough. And no offense intended," he told John, putting out his hand. "When I want something, I can be a little bit ruthless. At least that's what they say."

"No offense taken," John said, shaking hands. "I suppose it comes with the territory. Besides, you left me the one I really wanted. Can't argue with that."

Blake nodded and said, "Thanks again, honey," to Dakota. "And I tell you what—how about leaving your card along with my purchases? I might just need to get hold of you." And then he *winked* at her. Pushing his luck.

He lurched off and out the door, and Elizabeth asked, "Who *was* that?"

"Blake Orbison," John said. "Quarterback of the Portland Devils. Super Bowl MVP two years ago. I wouldn't have taken him for an art collector, but I guess he can afford it."

"I didn't get the impression that art was what he was most interested in," his wife said dryly.

"Well, you know," her husband said, "young single guy like that, with that much money? He's going to be cocky. He's on top of the world. His girlfriend was on the cover of the swimsuit calendar last year. Ah—so I heard."

His wife looked like she'd have words for him later, but she didn't say anything.

"Oh," Elizabeth said. "Football?"

"Yep," John said. "Super Bowl MVP's about as 'football' as they come."

He and his wife waited for Dakota to finish boxing up their flowers, and left with John carrying them, refusing Dakota's offer to ship them, and then it was just Dakota and Elizabeth again, standing in front of three pieces of glass that Dakota had now sold twice.

Elizabeth said, "I'd like ten pieces. I'll hang them for a month, and we'll see how it goes. And I'd like that to be exclusive in Portland."

Dakota resisted the urge to jump up, click her heels, and shout, *Yippee!* Instead, she said, "If you want an exclusive, you'll have to do better than that."

Elizabeth studied her for a long moment, and Dakota tried not to hold her breath. Finally, the older woman said, "Three months' exclusivity. And you'll replace pieces as I sell them."

"I set my prices," Dakota said. "Whatever you mark up is on top of that."

Elizabeth inclined her head. And that was it. Dakota had done it.

With a little help from her friends.

Date Night

♡

It wasn't easy to stay cool and collected, but Dakota managed it until she was out of the gallery, pulling her hand truck behind her. She headed over to Tenth, then got her phone out once she was safely out of sight and texted Blake.

Are you really headed to a meeting?

She got back, *Yep. How'd it go?*

I'm in. Was that cheating?

She waited a few seconds for the words to appear on her screen.

Only if they don't sell. Got to go. Sending car back for you.

She laughed out loud. They *would* sell. She knew they would, at least she knew it in this moment. And when she didn't, when she doubted…

Your work is exceptional. That's what Elizabeth had said.

Every day is a gift. Every minute. That's what *she'd* said. That was what mattered.

She didn't see Blake again until five o'clock. Until he walked in the front door of another enormous house, this one in Portland's Northwest district, home to more singles per capita than anyplace else in the world, or maybe that was just how it seemed. Another house made of wood and glass, with floor-to-ceiling windows, a whole lot of deck, and mountain views to die for. Not to mention a master bedroom with a bed that...

Well. In any case, when Blake walked through the front door and into his living room, she had a glass of red wine in her hand and another one on the coffee table. She was also lying back on a much nicer leather couch than the one in his Idaho house. And wearing his silk robe.

She waved her glass at him. "Hi, hot shot. How was your day? Did you make a million dollars?"

His eyes were gleaming, a grin forming on his absolutely bitable lips. "Well, yeah, wild thing. Probably so." He set his laptop bag down on a chair, then took his jacket off and tossed it, too.

"Because I only go out with very rich men," she informed him. "I'm a successful artist."

He was getting rid of his boots and socks. "That so."

"Sadly," she said with a sigh, "I had to tear up this check I got today. It was a really big one, too. I deposited another one, though. I bought a *very* expensive bottle of wine with it. I just need somebody to drink it with me."

"I think I could oblige." He was crossing the floor toward her now across all that expanse of living room. Limping, but not as badly as he had a couple days ago.

"Also," she said, "I borrowed this robe. I need to return it." She put a hand on either side of the silk robe and slowly pulled it open, making the moment last.

Blake stopped walking.

She stood up, let the robe fall off her shoulders, and tossed it onto the coffee table. "There's your robe. And here's your wine." Then she sank back down onto the couch, leaned back against the arm, and took another sip. "Why don't you come have a drink?"

♡♡♡

They didn't go out to dinner.

Blake was wearing the robe now. He'd had to put something on when the pizza guy came. He had his leg up on the coffee table, icing his knee again. He'd put a little too much strain on it, but what a way to go.

Dakota, on the other hand…

Dakota was wearing one absolutely devastating pair of black lace panties with a scallop-edged back, a tiny cluster of pearls nestled at the bottom of the v-shaped front, and, best of all, a black seam running down the middle. A seam that Blake had traced all the way around, rubbed into her, and generally had just way too much fun with before he'd taken that scrap of black lace off her and showed her what he was there for.

Yeah. Dakota was dressed for dinner. Because that was all she was wearing. And if there was anything sexier than a nearly naked Dakota, all long dark hair and bronzed skin, silver winking from her navel and her toenails painted red, eating cheesy pizza and drinking a little too much red wine on his couch, he couldn't imagine what it would be.

She was saying something, though, so he did his best to focus. "What if Elizabeth finds out you were, I mean *we* were sleeping together? There goes my beautiful showing. Did you think of that before you dropped by?"

He took another bite of pizza. Damn, that was good. Kale salad was fine, but pizza was better. And if it came from Lovely's Fifty Fifty, it was the best. "Nope. And it doesn't matter. If she does—*when* she does—she'll think about how I looked at you and what a horn dog I was, and think I tracked you down and went after you. Which would be about right. She'll think she set us up. What a mismatch, she'll say. The artist and the roughneck."

"You are not a roughneck."

He looked at her and grinned, and she said, "All right. Maybe you do a good job of pretending. A little over the top, wouldn't you say? 'At Home Depot, they wear aprons, so you can tell who's a clerk?' Not to mention, 'Bare's good, but sometimes you want to dress her up a little?' You sounded like a barbarian. And you do not have a house in Hawaii. Plus, you called my orchid a pussy."

"I did not. I carefully broke off. Besides, I meant in a *good* way. And sorry, darlin', but I do so have a house in Hawaii. On Kauai, if you want to know. It's got bare walls, too. Good bones and great skin, just as pretty as it can be, and it looks fine naked, exactly like somebody I know. But it'd sure be fun to dress her up a little, and I intend to do it. Which reminds me— pay attention, sugar, because this is a segue—that I'd like to take you shopping tomorrow."

"I already bought my glass. I had to celebrate somehow. I mean, besides the wine and this little item from La Perla, which I notice you appreciate."

"Oh, yeah. I thought I made that clear. I plan to appreciate you some more later on, too. My bed's a four-poster. You notice that?"

"I'm trying to have a conversation here." But her nipples had pebbled. That was the beauty of having dinner with a naked woman. You got all your signals straight-up. "I went wild," she went on determinedly. "At Bullseye. That's the glass place, and oh, Blake." She sighed. "It's so good when you can have exactly what you want."

"I noticed." He dipped his finger into his glass of wine, painted one taut brown peak with it, then did the other. He did some tasting, and *oh,* yeah. She was lying back, her fingers in his hair, and he had her going again.

"Wait," she gasped after a couple very nice minutes. "Wait. I need to tell you this." Which meant he had to sit up.

Well, damn. She had some beard burn going on, and it was a good look on her. He wanted to give her some more.

She said, "Elizabeth wants a dozen pieces to start, and if they sell, I'll need more. I only have eight flowers left, and no shells. No birds, either. I have to get to work. What if I can't deliver on time? She wants them in three months. Even if I only did shells… And I still have to paint your house, too. Maybe I should just fly back tomorrow morning. I could get your house done fast, before your parents come, even, if I worked enough hours, and then I could focus for a while. If Evan doesn't need me, I could take a couple weeks, just work straight through, and—"

He was laughing, and he had his hand over her mouth. "Darlin', stop."

He took his hand away, and she said, "Excuse me? Are you shutting me up?" Some sparks were flying from those brown eyes, and that wasn't bad, either.

"Well, yeah." He shook his head and took another drink of wine. "If I'd known this would happen, I wouldn't have helped. Tell you what—and here I go, bargaining again—you can just stop doing my house. Stop it altogether. *If* you stay with me tomorrow, because otherwise, I'll get too lonesome. I didn't sleep with you last night, and my tree-trunk bed scares me. I could have more bad dreams. So how about this. You keep those dreams away tonight, give yourself that break the doctor ordered—" He held up a hand again. "Nope. I heard him. You fly back with me tomorrow night, help me get past my fear of trees, and after that? You take off for a week or two and work on your glass. Get yourself started, so you stop worrying. And after *that,* you can come back and do my house, slow as you want. Use my hot tub after work, because, baby— next time you're in there like that, I'm coming in. I thought I was going to rupture something that night, holding back."

She was opening and closing her mouth. Shaking her head, too. "I don't even know where to *start.* First—last—you didn't hold back, not that I noticed."

"I had a whole glass of wine before I made my move. I talked for an hour, I swear. About half killed me, too. You were in this same robe with nothing underneath, and all I wanted to do was lay you down, untie that bow, and finish the job you started. I knew how bad you needed to come, and I knew I was the man to get you there. I finally got started, and what did you do? You ran out, that's what. I haven't ached that bad since I was sixteen. I thought I might need medical attention, like when you take too much Viagra."

"You have never taken Viagra."

"Well, no. But I've heard."

She took her head in her hands and pressed her palms against her temples. "I'm a drowning victim, you know. You're giving *me* an ache. A *head* ache. I am not going to stop halfway through painting your house. We made a deal."

"Only because I wanted you *in* my house. And now I'm unmaking it."

"You can't unmake it."

"I just did."

"All right. Here's the deal. I'll stay with you tonight, and I'll... wait. What am I agreeing to tomorrow?"

"I'm going to take you shopping. You've got to look pretty at my grand opening. You're my date."

"Excuse me? Have you invited me?"

He sighed. "What did I just say?"

"You have to *ask.*"

He took her hand, lifted it to his mouth, and kissed the backs of her fingers. Then he turned it over and kissed her palm. "Miss Dakota, may I have the pleasure of your company at my grand opening? And may I have the *very* great pleasure of buying you something almost as beautiful as you are to wear to it?"

She looked like she was trying to think about it but was weakening. He liked her weakening. "Yes, you may," she said. "Have the pleasure of my company, I mean. But I bought a dress. You saw it. You thought it was pretty, too."

"Trouble is..." He was still holding her hand, and now, he was running his thumb over her palm. He did like her hands. Slim and strong and capable, but when she touched you, you knew those hands belonged to a woman who felt everything she did all the way down to her soul. "Trouble is," he said again, keeping his mind on the job, "everybody's seen that dress. A woman needs a new dress for a special occasion. She needs new shoes, too. Killer shoes with sky-high heels and ankle straps. I do love you in ankle straps. I know exactly where to take you to get them, too."

"The car and driver," she said. "The jet. This house. And now you want to buy me fancy clothes? I feel like a courtesan."

"You kinda look like it, too, right now. It's a good look. You're not my mistress, darlin'. You're my girlfriend, and I want you to feel beautiful."

"Where were you thinking? How would you know where? There are some consignment shops that have gorgeous things. I'll have all day."

"Nope," he said. "My rules tomorrow. And how do I know? Research is my life."

$$\heartsuit\heartsuit\heartsuit$$

That was how Dakota ended up in a fitting room at Anthropologie the next day. Which, yes, was the right place, all the way down to the chandeliers and the soft indie music. Nothing about what you needed, and everything about what you wanted. About clothes that were art, and luxury that said you were thirty, not fifty, and you could afford it. Or that, just maybe, you had a guy with a jet. A guy who was sitting on the husband-couch, his elbow on its back and one booted foot stuck out in front of him, with a smile in his eyes for every dress you came out to show him.

A guy who said, "Pretty. But nope," every single time, until she put her hand on her hip in the gorgeous tulle-skirted, flutter-sleeved, beaded blush-and-black confection and said, "I'm getting worn out here."

"Nah," he said. "You're doing good. You just haven't found it yet. Come on, baby. Try a few more. I want you to knock my socks off, but what's more important—I want you to knock *yours* off. I want you to *know* that nobody there is more beautiful than you."

"This dress is six hundred dollars," she informed him. "I've never bought anything that cost more than two hundred dollars in my life. And by the way—your girlfriend was a supermodel."

He picked up a magazine, sat back, and opened it. "Yep. She was. My *old* girlfriend. And you're more beautiful. Sorry, but you are. And that's not the right dress. Color's wrong with your skin, and you know it."

When she put on the right one, she knew. And when she walked out to show Blake, he put his magazine down and sat up straight.

It was the flowers that had made her pluck it off the rack, and, yes, they were beautiful. Huge, lush, pink, full-petaled peonies, and they weren't printed onto their black background. They were embroidered. They were something she'd have created in her glass, and they made you want to stroke them.

But it was the cut that was selling Blake, she could tell. She cocked one foot and put her hand on her hip again, but she did it in a different way this time. Because this dress was perfect for her. One-shouldered and sleeveless, skimming and emphasizing her curves all the way down to the knee. And when she pivoted and showed him the back, with the pink ribbon belt tied in a bow and trailing nearly all the way to the slim-cut hem, he sighed.

"Yeah," he said. "Baby, that's gorgeous. See, now, look at your skin. Look at your shoulders and your pretty collarbones. You're classy, you're sexy, and you're everything any man could ever want."

"Silver-tongued devil," she said, trying to ignore the warmth that was spreading everywhere. Including to her heart. Especially to her heart.

"Nope," he said. "Honest man." His eyes were shining gold, her breath was coming fast, and she was falling hard. "Lucky man."

Future Plans

♡

They were on their way back to Wild Horse when Blake got the call.

Dakota didn't pay attention at first. She was looking out the jet window but not seeing anything, thinking up a schedule and a proposal and a plan. That is, until something in the tone of Blake's voice caught her attention.

"Yep," he said. "Good. Don't stop," and hung up.

"What?" she asked.

All the fun and sweetness she'd seen in him these past two days was gone. "You were right," he said. "There was broken glass on the beach. Right under the sand, in two spots. Two beer bottles' worth. One of them just at the edge of the water, like you said."

"Oh." The ice trickled down her spine as if she were under the water herself, still trapped. Her reaction made no sense, though. This was no more than the scenario she'd imagined. "What… what are you going to do?"

"Already got more cameras going up, and we're hiring more security. They've let the sheriff know about the glass, too, for what it's worth. What's that going to be, trespassing and littering?"

She hesitated, then asked, "Have they found out anything? About... what happened to me?" A question she'd avoided asking so far. When they'd been in Portland, it had all felt so far away, and all she'd wanted to do was forget it. But she knew Blake hadn't, and he wouldn't.

"He won't tell me," Blake said, confirming her suspicions. "Just says they're investigating, and I should butt out."

"Which you hate."

"I do. But at least there was nothing in the water under the boulders."

She did her best to get a grip on her emotions. "Then that's it. Whoever it was, they *did* focus on one thing—the swim area. And they wouldn't have thought it would be this bad. They weren't really trying to kill anybody, just disrupt things. And now you're on it, and you've beefed up your security, and they see that." She wasn't sure if she was trying to convince him or herself. All she knew was that she wanted it to be true.

"They'd better see it."

She waited for him to say something else, and he didn't. He didn't look like the impossibly charming man who'd taken her shopping, the man who'd held her hand walking down the street. This was the hard man under the surface of the charm, and he looked dangerous.

She shivered, and his expression changed. "Hey," he said. "You're all good. Nothing else is going to happen."

"I know it's stupid. It's just... sometimes, when I close my eyes, I can still see it. I try not to go back there, but I still feel it. Like... danger. Like it's still out there."

"I know," he said. "Because I do, too. But it's all right, baby. You're safe."

$$\heartsuit\heartsuit\heartsuit$$

The next morning, she went to see Evan.

"Hey," he said, setting down the roller in the living room of the Lake Street house. "You're back."

"Can you take a break?" She held up two paper cups and waggled them in what she hoped was an enticing manner. "Wolf Canyon's finest dark brew right here."

He took his cup and headed outside with her to sit on the steps of the wide wraparound porch. Barely past eight-thirty on this morning in late June, with a breeze coming off the lake. The water sparkled and rippled in the sunlight, a white boat carved a lazy semicircle through the water, and she took a sip of coffee and indulged in a dangerous moment of imagining that this could be her life.

Sipping coffee on the porch instead of going to work. Yeah, right.

"What's up?" Evan asked, bringing her back to reality.

She hesitated, not sure how to start, then said, "I have this thing. In Portland. With my glass." She told him about the gallery. She didn't mention Blake.

Evan got still—more still than usual—which meant he was emotional. Finally, he said, "That's great."

She waited, but that seemed to be all that was forthcoming. "I've got Blake's house to finish, of course."

"Need help?"

"No. He says no rush."

Evan shot her a glance, and she said, "Well, yeah. He's cutting me some slack."

"Uh-huh."

"But here's my plan. I'm going to pull out all the stops to finish his house around the grand opening of the resort on the Fourth. Then I want to take a month off painting." She didn't wait for Evan's answer, but hurried on. "If I could get at least three pieces done, then I could get back to the painting part-time after that, at least for a month. If we had Danny and José full time to help you, we could manage it even if we got quite a bit of work. I need to make sure I've got plenty of pieces in reserve if the first ones go fast. If they really sell."

Evan was just looking at her, so she kept going. "I know it's a lot to ask, but I wouldn't be all the way out of it. Blake wants to have a party at the house on the weekend after the Fourth for some of the people in town. He thought he could show off what I'd done—painting his house, I mean—and it would give M & O a push. We've never had enough of that high-end market, and this is exactly what we need to get it. I could still consult on the colors and do the sales part, and I wouldn't take a draw for the month. I'd take less after that, too. If you could keep Danny and José working..."

She stopped, because Evan had a hand up. "Hang on," he said. "What do you mean, you won't take a draw? What about Russ? What about the bank?"

"I've made almost ten thousand dollars on the glass just in the past month. I sold two pieces in Portland just a couple days ago. I charged a lot, and they paid it. I'm far enough ahead to do this, easy. I could take *two* months off. It's just having enough man-hours for you."

"So let me get this straight. Every bit of this hangs on Orbison. *He's* going to give a party, and you think that's going to get us contracts. You've made ten thousand bucks, but where has it come from? From him, I'll bet. And you want to count on that? That's your big plan?"

"The party idea is about ten days away," she said, trying to rally. "I think I can hold his interest for that long. Give me some credit. And the gallery isn't Blake. It's me. It's mine. My deal."

"Is it?" Evan's ice-blue eyes were steady on hers, looking too deep, seeing too much. "He takes you to Portland on his plane, and somehow, you've got the kind of deal you've never been able to land? Why don't I believe that?"

She was hanging by a thread, but she kept going. "It's not about what you believe. I've got an opportunity. I'm asking you if you're willing to work without me for a while. I'm telling you that I'll be doing my part to bring in business and do the initial work, so you won't suffer. If you get in a bind, I'll step up."

Evan set his coffee cup down on the step beside him, every move deliberate. "It's not about me, and it's not about the business. We'll get by. We always have. It's about you making a stupid decision. Orbison paid too much for a few pieces of glass because he wanted to get in your pants, and now you're ready to jump off the deep end."

All right. That was too far. "Oh really? Because I'm such an idiot that I can't make a rational choice to go after my best opportunity ever to do what I want most?"

"No. Because you're in love with him, and you're hoping too much."

The words punched the air out of her chest. "Maybe I am. So what?"

"So he's not in love with you."

Another jolt, and then her chin lifted. "He saved my life. And why couldn't he fall in love with me? Why not?"

"Dakota." Evan sighed. "All right. He got you out of the lake. He's an OK guy. He talks good and looks good and sounds good. He has a fancy house, he has a plane, and he can write you a big fat check and make you feel like all your problems are over. But how long is he going to be in Wild Horse once the resort opens? Have you asked him that? He's on vacation, or close enough. So, sure, go on and take a month. If you get us more work, that's great. But make it be about the glass, not about him. You don't have him, and you're not going to get him. He's not long term. It's not going to happen."

Her blood was heating, and not in a good way. "Wait a minute. When April got pregnant, did I say, 'Watch out, Evan, because she's not going to stick?' No, I didn't. But I thought it. I was scared the whole time she was pregnant that she'd take off before she even had the baby, but you were in love with her and I knew you wouldn't listen anyway, and even if you did, what could you do about it? So I shut up and hoped I was wrong. Which means that when she *left*, I didn't say 'I told you so.' I said, 'I'm so sorry,' and I helped you pick up the pieces.'"

"I didn't have pieces. I was fine."

"You were not fine. You were a mess. And I didn't tell you so. I didn't tell you it was bound to happen, because you'd picked the wrong person to love. I treated you like an adult. An adult who was my friend."

"I'm just trying to help."

"Well, you're not helping. Look. I know what I am. I know who Blake is. And yes, I'm…" She took a breath and said it. "Maybe I'm in love with him. But I don't have any illusions. That's *why* I'm taking this chance and throwing everything I have into it. Maybe he helped me get hung in that gallery, but if I sell there, it's because of *my* work. *My* talent. Nobody can make people buy. It's up to me to make sure that what I've got to sell is the best I can make it, and I'm going to bust my butt to do that. I'm asking you to help me. I'm not asking you to warn me about my broken heart. I know all about my broken heart. I can see it coming down the road exactly the same way you can. I'm asking you to let me do what friends do, to let me make my mistake and take my medicine, and then to be there when I've done it. Just like I'll do for you when you fall in love again."

"I'm not falling in love again."

"Yeah, Evan. You tell yourself that. You were made to be a woman's rock. That's the man you are."

He stood up. "You're wrong. Not anymore. I'll be Gracie's, and that's it. So—yeah. Take your chance. Take your month. Do what you have to do. And when Orbison's gone, I'll be here. And I won't say I told you so."

Too Much Blake

♡

Evan was wrong. Not about Blake, maybe, but about her. She went out with Blake on Friday night because she wanted to. For once, she was doing what she wanted. Broken heart be damned.

Or maybe because Blake said on Thursday night, when he'd come home to find her painting the downstairs bedroom and pulled her first into the hot tub and then into his tree-trunk bed, "So do I get to take you out on the town Friday night? Seems to me you've still got something to make up for."

"Excuse me?" she asked, trying to ignore the hand that was still lazily grazing her body from shoulder to hip, then traveling up again as if he didn't know how that was lighting her up. "I don't think I owe you anything."

"Oh, really?" He shifted onto an elbow and began to focus his considerable attention on her breasts. "Not even teasing the hell out of me with that perfume and those jeans that barely covered you, showing me what would happen if I unbuttoned one single solitary button, when I was supposed to be paying attention to somebody else?"

"Not my fault that you—" She sucked in a breath as he shifted lower, cupped her breast in his hand, and started to work with his lips and tongue. "Went out with the—ah—wrong woman."

"Mm," he said. "Hang on a second, darlin'. Let me get you a little closer to a 'yes.'"

Which was why, on Friday night, she was wearing those same distressed jeans, the little white blouse with its asymmetrical hem, and her platform sandals, walking into the Heart of the Lake with another big guy in jeans and boots. Except that this time, they were both with the right person.

And except that Steve Sawyer wasn't sitting with Jerry Richards tonight. He was with Ingrid.

Dakota saw them as soon as she followed the hostess onto the patio. Strings of white lights in the trees, candles lit on the tables even though it was barely dusk. And Ingrid and Steve.

She hesitated for one second, and that was when Ingrid looked up and saw her. Her bee-stung lips compressed, and she flicked her hair back over her shoulder.

It was the hair flick that did it. Dakota's chin went up. And Blake's hand was on her hip, his voice in her ear.

"That's my girl," he murmured. "Straight on through like the warrior queen you are."

Dakota did it. She put every bit of assurance she had into it, too. Her legs were long, and she used every inch to glide right past Steve and Ingrid and to the table where the hostess had stopped. A *corner* table. The best table. When she got there, she sat down, crossed her legs, and shoved her hair back over her shoulder.

I can flick too, she thought. *And I'm in the Fischer Gallery. Watch my smoke.*

If that hadn't been satisfaction enough, there was the look in Blake's eyes. He took care of business first, because that was Blake. "I think we're going to need a cold bottle of that Reserve Chardonnay of yours right quick," he told the hostess.

"You bet," the hostess said with the enthusiasm of a woman who'd been tipped very well in the past and knew there was more in her future. "Coming right up."

She took off, and Blake made it even better. "I didn't think I could like you any more or want you worse than I already did. I was wrong."

"Are they looking over?"

"Yep." He took her hand across the table and slowly threaded his fingers through hers. "And that woman's so jealous right now, it's turning her eyes green."

"She thought she had the pick of Wild Horse. Turns out she's got an also-ran."

"That's not why she's jealous. She's jealous because you've got what she'll never have, and it ain't Steve Sawyer."

"Oh, yeah? So you mean, not you?"

"Oh, no. That's not what I mean. I mean style you can't buy. I mean strong to the core and kind to the heart and loyal to the bone. I mean more woman than she'll ever be if she lives to be a hundred."

She couldn't breathe. "If you talk like that, I'll…" And then she couldn't think what to say.

Blake lifted her hand and kissed her knuckles. "I don't even need you to finish that sentence. We're just going to sit here and have our dinner, and we're not going to worry about what anybody else thinks or what anybody else says. It's not about them. It's about us."

After that, he set out to make her forget that there was anybody else on that patio. He made her laugh, and he looked into her eyes, and when she was sipping at the remains of her second glass of wine and shoving her hair over her shoulder again, he looked at the chain in her ear, sighed, and said, "You know what, darlin', I think we'd better be heading on home real soon, because I've got a long, slow date with your body tonight."

"Oh?" He didn't look impatient. He was sitting back, one elbow across the back of his chair, the other hand twirling the stem of his wine glass, his legs stretched out in front of him. "Is your knee all better?"

"My knee's going to do what I tell it to. And the headboard

of my horrible bed is all these branches. You ever notice that?"

A shiver went all the way through her body, and he sat there and watched it happen. "Excuse me?"

"I've had this vision ever since I swam with you that first day. Well, you could call it a vision."

Her eyes were narrowing even as she fought the smile. "Or we could call it a fantasy."

"Doesn't sound nearly as high-minded, though."

"Uh-huh." She took another sip of the kind of wine that made you think of hot summer days with the buzz of a lawnmower somewhere in the sleepy distance. Of a hammock in the trees and cool, starlit nights. Of lying on a blanket on the grass with your legs tangled up with somebody you loved and his hand drifting up under the hem of your shirt. Or of driving across a lake in the purple twilight wearing a pretty yellow dress, with a man behind the wheel who would take you away from it all.

Or maybe that wasn't the wine.

"So tell me," she said, drawing a languid finger around the rim of her glass. "What's the vision? Make it about me, though, because I'm the jealous type. If you slip up and put a blonde in it, it's not happening."

"I'm never going to put a blonde in it. Nobody but you. Starts with me taking off your librarian glasses."

Well, *that* was sexy. Not. "So far," she said, "this isn't going too well. Not looking too likely, I mean. I'm not wearing the glasses tonight. Maybe you didn't notice."

He had that smile in his eyes again. "I noticed. Do you want to hear my vision or just rain on my parade?"

She waved a magnanimous hand. She might have been the tiniest bit drunk. That tended to happen when you painted like crazy for nine hours straight so you could rush home and get beautiful for your customer before he saw you in your overalls and paint cap and the mood died right there. "Go ahead."

He looked around, then got up and moved his wine glass over a place, kicked the chair out, and sat beside her. "Now," he sighed, "this is so much better. Especially since this next part gets a little dirty."

She expected him to hold her hand. He didn't. He just bent his head closer and said, his voice so thrillingly low, sending spirals of desire all the way to her core, "In the next part, you're on your knees on my bed, and I'm taking off your shirt, watching you in that big mirror of mine. Got a couple candles lit, too, and, baby—your skin looks so pretty in the candlelight. I'm pulling that shirt right over your head and going for your bra. When that comes off..." He sighed. "That's even better. And then I've got my thumb on those silver buttons of yours. Those jeans are real, real low, and my hand's right there. Pop: one button goes. Pop: there's the second one. And then there's number three. And all of a sudden, there's just some smooth, warm, wet Dakota Savage. All for me, and I've got my hand exploring all of her, too, because in this fantasy, darlin', sorry to say, you aren't wearing any underwear."

She swallowed, and knew he was watching her do it. "Well, as it happens... you might be right. It's... ah... more stimulating, you know. And I thought you might want to..."

She saw his eyes go wide for just a moment, and she had to smile. Slow and sexy, and her hand was caressing the stem of her wineglass now. "Yeah, you like that, don't you? Because I'll tell *you* a secret." She leaned in and whispered it. "I want to please you. I want to push you. I want to make you lose control." And then she leaned back and asked, "So tell me. What happens next?"

If she'd thrown him off-balance, it hadn't been for long. He was running his hand along her arm, which was resting on the table. Just that barest touch along the sensitive skin of her inner forearm, and the shiver was starting somewhere down deep. She could swear he could feel it, too. "Well, I tell you what, darlin', since you asked so nicely. I've got you on your knees on my bed, topless, and I've got my hand in your jeans, working you up real good. Your hair's falling all around your face and down your back, and your mouth's open, because you're breathing hard. I'm getting you closer and closer. And then I'm taking my hand away."

She took a sip of wine and crossed her legs, trying to soothe the ache. And Blake sent his hand along her arm again. Wrist to elbow, the lightest, slowest touch. "And after that," he went on, his molasses voice rich and dark, "I'm pulling those tight jeans down that gorgeous ass. Right on down to your knees, and I'm pushing you onto your back. Those jeans are coming all the way off. That's when you find out what the branches are for, because, sweetheart..." He sighed. "I might have to tie you up tonight."

It was going to happen right here. She was going to have an orgasm at this table. She was squeezing her thighs together, and squeezing everything else, too. She couldn't help it. "You... might?"

"Oh, yeah, baby. I might." He drank the rest of his wine and raised a hand for the check. "Corner to corner. You're spread out for me, and you look real good that way. I've got you all night long. Ready for anything I want."

That was when the waitress showed up. Blake smiled at her, tucked his credit card into the leather folder, handed it back to her, and said, "I'd sure appreciate it if you'd run that real fast for me. I'm in a little bit of a hurry.'

♡♡♡

When they walked through the restaurant again, Blake's hand was on the small of her back. Right there on the side where her shirt was cut the highest, so his fingertips were grazing bare skin, and those tingles were spreading everywhere. Her hips were swaying, and she knew her pupils must be dilated like saucers. She was living, breathing sexual need.

He opened her car door, then went around to his own side and climbed into the SUV. He started it up and said, "Fasten your seatbelt."

She stared at him. "That's it? You're going to wind me up

like that and then not kiss me?"

He was trying to hide his smile, and he wasn't doing well enough. "I'm saving you up," he told her, swinging out into the sparse traffic of Wild Horse and heading for the lake road. "I don't want you to get diluted."

Her mouth was opening, and she snapped it shut. "Excuse me? You're saving me *up?*"

"Now, sweetheart," he said, "this is where you're just going to have to defer to the master, trust that I know a little bit better than you how to do this. If you're going to be putting yourself under my control and all."

"Did I say I was going to be doing that?"

He got the green on the last stoplight and started around the lake. "Didn't you? Or was that somebody else getting those shivers? If you're not going to be showing me how you're feeling, darlin', you really shouldn't wear such a skimpy little bra."

"You are…" She was still turned on beyond belief, but she was working up some outrage, too. "Where does my part of the deal come in?"

He sighed. "Now, see, I thought I made that clear. Your part of the deal is in offering up all of that pretty body of yours to me. Your part of the deal is those little whimpers you do, and the way you squirm. As much as you're going to be able to squirm when your wrists are tied to my bed and I'm holding you that hard, because you're going to spend a long, long time tonight with my hands on your thighs, spreading you open. Your part of the deal is to come hard for me and turn over when I tell you to. That's your part of the deal."

He was pulling into his driveway, swinging around the turns, hitting the button for the garage. She said, putting all her sweetness into it, "Are you sure about that? Sure that's what you want?"

"Oh, yeah, baby," he said, closing the garage door behind them. "I'm real sure."

"Then," she said, "you should think about one thing." She

was unfastening her seatbelt, and so was he.

"What's that?"

"How fast you can run."

With that, she was tumbling out of the car, running for the garage door. She could hear the explosion of his curse behind her and the sound of his car door slamming, and she laughed. "Kinda slow, aren't you?" she said over her shoulder as she headed into the house. "Shame about your knee."

Then she took off. Through the laundry room, then into the kitchen. She could hear him coming through the door behind her, and she picked up the pace. It wasn't easy to run in platform heels, but she did it. She swung around the kitchen island, then hung onto it and watched him.

"Not fast enough," she told him, and she was in the dining room now, across the expanse of all that stone and into the living room. Past the antler-legged coffee table and the giant couches to the stairway. Up the first flight to the landing. The sound of his breathing behind her. Getting closer.

He caught her halfway up from the landing. A hard arm around her waist, and she was turning, twisting. Being tackled.

"Got—" she began to say. *Got me.* But she didn't get the chance. She was sliding down one step, then two, on her hands and knees. One of Blake's hands was still around her waist, the other one pulling her shirt up. Yanking it over her head, then unhooking her bra with one deft hand and shoving it down her arms.

She started to turn, to say something. *Let's go upstairs,* or *Slow down, big boy,* or something. He said, "No," and he was shoving her back down. Then both his hands were on her breasts, and his mouth was in the hollow of her spine, between her shoulder blades, kissing her there, making her weak.

He pulled her down, and she went. Bumping on her knees, one more step, then two. She was on the landing, her hands still two steps above her, braced against the edge of the step. And he was unbuttoning her jeans, yanking them down her legs. All the way to her ankles. His hand was there, then, so hard and so urgent, and she was lost.

♡♡♡

Dakota. Hanging onto the carpeted step, her jeans pulled all the way down. He was shoving her knees apart with one hand, had the other one diving between her legs, rubbing hard.

No teasing this time. Nothing but now. She was pushing into his hand, panting, starting to call out. His palm was on the curve of her ass, urging her to open up more, and she was going. He had to... he had...

A hasty hand to unbuckle his belt, pull down his zipper, free himself. And Dakota on her hands and knees, rocking back and forth, asking for him.

He entered her hard, and she cried out. He was past hearing. He was hauling her hips back with one hand, the other hand on her again, driving her up with him. Higher and higher. Almost... there.

"Come on," he got out. "Come on, Dakota. Give it up. Give it to me." And she was going up, spiraling. Her sweet hips pumping, her hands shoving off like she was the one riding him. Like she was going to swallow him down.

He took her hard. He took her deep. She took it all.

♡♡♡

It was like she'd been struck by lightning. She was wrecked, her breath coming in shuddering gasps as the remains of the tremors rippled through her body. And she was sprawled under Blake with her jeans around her ankles, hobbled in every possible way.

"Uh..." he said at last, then swore. "Wait." He was working on the straps of her sandals, taking off her shoes, pulling her jeans the rest of the way off her, then standing up and taking her with him. "Come on."

He had all his clothes on, and she was naked. He had his

arm around her, taking her up the stairs, into his bedroom. He switched on the light by the bed, then fell onto the bed with her, wrapped her up tight, and kissed her, long and slow and sweet.

"OK?" he asked, brushing her hair out of her face. "Sorry. I didn't... I shouldn't have... That was too rough."

She smiled. She couldn't have done anything else. "Wow. You're so much more than I bargained for."

He laughed, and it wasn't very steady. "It was the running. You flipped my switch all the way to 'linebacker.' That was a sack all the way, and it felt so good to be the one doing it. You OK?"

"Yeah." It was barely a breath. She had a hand on his cheek, was kissing his mouth. "I'm OK. You probably killed your knee, though. And you know what you do for me? You push my buttons. Every single time."

He sighed, rolled onto his back, and pulled her to lie on top of him. "That's because I love your buttons. But darlin'." His eyes, his voice were sober now. "I messed up on the condom."

"Oh." A low, sickening lurch of fear. "Uh... I've been checked. But you..."

"Nah." His hand was stroking over her back, now, soothing her. "I'm all clean. Nobody gets tested more than an NFL player, and lately, seems I've been waiting for you. But what about birth control?"

Her heart had long since begun to pound. "No. I'm not... I haven't been on anything. I haven't been... it's been a while since I've needed it. I was planning to go to the doctor soon, once I finished your house. I should be all right, though. It's... I'm past the midpoint of my cycle. So I should be all right."

He rolled them again, braced himself on an elbow, and brushed the back of his hand over her cheek in one of those tender gestures that devastated her. "You're all right no matter what. Just tell me. It was my fault."

She nodded, suddenly too close to tears. The residue of the evening, of too much emotion and too much sensation.

Too much Blake.

There for the Taking

♡

Dakota spent the night, which was nice. Or necessary. Blake didn't want to admit how much he'd missed her the past couple nights. How could you get that used to somebody in such a short time?

It was the life change, he decided. In his playing days, he'd never been around enough to get into that kind of habit.

And then there was breakfast out on the deck on Saturday morning, with her wearing one of his white dress shirts and absolutely nothing else. That was good in a whole different way.

He said, "I had a thought, darlin', about that problem of yours."

She smiled lazily at him and adjusted her legs a little more comfortably across his lap. Which meant that he had to adjust his hand a little more comfortably up her leg, too. A polite man kept his left hand off the table. She asked, "What problem is that? My orgasm deficiency? Good news. I'm cured."

He gave her a slap on the thigh. "It's a miracle. But we'll keep after it. Complacency is the enemy of consistency."

She narrowed her eyes at him. "Did you make that up?"

He thought about it. "I guess I did. I'm getting smarter

327

every day. And here's the problem I was thinking about. You want to get my house finished before you start up on the art, because you've got this annoying stubbornness about you."

"Yep, I do like to fulfill my contracts. Call me crazy."

"So how about if I help? Here we are, got the weekend. We could have a paint date. It's probably a thing."

"Except that you're paying me to do it, and *that's* what's paying for my Glass Vacation."

"Call it an apprenticeship. You know you'd love to boss me around."

Which she did. Who knew that there was a right way and a wrong way to paint? He did, pretty much in the first hour. He got a whole lot messier than she did, too. His sole source of comfort was heading over to her ladder at noon and lifting her right off it. Which made her squeak, which was fun.

"Blake," she protested. "I'm *painting.*"

"Not anymore." He set her down. "Drop that roller, baby."

She put it in the pan, eyed him suspiciously, and said, "What?"

He already had her cap off and her overalls unfastened. "We're getting naked and going for a swim break before lunch, that's what. This is too much like hard work. Get that off." He was pulling his paint-splattered T-shirt over his head and working his shorts down his hips and over his bare feet. "You're falling behind, honey."

"I'm not swimming *naked,*" she protested, but she didn't sound too sure to him.

"In case you haven't noticed, I don't have any neighbors real close by." She was still working on her boots and socks, so he helped her out. Skinny little ribbed tank top, check. Bra, check. Overalls and thong, double check. "Now, see," he said when she was naked, "If you had a prettier bathing suit, I'd let you wear it. Unfortunately, I'm stuck with naked."

She had her hands on her hips. "Blake Orbison. I am not swimming naked with you."

He sighed. "I didn't want to have to do this, darlin', but…"

He lifted her again, and this time, he tossed her right over his shoulder.

Oh, yeah. She was squeaking some more, and he was heading out of the house and down the sloping lawn to the dock.

"We're naked," she was still moaning. "Oh, man." Which was when he tossed her in.

So, yes, the weekend had its moments. And even with his painting deficiency, they managed to get through a whole lot of it. Enough so all she still had left to go by Sunday night was his entirely oversized game room. Two day's worth, she'd told him, which was perfect. Deadline met.

This time, they ate dinner at Russell's. And Blake was leaving Dakota there tonight, which he wasn't one bit happy about.

"That's a first," Russell said, setting out another of those Russell-meals that said he'd never heard of fat grams. Enchiladas, refried beans, and guacamole. Russell's version of world cuisine. "Never had the customer help with the painting before. Most of 'em would be a menace anyway."

"Which he was," Dakota had to put in. "Luckily, the horror is over."

"Got to get back to work now, though,," Blake said. "My ego's too damaged anyway. I have to do something I'm good at. And starting Tuesday, things get crazy. Got a few football players showing up to give me some star power for my grand opening, or maybe just get some free room and board, and then my mom and dad are coming in from Virginia that afternoon. In fact, I had a couple thoughts about that while I was painting today. First one—most important one—is that I'd like you both to come over for dinner on Tuesday and meet them. The folks, not the players. I won't tempt fate."

He had to wait a few seconds, because Dakota was looking at her plate, then looking at him.

"They won't bite," he finally said, when the silence had stretched out too long. "It's dinner. You can do dinner. No different from me sitting here with Russ. Which is—OK, it was a little scary at first, but I got over it."

"All right," she said, and he let go of that breath. The one he'd been holding.

"And I thought you might give me a hand on the boat with the guys on Tuesday morning, Russ," Blake went on. "For a guide fee, of course."

"Nope," Russell said. Blake was sure he looked taken aback, and then Russell went on. "Friends don't charge friends."

"Now, see, if you'd tell that to Dakota…" Blake said. "The way she's gouging me on that paint job?"

"Oh, friends can charge friends to paint," Russell said. "But not to fish. That's too much like a good time."

"You haven't met these guys," Blake said.

♡♡♡

Which wasn't true, of course. As soon as Blake had spent an hour in their company, it was like he'd never left.

Three of them, the early arrivals, went out on the boat with him and Russell on Tuesday morning, and it didn't take long for the beers to get cracked and the trash talk to start.

Blake had left Russell in the cockpit to drive the boat and was on the mezzanine with DeWayne Johnson, who'd been catching Blake's passes since Ole Miss, but was catching somebody else's now. Anton Culpepper was kicking back with only one eye on his rod, not seeming too concerned about any possible salmon he might or might not be catching. And Eric Halvorsen was talking.

"DeWayne and Anton went and got married," the left tackle was complaining. "Pretty soon, there's going to be nobody to cut loose with except the rookies."

"Uh-oh," Anton said, lazily as always, his ball cap pulled low over his eyes. Anton never looked fast until he did. Saving his energy, he always said. "Somebody better tell Coach. Corrupting the youth. Could be time to dial it back, maybe.

Bein' married's a whole lot easier. Only one name to remember."

"Who remembers their names?" Eric said. "I just call 'em 'honey.' Plus, she'd want to decorate my house, and I've had enough decorating. I got a new house," he told Blake.

"You're kidding," Blake said. Eric was famous for having lived in a hotel for the past three years. He'd always said, "Why not? Maid service, room service, valet parking, full-time security, and two restaurants and a bar in the lobby. I don't have to hire anybody to make it happen, and I never have to worry that somebody's going to break in while I'm on the road. It's like magic."

"Only problem is," DeWayne said now, "That house is a flat disaster. Dude's got a pool table and a La-Z-Boy and a big-screen TV, and that's about it. You sleeping in that La-Z-Boy, man? Redneck paradise."

"Nah," Eric said. "That was before. I've got furniture now. I got this lady to do it. She backed up a whole moving van. I've got towels, even."

That set DeWayne and Anton off. *"Towels,"* Anton said. *"Look* out."

"I got these real ugly pictures, though," Eric complained. "She asked me what style, and I said, 'I don't know. Modern, I guess.' I meant, not like my grandma's house. I didn't mean *that.* Like this one? It's a red stripe. I mean, it's white, and then there's a red stripe. It's not even *straight.* Just smeared across there like somebody took a big fat paintbrush to it. And that's not even the worst one. I got a black square, too. I'm serious, man. Black square. The lady said it was modern. I said, when my mom sees it, she's going to say, 'Eric, honey, you got took. That ain't art. Nobody in their right mind would hang that over their couch.'"

Blake smiled. "Guess you got three choices, then. Go art shopping, get married, or have your mom come pick for you."

"Nah. She likes these things that look all... lit up. I can't explain it. Houses. They got too much light in 'em, like they're cozy or something. Light in the windows."

"And, man," DeWayne said, "you too ugly to get laid if you got that kind of thing on your wall. You better stick with the black square. Girl's gotta look somewhere else then, 'cause she ain't gonna be lookin' at no black square."

"I could buy one of those birds like you got hanging in your lobby, Blake," Eric said. "See, that *looks* like something. You can tell it's an eagle. It's not a house with cozy windows, and it's not a black square. It's a bird of prey, man. That's cool. Where did you buy it? Maybe I can order one of those."

When he'd brought Dakota's pieces home from Portland, Blake had hung the eagle in the resort's lobby. It just looked too good there, like the finishing touch. He was getting a little sign made to go next to it with her name on it, too. If he had his way, Dakota would have that stained-glass career sooner rather than later. She'd been made for something more than painting bathrooms.

"You can't order that," he told Eric. "That's one of a kind. But I know the lady who did it. She's painting my house right now, but she's an artist, up and coming. She does special projects, too. I don't mean she'd do exactly what you said, because she doesn't work that way, but if you said, 'I want an eagle,' she'd come up with something better than you'd have been able to imagine. But you should see some of her other stuff. I've bought three pieces off her, about the prettiest things you've ever seen. And sexy—whoa. Not black squares, and not houses with light shining out of the windows, either. I mean, serious stuff. I couldn't hang it in the resort, because you could call it downright erotic, but it sure looks nice in my bedroom."

He was about to say more, but he changed his mind. He realized at the last minute how that would sound. Like he was sleeping with his house painter, that was what.

"Huh," Eric said. "Well, hey. I should probably do that."

"Expensive, of course," Blake said. "Tell her you're a friend of mine, that I thought maybe she could give you a discount. Only three thousand."

"Sounds good to me," Eric said. "So where could I take a look at that?"

Blake finished off his beer. "She's painting my house, like I said. I've got to go pick up my folks at the airport soon as I get back, but go on and stop by and ask her to show you those couple things she did for me. Be sure to tell her I said three thousand. The eagle would be more, though," he thought to add. "And you'd have to wait."

With any luck, Dakota would be three thousand dollars richer by tonight. She could start letting go of that mental calculator Blake had seen whirring in her brain all weekend, no matter how many times he'd pulled her into the lake or into bed. She could start to see what he did, that she had a future out there waiting for her. All she had to do was take it.

A Failure to Communicate
♡

Dakota was painting trim in a frenzy, thinking that Blake's house had far too many windows. It was already past two o'clock, and she needed to be done by four if she was going to have time to go home and get dressed in time to come out again and meet Blake's parents.

Besides, she wanted it to be done. For his parents, and for… something else. Once she wasn't working for Blake anymore, she'd find out what they had, or what they didn't. Once he had to make an effort to see her.

Her stomach dropped at the thought, but that was why she needed to know. That was *exactly* why.

In two days, the resort was opening. And then what?

He's on vacation, Evan had said. It wasn't exactly true, but it was partly true. Blake had two other houses—at least two she knew about. And his home was in Portland. This was a vacation house, and he wasn't going to stick around much longer. He'd complained about his furniture, but he hadn't changed it. People who actually *lived* in a home, who hated their furniture and could afford to replace it—they did it. People who were visiting didn't bother.

At least she assumed that was how it would work.

It took a while for the voice from upstairs to make it into her consciousness. There it was again, though.

"Anybody home?"

Blake. He was supposed to be picking up his parents. Did he… maybe he wanted her to go with him. Maybe…

She put her brush hastily away and pulled off her cap. On her way to the stairs, she unsnapped the bib of her overalls. Whatever he said, she knew her overalls weren't in any way cute. Her orange tank top, though, was. At least he seemed to think so.

She ran up the stairs, calling out, "Right here," then got to the living room and rocked to a stop.

There was a man in the kitchen, and it wasn't Blake. It was somebody bigger. Probably six-five, and *huge.* Blonde hair and a flattened nose, wearing board shorts and a T-shirt, enormous hands hanging by his sides.

He turned and looked at her out of narrow blue eyes, and she had an icy moment of pure fear before she whirled and headed for the door.

"Wait," he said in a voice so deep, it was as if it was coming out of the bottom of a barrel. "You're the painter. Sorry if I scared you. Blake said to come on in."

"Oh. Yes. I am." One of Blake's teammates? Blake had told him to come on *in?* Like Dakota would be fine with having some huge, strange guy walk in while she was alone?

She stayed where she was and willed her heart to settle down. She wanted to fasten her overall straps, because whoever this was, he was looking her over too closely, and her tank top was too low. She didn't, because it would have looked defensive. "Can I help you?"

Now, he was smiling. It wasn't a hugely better look for him. "Blake said you do art. Sexy art."

"Excuse me?" He'd come over from the kitchen now and was standing too close, like nobody had ever explained the concept of "personal space." She took a step back.

"Sorry," he said. "Guess I'm supposed to say erotic. Erotic

stained glass. That's what he said."

"What?"

"I saw that eagle, and I was thinking something like that. But then Blake said you'd done sex— I mean, erotic stuff, and I thought that'd be even better. He said I could ask for what I want."

Something cold was happening in the pit of her stomach. "What exactly did he tell you?"

"I told you. That I could tell you my idea and you'd do it, so here it is. It's like, the Kama Sutra."

"Uh… I think you might have…" *What?*

"Not all of it," the guy hurried on to say. "Just five or six positions. Sort of, you know, subtle. I mean, if it was stained glass, she might not even notice what it was at first. Then she'd look closer, and —boom. Hit her right between the eyes, get the mood going right there. And I'm asking her what her favorite one is, see, making it like a menu. I'm thinking oral both ways, then you got doggy style, and one with her legs up over my shoulders. Reverse cowgirl, maybe. That'd be good. And something where you can tell it's anal, get that conversation started in a classy way. That's six, right? Basic stuff. Does she like to ride, or does she like to be on her knees? That's, what do you call it. Empowerment."

She couldn't believe it. She could not. "Let me guess. You've got a stripper pole in your bedroom."

His eyes got a faraway look. "Damn. I never thought of that. That'd be good, too. I never had my own place before. Blake said three thousand apiece for the pictures. So that's, what, if there's six? Eighteen thousand?"

Time to shut this down. "You've been given wrong information. I don't do that."

"Blake said you did. Said I should ask you. It'd be classy. Just the position, not like I'm asking you to do her tied up, or some kind of spread beaver shot or anything. So which ones would turn you on best if it was you? I mean, getting oral, obviously. But what else?"

"Nothing," she said. "I think you need to go. You have the wrong idea of what I do."

He scratched his head. "Well, shoot. Blake said…" His expression cleared. "Wait. He's pranking me, right? He knew I'd think you were hot, and he's trying to make me look dumb so it'll be harder for us to hook up." He laughed. "Damn. He's a sneaky bastard. OK, forget all that. So when do you get off here? I'll buy you a drink out there at the resort, we can talk about you doing one of those eagles for me, and maybe you'll feel like helping me make my list. Now that Blake put it in my head, I want that art bad."

"I'm not interested." She wasn't getting a menace-vibe anymore. She was just mad.

"Aw, honey, come on. I meant it about the eagle, that I'd buy that off you. And if we did hook up, it wouldn't just be about me. I meant that, about the menu thing."

"Blake shouldn't have shared my information with you." It was as cold as she could possibly make it, and now, she *was* fastening her overall straps. "I'm not interested either way. Any way." Blake couldn't have said anything to make this cretin think she'd do something like that. He *couldn't*. Blake wouldn't do that to her.

"Oh. I get it," the guy said. "You and him are…" He made a motion with his hands that she'd like to think meant something other than what she knew it meant. "Hey, that's no big deal either. He doesn't mind sharing, if that's what you're thinking. Not unless it's his girlfriend."

The blood was leaving her head. "Well, maybe *I* do," she managed to say. "And that's it. Get out." It wasn't her house, no. But she didn't care.

"Man." The giant was shaking his head. "See, now, at least I'm straight up. I'm real sorry. Blake's… he's on the marriage plan. I guess he didn't tell you that, but hey, I like you. I mean, really, not just because you've got a good body. You're feisty, and I like that. Kinda exotic, too. But Blake… nope. He's looking for this certain woman, see. I mean, not just for fucking. For marrying. The conservative type, you know. Somebody with her own money and a big-time job, so he knows she's not a gold-digger. I shouldn't tell you, but like I said, I like you. Plus I need to get him back for setting me up like that."

She wanted to put a hand onto the back of the sofa, but she didn't. "And you know this how? The same way you knew I'd make your porno art?"

"Well, because he said. He's been saying that for a while. Sorry. It's not like it's a secret. So—hey. I'm going. Sorry if I made you feel bad. If you want to have that drink, just have them buzz my room. I'm here two more days."

♡♡♡

It was almost six by the time Dakota got home. She parked the truck and opened the front door, and when Bella rushed to meet her, she gave the dog some extra love and had to force herself not to drop into a heap on the floor and bury her face in Bella's fur. She'd kept it together on the whole drive home, but she wasn't going to be able to do it much longer.

"Hey," Russ said, coming from the hallway as fast as his hobbling gait would take him. "Where've you been? It's almost time to leave."

He was in a white button-down shirt, dark slacks, and the string tie she'd bought him last Christmas, with a sterling silver and turquoise clasp. His hair was flattened down and combed so neatly, and the lump was rising in her throat. Russell, dressing up, getting his hopes up that this was going to work.

Or maybe that wasn't Russell.

"I'm…" She lifted her arm and let it fall. She'd thought going for a swim would help. It hadn't. "I'm sorry, Dad. We're not going."

Russell's blue eyes were too shrewd. "Why not? Don't tell me you had a fight with Blake. How? He was on the boat until almost two, and then he took off to Spokane to get his folks.

Which means if you had a fight, you did it on the phone, while the man was driving. You don't fight on the phone where you can't see the other person and they can't see you, and you sure don't do it in the car. All that does is mess you up. If you're going to have a fight with him, do it face to face."

"I didn't... we didn't have a fight. I just... I found out some things. And I can't go."

"Uh-huh. What things?"

She tightened her towel more securely around her middle. "Not now. I have to take a shower. I can't tell you now. I can't..." Her chin was wobbling, and in another minute, she was going to be crying. She needed to be alone when that happened.

"What, so you're going to run away? Not even going to face it?"

"Dad, I..." She was too close. "If I tell you, I'm going to cry."

"So cry. So what? Think I'll care?"

She tried to breathe her way through it. "I heard some things. He... he doesn't love me. He's got a whole other... plan. It's not me."

"Bullshit."

"He does. He wants to marry..." The sob ripped through her. "Somebody else. And he's been... talking about me. I'm just... I'm just for... He told him I was..."

She couldn't go on. The tears had come for real. Her chest was heaving, hurting in a way that was worse than drowning, and she couldn't hide them. She had her hands over her face. "I can't... It hurts too *much.*"

Russell's arms were around her, and that was worse. All the tears she'd held back, the pain she'd kept at bay so she could finish Blake's house, so she could be done and get *out*—there was no keeping it at a distance anymore. It was here, and it was swamping her. All her stupidity. All her foolish hope. All her exposed heart.

She was lurching into the corner of the room, because she

couldn't stand Russell to see. Pressing herself into the corner like it could hide her, like she could dissolve. Bella was right there, her muzzle pressed into Dakota's knee, and all that did was make her cry harder.

Russell was still there, too. She wished he'd leave, and she wished he'd stay. He was patting her clumsily on the back, saying, "It's OK. It's going to be OK."

"*No,*" she got out. "It *isn't.* I'm never going to... I'm never..."

"Yes," Russell said. "Listen to me." He turned her around, but she kept her hands over her face. She couldn't stand him to see her like this.

Russell said, "You're never what? You're never going to shake it? Sure you are. You've shaken it all so far. So you broke up. So what?"

"I haven't. You don't know. I *haven't.* It's the same. It's just the same. I'm always going to be..." Her chest worked to bring the word up, but when she did, it was a whisper. "Trash."

Russell reared back. "Like hell you are. Like hell. If he says you're trash, *he's* trash."

"I can't shake it, Dad. I can't. And it hurts too much. I need to... I need to take a shower." She had to keep going. She couldn't let Blake win. She couldn't let him beat her down. Not again. Not this time.

"You take a shower," Russ said. "And then you talk to him. You don't let yourself go down without a fight. I said not to fight on the phone, and I meant that. So you tell him face to face. You show him what he did. You tell him he was wrong. You give him a chance to tell you, too."

"I already know."

"You think you know. You love him, right?"

She was going to break into a thousand pieces. She was going to shatter.

Russell didn't wait for an answer. "If you do, you give it a shot. And if you were right… you tell him what he did. You tell him he's a piece of shit. You let him know. You go take care of your business, and if you go down, you take him with you. You go down swinging."

The Chickens Come Home

♡

The phone rang right about the time Blake was getting ready to make the call.

"Hey, baby," he said. "Are you on your way? I just realized I owe Russell about ten dinners by now. My dad's cooking this one, which means it'll actually be decent."

"I need to talk to you."

The words hung there, and he'd stopped with his hand on one of the sliding doors to the deck. "Sure. What is it? Something wrong?"

The resort, he thought, and his blood went cold. He asked, "Did something else happen to you? Something bad?" He should have warned her. He should have told her already.

"I need to talk to you," she said again. "Come meet me at City Beach."

"What? Baby, my folks are here. Dinner's almost ready. Come on over and tell me here."

"I'll be at City Beach in five minutes." She sounded like a robot. Cold. Dull. Nothing at all like his warm, passionate Dakota. "I'll be leaving there in fifteen if you haven't showed up. Your house is finished. And don't call me 'baby.'"

"Dakota? What? What happened?"

It took him a good ten seconds to realize he was talking to a dead phone. He stared at it. His finger hovered over the button to call her back, but he didn't.

He went back into the kitchen and said, "Sorry, guys. Something's happened. I have to go see Dakota."

His mother's head went up. She'd been sitting at the breakfast bar with her wine, but now, she set the glass down. "What's wrong?"

"I don't know. I'm going to find out. Don't wait on me for dinner."

♡♡♡

She was standing near the water.

The clothes she had on weren't anything close to "dinner with the new boyfriend's parents," either. She was wearing the sage-green embroidered top she'd worn the first time she'd come to his house, a pair of short cream-colored shorts, and flat sandals, and her hair was wet and twisted up into a clip. That was a very bad sign.

He got closer and saw that she wasn't wearing makeup, and she had her glasses on. That was a worse sign, but the look on her face was the clincher.

"Dakota." He caught the *baby* on the way out of his mouth. "What's wrong?"

"Let's see." Her voice shook on the words with what looked way too much like fury. "That you told your teammate to come to your house so I could make porno art for him, since that's what I do? That you made me think you cared about me and then told everybody else that I wasn't..." She took a breath and went on fast. "That I wasn't good enough? That I wasn't the kind of woman you wanted to marry? That I was just for fucking. That you want to *share* me. With your *teammate.*"

"*What?*" He shook his head like that would help. "I don't know what you're talking about."

"No?" She came closer, then, and shoved a flat hand into

his chest. "I was *there,* Blake. I heard what you said. Did you send him on purpose? Maybe you were sorry you'd asked me to meet your parents. Maybe you realized you'd be *embarrassed,* because I'm not—what was it? A classy woman with her own money and a big-time job? Well, no. I'm not. I'm a house painter whose stepdad is an alcoholic who can't keep up with his mortgage. My parents weren't married, and my mom slept around and had two kids by two different guys, and then she dumped us. My father's back in prison again, and he'll probably be there most of his life, and it doesn't matter, because I don't know the guy. I've got no DNA anybody would ever want. I've got tattoos, I've got too many piercings, and I didn't go to college. I've got nothing that means anything at all in your world. But I'll tell you something. I didn't ask for this. I don't deserve this. Just because two guys thought I was trash, just because I've been violated and hurt, just because I *shared* that with you, that doesn't give you the right to do it again. That doesn't mean I'm there for every man to share and fuck and throw away and *talk about* and treat like trash. I never signed up for that. I'm a person. I have feelings. All you had to do was leave me alone. If I'm trash… " Her voice wobbled, and there were tears in her eyes, and he couldn't stand it. "Why couldn't you just leave me alone? Why? Why did you have to make me feel like trash again? What did I do to you?"

He'd been trying to break in since she'd started, but she'd kept going. Now, he said, "Dakota. Baby. No. No, I didn't."

He'd thought it had hurt when he'd seen her on that hospital bed, and it had. But that day, he'd known she was getting better, that she would come out of it. Now, though, she was shrunk in a way she hadn't been then, and he couldn't stand it. "I didn't say that," he went on desperately. "I wouldn't have said that. Never. That's not how I feel. Tell me what happened, and I'll make it right."

It hit him, then. "Eric. I sent him to the house. What did he say? What did he tell you? What did he do?" He was going to kill him. He was going to flat *murder* him.

"You know what he said. He said what you said." Dakota had her arms wrapped around herself now, like she was holding herself together. "If you forgot what that was, he can tell you. He remembers it all."

Blake was in two spots at once. He was aching, because Dakota was hurting. And he was mad, and getting madder. "Really? *Really?* Everything I've said, everything we've done, and you're going to believe one barely literate redneck left tackle who has to get extra tutoring to remember which one's his locker, never mind the playbook? How about what *I* deserve? Don't I deserve a little more faith than that? Come sit down and *tell me.* Right the hell now."

He didn't wait for her answer. He had her hand in his and was marching her across the sand, over the grass, up to the picnic table. He sat her down on the bench and said, "Now. Tell me."

She did. When she spelled out Eric's request, Blake's mouth opened, then shut again. He had no words. And when she told him about the marriage plan, about the sharing... he lost it.

"No," he said. *"Hell,* no. That isn't what I said. Well, it is—the marriage plan—but not now. Not lately."

Dakota put a hand up to her head and rubbed. "All right," she said, sounding so tired. "You tell me. Tell me what I ought to have heard."

"First—all right, I said you made sexy glass, because it's true. I meant my shell and my flower. I told him to *look* at it. Maybe I should've realized that Eric's about as subtle as a garbage truck and twice as dumb, but go figure, I didn't. He never said anything to *me* about sexual positions. What kind of moron would even *think* of that? I can't believe it. He's a cretin. I'm going to..." He cut himself off, because that wasn't what was important. "And the other stuff? I don't mind sharing? I sure as hell *do* mind sharing. I don't share. I told you. We're exclusive."

"Except when you're not."

"No. And all right, maybe before, when I was younger, I

wasn't as… discriminating. But I never hurt anyone. I never humiliated anyone. Maybe I slept with some women who were looking to have sex with a quarterback, and maybe they were looking to have sex with somebody else, too. Maybe I did a whole lot of stupid things, in fact. But I'm not doing them now."

This wasn't working. He shook his head in frustration. "That isn't what matters either. Damn. I'm trying… I can't think how to say this. That isn't what you mean to me. It's not about sex. Not *just* about it. It's that you got hurt, and I can't stand it. Because I love you."

The word was out there, and he took the blow straight to the gut. Dakota looked just as stunned, then seemed to shake herself and said, "Except that I'm not right for you. It doesn't change that I'm not all those things you want."

"No," he said, and saw her flinch again. "You're not. Because I was stupid. I thought I could make some kind of list, and I'd find the right woman that way. I thought I was being smart, and I wasn't being smart at all. When my knee went out, though…" He couldn't look at her, not for a minute. "I wanted it to be different. I kinda went down the rabbit hole for a while. And then I came out, and by the time I did, I didn't have a girlfriend. I knew that everything had changed, that I needed to be a different guy, that I needed to have a new life, but I couldn't think how. That was part of the new life. I don't know how to explain it any better than that except to say that I was dumb, but maybe I'm not as dumb now."

"Are you still looking?" Her eyes were steady on his, her face at its most regal, its most severe. Dakota, strong. Dakota looking reality in the face. "If you are, Blake—come on. Tell me. I can't stand to be lied to. I can't stand to be made a fool of. Respect me enough to tell me the truth."

"The truth is that I don't know anymore. I don't know what 'perfect' looks like, except maybe I do, because it's you. You're nothing like what I thought I needed, and you're everything I've wanted. And I don't know what that means, except that I know I can't let it go. And as soon as we finish here, I'm going to go kick Eric Halvorsen's ugly ass, except maybe I shouldn't. Maybe I should kick my own."

"Oh." She swallowed hard. "If you mean that, could you say it again? Because, Blake... it hurt so bad."

"Oh, baby," he said helplessly. He watched a single tear spill over and make its slow path down her cheek, and it sliced him to the heart. He couldn't stand it anymore. He took her off the bench and into his arms. "I'll say it again. I screwed up. I'm so sorry. And I love you."

It took a long moment. And then her arms came around him, her head was resting on his shoulder, and he was holding her tight. Holding her hard. Holding her like he'd never let her go.

Getting the Best

♡

Dakota cried some, and Blake didn't seem to care. He just held on.

Finally, she pulled back, tried her best to clean up her face, and said, "I don't... let people see me cry. I *never...*"

"Yeah," he said. "I know. You don't let down your guard. Do you know what it means to me that you'll do it with me?"

"Well, no."

"It means everything, that's what. And what'll mean even more is if you'll hustle up and pick up Russell and come for dinner and meet my folks."

"You'd take me like this to meet your parents? You're crazy."

"Sure I would." He had his phone out and was texting. "If they've eaten already, they can sit with us. They won't care, and neither will I. And if this is a test, I pass, because you're beautiful."

"Blake." She had to laugh now. "I am not beautiful. I've been crying. I'm wearing my glasses and no makeup, and my hair's still wet. Nothing about me is beautiful."

He sighed. "Now, see, honey, this is where you need to defer to the master again. *Everything* about you is beautiful, and

I guarantee my parents will think so too."

"Yeah, right."

"Yeah. Right. Because they know how to judge. Just like me."

That was why, fifteen minutes later, she and Russell were climbing out of the pickup in Blake's driveway. With Bella, because Blake had insisted on that, too. And Blake was standing in the driveway waiting for them.

Dakota had contemplated taking ten minutes to get at least acceptable. Of course she had. But in the end, she'd done as Blake said and come as she was. She couldn't even have said why. Maybe because she knew their dinner was late already, and maybe because she needed to show them—and him—her unvarnished truth, and know for sure whether that was good enough.

Blake didn't seem too concerned. He said, "Hey, baby," kissed her again, then shook Russell's hand and said, "Thanks for coming. Thanks for bringing my girl."

Russell looked at him without a smile, and Blake met that hard gaze. "Dakota said she changed her mind," Russ said at last. "She can always change it back. She deserves a man's best."

"Yep," Blake said. "She does. I already told her so. And when I make a mistake, I fix it, and I don't make it again."

Russell nodded. "That's all right, then." He hitched up his pants. "Let's go."

Blake's parents weren't so scary, either. His mom— Margaret—went straight to her knees after she'd said hello to Russell and Dakota, started patting her thigh, and within ten seconds, had Bella on her back getting a belly rub.

"There she goes," Blake's father, Elliot, said. He was a tall, slightly stooped man with a shock of white hair, glasses, and a downright courtly manner. "Dogs and children love Margaret. On the other hand, most everybody else does, too. It's all in the nonverbals."

"Not everybody," his round little wife said with a laugh,

standing up and dusting off her hands. "You know better, Elliot."

"Well, yeah," Blake said. "Crazy people."

"Stop talking about me and come eat," Margaret said. "I'm so glad we got you here after all. I've been dying to meet both of you. Blake's told us so much about you."

Soon enough, Dakota forgot her lack of makeup and her less-than-suitable dress. Blake's parents had that effect. His mother's rapid-fire delivery, her lightning changes of subject, combined with his father's slow, dry interjections.

"Real good food, Margaret," Russ said at one point, taking another bite of apple cider chicken and mashed potatoes with crispy interjections of sautéed Brussels sprouts. "I'm more along the beans-and-franks-line, so this is a real treat."

"Oh, that isn't me," she said with a laugh. "Elliot cooks. I burn."

"Could be true," Elliot said. "It started out of pure desperation. Early on there, I'd think I was getting dinner. Then Miss Margaret here would get a phone call, and I'd be faced with something purely terrible. My Lord, the things she burned. And then Blake came along and took all that feeding. Somebody had to do it, or it wasn't going to happen."

"We weren't expecting a football player," Margaret said. "Oh, my goodness, we weren't. We were just so thrilled to get that little boy, and he *was* little. Undersized. Right skinny, really. His birth mother probably hadn't been getting enough nutrition, poor thing. But oh, how he grew, and how fast he developed, too. He did everything too early. Rolled over, sat up. Blake didn't start walking. He started *running*. At ten months. When he was three, he could dribble a basketball. You'll think I'm exaggerating, but you never saw a child like him. We knew we had something special on our hands. I should've brought the album to show you, Dakota."

Blake groaned and put a hand over his face. "Mom. Please stop. Dakota doesn't want to see my baby pictures."

"No?" Dakota couldn't help laughing. "And yet I find I do.

I *totally* do. Especially if he's in the bathtub or wearing a ladybug costume for Halloween or something equally humiliating."

"Not as many pictures as there ought to have been," Elliot said. "He was usually out of focus. Always running away."

"It wasn't a ladybug," Blake said. "It was a mouse. An extremely manly mouse. And I'm changing the subject. Dakota's pretty much a prodigy herself, Mom."

"Oh, I know," Margaret said. "Blake already showed us your beautiful art."

"I've got an eagle out at the resort that has to be seen to be believed," Blake said. "I'll take you out in the morning and show you."

"How's everything going with that?" Elliot asked. "Blake told us what happened to you," he told Dakota. "Terrible thing. I'm glad to hear it's taken care of now."

Dakota saw the moment when Blake's expression changed. "What?" she asked him.

He hesitated, and she said, "Something's happened." The cold was right back in the pit of her stomach, and she was clutching her fork too hard. "Tell us."

He took her hand under the table, and she was glad of it. "I do feel like I need to tell you," he said. "Just in case, since it was you it happened to before."

"Of course I need to know," she said. "Of course you need to tell me." She didn't want to hear, and she needed to.

"It's worrisome," Blake said. "When we were talking with the sheriff, Dakota suggested that somebody could dump something nasty on the lake bottom under these boulders. The too-high kind of rocks that kids tend to jump off of. She was talking about something spiky, where somebody could jump and get…" He hesitated again. "Impaled."

His mother made a sound of distress, and Dakota had stiffened. Blake squeezed her hand and said, "Yeah. So you can guess. We didn't find anything at the time, but I've kept them checking, and yesterday, they pulled something up all right.

351

Part of a crib frame. Upside down, legs sticking straight up. One of those legs was sharp, and a couple of the springs were broken off. Looking accidental, but you know it's not."

Dakota didn't say anything. She couldn't. But Russell did. "Evil. Pure evil."

His parents looked like they agreed, and Dakota said slowly, "But wait. That's too coincidental. All right, the broken glass. That was obvious. But this—*after* we'd talked about it? *After* you'd looked for it?"

"Yep," Blake said. "That's what I thought. We didn't spread that around, either. We told the sheriff, of course, and I told Walt Crane, my head of security, what we were looking for, and he told his guys, obviously. That's it. And a week later, it's right in that spot."

"People talk, though," Margaret said. "The more sensational something is, the more they talk. And the idea that someone would sabotage a brand-new upscale resort… that would be interesting to anyone."

"It's not that likely to get from a security guy to a radical environmentalist in six days," Blake said. "That's not the same social circle."

"Oh, I don't know," his father said. "If it's family."

"True," Margaret said. "The brother-in-law nobody can stand. The crazy cousin. But it's worrisome all the same. Are you saying it could be aimed at you personally, honey?" she asked Blake. "Or through Dakota? Surely she's not jumping off boulders."

"Not anymore," Dakota said. She was trying not to show it, not to shake. But her breath was coming short, and she was tangled in the net again as if it were happening right now.

Blake said, "I knew I shouldn't have told you. But be careful, baby. Swim at City Beach, and that's it. Watch your back when you're out and about. Lock your doors. Or you could come stay out here. I just don't like this."

"If anybody's in danger," she said, "it's you, not me."

"Nope," Russell said. "A man will risk anything for himself.

He can't take it happening to his woman. That's going to be worse every time."

"I'm not Blake's woman," Dakota said.

"Oh, yeah," Blake said. "You are. And whoever this is will know it. They know who pulled you out of the lake. They know who's been taking you out. And Russ is right. Having it happen to you would be worse. It already *was* worse."

"You obviously have people checking, though," his father said. "When was that dumped, do you know?"

"Sometime this week. We've got cameras, but it must not have been obvious. Plenty of boats passing that spot, and a crib frame—that's small. Run the boat in close, dump it over the far side. Nobody saw anything in time to save the tape, anyway. It gets recorded over."

"What I don't like," Dakota said, "is that they're... taunting you. They know *you* know it's not an accident, and that the sheriff does, too. A bed frame was your *idea,* or mine, which is the same thing. They're saying they don't care anymore. That's different from the glass and the net. It's escalation."

"Yep," Blake said. "So—want to move in for the week, while we're opening?"

She laughed. "No. That's silly, Blake. You won't be around that much longer. If I moved in, it'd look like *more* than it was. I mean, *we* would. It'd do the opposite of what you're saying. You're going to open the resort, and after that, you won't be here that much. You can't be a target, or you would have been already. Which means *I* certainly won't be a target. The resort might be, but you're watching for that. You're doing all you can."

Blake looked like he wanted to say something else but wasn't sure what. His mother said, "Well, that's just awful, but all the same—I wish Victoria could have come out with us, Blake, and seen how beautiful it is here. Blake's sister," she explained. "She's a chemist, and she's in the middle of a series of experiments. At the University of Virginia, like her dad."

"Fortunately," Elliot said, "linguistics professors are

flexible. I need to be, to accommodate Margaret's schedule."

The conversation changed, and the moment passed. And an hour later, Dakota said, "We should go. It's getting late."

When they'd said their goodbyes, Blake headed outside with Dakota and Russell, and Bella tore herself away from Margaret and came along. Russ opened the door of the pickup, told Bella to jump up and hauled himself inside, said, "I'm not looking," and slammed the door.

Blake smiled. Then he took Dakota in his arms, gave her a long, slow kiss that had her melting against him, and kept his arms looped around her lower back. "Thanks for coming," he told her. "That's not enough to say, but I'll say that."

She couldn't see him very well in the deep purple twilight that lingered so late at this time of year, this far north. She didn't need to see him, though. She heard the warmth in his voice, and she felt the security of his arms.

"Thanks for insisting." She felt a little shy, still. "I like your parents."

"They like you, too. And they like Russell."

"How do you know?"

"Because they're my parents. Because if they didn't, my mom would be giving me these little looks. *Concerned* looks. 'Oh, my Lord, what's Blake gone and got himself into now? And how am I going to set him straight without him realizing I'm doing it?'"

She laughed. "Really?"

"*Oh,* yeah. You could say I've had experience. You're the real deal, though, and they both know it. I'm all good." He gave her another kiss. "Well, not *all* good, because I'd still rather you stayed."

"Mm." She rubbed her cheek against the soft cotton of his shirt. "I need to get started on my glass tomorrow, though. And I need to get myself beautiful for your grand opening on Thursday, too. You're not allowed to see until the end. I *do* want to knock your socks off, as much as I can when you bought me the dress and the shoes."

"You can. You do." He smoothed her hair back where a lock had fallen out of the clip. "Will you do something for me?"

"Probably. I don't seem to have much self-restraint."

He laughed, low and soft. "Wear your hair up. I want to see your pretty shoulders in that dress. I do love your skin."

"You also want to take my hair down afterwards. I haven't forgotten that your parents will still be here, by the way."

"And I'm still going to take your hair down. They know I'm a big boy. They also know I'm in love with you, because they're smart like that. But you know, darlin'..."

"What?" She was floating some now. On the warmth of the night, the shining points of light beginning to appear now, including that brightest one, Venus. On the warmth of Blake's arms and the tenderness in his voice.

"There are a few words you haven't said to me," he said. "And I'd sure like to hear them, if you've got them in you."

She put her hands on either side of his face. He'd shaved for her again, or for his parents, but she thought it was for her. She traced her thumbs gently over his jaw and said, hearing the catch in her voice, "I've got them in me. But it's scary."

His arms tightened. "I know it is. That's why I jumped first. But if you want to jump in yourself, I'll be right here to catch you. I promise."

She looked up at him, but there was nothing to fear in that face, or in his arms. Not right now. "I'll tell you, then," she said, because she couldn't have stopped herself if she'd tried. "I love you, too. I've been falling in love with you for so long. When you came to find me after Evan interrupted us that time, when you asked me to give you another chance... maybe that was when I started for real. When I saw that you cared enough to try that hard. And now, I'm in so deep, I don't even know how to get out."

"Yep." He sighed, and he didn't let her go. "That's about it. Guess we'll have to keep holding on. Keep making that spot a safe place to land. That's what I want to be for you, and, baby… if you could do that for me, too, that'd be good. That'd be just about everything I could ask for."

Her heart was so full, it was going to overflow. She pulled his head down and kissed him. "I love you. And I'll see you Thursday. And no, you don't have to come get me. You'll be doing all your grand opening things. Russ and I will come out there and find you in all your glory, and when we do, I'll do my very best to knock your socks off. You wait and see."

Questions and Answers

♡

It was after eleven, and Blake had a full day tomorrow, but he couldn't sleep. His parents had said goodnight more than an hour earlier, but he was sitting at the edge of the deck, his feet on the rail, looking out at the blackness that was the lake and the mountains, and the impossible, heart-aching blaze that was the sky.

He heard her behind him. He didn't even need to turn around. "Hey, Mom."

"Hi." Her hand gripped his shoulder, and she kissed him on top of his head. "Want some company?"

"Sure."

She pulled up a chair beside him and sat. In her robe and slippers, her curly brown hair undisciplined at the end of her own long day, all of it as familiar and comforting as warm bread out of the oven.

He said, "More wine in there. Want me to get you some?"

"No, thanks. I've had enough."

He sipped at his own beer. "I'm surprised you couldn't sleep. Three hours of time change is no joke."

"Hard for me to sleep when I know one of my kids is struggling."

He laughed softly. "Is it that obvious?"

"To me. I noticed Dad and I were the only ones drinking tonight, by the way. Is there a reason for that?"

"Yeah, but it's not me. Don't worry." He hesitated a moment, since it wasn't his story to tell. But this was his mother, and nobody understood weakness better. "It's Russell. He's been sober almost fifteen years, but I guess it's still a fight. Dakota won't drink around him, so it doesn't seem right for me to do it."

"That's a hard fight. And a good fight."

"He's a strong man."

"Like his daughter."

"Stepdaughter, actually. Her half-brother was his. Riley. He died in Iraq about eight years back."

His mom took a breath. "Oh, my."

"Yeah. Tough times."

"I noticed that Russell's been injured, too. And you want to make it better for both of them."

He had to smile. "You don't mess around."

"Messing around doesn't get anybody anywhere. Want to tell me about it?"

"It's confusing."

"Most important things are."

He tried to marshal his thoughts, but they refused to be herded, so he just spilled them, messy as they were. "When I had to retire, I decided it was just as well. I was thirty-four. I wasn't going to get many more seasons anyway. And it was time for me to change. Time to move on, do all those adult things."

"You don't think you'd been doing adult things?"

"Some, sure. Football's a game, but it's hard work."

"Of course it is. It always has been, the way you've done it. So what wasn't adult?"

He glanced across at her, but she wasn't looking at him. She was looking up at the stars, her hands folded in her lap. It reminded him of the way she'd used to be there, standing in the kitchen after school, after practice. Folding clothes, doing the dishes. Not demanding anything, but there to listen if he wanted to talk. "You're a good mom," he said.

"I know. So what wasn't adult?"

"Oh, you know. Women. And the nine to five. Living like other people live. I made this…" He laughed softly. "This checklist for the right kind of woman. The right wife, the right mom. I was going to find her. I sort of did, but she was never right after all, or I wasn't. And then I met Dakota."

"Mm-hmm."

He sighed and took another sip of beer. "She's nothing like my list. Not one single thing. But her heart… it's… I just…"

He got stuck, then, the way he always did when he tried to think about this. "I just *like* her," he finally said. "It's better when she's with me. I leave, or she leaves, and I miss her too much. And it doesn't stop."

"I imagine not. I imagine it gets worse."

"Yeah. It does. I thought it was physical, and it would… burn out, if we could just get started. But then we did, and it hasn't burned out." He rubbed a hand over his chest. "It's worse. It *aches.*"

"And? Are you worried she doesn't love you as much as you love her?"

That knocked some breath out of him. "We just said it tonight."

"Mm." She sounded sleepy. "Saying it isn't the first step. For somebody as cautious as you, it's probably the *last* step."

"I'm not cautious."

"Oh, honey. Why do you think you aren't married?"

"Because I was having a good time. Because I never found the woman who made me want to give up the good time. Because of who I am genetically, probably. My wild side."

"I'll tell you why. Because you wanted to wait to be sure. That's caution. It doesn't matter how much you're willing to get tackled or how many businesses you start. That's your body and your head, not your heart. Your heart's in a whole different country. Your heart's uncharted territory."

He tried to think of something to say about that, but he couldn't. She was pretty much right. At least that was how it felt.

After a minute, she went on, "So you love her, and she loves you, and you want to take on that new life. You want to move on. But…"

"But she's not right." It was out there, and it was the cold truth. It was impossible.

"Hmm. How?"

"I want to do it the right way. I know it's time to settle down and have that adult life, where I focus on the business, but I go home to my wife. Where I have kids. And Dakota… she wants the opposite. She wants adventure. She already has the kind of life I want, and it isn't right for her, and I *see* that. She wants to travel and see the world. She wants to… I don't know. Swing out on vines into the water in some rainforest. Swim with dolphins. Go to Antarctica, probably. Dream up her glass, and make it, and get somewhere with it. So how do I ask her to choose something else, when I see her dream, and I see it's right for her? When she's given it up for Russell already? How do I ask her to give it up again for me?"

"Is that what you'd be doing?"

He felt a stab of annoyance. "I just said. It's exactly what it would be. It's bad enough now. I'm restless enough. I need a woman to help me with that, not somebody who's even more restless than me. She's the right woman, and she's exactly wrong. And I think she knows it."

"That thing she said tonight about you going away soon, you mean."

A lurch of his heart. "You noticed. And what can I say? 'No, I'm not'? Of course I am. 'Come with me'? She can't. She's got Russell. And anyway—what? She's flying around with me, sleeping in hotels? How's she going to do her work?"

"It does seem like you think you have a problem."

Another stab of irritation. "I don't think. I know."

"Or," his mother said, "it could be that you're looking at it the wrong way around."

"Like what? I've looked at it every way. I've done nothing *but* look at it."

"Let me ask you a question, then. You think an adult life has to look like your dad's and mine, like some idea you have of 'family life' and 'marriage' and how those things are supposed to work. Is that about it?"

"Of course."

"Why?"

"*Why?* What do you mean, why?"

"I mean, do you imagine that's the life everybody would have if they could choose it? Or is that their life because they have no choice? What kind of life would you choose if you could have exactly what you wanted?"

"What?" This wasn't helping a bit. "Why can't you ever just answer, instead of asking more questions? I have enough questions."

"Oh, you probably know that, too." She stood up, stretched, and yawned in her fleecy robe and slippers. "Because my answer doesn't matter. What matters is *your* answer." She bent and gave him another kiss. "Goodnight, honey. I think I can sleep now. I hope you can."

He put his arm around her waist and said reluctantly, "I'm never sure whether you're incredibly annoying, or you're brilliant."

She laughed out loud. "Oh, honey, I imagine I'm both. Just like you."

Where There's Smoke
♡

It was the Fourth of July, his resort was opening, and it was crazy. Blake was a veteran of opening days, of events, of pageantry. This was different, though, and it was new. This was *his* event. And Dakota hadn't arrived.

The grand lobby of the resort was a sea of people. Townspeople and hotel guests, and here and there, an oversized hulk representing the NFL. People drinking and talking, seeing and being seen, being photographed for every bit of media his publicity department had been able to come up with. All those people, but no Russell, and no Dakota.

"Hey. How you doin'," he said to the mayor. He shook hands and saw the mayor's nephew, one Steve Sawyer, near the entrance, part of a group clustered around Dakota's eagle. He hoped they noticed the plaque on the wall, realized who'd made that thing, and burned.

He didn't see Steve's cousin the sheriff, but he was here somewhere, too, together with two deputies. Supplementing Blake's security force, he hoped. So far, the night had been uneventful, and he wanted it to stay that way.

The mayor said, "This is quite the turnout. Did you sell out the hotel?" But Blake barely heard him.

There she was, coming through the front door with Russ.

Russell was wearing his turquoise string tie and white shirt again. And Dakota? Dakota was wearing her dress. Black, with huge pink flowers. And the shoes. Four-inch heels, a delicate ankle strap, and the top cut out in a dainty flower pattern all the way to the pointed toe.

Those shoes were black, and they were killer. All that body, all that bare leg in four-inch black heels… Lord have mercy.

She'd turned, then, to talk to somebody. Evan, in a white shirt and black jeans. Cowboy black tie. Blake wasn't looking at Evan, though, because he could see Dakota's back now. That pink ribbon drifting down to her hem, the curve of her hips. The devastating flash of honey-colored skin from her bared shoulder, the wing of her shoulder blade. And the vulnerable, sweet nape of her neck. He could see that because her hair was up, pulled softly into a knot that was just rumpled enough.

She'd worn her hair up. Just like he'd asked her to.

". . . wouldn't you say?" the mayor asked.

"Excuse me," Blake said, and took off.

It took him a while to get to her. People turning, men putting their hands out to shake. A question about football, an introduction.

No, not a while. Forever.

Blake was near the door at last, and there was one last obstacle. Ingrid, talking to Dakota like they were friends.

"I'm sorry you heard that," Ingrid was saying. "Melody can be so bitchy, I know."

"Excuse me," Blake said again. He was going to be civil, because this was a small town. Even though it was the last thing he wanted to be. "Hi," he said to Ingrid. "How you doin'. I need to borrow this lady a minute." He had Dakota's hand and was pulling her to one side of the crowd, then turning his back on the room.

"Thanks," Dakota said. Her eyes were flashing dark fire. She was made up tonight, eyes and lips and cheekbones and smooth skin. She'd dusted her shoulders and chest with some sort of sparkly powder, too, and she glowed and glistened like she'd been painted. "I shouldn't care, but the *gall*. Like she can open her eyes wide, act so innocent, such a perfect girl, and say she didn't mean it, and I'll be grateful because the popular girl's talking to me." She took a deep breath and put a hand to her hair. "That's enough of that. I'm not letting her wreck my night. Are your parents around? I should say hello."

Blake had to laugh. "Now, honey, I'm a little insulted. What am I, the furniture? Here I shaved just for you, wore your favorite outfit, and you not only don't notice my gorgeous looks, you want to go talk to my mom?"

She was laughing now herself, her mood shifting just that fast. "Right. There are probably three hundred people here, and you shaved for me."

"Yep." Now that the moment had come, his heart had picked up the pace. "Because as soon as I saw you, all those people faded out, and right now? They're gone. You look real pretty, baby. Those are the shoes, and that's the dress. We did good. You almost knock my socks off, in fact."

"Almost? Excuse me?" The fire was back. "This is my best effort. This took hours. This is as good as it gets."

"Uh-huh." He pulled the box from his pocket. "See, now, I think we can do better."

He'd planned on doing this in a back room. When he'd seen Ingrid and Steve, though, he'd known he had to do it here. He opened the velvet box. "Take off those earrings, and we'll see."

Her mouth had opened. "Blake. You're kidding. Are those *real?*"

He put his hand to his heart and staggered. "How about just shooting me right now, baby?"

"Sorry. I just…"

"Still waiting. Take those out and put these in. I want to see."

Finally, she did it. She unfastened the delicate triple hoops in her lobes first, then took care of the chain up above. He held out his hand, and she put them in his palm.

And then he got to watch her take two one-and-a-half-carat diamond studs out of the box and fasten them into her ears, one by one. "I can't believe this," she said. "You said... I never thought..."

"Less talk, more action," he said. "Do the rest."

"I need a mirror." She laughed, and surely only Dakota would laugh at a moment like this. "Blake. You're *crazy.*"

"Yep. I seem to remember telling you so. Wait. I think I said 'crazy about you.' That too." He had her hand again and was taking her over to an ornate mirror set between potted trees, decorated with tiny white lights tonight. "Here you go. Show me."

She fastened them into her ear, then. Twin diamond-studded hoops, and a chain that appeared to be made of tiny diamonds. "Where did you *get* this? It's so beautiful, I can't..."

"Had it made, of course. I did it when we were in Portland. I've been wanting to see you like this for so long, and now I get my wish."

She turned to him, all sparkle and flash, and smiled, and his heart just about left his chest. "Well, thank you." And then she laughed. White teeth, cheekbones, dark eyes. Full of fire. "Thank you very much."

"You're welcome, but you can't really thank me for this. I had to do it. And, baby... *now* you knock my socks all the way off, because it seems you're just too beautiful."

"Thank you," she said again. Her mouth was trembling a little, even though she was smiling. "I'm trying not to cry and wreck my makeup. Thank you."

"See," he said, "the problem is—if you're going to look at me like that, I need to kiss you. And I can't kiss you here. It's what you'd call a dilemma. I'm going to have to settle for keeping you right beside me all night long. And by the way." He grinned at her, because he had to do that, too. "Melody and Ingrid? They're both watching."

♡♡♡

If Dakota had ever had a better night, she couldn't think when. She even had the satisfaction of having Eric Halvorsen come up to her and say, scratching his chin, "So, uh... I guess I screwed up. Sorry."

"You think?" Blake asked. "But then, I screwed up some myself. I should've made the situation much clearer. Dakota, this lump of meat is Eric Halvorsen, offensive tackle, who protects his quarterback except when he doesn't. Eric, this is my girlfriend, Dakota Savage. Dakota's an artist. Is that better, sweetheart?"

"Hello, Eric," Dakota said demurely. "And, yes, that's much better."

Eric said, "So maybe we can forget about the, uh... position thing. Except if you know some other stained-glass person who could do it. I still think it'd be cool."

"The question is, though," Blake said, "whether any woman in the known universe would think it was cool."

"Well, not *her*," Eric said, pointing a thumb at Dakota. "But that's the *point*. It's *for* a woman. It's a *menu*."

Blake put a hand over his face and groaned. "No. Just no."

"You're not a woman," Eric said. "You don't count." He asked Dakota, "Don't you think?"

"Sorry," she said, trying not to laugh. "But if it were me? I'd be thinking, 'Kill me now. Just kill me now.' And then running. But then, I'm not... ah... attracted to football players."

"Excuse me?" Blake asked.

Eric ignored him. "Oh." He looked crestfallen for a minute, then said, "Well, at least I didn't waste my money."

Pretty much the best night ever.

There was only one tiny hitch. When the crowd finally headed outside into the lingering twilight for the fireworks display over the lake, she took advantage of the moment to hold Blake back and say quietly, "I should probably wait to tell you this, but I'm going to be raining on your parade later tonight. You know that issue we had last week? It's not an issue."

He looked confused, and she pulled his head down and whispered in his ear, "Condom. Or not. I'm not pregnant."

"Oh," he said, and that was all.

She didn't say anything else. She wasn't about to tell him about the unexpected wave of disappointment she'd felt. She'd tried to pass it off to herself as regret for wrecking his big night, but she couldn't fool her heart. Her heart... it wanted so many things. Freedom and adventure and fun and *glass*. But it also wanted Blake. And Blake's baby.

Stupid heart.

She shoved her heart aside and said, "I went to the doctor, and you don't have to worry about that anymore. Meanwhile, the timing could be better. Sorry I'm out of commission."

"Aw, no, honey." He wasn't bothering to whisper. "Not unless you want to be. Not if it's up to me."

If she'd been the blushing type, she'd have been doing it. She couldn't swear it wasn't happening, and she was revealing enough skin to show every inch of it. "You don't want that."

His eyes were lighting up again, and he had an arm around her waist. "I'm a football player, baby. It'd take more than that to put me off. That's nothing a towel and a sense of humor can't fix. There's nothing in this world outside of a 'no' that's going to put me off you tonight."

"You're not getting a 'no.'" She had to be blushing now, and she couldn't help it. It was the look in his eyes. He got her every time. And whatever happened after tonight, tonight was good. Tonight was perfect.

He seemed to feel the same way, because he sighed. "I knew this was going to be a good night." His hand drifted down a little until it was resting just above the curve of her bottom, and then it stopped. "We're watching these fireworks, because I've got no choice. And then we're going home, and I'm locking the bedroom door, laying you down, and taking everything off of you except those earrings. And I can't wait."

They did go outside, and Blake was surrounded again. The fireworks show started, and it was spectacular, but what Dakota felt, through every thunderous explosion, was Blake's hand around her waist and the diamonds in her ears. And what she saw through every shower of stars was the look in his eyes when he'd given them to her.

She felt the moment it changed, too. When his arm stiffened around her and his hand went to his pocket and pulled out his phone.

Something was wrong. He was turning, shoving the phone back in his pocket, starting to push his way through the crowd. And she followed him.

♡♡♡

It was all just fine until Blake got the call. The fireworks, the crowd, the lake. And Dakota beside him. And then his phone buzzed in his pocket.

"Hello?"

He had to press it hard against his ear to hear. "This is Logan Mansfield. I'm over at the northeast end of the property. You said to let you know if we spotted Jerry Richards around, and I think I just did. Saw him going around the corner of the building."

"You sure?" Blake was already turning. He'd given those orders a long time ago. He hadn't expected his former chief of security to turn up tonight.

Or maybe he had. He'd expected *something* to happen. But his money had never been on Jerry. It still wasn't.

Logan said, "Not a hundred percent. He's wearing a ball cap. I could swear I recognize his walk, though. Hang on."

Silence on the other end, then, at least Blake thought so. It was too hard to hear. The fireworks were going off, the crowd oohing and ahhing. Laughter and cheers and shouts. He was pushing through the tight knots of spectators with his free hand, trying to get out of it and call Walt, his new chief of security, when he thought he heard something.

"Hey." It was a shout from the phone. "What are you doing? You can't—" That was all. And Blake was almost through the crowd.

He'd cut through the building and call on the way, he decided. He shoved through another knot of people, and there in front of him, blocking his path, was Steve Sawyer. Not with his wife now, but with a bunch of good ol' boys. His posse, probably the same guys he'd been hanging around with all his life.

"Leaving your own party?" Sawyer asked.

"Not now." Blake kept moving, but Sawyer stepped to his left and blocked him.

"Blake?" The voice came from behind him. Dakota. He'd forgotten all about her.

Sawyer had seen her too, because he said, "Bud, you don't have to be in a hurry for that." His boys closed up around him. "All you need is a few trading beads or some firewater, and she's good to go. Isn't that right, Dakota?"

Sometimes, you made a plan. Other times, it was instinct. When you saw that unexpected receiver about to get open and you let the ball go, your arm and your hand seeming to act independently of your brain.

That was what happened this time. Blake's arm had gone back, and his fist had gone forward. It met Sawyer's grinning face, and he dropped to the ground. Just like that.

Blake reached back and grabbed Dakota's hand, stepped over Sawyer, and took off. He wasn't thinking anymore—about calling Walt, about anything. He was through the hotel lobby, out the front doors, and turning right, toward the northwest corner of the building. Toward the spot where Logan had spotted Jerry Richards in a place he shouldn't be.

The resort's forecourt was deserted except for a solitary bellman who'd drawn the hard duty of missing the action out back. Blake snapped at him as he passed. "Call Walt Harris and tell him to get to the northeast corner and bring his troops," and then he'd let go of Dakota and was running. Not fast enough, but as fast as his knee would let him.

Why? Because there was something happening up there. A shower of sparks where there shouldn't be sparks. And then flame.

There's Fire

♡

Stupid shoes. Dakota couldn't keep up.

She wasn't even halfway to the end of the building, having fallen far behind Blake, when she saw the sparks. Her first thought was, *How could that go off that wrong? It got shot all the way over the building?* But how could a firework be shot exactly backwards? How could it land there?

She didn't wait for the whirling thoughts to settle, just grabbed her phone from her purse and dialed 911.

"Operator," she heard. "What is your emergency?"

"Fire at Wild Horse Resort." She was breathless from running, but she didn't stop.

"Ma'am, there's a fireworks show tonight."

"No. It's not the fireworks. I'm here. The building's on fire. It's burning. Tell them to hurry."

"What area of the building is this? Are you sure?"

"The front. Outside. They'll see it. I'm sure. Send them now. I've got to go."

The phone missed her purse when she tried to put it back. She heard it clatter to the ground behind her, but she couldn't stop to pick it up. Blake was up there, backlit by the flames, and he was grappling with somebody. And then he was going

371

down. Into the fire.

She forgot about the shoes. She dropped her purse and ran. Straight into the man who was bending over Blake, raising something overhead. She was screaming, and as he turned, she kicked.

Side of the knee. She got him there hard, he staggered, and his arm came down. He was holding a hammer. She saw it in a split second, his body backlit by the flames. The steel head struck her forearm, and the world blossomed into white-hot pain. But she was still going, her other knee driving into his groin, and he was down. On his knees.

Blade of the hand to the neck. She chopped, and he went down on his face. *Kidneys. Hard.* She was kicking him again and again, the toes of her shoes meeting heavy flesh.

Jerry Richards. Who'd hit Blake with a hammer. Jerry was down, but where was Blake?

She turned and saw him. Crawling on both hands and one knee. *Toward* the flames. Her arm was screaming at her, but she was running to Blake. The world had closed to a tunnel, and only he was inside it. He was all she could see.

"Blake!" She shouted his name, and he turned. His teeth were bared, his eyes staring. "Get out!" she said. "Come on!"

She put her good hand down for him, and he gasped. "No. Guy. Get the guy."

She saw him, then. A man in jeans and boots and a black T-shirt with SECURITY in white across the front, lying next to the flames that were licking up the building. She ran to him, got his ankle in one hand, and started to drag him away, and Blake was there, grabbing the other ankle. He was moving backward now, still in that horrible crab stance. And then they were dragging desperately at the dead weight of the body, getting him clear. Getting him out.

♡♡♡

Blake heard shouts, running feet, the wail of a siren. And another thing. Eric Halvorsen, yelling like he was on the field. *"Whoa whoa whoa!"*

Blake tried to turn, and his knee collapsed under him. He couldn't get up, and he couldn't get clear, but he could see Dakota, and he could hear her. Her left arm was hanging by her side, and she was shouting to Eric, "Hold him down! Get him down!"

Blake saw him. Jerry Richards, on his feet again. Coming at him with a hammer.

Which was when Number 72 took him out. Blake's blind side tackle, doing what he did best. Protecting his quarterback.

♡♡♡

For Dakota, it was a very long night.

First, there was all the confusion as the paramedics loaded Logan Mansfield, a security guard who was surely due for another raise, onto a stretcher. Logan was groaning, and that was so much better than the motionless figure she and Blake had dragged away from the building. Dakota could breathe a little as she tried to explain what had happened to the sheriff, no doubt making a disjointed mess of it.

Jerry Richards, bully and coward, had his own ambulance. She'd hurt him, but Eric had just about destroyed him. Three hundred pounds of Eric, tackling Jerry onto blacktop. That would've hurt. And Dakota wasn't one bit sorry. That was what excessive use of force looked like if you were on the receiving end, she guessed. And karma was a bitch.

There weren't any ambulances left, so she and Blake sat on the sidewalk on one side of a makeshift barrier and waited as the firefighters worked to put out the blaze and the spectators talked and exclaimed, taking in their second spectacular show of the night.

Her arm hurt. It hurt a lot. But Blake's knee hurt worse. His face was taut with pain, his teeth gritted tight, and he had his hand around his knee like he'd hold it together by force. That is, until a paramedic finally slapped a mask on his face.

Dakota watched Blake's face relax, his eyes go fuzzy, and took his hand with her good one. "Hey," she said, "you're all good."

His eyes shifted above the mask, and she said, "Yeah. We both made it. How about that? I wrecked my shoes, though. I expect…" She had to breathe a few times herself. "Replacements."

Finally, they made it to the hospital, where a doctor set her arm, which was no fun, and she sat in a waiting room for hours along with Russell, Evan, and Blake's parents, which was worse. It was a long time later when she was finally sitting beside Blake's bed in a curtained cubicle and holding his hand as he emerged from yet another knee surgery.

His eyes were still fuzzy, and his voice was a croak. "Your arm," was the first thing he said. "Cast."

"Yep."

"Going to have to… what about… your glass."

She laughed. "Oh, Blake. Yeah, that's a delay. But I think you're worth it."

"Jerry. He had a… hammer."

"He sure did."

"Security. The guy. Uh… Logan."

"He's badly concussed, but he's going to be all right. You got there in time." She lifted his hand to her mouth and kissed it. "Good job."

"He was coming after me. Jerry. Going to hit me in the… head. I remember lying there. I remember the… hammer. What happened?"

"Well, could be I took Jerry out. It could be."

"You?"

"Yes. Me. I was assaulted once. It wasn't going to happen again if I could help it. I've been taking self-defense courses for a long time. Turns out they're Blake-defense courses too. Good thing, huh?"

"Going to have to… keep you." His words were slurring now. "So… fierce. So… strong."

"Yep." She put her good arm gently around him and laid her cheek against his. "I am. You see… I'm Lakota."

Our Best Life

♡

Blake hung around Wild Horse longer than he'd planned.

In the end, he just hired a few nurses to come in around the clock. Anything else was inefficient when you had three patients.

There was him and his knee, but he was used to rehabbing his knee. There was Dakota's arm, too, though, and she wasn't the best patient. She kept getting frustrated. But at least she was staying at his house, which meant she was able to go for long walks around the lake and dream up enough pieces to fulfill her commitment to the gallery. "If only I could *do* them," she kept saying, as she worked on her physical therapy with renewed determination.

Blake just smiled and took her occasional grouchy mood in stride. He'd been there, and he knew what it was like to long to do the one thing that mattered most and not to be able to do it. He also knew that once she got back to it, she'd be throwing her whole self into it, and that it would all be good.

Then there was Russell. He had it the worst after his complicated, impossibly delicate back surgery, and he complained the least. But he got better, and then better still. It was a slow rehab, but he took it, as he said, "One day at a time."

Blake now had a criminal record, too. Yes, he did, though it could have been worse. The prosecutor had talked about "aggravated battery" for that punch in the nose. It had actually knocked Sawyer out, which Blake was pretty proud of, especially after it developed that Sawyer had held him up on purpose. He found that out because Sawyer and Jerry Richards couldn't wait to rat each other out.

Unfortunately, Sawyer couldn't be nailed down hard enough. Blake had always had trouble imagining the man risking his entire reputation and livelihood to destroy the resort just because Blake had fired his painting team and asked questions about Russell's accident. It hadn't made sense for such a self-involved guy. Which was why Sawyer had limited his efforts to encouraging Jerry and offering a helping hand here and there. Unfortunately, that meant that the max anybody could have pinned on Sawyer was driving the boat while Richards dumped the crib frame over the side, and as his cousin the sheriff said, "That's not even littering. Just aiding and abetting littering."

On the night in question, his "aiding and abetting" had amounted to getting in the way of anybody important leaving the fireworks display before Richards had a chance to set off his "accidental" firework on the other side of the resort. The fact that it had been Blake who'd been leaving had just made Sawyer a little more zealous in carrying out his part.

In the end, Blake's attorney pleaded his case down to simple battery, Blake paid a fine, and that was the end of it. As far as Blake was concerned, a fine and some reconstruction on the resort were a small price to pay for knowing it was all over. He'd have paid a lot more to get the chance to hit Sawyer a few more times, but at least he wasn't quite as pretty as he'd used to be. His nose had a definite bump in it now after being broken by both Riley and Blake. That was satisfying.

It was also satisfying that Jerry Richards was in jail and would probably be going to prison. And if Blake paid a visit to Sawyer's house on his crutches early on and suggested that, given his part in the whole deal and the fact that the entire town knew about it, it might be wise for him to get out of town and stay there? If three oversized specimens of NFL muscle went with him to do it? The sheriff didn't have to know about that.

All of that took a while to happen, but by Thanksgiving, Sawyer had moved to Coeur d'Alene with Ingrid, Richards was still in jail, and Dakota had recovered enough to finish six glass pieces, which were hanging in a Portland gallery with a couple of the earlier ones. Only a couple, because she'd sold five in the first month, and was in the process of replacing them.

This Thanksgiving turned out a little different from every past one Blake had spent, though. Or a lot different. For one thing, it was the first time in sixteen years that he hadn't spent the holiday either playing a football game or getting ready to play one. And for the other, he'd flown Russ and Dakota to Charlottesville to spend the holiday with his family. That was good. The day after Thanksgiving, he took Russ out to breakfast at Ace Biscuit & Barbecue, which wasn't.

Oh, the food was tasty enough. Blake just didn't seem to have an appetite.

Russell was tucking into his fried chicken, waffles, fried green tomatoes, and sweet tea like he'd been kept out of heaven too long and the angels had just opened the gates. Finally, though, he glanced at Blake. "You're not eating. Knee bothering you?"

"No." Blake rearranged his plastic silverware one more time.

Russ shot him a look. "Spit it out, son."

"Right." Blake shook his head at himself and dove in. "Here's the deal. I'm planning to ask Dakota to marry me, and I'd like your blessing to do it."

Russell stopped eating, which was some sacrifice. "Do you need my blessing?"

"No. But I'd like to have it. I want Dakota to have everything she wants, and she'll want this."

"Well…" Russell said slowly, and Blake thought his heart

was going to gallop straight out of his chest. "It's been, what, six months?"

"Yep. And that's long enough." Blake cut himself a slice of biscuit, ham, and gravy, and then didn't eat it. "I knew after three weeks. I just didn't know I knew. When I saw her in that hospital bed, though, I couldn't have known any clearer. And since the Fourth, it's been just about killing me not to be married to her. I want to know *she's* sure, though. I decided to wait until she'd sold some more of her glass first, so she'd know she had a future. So she'd know she didn't have to choose me to get it."

"Huh." Russell sounded dubious. "That's a whole lot more high-minded than I'd ever be."

Blake had to laugh. "All right, maybe that's a little bit of a lie. Maybe I was scared she'd say no. Maybe I still am." He sobered again, because this was too important. "I'll give her a good life. You have to know that."

Russell thought a while, which was a while too long, then said, "I don't care so much about that. Dakota can make it on her own. I care that you give her your best, and that you don't give it to anybody else. That would flat-out destroy her. She's had enough broken promises in her life. If you let her down, you'll answer to me. I like you fine, but that little girl's my daughter."

"I'll be making some promises," Blake said. "Some vows. I'll make them in front of my family, you, and God, but I'll be making them *to* Dakota. I haven't always been a perfect guy, but I've always kept my promises. I'll be keeping these. You've got my word on it."

"Then, son," Russell said, "I guess you better ask her."

"I guess so." And never mind that the thought made those butterflies rise again, worse than before the biggest game of his life.

"When you planning on doing it?" Russ asked. He was getting back to his breakfast now, and Blake decided he'd better start in on his own. He didn't get to Charlottesville often enough to pass up biscuits and gravy done right.

"Well," Blake said, "I tell you what. Here's my plan."

♡♡♡

Two weeks later

Dakota couldn't stand to wait for the boat to reach the shore. She needed to be in the water again, because it was warm, and that shoreline wasn't fringed with cedars. It was edged by palms and ferns and a Four Seasons hotel.

A Four Seasons hotel in Costa Rica, to be precise. She was here, and she'd explored the rainforest canopy and seen more birds than she'd known existed. She'd jumped into an impossibly blue plunge pool at the base of a waterfall and been overtaken by the soul-deep vibration of the roaring water. She'd hiked on a volcano, and she'd snorkeled in the Caribbean. And today, she'd swum with dolphins, and that had been the best of all.

Everything she'd imagined had come true. And more.

How could a woman stand still and wait for a boat to dock with that kind of happiness fizzing inside her? She was jumping over the side on the thought and swimming for the beach. When she heard a shout behind her, she turned in the balmy water and shouted back to Blake, "Why are you still up there? Why aren't you racing me?"

He dove right in, and she laughed out loud and swam hard. She didn't beat him even with her head start, but she gave it her best shot.

By the time the boat had docked and Blake's parents and Russell had made their leisurely way to the resort's veranda, Blake already had a daiquiri in front of her, and she was leaning back in her cane chair in her brand-new yellow bikini, playing with the tiny little beach umbrella in her drink and teasing him.

"I'm going to beat you one day soon," she told him. "Just wait. I'm practicing."

"Oh, yeah, wild thing," Blake said. "You tell yourself that."

Russell joined them first, because that was how fast he walked these days. "You did good, son," he told Blake. "Keep her on her toes."

"Hey," Dakota protested.

Blake's parents followed close behind Russell. "Well," Margaret said as Elliot handed over the beach bag Blake had left behind, "that was fun."

"I'd call that the highlight of the trip so far," Elliot said, picking up his mojito and taking a sip. "Although the drinks aren't bad."

"No," Dakota said, "that wasn't the highlight. That was the best thing ever. That was one from my bucket list." She smiled at Blake, he smiled back at her, and her heart turned over one more time. "Thank you. I love you. Have I mentioned that?"

"Just because I took you to swim with dolphins?"

"Maybe." She was so happy, she thought she might float away. "Or maybe because you do all those things Evan said once. You look good, you talk good, and you sound good. Or maybe, just maybe, it's more than that. Maybe it's that you make me laugh and hold my hand and make my life so much better. Maybe because you've got the sweetest heart a man could ever show a woman, and you keep showing it to me and telling me it's mine. Maybe because I'm so grateful to have you, it scares me."

Everybody else was smiling, but Blake wasn't. "That's a pretty good declaration, darlin'," he said. "Sounded like you meant it, too."

"Because I'm reckless," she said. "I'd have to be, to say that in front of everybody. But then, Dad told me something once, too. He said that if people didn't like all my Dakota, I should go find better people. And I did. I found you."

"You did." He wasn't looking at her, though. He was rummaging in the beach bag, and she got a pang of unease. That probably *had* been too reckless. Too much, as always. Too intense. Putting him on the spot.

He stood up, and she thought he was going to make an excuse to walk away.

Reckless. Wild. Too much Dakota.

He didn't walk away, and he didn't make an excuse. He was kneeling on the patio. On his good knee. And he was holding a box.

She couldn't breathe. She couldn't move.

He took her left hand right there in front of everybody, and when he started to talk, he was trying his best for his usual amused drawl, but he wasn't making it. Maybe because his voice wasn't quite steady.

He said, "Seems to me it's almost Christmas, darlin'. And you're probably thinking, what do I give Blake? Can't give him a robe, because he won't wear it. Can't give him a tie, because it'll never make it out of the closet. So I have this real good idea. Seeing as I love you more than life itself, and being where you're not is doing its best to kill me, I think you should marry me. That's what I want for Christmas, for you to come to Virginia again and marry me out there. Turns out I've got a church and a minister just waiting to do it."

He opened the box with his thumb, then. And she stared. That... that *ring*. It was three intertwined circlets studded with diamonds, and there was a stone in the middle that was... that was...

She couldn't look at the ring anymore, though, because she had to look at Blake. She asked, "You mean... now? What? For *Christmas?* That's... uh... less than two weeks away." The hand he was holding was shaking, and Blake's eyes were shining gold.

"That's what I mean," he said. "But I should say the words, I guess." He laughed, and that wasn't steady, either. "Miss Dakota, I truly do love you, and I surely hope you'll agree to marry me."

"Yes," she said, and watched his smile come. Watched it grow. "Yes. Of course I will. Of course I do. I love... I love you. But, uh..." She couldn't think. She had a hand over her mouth, and she couldn't hold herself together. There was no way. "But... Evan. A dress."

He sighed. "We'll get Evan down there for it. I hereby accept Evan, even though I'm not sure he accepts me. And I tell you what. My grandma had this dress, sort of a mermaid deal, and I think it'd look real pretty on you. Seems my mom's been hanging onto it, because it did all right by her own mom. There's sixty years of marriage in that dress, and seems to me we could probably take it over a hundred. We could even pass it on if we wanted. I'm going to want some babies, and I hope you'll want to make them with me. I sure would like a little girl, and if I got a son, too... well, I'd have just about everything a man could want."

"But... but..."

He was still talking. "I hear you thinking it, because I thought it, too. What about your adventures? What about your work? See, the good thing about babies is, they're portable. You can carry them through rainforests, and you can walk through Paris in the rain with them. I want to give you adventures, and I want to give you babies. I want to give you everything you've ever wanted."

She was smiling, or she was crying, or both. And so was his mother. Russell and Elliot were just sitting there looking smug. And Blake was sliding that ring onto her finger and threading his fingers through hers.

"Here's an idea to ponder," he told her. "I've been thinking about this for a while, ever since my mom asked me some questions that got me started. We don't get one life. We get lots of lives. Lots of choices. We've already had one of ours, and now we're looking at another. And we're lucky, too. We're lucky all the way around. We get to start on that new life together, and we get to pick how it'll be. We get to live our best life. Our choice. Our rules."

"But... your work," she said. "Your traveling."

"I haven't been doing it so much lately. You notice that?"

"Yes, but..." She didn't know what to say. She got

adventure *and* babies? And Blake? It was too much.

"Seems I was running around," he said. "Trying to fill up my life. But I'm thinking I was looking in the wrong places. I want to try it differently now. I want to try it with you, because I have a feeling that'll turn out better. And someday, when we have a baby or two and it's time for them to go to school? Then we decide what our next stage looks like. In the meantime, I've got all these houses just going to waste, and I've got a couple boats, too. If Russ wants to use that one sitting at the dock in Wild Horse to do some guiding, that'd be good. Meantime, you and I've got some cruising around Hawaii to do, and I've got some houses that need glass studios built in them, so you can get inspired and go to work."

She knew what she was doing now. She was laughing. "Blake." She stood up, tugged him to his feet, and went straight into his arms, and he held her. So close, so tight, and a whole lifetime's worth of secure.

She put her palms on his face, smiled into his eyes, and said, "Silver-tongued devil. I don't need you to sell me. I'm already sold. You had me a whole long time ago. You had me jumping off the rocks, and you've had me ever since."

He smiled down at her, and there was a lifetime's worth of tenderness in that smile. "Badasses gotta badass."

Surely one heart couldn't contain this much happiness. It was impossible. But it was real. "Yes, they do," she said. "They surely do. And they gotta do it together."

Acknowledgments

♡

Thank you to my alpha read duo, Kathy Harward and Mary Guidry, for their help and inspiration as they read along with this book.

Thanks to Barbara Buchanan, Carol Chappell, and Bob Pryor for their feedback, and a special thank-you to Phalbe Henriksen for proofreading the story.

A thank you as always to my wonderful assistant, Mary Guidry.

Thanks to my husband, Rick Nolting, for everything: for reading along (always heroic), for keeping absolutely everything else in our lives going, and for his love and support.

Thanks to the staff at Meal Ticket, my favorite Berkeley restaurant, for feeding the author so well and putting up with me drinking so much of your terrific coffee.

And finally, thanks to my readers for taking a chance on a new series with me. Without you, none of this would be possible. I appreciate you.

Other Books from Rosalind James

The *Portland Devils* series
Dakota & Blake's story: SILVER-TONGUED DEVIL

The *Escape to New Zealand* series
Reka & Hemi's story: JUST FOR YOU
Hannah & Drew's story: JUST THIS ONCE
Kate & Koti's story: JUST GOOD FRIENDS
Jenna & Finn's story: JUST FOR NOW
Emma & Nic's story: JUST FOR FUN
Ally & Nate's/Kristen & Liam's stories: JUST MY LUCK
Josie & Hugh's story: JUST NOT MINE
Hannah & Drew's story again/Reunion: JUST ONCE MORE
Faith & Will's story: JUST IN TIME
Nina & Iain's story: JUST STOP ME

The *Not Quite a Billionaire* series (Hope & Hemi's story)
FIERCE
FRACTURED
FOUND

The *Paradise, Idaho* series (Montlake Romance)
Zoe & Cal's story: CARRY ME HOME
Kayla & Luke's story: HOLD ME CLOSE
Rochelle & Travis's story: TURN ME LOOSE
Hallie & Jim's story: TAKE ME BACK

The Kincaids series
Mira and Gabe's story: WELCOME TO PARADISE
Desiree and Alec's story: NOTHING PERSONAL
Alyssa and Joe'sstory: ASKING FOR TROUBLE

About the Author

♡

Rosalind James, a publishing industry veteran and former marketing executive, is an author of Contemporary Romance and Romantic Suspense novels published both independently and through Montlake Romance. She and her husband live in Berkeley, California with a Labrador Retriever named Charlie. Rosalind attributes her surprising success to the fact that "lots of people would like to escape to New Zealand! I know I did!"

11029040R00233

Printed in Great Britain
by Amazon